I0772323

The Darkness and the Deep

Cover Design Midnight Mall

Cover Photo by Lance Reis on Unsplash, Published on November 18, 2023: Back Cover Photo, by Lance Reis on Unsplash, Published on November 17, 2023

IMPRINT: Midnight Mall

Library of Congress Control Number: 2024921824

ISBN: 979-8-89626-000-4 (**hardback edition**)

ISBN: 979-8-89626-002-8 (**paperback edition**)

BISACS:

FIC009110 **FICTION** / Fantasy / Arthurian

FIC009120 **FICTION** / Fantasy / Dragons & Mythical Creatures

FIC027150 **FICTION** / Romance / Historical / Medieval

The Darkness and the Deep

Nora Dempsey

M . I . D . N . I . G . H . T   M . A . L . L

Chapter One

Drusilla knew she should have just jumped, but when her eyes stole down, and the sliver of Moon—low then, and now so high in the sky it was embarrassing—reflected maddeningly off the glossy black water of the canal, she knew it was death staring back.

Water, driven by the tide, or perhaps by whatever moved within it, lapped against the pylons that held the building up. Held up all the buildings. Water instead of streets, two stories and the height of the roof below her. More rooftops stretching out from her in all directions, like broken fragments of some great, labyrinthian wall, and she, Theseus, in its center with no thread.

Get up, she begged herself.

But she could not pry her iron grip from the roof's edge, too acutely aware a single misstep, and she would be in that water. And she had no doubt that would be the end of her.

Why Venice of all places?

The very thought made her want to concede the impossibility of the task before her. All the air was gone from her lungs, and she was finding it difficult to take the next breath. It would be so easy to slink away, return to Britain, and forget her reasons for being here

Except her reasons were noble, compelling—her conscience would not allow her to leave tonight until the man she had come to kill was dead, or she was. There was no third option. And with that, she had answered her own question—Count Nolan was in Venice.

Drusilla's hands ached with cold and inaction. Her lips were numb. Was that from the cold, too, or a byproduct of hyperventilation?

"Get up." Outwardly, a simple command barely whispered. Inwardly, a scream, a battle cry. A final and desperate plea.

She stood. Paced back, heart pounding. Readied herself for the jump. Shook the tingle out of her fingers.

This, at least, she could do openly. Drusilla wore all black, blending into the night. Just another outcrop of roof. A chimney or gable. A night heron come to roost.

But just in case, a mask covered the upper half of her face—further insurance—black leather trimmed in blacker lace. Unlike the inhuman masks she had always detested, this one was elegant, and necessary should she be spied.

Luxurious, brown-black hair that, when combed out, descended to her waist, and then a half-foot more, tonight, sat upon her head like a crown. Heavy braids pinned out of the way, men's clothes for practicality—she had tried climbing a building in a dress once. It was needlessly difficult. And though she could be hanged for wearing pants if caught, she could be hanged for a good many offenses this night if captured. One more charge would hardly matter.

But to have any chance of success, it had to be now. A tinge of exotic blue colored the star-choked sky, lacing drifting clouds in silver. Morning was coming.

Anxiety pounded through her veins. Just keep your eyes on the next roof. Do not look down.

Drusilla ran towards the edge.

Leaped...

And looked down.

Morbid curiosity had won.

Glassy black water rippled, distorted stars sliding maddeningly over crest, slipping into valley. Heart stopped, stomach balled in fear—and though it was too late for damage control, she squeezed her eyes shut...

And hit the opposite roof, somersaulting, coming to rest. Frantic fingers searched out purchase, something, anything to hold on to. But there were only the slate tiles of the new roof. Count Nolan's roof.

Had that raised an alarm?

Perched low, she waited, listening, fearing she had undone all her long preparations, heart pounding in her head as it resumed beating, or had it been hammering the whole time, and it was her mind which had hung suspended in time?

The world was darkness and the rap of her heart.

Be calm, you're on the other side.

Deliberately, Drusilla brought her breath under control, and with it, her heart followed, giving herself the space to, once again, monitor her surroundings. The distant creak of ship timbers, the whisper of the late spring breeze, the lap of water.

Thump. Thump.

Fingers located grooves in the cool slate and dug in.

Quiet.

No shouts. No murmurs or scurrying below to indicate she'd been heard. Willing her eyes open, she saw no defense being mounted. Another long moment to be sure, and then she conceded. This small victory was hers.

She could breathe.

A moment. That was all she needed. A moment more, to pretend what was happening next was not. She had never killed before.

For her dinner, yes. The beasts of the field. The bounty of the sea. But a man...

She needed distraction.

So little time remained, and yet she could not proceed in this state of mind. One more moment to find her center. One more attempt to stop the spiral.

Casting her eyes about, she looked at the city and the wide and placid lagoon beyond. The Passageway of the Seven Seas.

Yes, that would work.

The achievement was modern beyond compare. The audacity of it, brazen and reckless. Had Atlantis not been warning enough? Or Egypt's own Alexandria, half of it now below the waves? The Day of Horror was still commemorated there by the descendants of those who had survived and witnessed it. And what of the tales of Poseidon taking whole cities under? Was there no seed of truth in myth?

Portions of Drusilla's hometown had been taken by the sea. But that was centuries ago. And the seas here, tonight, were calm. She inhaled, slow and deep, filling her senses. Salt air, hints of lamp smoke, fragrant and exotic blossoms of the Adriatic. The faint hint of algae and the sea...

The canals.

Not helping. Look at anything else. Think of anything else.

Drusilla lifted her eyes. Took in the lagoon. Pinpoints of lantern light—some fixed, some bobbing to the rise and fall of ships at moor. More than a hundred islands interwoven by the sea. A hundred or more islands connected by bridge and waterway. It made as much sense to her as houses in trees, waiting for the first gale to send them all crashing down.

Drusilla would be glad to be away from this place. Glad to be done with the whole business. She had been at it four months. And four-month's time had brought her within striking distance. It had brought her to this nine-foot gap.

And across this gap slept the man who must die.

He was masquerading himself as a Vandal baron by the name of Eigel. She had tracked him from London Town, across the channel to her childhood home, the little seaport of Ys, in Merovingia. Then down the coast to Spain, following the path of young misery he had carved in his wake. She had visited Florence a month ago, and it was there she had begun to generate rumors of an assassin who was looking for the count. She had dropped his real name, not that of his false identity, Eigel.

Innkeepers, barmaids, merchants and sailors, she let the rumors fly upon the winds of gossip. The count's days were numbered, and she wanted him to know it. She wanted him to dread it and possibly to run from it. Or to prepare for it. Either way, his action would betray his location to her.

As it had.

She was here, and he was in trouble.

But there was work to be done yet. And work meant tools. Though she had prepared methodically for this mission, anything could have been lost climbing, or in that tumble. While her mind was blanked out—

Check your gear. Don't panic. Everything's fine.

This final lie stretched credulity a bit too far. But the familiar press of marbles against her thigh reassured her of the pouch still residing within her left pocket. Of all her essential items, they would have been the most easily lost. Several dozen perfect glass spheres.

What should be in her right pocket, she couldn't be as certain of. Unlike the marbles, she couldn't feel its press against her body, and she worried it might have fallen out in her jump, or come open and spilled away.

But the pitch of this roof was steeper than the one she had just abandoned, and checking meant freeing a hand. Right now, Drusilla only wanted to hang on.

Both pockets—at least that was the presumption—contained marvels from Helven, an artisan community nestled in the long shadow of the Accursed Mountain in the Italian Alps. And though the reputation of the mountain was terrible and fearsome, the people of that village were always warm and welcoming to Drusilla.

She was one of their best customers.

Bringing glass of this caliber, glass which could be obtained nowhere else shy of Phoenicia, home, was how she kept her purse fat. One of those ships, bobbing in the Venetian tide, in fact, held crates of glass of every size and purpose in its belly. If she survived this night, she would bring it to the markets of London Town.

But that was a big if. It was time to get on with it.

Peeling a hand from the slate, Drusilla reached into her right pocket.

Yes, the velvet pouch was intact.

It was an experiment. Drusilla had purchased a goblet of leaded glass and crushed it to a rough powder in her mortar and pestle. The circle of purple velvet was bound by a slim black cord tied in a half bow. A single tug at the right end, and the bag would fly loose, unleashing the powdered glass.

Carefully, she next checked her hairpins. Amongst her most prized possessions, they were of her own design and crafted to a very specific purpose. The ornate hairpins doubled as lock picks.

Relief washed over her, finding them still in her possession and not at the bottom of the canal.

Lastly, she checked the dagger which hung from her belt, at her side, a ten-inch narrow wedge of finely crafted steel—a metal few people knew of and fewer still possessed. A new technology still largely regarded as mythical by all but a handful. Amongst all her possessions, this was her prize.

Everything seemed in order.

Time for the window.

Earlier reconnaissance had informed her of its location, small but passable, looking out from the third-story loft, just below the roof's eve. She could enter there.

Drusilla crawled to the edge and peered over.

The canal was below.

Her stomach did another little flip and she felt ill.

Water had a sound, and the lagoon around her was endless with it. Every building surrounded by it. Dipped in it. Water of unknown depth hiding unknown things. Colder and darker than the night itself—

Stop.

She was obsessing again.

Maybe it's locked, she thought. An attempt to distract herself. A carrot instead of the stick.

Drusilla liked picking locks. She was good at it. What challenge it would be to pick a lock whilst hanging upside down over the side of a building!

Had she ever encountered a keyed lock on a third-story window before? Or any window, for that matter? She couldn't think of a single instance. She'd never even heard of such a thing. But there was a first time for everything. She could hope.

What she found was a simple latch, and her dagger's slim blade made short work of that. With a gentle push, the window swung open.

It was time.

Drusilla depended head and arms over the edge, reached through curtains, lazily flapping now in the liberated breeze, and peeked in.

No light within, save what the moonlight provided, but that was sufficient to reveal there were no further obstructions to her entry, and that it was vacant. Good enough.

She retracted herself to the roof. Flipped around, feet first over the edge, then, rushing to act before thinking got involved, swung herself through, landing face inward within the darkened abode.

Safety.

Drusilla stifled a laugh.

The absurdity of it. Safe? She had been spared the water, and for that she felt relief. In the home of her enemy, no less, and she an intruder.

What was wrong with her?

She took a moment, eyes adjusting, collecting herself, and once again, listening for any telltale sound she'd been heard. When she was satisfied her presence was unknown, she oriented herself to the room.

A large study, desk in the near corner, shelves filled with string-bound collections of vellum, scrolls stacked in their sconces, maps of the explored corners of the world upon the walls. She crept to the shelves—eyes now adjusted to the near dark—pulled one piece, then another, making cursory examination of the menagerie.

Slowly, the various works revealed themselves; titles in Latin, Greek, and a dozen other languages composed the worldly collection.

Impressive. The count had been busy. How many lives had he ruined in the building of this new life? How many shores?

She pushed it aside for now. The past could not be remedied. She was here to make sure Nolan had no future.

Still, the collection itself was remarkable. Drusilla was literate in half a dozen of the languages represented. She "borrowed" a few of the smallest treatises, folded parchment texts, shoving them into a spare pocket. The count wouldn't be needing them.

Well, if he lived, he could have them back.

She inched her way further in, away from the canal beyond the window. The remainder of the room was borderline spartan. Of course, the "baron" had just moved in. Was probably sleeping, in fact. How to remedy that?

Drusilla's eyes raked her options, selecting an oversized piece, annotated vellum maps stitched and bound curiously between covers fashioned of leather to form a thing most rare.

An actual book.

Leafing through it revealed it to be an atlas of the military campaigns of Alexander the Great. Lifting it to shoulder height, she gauged its considerable heft, then dropped it upon the floor.

The sound it made was quite impressive. That might do it.

She turned an ear to the silence and waited. Speculated.

The house was full of creaks and groans, as any house was. The water outside, ever-present. The smell of the sea—the night breeze. All these had to be filtered out in order to find the affected change.

The "baron" had many dark secrets. She found it interesting to entertain whether he would involve his privateers, or come to investigate on his own.

Waiting, listening, Drusilla stepped cautiously to the open window, peering down the alley to the street crossing the front of the house, but she could see no guards.

The canal below made its presence known, lapping against the walls of this building and the one across the way. Against the pylons, making horrid little slaps and gurgling sounds...

Movement from within the house brought her out of the paralysis. Footsteps, slight and practiced, upon the stairsteps.

Drusilla took another deep breath, centering herself. But it was thoughts of Carlotta, now, which invaded her serenity, forcing adrenaline to rush to her veins with urgency.

Carlotta was the reason she was here.

She choked back a flood of raw emotion. Hatred, loss, anger. "Anger defeats the angry," her sponsor, Roland, had told her—only once. But she had never forgotten it.

All right. Anger later then. For now, she would be infinitely calm.

The door to the room opened quietly. Closed again. Smoke from a punk wafted into the room, a candle was lit, then two, three. Light and shadow danced, competing for attention.

"I could call the guards," came the count's voice, rich and deep, filling the room.

Alone. He did value his secrecy then. She was glad.

Drusilla stepped towards him again, deliberately putting distance between herself and the canal. He held a sword in one hand, Spanish in design, a long, slender spatha, most likely as sharp as iron could be. Pity for him, even with all his money and influence, steel was an unattainable thing. In his other hand was the smoldering punk. He set it down on a far table, revealed in the new light, where it would cause no harm.

The count was in an expensive dressing gown worn over a nightshirt. Not quite in keeping, he also wore a sword belt and high cuffed black boots. He appeared to be in his forties. Drusilla remembered him being younger. It had been some time.

The count raised his sword, leveling it to Drusilla's heart, a long dagger still hanging limp at his side. Obviously, he didn't consider her to be much of a threat—yet.

Fourteen feet separated them.

"They'd never get here in time," said Drusilla, all calmness now.

Count Nolan sounded irritated as he spoke again. "Who sent you?" His face, contorted in the low firelight, reflected a mixture of power and pain.

"You left a lot of devastation in Ys," said Drusilla. The mere mention of her hometown stirred up memory and emotion long buried.

The count was no less immune. Even by candle, she was certain he paled a shade or two. His grip tightened upon the sword, and he brought the dagger to bear upon her, also snickering sharply in the light as it slid from its leathern repose. His reputation as a swordsman was not unknown to her. Many a veteran warrior had perished on those blades.

Drusilla didn't care. The game was on. This was it. Only one of them would leave this room alive.

Time to kill the bastard.

Chapter Two

D RUSILLA SHIFTED HER FEET. Things could go quickly from here. She needed to be ready. But if she could extend the parlay just a little longer... she wanted to unsettle him.

"Carlotta was Duke Halsten's niece," she said, coming a step away from the window into the firelight. "In fact, it seems she was well liked by quite a number of people."

Again, she felt the irreversible twinge of loss. But her words affected him too. The count's jaw tightened.

"I remember you," he said. "You're no longer a little girl. Take off your mask. Let us see what time has made of you."

"It's you who should be worried about time." She took another step forward. Ten feet separated them.

The count's mannerisms seemed to shift. Was that fear?

"Leave right now," he said.

Yes, definitely fear.

"I'm afraid I can't do that." Drusilla slid a hand into her pocket, striving to make the action subtle, unnoticed. "I still have business with you. Count Nolan."

The count sneered. His true name seemed to bring him pain, and was that resolve?

"Ah, yes. I do remember you," he said, his voice injected with new confidence. "Little Dru, so terrified of the water."

Drusilla's mind recoiled. Dru was Roland's name for her. It made her skin crawl to hear him speak it. He had no right. But that alone had no bearing upon her rapidly slipping composure. His mention of water, on the other hand, unnerved her, struck to her core in the most basic of ways. It was an idle comment—an empty threat, of course. She was secure within this room built upon sturdy pylons. In fact, the whole front of the building, the bulk of it, rested on the land.

All true and sound reasoning, yet still, her awareness of the open window was now foremost in her mind. How quickly he had located and struck at her Achilles' heel. She had to pull herself back from that darkest edge of her mind, towards which he was so skillfully driving her.

Hold it together, Dru, she told herself.

The count advanced another pace. From where he stood, arm outstretched, the sword point was a mere yard from her heart.

"It will be my supreme pleasure to toss you into yonder canal," said the count. He lowered his voice to a near whisper. "Can you hear the water lapping? Yearning, hungry?"

Drusilla edged from the center, into the room's corner, if only by inches. Heart pounding now, hammering away. Vision closing down to a tunnel, Count Nolan filling the whole of her perception.

Water lapping at the building's pylons, eroding them one lick at a time. The horrid slap and gurgle, the interplay of water between buildings. Greedy. Waiting. Patiently seeking...

"I'm not afraid of you," said Drusilla, but heard no conviction in her own words.

"Aren't you?" He knew her fear. Surely it was obvious. She ached to abandon this place, flee to the comfort of the forest, or London Town, or... or anywhere but here.

She felt her lower lip quiver. In response, his mouth twisted cruelly. "Your whole life, you've feared the water." He paused, savoring her discomfort. "Now, your worst nightmares are about to be fulfilled."

Drusilla bumped into the windowsill, her back colliding with it. She nearly lost her footing. Had she been on the retreat the whole time? In her terror, the count maneuvering her there? There was no denying it.

A puppeteer commanding cruel strings, he had put her there.

Revulsion filled her as she glanced backward, over her shoulder, to the dark water below. A whimper escaped her lips as though she were a child again.

She had been a child the last time she had seen him. Carlotta had been a child…

Drusilla's hand sunk deeper into her pocket. The press of marbles helped to center her, if only by a minuscule amount. She snapped her attention back to the present scene.

"That's it," said the count, as though supping upon fine delicacies. "There's nothing in this world more beautiful than a terrified girl!"

He lunged in—

She tossed the contents of her pockets, ducking as his sword sliced wildly past her ear—marbles, a swirling chaos, under his unpinioned boot heels.

Down crashed the count, howling rage as he went.

That'll wake the house, thought Drusilla, part of her mind back from its binge of terror. And in an instant, she was back in action, seizing the contents of her other pocket.

Count Nolan was temporarily akimbo, weapons flailing for purchase. Drusilla swung the velvet pouch downward, holding on to a single end of the black cord. The pouch began to unfurl even before striking him squarely in the face.

Coarse, glittering dust exploded into the air. Drusilla recoiled to the room's far corner, sinking into darkness.

"I remember you too." Drusilla watched the scintillating cloud of dust dancing in the candlelight. It evoked a memory of snow drifting off the convent rooftops in Ys. A little girl staring out at the winter night from behind her pane of glass, mourning the death of a lost friend. The wind howling fiercely outside. It was the winter of Carlotta's death.

But it wasn't the wind howling now, it was the count striking out blindly with his weapons. A cloud of glass shards sucked into his mouth and nose as he did so, swirling, sparkling. He coughed, a stir of glinting powder churning violently before his face. The dagger twisted from his hand, clattering to the wooden floorboards.

Drusilla pressed herself deeper into the corner, waiting…

The count swung again with his sword, blindly, less physicality than before, his other hand wiping at his eyes—leaving a red smear.

"I'll dispatch you to Hell!" the count managed in a raspy dissemblance of his former voice. A fit of coughing took him, filling the air before him with more glinting powder, no longer pristine, but tinged with red mist. His whole body wracked with agony.

"Me, burn?" Drusilla laughed, adrenaline revisiting her in full force. "I remember you too. I remember what you did, you depraved son of a bitch. Carlotta was my friend."

She rose to her feet, an ebon shadow pressed still to the corner, but erect now, once again in full control of herself. She spat her contempt at him. "Enjoy the fire."

The count's coughing became screaming. Heavy droplets of blood accompanied the stir of glass. The sword dropped from his other hand, both clawing at his ruined eyes now. Hands leaving crimson prints on the floor, unable to get up. Trying. Failing.

Somewhere below, people in the house were stirring now. There were murmurs, shouts, footsteps rushing—

The bang of doors flung open in haste.

Good. A large house full of echoes and chaos. They knew things were clearly amiss, but hadn't yet pinpointed where.

Gasping, the count tried to call out, and was besieged with another fit of coughing, blood spraying from his mouth. Crimson drizzling from nose and eyes.

Drusilla looked to him, then to the door and back again.

She went to sheath her own dagger, and realized she had not drawn it, then leapt from the corner and seized the count's. Her hand was shaking, but she didn't need a steady hand for this—in one deft move, she spun the blade around and plunged it through his throat.

The footsteps were dangerously close now. The whole house in a ruckus. Time, Drusilla realized, was extremely limited.

She knelt by the count, retrieving her two pouches.

"Shhh," she said, putting a finger to her lips.

The count's body convulsed a final time, then went slack, save for his neck, which was kept twisted at a most unnatural angle, being pinned to the floor.

Drusilla moved to the window, climbing out, pulling herself to the roof, a worried glance cast to the water of the canal below. She was trembling, unsure of the reliability of her legs so needed for her escape.

A footfall within the room below encouraged her to try. Gasps of horror, then shouting. She couldn't be here anymore. Heedless of her chances of success, Drusilla fled, rooftop to rooftop, needing only to be away from here.

Chapter Three

T HE SEA TOSSED THE small sloop roughly. Drusilla sat top deck, back to the forecastle, huddled against the cold and her own deep-seated fears. She was wrapped in a cloak of black oilskin, hair down, drenched, and miserable.

Every ocean voyage was the same, and she had made many. This was about as bad as it could get. The whole of the ocean lay beneath her in all its mystery. The thing about deep water was, in its vastness, it housed the unknown. Any terrible thing could be down there.

Captain Childebrande stood at the wheel, a commanding presence in his dark garb. A blonde-bearded man of mid-thirties, he was full in strength, large and rugged, possessed of powerful hands and thick forearms. Beryl-blue eyes raked the world like a falcon locked on prey, but when they fell upon her, there was always kindness.

The *Black Swan* was his ship, and in his masterful hands, she had brought Drusilla to Italy. Now, they were returning to her adopted home, to Britain.

A wave crashed over the main deck, and though Drusilla was steps above it, only an observer watching it slosh back into the sea, she became fearful the next wave would be higher, and take her too. The very thought chilled her to the bone. But neither could she spend the voyage below decks with the sounds and feel of the ocean all around her. She had tried it. It felt like a tomb.

So she sat, clinging to the small comfort the door jamb offered, watching the waves swell and recede all about, drenched, terrified, and mostly immobile. She hated herself for giving into such cowardice. What a loathsome creature she must appear. Still, there was no better solution she could contrive. It would have to do.

Another wave. This time bigger.

Drusilla pulled the cloak closer about her, casting a glance towards the captain, terrified this one had surely taken him.

"I'm here, m'lady." His voice rumbled like far off thunder, carrying past wind, sea, and terrors born of dark imagination. Lashing off the wheel, he moved to stand over her, seemingly unconcerned in the crossing.

Drusilla returned him a grateful look.

"Until the weather calms, we had both employ safety lines. That is, unless I can talk you into taking a bit of rest," he said. "I know how's you don't like the belowdecks. I don't blame ya. Takes some gettin' used to. Why don't you take your comfort in me cabin?"

As the captain talked over the churn of the sea, he tied a line to the mainmast, and then around his own waist. He was just finishing the complex knot, and reminded Drusilla, at that moment, very much of her own late father. She knew the knot. She knew all the knots. Not their names, just how to do them. Every time her father had been agitated, he would take a length of rope and tie. One knot after another. Drusilla suspected he had known she watched him. If so, he had never let on.

"Can't be none too careful," the captain explained, breaking her reverie. The knot was complete.

Drusilla felt miserable asking her next question, but her body ached to the bone, literally hungering for sleep.

"Do you think I could do both?" Fighting her urge to cower in the doorframe any longer, she rose.

Drusilla was tall for a woman and found herself eye to eye with Childebrande. There was more concern in his features than he was letting on. He really was a kind soul and had taken to her in what she envisioned as a fatherly way.

He patted her shoulder, a friendly gesture but no more familiar than that. She had portrayed herself as an aristocrat to him, and he seemed to respect her higher station.

"I don't see why not," he said, grinning. "I'll be most judicious with the length. Just enough to get you through that cabin door and into bed with you. How long has it been now? Right near two days, I imagine."

Drusilla nodded, waiting in the doorframe for him to return with rope. Another wave washed across the deck of the low ship, and for a moment, she imagined the unthinkable task—bringing this ship into port alone. If it came to that, she didn't hold much hope. It was a river boat as much as a seagoing vessel. A hybrid capable of both, and therefore, not quite suited to either. Childebrande was quite capable, but herself...

As quick a study as she was, as much as she had observed him at work, it was just—the ship was so small and the ocean so vast.

These were not the kinds of thoughts she should be entertaining right now. She knew it. Was embarrassed by it. She had been taught better than this. Her horror of water was one thing she had kept hidden from Roland, even when all her other faults had been laid bare. But what she could not hide, he had tempered and wrought into something finer, always demanding more from her than she thought she had to give. In this, too, she knew by experience's own hand, she could prevail. Somewhere within her, she would find what was required to survive.

The sea was not within her means to control. Nor was this tiny ship. In those things, she need only trust. She could not disgrace all that Roland had made of her by hysterical action.

Roland had taken a chance with her when others would have sent her to the gallows. Drusilla had been nothing but a petulant runaway, and a poor excuse for a thief, when he'd first encountered her. He'd mentored her, sponsored her, molded her into something more fine and noble than she'd ever dreamed she could be. She breathed in the salt air. Her senses filled with oiled Lebanese cedar, musty rope, the whip of sail cloth harnessing the driving wind.

Bringing them home.

Drawing to her full height, she choked back the terror, raising her eyes to the toss of grey-blue madness that was the sea, challenging herself to face it.

Her knees nearly buckled. Her grip tightened to white-knuckle upon the doorframe. There was nowhere to run. Her lot was already cast. She wanted to retch.

Childebrande returned with a length of hemp secured at one end to the mainmast. Already, she found her eyes casting downward again, searching for that anchor that nothing at sea could provide.

"Trust the sea, m'lady. She's a fair mistress. She'll bear us home. I've seen much worse and come through things just fine. The *Black Swan* is Phoenician built. They don't make 'em like this anymore. She's a true explorer, this one. We'll see the shores of Britain again. I promise ye."

"You are, of course, correct, Captain," said Drusilla, keeping her eyes low and grounded. Injecting as much measured rationality as she could muster into a voice which still betrayed her baser wont to flee. High, grey swells churned all about the little ship, a ship floating precariously above unimaginable, crushing depths.

"To bed with ye," he said, opening the door behind her.

He guided her with strong hands, his footing as sure upon the deck as hers had been upon the Venetian skyline.

"If you have need for anything, you have as much rope extra to let out as ya need. Just make good knots, like the one you just saw me do. I imagine you could do that again if needed, couldn't you?"

Drusilla nodded. His insights were good. She was a quick study—a disciplined student—and had the knot not already been known to her, it would be now.

"Try to sleep," he said. "You have no worries here on my ship."

Drusilla took the captain's wrist firmly. "Thank you."

The captain only smiled, giving a little shrug, and put her, and her lifeline, safely on the other side of the door.

She fell as haphazardly as a tossed sack of grain, hitting the pillows and collapsing at once in surrender to her exhaustion.

DRU'S MOTHER STOOD IN a golden field of rye, waving goodbye. Why was she saying goodbye? Mother, you don't have to leave. Why?

She reached out longing arms towards the retreating woman, but was led off by her brother, Bartholemew, instead. They passed through a forest, and Dru started to forget her want for mother. She felt safe in the forest, enveloped, protected. It was cool and green, and far from all the noisy people.

Besides, Bartholomew was one of her favorite people, after Mother and Father, that was. He was fun. They always did fun things together. As long as they stayed in the forest, they would find wondrous diversions, she was sure of it.

But they did not stay in the forest. Bartholemew led little Dru to the forest's edge, to a meadow full of wildflowers and butterflies. It was lovely, yet filled her with such a sense of dread. Why, she did not know. But she did not want to be here.

Over a low hill, they climbed, and found themselves overlooking a shimmering lake dancing with sunlight.

Bartholemew became excited.

"Look, Dru," he said, running now towards the water.

Something wasn't right. The child, Dru, was unalarmed, but Drusilla was terrified. Why did this place hold such terror for her?

DRUSILLA WOKE, SOAKED AND trembling, this time in her own sweat. A cry escaped her lips. What she said, she didn't know. But she was fully awake now, struggling to compose herself.

Sunlight slanted through imperfections in the porthole shutters. Drusilla checked the rope. It was still securely knotted to her waist. She was tired, though no longer exhausted, and knew no more sleep would come to her this day.

Gathering courage, she went to a window and let in the sunshine. Blinding blue and white resolved to Sun, sky, and water as her eyes adjusted. The sea was calmer now, a relative state which did nothing to assuage her unease. She turned away, seeking to find some center of calm, which remained entirely elusive.

Drusilla pushed back limp curls and mopped some of the sweat from her forehead with her palms. She must look a frightful sight.

She took inventory of the room. Her oilskin cloak was in a thoughtless heap on the floor, and instead of a ewer and washbasin, the captain had a bucket on the floor. But the water was clean, and she made use of it as best she could. At least she could have a fresh face.

Time to face the day.

Opening the door, she stood in its frame, staring first at the deck, then lifting her eyes high enough to see the captain's feet standing dutifully at the wheel. He no longer sported a safety line.

She wondered, briefly, if he had secured himself only for the sake of her pride. Feeling a little stung, and despite her uneasiness, she began tugging at the knots at her waist. From her peripheral vision, Drusilla glanced at the water. Undulating blue dominated every direction out to infinity. Her fingers protested her will, heart racing, knees suddenly weak.

An involuntary gasp escaped her lips.

"M'lady, are you well?"

She forced herself to look up.

"I am," said Drusilla, knowing she was not.

"Look," he said, raising an arm. "Britain."

Looking up, she saw only sea, but then, with the swell, a distant, green island of stability emerged.

"Britain," said Drusilla, with unabashed reverence. "Thank God."

"Aye," said the captain, his own tone touched with reverence. "And the Lady as well."

He looked at her fingers, fidgeting nervously with the knotwork. Heat branded her cheeks.

"Might just as well leave it," he said, indicating the safety line with his gaze. "Won't hurt none."

She renewed her efforts, tugging at the knot with fingers that wouldn't obey. "If it's not necessary..."

"You never know," he said, kindly. "Leave it be.

"Sun'll be late in the sky, afore we reach shore." Childebrande had expertly shifted subject before too awkward a silence developed, and she was grateful for it. "The winds are calm, but they'll pick up. The day is young yet. That little spot there..." and he tried to point something out Drusilla couldn't distinguish from the rest of the coast, "that's Elver's Pool. Isn't that where ya asked me to put you ashore?"

"It is," said Drusilla, admiration for the man's expertise.

"The horizon can deceive, and many a shore looks the same from a distance. But the stars," and he winked at her, "they never lie."

Drusilla managed a smile for the man, though she felt as much dread in the calm weather as she had in the storm. Deep water was deep water, and sometimes the calmest waters were the most terrible.

She closed the cabin door, and sat with her back to the deck, taking up the slack of rope and knotting it off.

"Make yerself comfy. It'll be half the daylight, yet."

"I leave it in your capable hands," she said.

The captain threw back his head and laughed. "You've got some spirit in you, you do. I think you possess more courage than ya give yerself credit for. I do at that."

Chapter Four

A SMALL TOWN SAT upon a gentle hill rising from a natural harbor where afternoon sunlight sparkled off the fast and wide River Mersey. Seabirds circled the activities of local fishermen, the snap of sailcloth competing with their cries.

They had traveled the coast for days without her knowing it, until the last day of their voyage, finally leaving the Hibernian Sea to come inland. Soon the river had brought them to the town of Elver's Pool, named so because the waters here were teaming with the creatures. Little serpentine exaggerations of tadpoles churning the water with their activity. It was quite horrible to watch them. And the captain was quite enthusiastic on the subject. "Plenty of eels, too," he said. "Good eatin', them eels. A local specialty."

Drusilla was more than acquainted with the creatures. Having grown up in a seaside port, and oft helping with the domestic preparations, she had seen every facet of the sea's bounty first hand at the fishmonger's or upon a cutting board or plate. Familiarity only made the image, which came unbidden to her, all the more vivid. Waters filled with swimming snakes, and the promise of a plateful, their glassy eyes draped in oily black skin, staring back at her come dinner. Just what she had longed to hear.

The *Black Swan* drifted lazily to dock. Being a small enough ship, and agile in the captain's hands, he brought her within arm's reach of the pier before grounding her by use of anchor and tie-off lines. Drusilla sighed, unaware till now she'd been holding her breath, grip white-knuckle on the doorframe.

Despite the continued sway of the deck under her feet, Drusilla forced her hand to relax—they were, at least, moored to the land—and took stock of her surroundings. Fishing craft, explorer craft, craft for charter. Most at anchor. Some drifting by, a painful reminder of which side of the land she was on. Fishmongers were doing a brisk business along the main harbor street. Other merchants too. Nothing like London Town. But all the basic necessities of life could be met here.

Even from here, Drusilla could smell the rich, earthy tones of the world carried to her upon the salt air. She heard gulls, lapping water, and wagon wheels bouncing along packed dirt roads to the voices of merry people, her adopted countrymen, going about their day.

Farmers manned stalls, produce of every color, testament the gates of summer had been swung wide. Townsfolk and sailors mingled, seeking reprovision and haggling over price, unconcerned by the lazy saunter of the occasional guard patrolling the streets. The Romans had fled Britain two centuries before, but this town retained that Romanized feel.

Beyond the budding town were lush, ancient forests so common to this part of the isles. Drusilla's heart ached to be away, and into those woods, but there were other matters to attend to first.

"Will you be coming ashore, m'lady?" It was Childebrande.

"Momentarily. I'll take a little privacy below decks first."

When Drusilla emerged, she was transformed. Yellow silks clung tightly to her body, accentuating her svelte figure, the neckline plunging just enough to hint at a swelling bosom beneath. Her hair was done in twisting coils, cascading down her back in neat ringlets. A carved silver comb depicting scenes of courtly love sat high upon her crown, sparkling in the afternoon Sun.

Her face was scrubbed and clean, her cheeks freshly pink from the attention. And after the fashion of her upbringing, a bit of pigment darkened her lips subtly, a healthy rose color offsetting the vivid green of her eyes.

Her sleeves were green also. Of a bliaut design, they descended to points near to floor length. The dress had cost her a small fortune. It was exquisite in the detailing. Under the hem, mostly unseen, she wore comfortable black "adventurer" boots, as she called them. They, like her saddle, and her lock picks, were custom. There were times in her travels when she realized life could be made easier by some small modification to an existing device. A little coin in the hands of an artisan, and an apt description of what one wanted, and much could be achieved.

Her boots, for instance. They were as comfortable as the more customary slippers worn by most women, yet afforded so much more protection and support when terrain became rugged or the way challenging. In short, they delivered so much more.

Captain Childebrande gripped the rail when he saw her. She'd never seen him unsteady on his feet before. To be fair, she'd hired him cloaked and at night wearing much more rugged attire.

"M'lady." The whisper escaped his blonde-bearded lips. He gave her a deep bow, then laid out a gangplank. She hesitated. That narrow strip of ocean, between ship and pier, held incalculable terrors. One slip, and she would be plunged downward to her death. Her heart pounded, mercilessly prompting her to flee. How was she to accomplish this final task?

And then Childebrande took her hand.

He knew.

Of course he knew.

Drusilla closed her eyes, and he led, putting her safely on the land side. And although the echoes of the sea persisted, no longer did the world rise and fall with such intensity. This was terra firma. She wanted to fall to her knees and embrace the lovely, lovely earth beneath her. Instead, she straightened, attaining her full height.

Breathe, she told herself, inhaling the sweet loam of the earth, the fragrant things which bloomed and rioted, filling the land with every color. It calmed her and brought her joy.

Only then did she open her eyes to the new surroundings, and knew that she was home.

The local peasantry all moved for Drusilla and Childebrande, occasionally daring to offer her pleasantries. Fine clothing had its advantages. She was, by appearance, a marked cut above anyone else of this small, British seaport.

Through the morning crowd, Drusilla's footman, Percival, came running up to greet her. His young enthusiasm infected her mood, drawing a warm smile from her lips. It was good to be home.

"My lady," he said, skidding to a halt, his mop of black hair flopping over animated gray eyes as he bowed low.

"Percival," she genuflected ever so slightly. "Arise, lad. Where's Master Linus?"

"He waits with your coach. We saw the sail."

Drusilla turned to the captain. From a pouch at her side, she removed several small coins, placing them in his hand.

"It's more than we bargained for," he said.

"It's just right," said Drusilla, then to Percival: "Go with the good captain. Unload my wares and put them on the coach. Some of it's glass, mind you. Then come fetch me at the inn." She felt safe saying that. The possibility of this town having two inns was remote.

"Captain." She curtsied to him, and he bowed even more deeply this time.

"M'lady," and he was off, the tall, gangly lad, Percival, just coming into his manhood, tagging at his heels.

DRUSILLA FOCUSED ON THE tankard of milk in her hand, trying hard not to feel the rise and fall of the room. Trying not to see the River Mersey out the tavern window. She had yet to acquire her land legs; the world had not yet settled down.

She planted her feet more firmly under the table-for-two she currently had all to herself, the scattered crowd, enjoying their repasts, their drinks, laughing amongst themselves, but careful not to meander too closely to her. From the distance they kept, and the care they took when near her, the threads of their conversations were easily lost to the shuffle and clink of an active end of day celebration.

Drusilla watched the Sun make its appearance as it sank below the eves of the building, traveling west across the Mersey, and the water, close as it was, finally seemed far enough away. The undulations that made the land seem as though it bobbed upon the sea were becoming less and less noticed.

She took a pull of cold milk, and was pondering if maybe there were two inns, when Linus walked in, crossed the planked floor, which was only slightly heaving now, and gave her a cursory bow.

"My lady."

"Master Linus," she said, extending her hand across the small table, and bidding him to sit. "Pray, have a drink before we depart. Is everything in order?"

"All is prepared."

He hadn't taken his eyes off her since entering. Not until now, as she registered the look. Linus glanced away, color invading his already ruddy cheeks. He was a good, honest man.

"May I say, your journey has done you nothing but good."

Drusilla smiled warmly. Linus had been in her service three years now, ever since the ending of her apprenticeship to Roland the Just, her sponsor and dearest friend. Linus was in his early forties, uncommonly fit, balding with short cropped hair, and possessed of a generally happy disposition. And he was wickedly good-looking. There were times she regretted the pretense of her higher station, and this was certainly one of them. "Thank you, Linus," she said, and to hide her reaction she called to the innkeeper.

The man behind the counter, a stout fellow in his prime, responded. "More milk, my lady, or something for your gentleman friend?"

Drusilla looked to Linus, eyebrow raised.

"House Ale," he said. His glance shifted to and fro about the room. Three years, and he still could not take his ease with her. Social stationing was as inbred a part of his nature as was courtesy and loyalty. Linus always dressed nicely for a coachman, but he was no courtier. If he were, Drusilla wouldn't like him nearly so much, but even courtiers received perfunctory courtesy from her.

The two enjoyed their drinks in companionable silence, then repaired to the coach, waiting in a side street nearby, where Percival kept a vigilant eye to the surroundings, and where, fortunately, the Mersey could not be seen.

Her coach was glossy white, made to seat four, even six comfortably enough—benches padded in soft, dark brown leather—the walls, quilted royal-purple velvet. Gold paint trimmed the outer carriage in gleaming brilliance. The canopy, a dark green, followed a double-S curve, tilting upwards at the front and rear, all intricately carved. Wheel fenders were also dark green, the wheels themselves black rimmed with white spokes, and hubs painted in a golden starburst pattern.

And those same wheels... they turned as effortlessly as anything made by man. The suspension, unparalleled, gave a ride to be coveted. Matched with the remnants of three attempts to conquer the land—a network of Roman roads—nothing anywhere else on land, not in all the countries she had been to, traveled as smooth or as swiftly.

It was crafted in the small community of St. Stephen's upon Moray, in Caledonia, north of the Antonine Wall near Inverness. But no local ever attempted that mouthful. To them, the town was called Lion's Gate. The hometown of her dear friend, Camille.

It was on one of Camille's visits to London Town that she had first seen her friend's coach, not in the white, gold, and green as Drusilla's, but in her family's ancestral pattern and colors of robin's egg blue, cream, and silver—a thing of absolute beauty which had inspired the commission of her own.

On each of those visits, the two of them had been inseparable. But on her most recent trip, bandying about some pretense or another, she had practically ignored Drusilla, spending an inordinate amount of time in Roland's company. So much so, she would hardly be surprised if she discovered them married in her half-year absence.

How nice it would be to have her a permanent resident of the town she loved.

A stray bit of sunshine found its way into the alley as she approached the horses to greet them. Four dappled grey stallions, fine Coursers, all belonging to Drusilla. Together, they pulled the carriage, but were also excellent single mounts, trained to respond to tongue-clucks and other subtle signals. Additionally, they were capable of grazing themselves without fear they might stray too far afield, and came when summoned by whistle.

Her favorite was Polaris. He had a lovable way of nudging her when she needed it most that endeared him to her heart.

Before getting into the carriage, she said hello to each of them. There was also Perseus, Orion, and Ursa Major, nicknamed "Major". All named after stars. And all visibly happy to see her. In truth, she had missed them just as much. An accomplished horseman, they were as much a part of her trade and training as was the dagger hanging at her waist cord.

Linus helped Drusilla to her seat, and before closing the door, inquired where they were going.

"To London Town, all haste," said Drusilla, and once the door was shut she drew the black curtains against the western light, looking out to the east instead, to the cool green forests as they bounced along the dusty road.

The afternoon warmth and lull of the carriage began to make Drusilla sleepy, and she stretched out upon the leather cushion, employing a few silk pillows to make herself more comfortable. Her love of the forest put her at ease. She could ride ahead, reach town in two days, but there was no need for it. She had no dread of the week-long journey ahead. On the contrary. Camping in the woodlands, traveling through forest and amongst the green hills was something of a holiday for her. And though she longed for home, it would come in its own time. Though they would not dally, she secretly relished the days ahead.

On the second day, they made the turn south, towards the walled citadel, her adopted hometown, London. Drusilla adjusted the curtain to take full advantage of the last sinking rays of light.

Orange and salmon blossomed over the treeline, and golden light slanted through the forest, silhouetting the trees in darkness. Drusilla held up her right hand to the Sun, the silver band on her ring finger glinting brightly. Her *Order of Arthur* ring.

Even in near dark, it shone with an internal brilliance. It wasn't actually silver, nor was it any of the other commonly known metals. It was steel—a type of steel anyway—passed to her by generations of trust, even as it had been given to King Arthur at the appropriate time.

She recalled the riddle, the riddle of steel, it was sometimes called. Late in her apprenticeship to Roland, he had taught her, and later quizzed her. It was a sacred trust.

"What is the riddle of steel?" Roland had asked her.

"He who pulls the sword from the stone shall rule all of Britain," she answered.

"And what is the stone?"

"It is iron ore, my lord."

"Good, Dru, you paid attention. That is well." The way he had smiled at her that day had meant everything to Drusilla. "And how is it pulled?"

"By fire. Intense fire."

"And how is this achieved?"

"Bellows. A fire must breathe to be hot, and it must be contained in a furnace, so as to shield it from the cooling elements."

Roland was clearly pleased with her. It was a happy memory. A happy time.

His questioning continued, knight to squire. "And what is the secret ingredient which makes it superior to iron, superior to weapons of copper, or brass, or bronze?"

"Charcoal. One-fortieth-part, blackest charcoal."

"Yes. This will make steel. A secret we must always guard. For there are men in this world who would wield it for might alone. It gives a terrible advantage over other weapons."

Drusilla thought on this. She knew it was true. Where she came from, women weren't valued enough to be taught reading, and yet it wasn't a terrible society. What would men who craved real power do with such a technology as steel?

"And how do we achieve the ex-caliber, the metal superior even to steel? The metal which shines with a just and brilliant white sheen. The metal which is not a metal, for it loses its weight while gaining strength and beauty. The metal with soul. How do we make the metal with soul?"

Drusilla was suddenly alert. This was no mere exercise. She had passed another rung in her training. Roland was about to give her a secret—one not lightly given. Her heart swelled with pride at the trust she had earned that day.

"You have not taught me this, my lord."

"You are ready to learn, my protégée. The secret must not be lost. Listen well. The ex-caliber is achieved by heating the blade to a red-hot glow, then quenching its thirst in water and ice. It must be cooled such that you see transmissions of light pour forth. The blade itself will sing as you do this."

Drusilla was fascinated. "Sing?"

"Yes, sing. It is so, I have witnessed it. A pure, shrill note of ecstasy as the blade sheds its crudeness and becomes pure by the sudden quenching. And it must be repeated. For the more times you work the blade in the fire, kneading the steel with hammer and tongs, then quenching it rapidly thereafter in the drink, the finer it becomes, and the more brilliantly the soul of the steel shines forth."

"Arthur had such a sword? Are the stories true, then?" Her curiosity was a burning excitement.

"Indeed, he did. Not all of the stories are as the popular tellings would have you believe. But the sword, yes. It was given him, along with the secret, and now I share that secret with you."

Drusilla's mind danced anew with the recall of all those fabulous fairy tales. Some of them were not tales. It was an amazing revelation.

Roland had known Arthur. In the final days. He had been a squire to Gwaine, a lad of ten, when those final, tragic events had broken the table, and the knighthood. Much had been lost that day to the world. Camelot had been an ideal, shining in an otherwise dark time.

Drusilla removed her ring, read the inscription inside, engraved in the secret Druidic runes:

"To Dru, first Dame of the Knighthood. Might for Right. To uphold this principle is our finest purpose."

The writing was absolutely tiny, the ring flawless, silver-white. Never tarnished by time.

Roland had shared the secret with her that day, but more than that, he had passed the torch of responsibility. She was a knight now, of Camelot. And though Camelot was no more, it lived on as an ideal. It lived on through her.

"Such a sword cuts more than flesh," Roland had said that day. "It rends armor like it were not there. A sword of such caliber cuts time."

"Cuts time. Surely you jest, my lord?"

"I do not. The sword must be quenched more than a hundred times, a thousand times even. But it will cut time if the process and intent is followed."

"I don't understand."

"Such a blade disturbs the very essence of things, cutting not just crude matter, but the energy that binds it together. It sweeps through time, and hews things as though a spirit—not steel, but something infinitely finer.

"Anything that challenges such a blade, falls away." Roland regarded his protégée. "You have a fine mind, Dru. But even I do not understand the workings of the ex-caliber. Yet, I assure you, it is so. And now you know how to construct such a blade.

"Never do it. Never, until the world is right. The world, such as it is, is not ready to receive such knowledge. Carry the knowledge. Pass it on when you find one equal to the task, fair of mind and pure of soul, ready for the mentoring. Each generation carrying our torch through these dark times, until an age of enlightenment should grace the world again."

"I promise, my lord, to never forget, and to never divulge, except according to how you say."

"No other caliber of steel withstands the ravages of time. Unless kept oiled and clean, they will rust away, powdering to nothing but the red dust of earth. Only the ex-caliber withstands this test of time."

"Must I never make one?"

"I trust you more at times than even I trust myself. If you decide to fashion such a blade, do it from the purest of motives. And when its cause is done, cast it into the hearth fire of the Earth herself, or the deepest and most remote lake or sea. Do not let such a blade abide unattended in dark times.

"Arthur's sword lay hidden in a lake for countless ages of time until the world was ready again. The Merlin thought that time had come. The time of Camelot. But it was fleeting. A single, brilliant spark. Barely enough to light the dark corridor of history."

"The edge it gave Arthur was a needed one, and great indeed. Surely The Merlin's choice was not a vain one?"

"Perhaps not," smiled Roland behind his heavy blonde mustache, sky-blue eyes adoring her, then looking quickly to the ground.

He was a shy and gentle man. A capable knight, also, and a man of great courage. She loved him dearly and thanked God he had taken her in near a decade ago—a lost and wandering waif of fourteen.

The days passed, camp was made, and broken. Percival and Linus variously attended to the driving. And Drusilla took advantage, reading from the works she had taken from Count Nolan's library.

They were texts on alchemy and natural philosophy, subjects of great interest to Drusilla.

At some point, on the sixth day of travel, Drusilla had dozed off, and woke now to the sounds of other horses drawing chariots, carts, and the like. Her carriage was a rare creation and often drew gazes of curiosity and wonder. She drew the curtains, and peered outside, straightening from her repose.

"London Town," she breathed. This was home. Drusilla would not sleep now. The town enchanted her. There were familiar sights everywhere, and one or two new ones. She had been away for near half a year, tracking the count, and meting out justice to him.

The markets were closed. She would have to vend her glass in the morning. But Roland would be up. He had always been a bit of a night owl.

Drusilla tapped the roof of the cab.

"Yes, my lady," came Linus' response from the driver's seat.

"Pray, make haste, Master Linus," she entreated. "Quickly now, to The House of Roland."

She heard the answer in reins and hoofs. She would see Roland tonight.

Chapter Five

The House of Roland the Just stood facing the western shore of the River Thames. It was a large structure, built in the style of the Romans, but heavily influenced by Saxon design as well.

As Drusilla suspected, there was still light and activity within. Leaving mundane matters to Linus and Percival, she leapt from the carriage and rushed to the front door, banging the knocker loudly.

The door, like the house, was solidly constructed. Already fifty years old, she suspected it would be here another five hundred or more.

The old servant who answered the door immediately recognized Drusilla and fell to his knees.

"Oh, forgive an old man," he said, his voice atremble with emotion. "But you've been gone so long. We'd begun to fear the worst, dear child."

"I'm fine, Milton. Please get up."

Milton stood, wiping a tear or two from dark, age-lined eyes set beneath brows that had been steel gray when she had departed, but now were flecked through with white. "But where are your bags, my lady?"

"Linus is taking care of everything. Don't you worry. Is the master of the house awake?"

"Yes, yes, of course. I'll tell him immediately. Please make yourself at home."

Milton turned to leave, then paused. "God bless you, Lady Dru, but it is good to see you."

Drusilla smiled. It was good to be home.

She walked across the hall, taking in all the old and familiar things that filled the spaces and made it home. A suit of bronze armor belonging to Roland's grandfather stood next to the stairs. Shields, swords, and tapestries decorated the walls.

There was a vase from Athens purported to have belonged to Aristotle, and in one corner, the prow head of a Saxon ship, all that had been saved of a once mighty vessel.

"He's in the great hall," said Milton, returning. "Come at once."

Drusilla followed him, and soon found herself in the centerpiece of the mansion, a great throne-room-like hall, at the end of which sat Roland upon a mighty dais, in the very chair Sir Gwaine once sat upon at the Round Table. Two other chairs sat empty, one to each side of his.

Torches lit the length of the hall, which was impressive. Roland looked like one of the old kings, sitting regally, short cropped blonde beard under a long and curving blonde mustache, his waist-length hair in a single braid down his back. But it was his eyes that always drew her attention, though, always so thoughtful, so wise under those bushy red-blonde brows.

"My lord," said Drusilla, falling into a respectful curtsy.

Roland stood from his chair, rushing towards her.

"Come now," he said. "No formality between us."

He smiled, or so it appeared beneath his long whiskers, and held out his arms.

They embraced. He smelled of leather and forge smoke, and of thyme, the soap she'd bought him in Saxony. The mingled scents brought back a flood of memories. This was home. She was safe behind the walls upon the Thames.

After a long and unreal pause, he held her at arm's length. "It really is you," he said, life returning to the grey-blue of his eyes.

"Were you expecting someone else?"

Roland leaned forward, conspiratorially. He spoke in a stage whisper. "I would have rushed to the door and met you personally, but I didn't have the strength to bear another disappointment. Milton has announced your return three times prior. I'm afraid the old chap's getting on in his years."

Drusilla laughed. "Well, you're certainly not. You don't look a day older."

"In six months, I should hope not," said Roland. "But you'd be, what, twenty-one now?"

"Twenty-two. And you are?"

"Old enough to be your father, or nearly so. Let's talk no more of age. Come, sit by my side and tell me of your journey."

Drusilla joined her mentor, taking a seat beside him. The chair was strangely like his. She studied it, then looked to him and back again.

"It is," he said. "I was able to find two more. That one there," and he looked to his left, "belonged to Kay. And you sit where Lancelot himself once did."

"You lie," she exclaimed, laughing to soften the accusation into a tease.

Roland held his hands wide in submission.

"Lancelot?"

Roland nodded solemnly.

"Once, he was Camelot's finest knight. And now I seat you there."

A chill passed through Drusilla's body. She moved to rise, but Roland stayed her with a gentle hand.

"Arthur himself would not begrudge you that chair, Dru. Sit.

"What news of your mission?"

"Count Nolan will never hurt young girls again."

What remains when vengeance has been dealt? Melancholy. Loss... Putting an end to that monster had not erased the pain, but it had cooled the heat of her anger.

Roland, unaware of her thoughts, took the news well, visibly relaxing.

"And your travels?"

"I tracked him to Venice. He was living under the name Baron Eigel."

"So, he demoted himself. Clever. Not a move one would suspect. But how did you find him?"

"I followed the trail of wrecked souls," said Drusilla.

His haunted, blood-slicked eyes, staring sightlessly at what? came unbidden to her mind's eye. She had not an ounce of remorse for what she had done, but still, the sight persisted. How long it would linger in her memory, she didn't know. A small price to have accomplished the deed.

Both were silent for a time.

"He had a library. I brought you three of his smaller pieces. I would have taken them all, but I was traveling light. Two addressing alchemy, and one on natural philosophy. I think you'll find them most interesting."

"Count Nolan is a notable swordsman. Not that I question your skill, but his reputation in single combat is unparalleled. How did you defeat him?"

"I reduced him to the helplessness of a child," said Drusilla, thinking back once more upon the horror she had inflicted upon him. Thinking it poetic. "A secret I will share with you sometime. But something is troubling you still, dear friend. Pray tell, what is it?"

Roland's lips grew tight, and he looked suddenly very far away. He sighed deeply, and when he continued, it was with labored effort.

"It's Camille."

Drusilla fell from her chair to her knees, grasping his hands in hers.

"Tell me she's all right."

Roland, barely able to speak now, went on. A knot in her gut formed, then twisted, but she did not show it, steeling herself against whatever terrible revelation might be coming.

"She missed a scheduled communication. Even from this distance, we are only six hours apart by pigeon."

"How long has it been?"

"Six days. Six terrible days," again he sighed, but forced himself continue. "Of course, I did not wait that long to take action. I called upon Sir Atreus the same day the pigeon failed to arrive."

She knew Atreus. A good and noble knight, another of Roland's protégés, whose education had overlapped her own.

"He is but twenty miles from her last location, and the reason I know Camille. What good that I should ride the eight or ten days, neglecting duties which would jeopardize many lives, when Sir Atreus, who resides upon the North Sea in Nairn, could be there the same day my pigeon arrived?

"But his second pigeon never came. Now I fear for him as well."

Drusilla understood the situation. Many disparate warlords ruled the various parts of Britain. Kings rose and fell as the tide. But only The House of Roland, unconcerned with rule or conquest, upheld civilization itself.

And, like their order, did so without drawing attention.

"I would go… ride out tonight." His words were at war. Every impulse as a man measured against his duty to all that remained of Camelot.

"I know that you cannot."

Drusilla tightened her hands on his, knowing he would never ask of her what must be done. Say what you will of knighthood—and she had paid her dues as any other—he protected her more than any of the others, because she was a woman.

There was no resentment in her observation. But neither could she wait for a request that would never come. "I'll attend to matters at once. What are the particulars?"

"That is not why I shared this with you," said Roland, giving her hands the indication there was still strength within his own before letting her go. "The Order of Arthur does not exist to serve my personal whim."

"No, it does not," said Drusilla forcefully, continuing to kneel before him. "You're in no state to be deciding such things. Respectfully, my lord, the particulars. Let me judge whether it is a matter for my consideration."

"It is too dangerous."

"And how well did that argument go over when I announced I would end Count Nolan?"

Roland nodded, and she saw in him a lifeless, beaten shell of his former self. How he must have suffered these last six days. That he and Camille were on the verge of marriage, she was now almost certain, and she cursed herself for having been away so long.

That he and Camille should unite? Both deserved that happiness. What could have befallen her dear friend—and Atreus as well? She prayed it was nothing more than a peregrine, sparrowhawk, or kestrel which had discovered the route of their pigeons. As terrible as that would be, it measured not against the lives of their friends.

Roland took a moment to compose himself, then spoke.

"I sent for her, Dru. By her father's consent, we were to be wed. Her carriage experienced trouble near Loch Ness, at the border of the Pictish lands to the north.

"She was taken in by the MacKay brothers who govern Foxborough

Keep upon the loch, and the surrounding fishing village and town, also known by Foxborough.

"Here is her last letter to me..." said Roland, too choked up to continue. Instead, he merely handed it to her, and was silent.

Taking the letter, Drusilla silently read, hearing Camille's familiar voice speak the words:

> *My dear Roland,*
>
> *How I miss you, darling, and long to be with you once and for all.*
> *The MacKays are tending to my every need, whilst repairs continue on the carriage. They are not a real town, and lack for the services of my beloved Lion's Gate, or my soon-to-be home, London Town. How it rolls off the tongue!*
> *Be patient, my love. They say a day or two at most, and I will be speeding to you.*
> *I keep your safety and well-being in my prayers,*
>
> *Yours most affectionately,*
>
> C.

The letter had been neatly folded for the pigeon to carry, a postscript stating to expect her next communiqué in two days' time—or upon departure, if that came sooner.

Drusilla looked up from the letter to find Roland's head buried in his hands. Tenderly, she placed a hand upon his shoulder, and as he looked up, gave the letter back into his possession.

All that she had suspected was confirmed. No wonder that he had suffered.

"Can you be certain it is written in her hand?" asked Drusilla. She knew it was, but in a matter this grave, she desired a second opinion.

"Without a doubt." His voice was a whisper.

"My dear friend, I will go at once. If ever a knight errant had a quest laid out for her, this is it."

Roland met her gaze squarely. His eyes were moist, but his face stoic and resolved. "Damn my duties here," he said, hand curling into a tight fist. "Damn my duties… I was a fool not to go in Atreus' place, to have let so much time slip by… Never wear the crown, it is a shackle…"

"I know, my lord. Do not trouble yourself. Whatever can be done for Camille will be done. I promise you."

"Remember our Creed."

"Might for right," said Drusilla.

"Never for its own sake," he added, patting Drusilla's hand a few times, then straightened in his throne-like chair, the chair of Sir Gwaine.

"We are the keepers of the flame. It is a dark time our country faces, made harder by the fact that we still remember the enlightenment that was Camelot."

"Those days will return," said Drusilla.

Roland nodded his acknowledgment.

"Someday they will write of this time," said Roland, sounding very far away. "And they will call it a dark dream."

"It is a hopeful time, my lord," said Drusilla, rising to her feet, facing her mentor and dear friend. "Is that not why we do what we do?"

"If anything can be done," said Roland, "I know you are the one to best accomplish it. You are my first knight, my right hand. Go with God."

Drusilla curtsied, spinning on her heel, leaving the hall with some haste. She didn't want Roland to see that her eyes, too, had misted over.

CHAPTER SIX

ROLAND SUPPLIED DRUSILLA WITH papers, coin, and a plausible cover for arriving at the loch. She was Lady Drusilla of Merovingia, traveling to Inverness, to a festival, but finding the loch to be much more enchanting, and being weary from travel, had decided to go no further, if she could but impose upon their hospitality.

The latter part was a stretch, but she would improvise.

The carriage was provisioned for the eight to ten-day journey. To accomplish such fast travel, she would take a second team of horses, changing the workload out at four-hour intervals. Four Hibernian Hobbys, dun steeds, their yellow-tan coats and black manes, majestic in the sunlight, would provide the effort. Once again, she was grateful for Roman infrastructure. Without good roads, the journey would be one of months.

As Drusilla oversaw the securing of the pigeon cages to the roof, she noted the interaction of the two groups of horses—her familiar dapple grey Coursers, and the Hibernians. Until last night, the horses had been apart six months. And though cautious at first, they were soon socializing.

She was relieved. The eight animals would work well together.

The night before, Drusilla had informed Linus and Percival of her intended journey, and that it may indeed be perilous, though she shared no details. "You needn't go," she explained. "I can give you good letters of reference and three months' severance each—"

But that was a sentence she was unable to finish. They were both insistent upon going.

After settling that, by cloak of night, she had given her longbow a good rubbing with linseed oil before securing it, again, in the hidden floor-hatch of her carriage. It was a place known only to her and the carriage makers at Lion's Gate. And the carriage makers of Lion's Gate were sworn to secrecy.

Nothing remained to do in her beloved London Town. It had been a short reunion. Less than a day. It was time to set off.

She bid Roland to sell her glass wares. They should fetch a sound price in the town market, and more than cover all her expenses. One goblet, she kept, however, crushing it to fine powder with her mortar and pestle—refilling her velvet pouch. A shame about the marbles. She would have liked to have more of those.

The greenery along the drive was an endless source of wonder for Drusilla, as the carriage wended its way through field and forest, day after day. The riot of nature continued to change on the way to Loch Ness, the land becoming steeped and rocky, pigeons cooing gently in their wicker cage, sway of the carriage lulling her into a drowsy state. The monotony of wheel and hoof, sounding on the forest loam, often put her to dozing.

Today was no different. She felt herself quickly drifting away, and so laid head to pillow, curling her legs up and under her skirts, upon the sun-warmed leather bench. Breathing slowed, as did mind, as she let the laziness of the day claim her.

DRU WAS IN THE meadow again, with Bartholemew. He had been telling her stories of mermaids and kelpies, lost treasures, and noble doings of knights and adventurers.

She was having a good time, but then he left her there all by herself. She was so young, so frightened. He called to her from the water as he showed off and swam for her.

Suddenly, the sky became dark and menacing. Below her, the deck of a ship pitched and tossed upon a hostile sea.

No longer the child, Drusilla tried to hang on, but the deck rails were slippery. It didn't matter that she had her adult strength, she could find no purchase.

She looked hopefully to the ropes tied about her waist and legs, but the knots were coming loose. She slid across the deck, a leg, to her horror, going over. Cold ocean water rushed the deck, washing the captain overboard.

She was alone.

The rope was nothing but a loose coil about her ankle now. She was in her underclothes and soaked to the bone.

She grasped desperately to the pitching rail, but it gave way, and she was plunged into the sea.

Drusilla tried to scream. Cold salt water invaded her lungs, seizing her chest with paralysis. Flailing, she sank into the darkness. Into the cold, crushing depths—

SHE AWOKE, GASPING FOR air, nails clawing into the plush leather of the coach, seeking purchase.

Forcing calm upon herself, she drew back the curtains, letting the afternoon light into the carriage, and was confronted with the sight of a deep mountain lake falling steeply away from the narrow road they traveled. Drusilla recoiled to the opposite end of the coach, drawing sharp breath, eyes wide with terror.

"Is my lady all right?" asked a familiar voice. It took Drusilla a moment to place it as Percival's.

Drusilla calmed her breathing before a reply.

"I'm fine, dear Percival. What is yonder lake?"

The lake was long, twenty miles or more, stretching out between two ranges of mountains. A rugged country, not like the gentle south of this blessed isle.

"'Tis the loch, my lady. Loch Ness. We draw nigh our destination."

Chapter Seven

T HE LOCH COULDN'T HAVE been more than a mile or so wide at its best. Drusilla studied its shore, Sun playing spectral tricks upon the water. Studied the way those mountains plunged abruptly, steeply, into those waters, it had to be very deep.

Straightening her costume, and checking her hair, Drusilla opened the opposite curtains, and was confronted with a highland meadow penned in by crag and forest, the mountain range rising behind it. It was a lonely-looking place. And as she thought of the vast, virtually unpopulated, tracts of forest they had passed to get here, she amended her assessment: not lonely looking; there was a pervasive feeling of loneliness.

Drusilla shook away the melancholy which followed—either causally, or something else, she didn't know. There was no time for overwhelm, or sadness—whatever had brought it on. She needed to mentally prepare herself for her role.

She was here without invitation. She must ingratiate herself to the lords of Foxborough Keep, and quickly. She would probably only get one chance. And if she failed, she would have to do all her investigating skulking around by stealth and by cover.

She took her mirror, a small, polished piece of silver, and checked her appearance, taking all care to look her best.

She was wearing another of her dreadfully expensive creations, as they had anticipated this to be the day of the arrival. A purple velvet cropped jacket over a white satin dress with purple pinstripes on the skirt. It was cut even lower than the yellow dress, and the buttons of the jacket stopped at the neckline, adding nothing to the outfits' modesty.

She hoped the people of Foxborough were not prudish.

To complete the look, she wore white leather gloves, her comfortable adventurer boots, and tied a purple ribbon in a complicated, weaving pattern through her wavy, dark hair. A little lip powder, and, well, that would just have to do.

The keep was a rambling affair, built upon a terrace of uneven stone directly at the edge of a steep cliff overlooking the loch to the northwest. It was several stories in height, and patrolled from the high, crenelated walls by archers in Celtic armor with their characteristically pointed helmets. Two guards with halberds stood watch over the gatehouse, a square tower with an iron portcullis.

Linus brought the carriage up to hailing distance, and reined in the horses. The four follow-alongs—at the moment, the Coursers—brought themselves to a stop at the end of the procession.

"State your business," he was commanded by one of the guards.

Drusilla could not help but notice the arrow slits in the towers, a particular glint of light catching out a poised arrow tip within. Behind her, she could hear the six pigeons gently cooing, unaware of the building tension.

"The Lady Drusilla of Merovingia wishes to take repose within your keep," said Linus, just as she had instructed him. Good man. "She is weary from long journey, and has taken a fondness to your lake."

"Wait," the guard called out.

A message was relayed within. And then they waited. The men upon the walls watched them hawkishly and with ill intent. One minute passed, and then another. The art, in the waiting, was to look unconcerned and possibly bored. Drusilla did her best, all the while sizing the terrain for options of retreat. The outlook was grim. Should things turn against them now, they were as good as dead.

As abruptly as the period of silence had begun, the portcullis began its slow grind upward, and the carriage was ushered in. Drusilla observed murder slits cut in the masonry overhead as they passed under the tower, and into a Mediterranean-style courtyard, laid wall to wall in stone, with little earthen spots left untouched and bordered. From these, grew trees and shrubs, and a variety of exotic plants not local to the area. A pomegranate tree, in particular, caught her eye. She hadn't seen one of those since Milan. Nothing here belonged. She recognized the whole menagerie as being native to the warmer climes of the Earth, Italy and Greece in particular.

Two men crossed from a massive, iron-reinforced door across the courtyard, trailed by six, no, eight men in Celtic armor, looking more like special bodyguards than regular soldiery.

The two could easily be brothers. The MacKays, by her guess. Both were tall, having long, dirty blonde hair, and dressed after a fashion, like rogues—tight leather pants and high black boots, white shirts open and loose, a sword and dagger each hanging from wide, silver-buckled belts. The bigger man was handsome, built like Adonis himself, with a wide grin full of white teeth. His eyes were a stormy blue, his skin a swarthy olive.

The other was nearly as tall, leaner, but by no means lacking strength. His eyes were hazel or brown. It was difficult to tell in the slanting sunlight. His nose was more hook-like and narrow. He was less bronzed, yet still healthy looking, and might also have been considered handsome by some, but in a less traditional sense. He quirked a smile her way, or was that just a squint against the Sun?

Both men approached her carriage.

Drusilla forced herself to take a languid position.

The larger man held out his hand.

"Bayden MacKay, lord of all you see."

Modest.

"Drusilla of Merovingia, recently of London Town." She held her white gloved hand out the carriage window.

He took her hand in his and kissed it tenderly. "I'm enchanted."

Drusilla squirmed a little. She had never been good at courtly games. She forced a smile, and looked to the courtyard beyond, hoping to appear aloof.

"Forgive me," he said, releasing her hand, and opening the door for her.

Again, he offered his hand and helped her down. Drusilla was tall, but next to this man, she felt petite.

"It's magnificent," she said, looking about. "Not at all like the surrounding fiefdoms. I see you've had exposure to the classical world."

Something dark and brooding churned behind those lake-blue eyes. Something that chilled Drusilla to the bone. He was reading her. Did he not appreciate her comment?

"You are not well," said Bayden.

Drusilla withdrew her trembling hand.

"'Tis the weather, my lord," she said, making the easy excuse. "A bit chill by London standards."

"Of course," said Bayden. "The high mountain air takes some accustoming. Pray, come within." He beckoned with a wide gesture to the sweeping estate built upon the crags above Loch Ness, within an imposing fortification of stone.

The other man cleared his throat, a wildness in his dark eyes.

"Ah, yes. Where are my manners," said Bayden. "This is my brother, Ludo."

Ludo sneered and also took Drusilla's hand. Her other hand. He took pains not to kiss the same hand his brother had.

Interesting.

"Merovingia?" he said. "Your English is certainly passable."

Charming.

"I only mean to say," Ludo pressed on, "that it's obvious you're a foreigner."

"I'm a bit of a transplant," she said, eyes straying again to the exotic foliage of the courtyard.

"Well, let us make you at home," said Bayden. He seemed pained by his brother's discourtesy. Or perhaps it was only a lacking social aptitude on Ludo's part. The way he looked at her, he hardly appeared to be harboring any desire to alienate her.

"Come," said Bayden. "Let us acquaint you with our home." He motioned forward a servant who looked to be familiar with hard labor. "Take the horses and carriage to the livery. Show her servants to quarters befitting their station."

Drusilla found Linus' eyes. She hoped he could see the unspoken apology in hers.

Tour begun, they proceeded through the far door, the one from which the brothers had come, and into the main hall of what Drusilla guessed was the centerpiece of this keep. The ceiling was two stories high. A staircase to her right went up, making the turn left to a balcony halfway up overlooking it all. Behind the overlook, a hall cut tangentially, presumably leading on to a great many rooms and possibly other corridors.

They traveled instead, underneath the staircase, through an arched passageway, and into a vast and open ballroom. The floor was made from polished marble, dark grey, and light golden white. There was easily enough space for a hundred people or more to dance simultaneously, and still a place for musicians, and for tables of food.

Drusilla gasped.

"It's breathtaking," she managed.

Bayden smiled, ushering her back towards the main house, but something caught her eye. Through a series of pillared archways was an outdoor courtyard. It appeared to overlook the entire valley. Why had he redirected the tour?

He showed her many other facets of the house. A large kitchen with a generous hearth and every manner of utensil required to feed a kingdom. Servants were often seen, but seemed to know their place very well here.

There were many bedrooms, most of which resided on the second or third floors. And there were other rooms which served functions, such as music rooms, weapons practice halls, and a sewing room with spinning wheels, skeins of cloth being made by servants as the little tour passed.

At one point, Bayden told the eight bodyguards to go and find something more productive to do. Drusilla was glad she was perceived as no threat here. That would make her job of investigation much easier. She had to be careful, though. Trust easily gained was just as easily lost.

The brothers took her to a grand den of sorts that reminded her at once of a hunting lodge. They entered by a massive oak door carved with murals and borders consisting of exotic animals and a menagerie of even more unlikely monsters. Within, there were animal trophies on walls or stands, including a great brown bear, its now defenseless claws raised high, mouth agape.

Heavy maroon drapes ran ceiling to floor, glowing with the sunlight of windows behind them. Filling in the spaces between were portraits, one in particular, a powerfully built man of forty, a Roman general bearing strong resemblance to the two brothers; tapestries depicting strange and presumably mythical beasts; and weapons and shields of antiquity suspended upon iron hooks driven into the stone. There were scrolls here, too, and maps both rolled up and displayed. Chairs and small tables, arranged in casual formations, evoked a sense of escape and ease.

But the thing which dominated the room and commanded attention was a great stone fireplace, roaring fire within. The stonework, worn old river stones, went straight up to a fifteen-foot raftered ceiling. The fireplace itself was eight foot across and five high, not counting the hearthstone, and threw off pulsing waves of heat which were surprisingly welcome, even in late May.

Caledonia, Drusilla was reminded right down to her bones, was not London Town.

Above the fire, a mantel, a solitary slab of green-grey stone crossed the top and somehow spoke of eons of submerged existence in the loch. And above it, hanging on a brass nail, was the most curious object in the room, for it was wholly unidentifiable—a tawny colored horn mottled in places with a rusty red dappling. Affixed to it was a leather strap. Hollowed and fitted at both the narrow and wide ends by copper rims, it was maybe fourteen inches, narrower than it was wide, like a claw, curving as it tapered, but from what animal she couldn't venture a guess.

Its place of prominence in the room amongst so many other curious objects lent it even more mystery. Ludo, in particular, seemed to pick up on her interest.

"It's a wyvern horn," he said, his eyes inscrutable.

Was he having her on?

"How did you come by such a thing?"

Bayden stepped between them, a look of disapproval vaguely masked. "Most likely from a cow suffering the pox. But it's been in our family for generations untold. The whole thing would likely crumble if touched. Aside from its aesthetic qualities, it's quite useless."

Drusilla watched his eyes with interest. Even lacking the evidence of the horn itself, she knew he was lying. But why?

The leather on the horn was by no means ancient. It had been redone no more than ten years ago. The copper bore not a trace of tarnish. And the horn, yes, that could be old, but certainly not fragile. It had a fine luster, the look of recent oiling and care. It was a thing used. So why lie about it?

Massive logs snapped and popped, sending off embers. They must forest far and wide to feed this monster, for she had seen no deficit of greenery in the surrounding lands.

"No more talk of wyverns, brother," said Bayden, crossing the room to a map displayed on a small, angled scholar's desk near a heavily curtained window. He made pretense of studying some detail or other.

Ludo did not seem to appreciate being chided so, but held his tongue, changing the subject instead.

"You've traveled," he said, a strange hunger in his eyes.

"I've been blessed."

"Have you been to Rome?"

She wasn't sure how much to reveal about herself. Stick close to the truth where possible, she reasoned. Easiest way to keep her story straight and come across genuine.

"I haven't. I hear it's full of wonders."

Ludo lit up. "We've been to Rome, my brother and I. Lived there a while. We had to speak Latin."

"The Colosseum?"

Ludo's eyes narrowed. They looked red in the shifting firelight. "They loot it mercilessly, the native rabble. For its masonry. Still, there's nothing to compare. It was..."

Again, Bayden interrupted, taking advantage of Ludo's moment of silent reflection. "A barbarous people. Their entertainment measured in lives. Certainly no place for a lady of Drusilla's refinement. Or do I speak out of turn?"

"I prefer the quieter reaches of the world," she said, her mind reeling with images of the combat she'd known, the men whose blood she had shed. The life she had taken.

Bayden looked ready to say something else. Ludo quietly seethed. Neither got their opportunity. A servant woman, mid-twenties, dark hair pulled back in a braid and kerchiefed, curtsied at the door.

"I beg pardon, my lord." She waited, eyes cast down, hands holding her aprons in genuflection.

"My apologies," said Bayden, beseeching Drusilla's understanding. "A matter of importance, I'm sure, lest I would not be bothered with it." His voice had taken on a dangerous edge.

"Of course, my lord," she smiled for his benefit, but only till he turned away. He radiated a sense of raw power that kept her ever vigilant in his presence.

Ludo looked amused by the whole proceeding, and angled himself such to inject himself into the event. In their distraction, Drusilla simply slipped away.

Of course, that's what she hoped it would look like to them. Her purpose was to find that courtyard again, and determine why it had been left off the tour.

Being dressed so high-born, Drusilla was not accosted in her wanderings, though she kept an eye out for the bodyguards. She was quite sure they didn't care how she was clothed. She was a newcomer, a possible intruder. It would take time to win them over.

Drusilla found her way back to the main stairs, crossed underneath, and found herself, again, in that marvelous ballroom. It felt strange being here all alone. The vast hall was an exceptional amphitheater. Musicians placed in the right spot could fill the entire hall with sounds of merriment.

Drusilla didn't linger long in the hall, however. She went straight across the ballroom floor to the pillared archways, each with a set of iron-reinforced, glass-mosaic doors—all swung wide open and locked in place by bolts.

More evidences of Rome.

A breeze whipped her hair, and pulled at her dress as she stood, half in, half out, examining the glass. The mosaic was artful, suggesting themes of woodland and fairies, but not explicitly. The images could also just be shapes...

And they were done in only two colors: clear and gold. Neither she recognized from her imports. Perhaps the two brothers had joined in the looting of Rome.

She chuckled at that, and stepped out onto the golden-brown stones of the courtyard, gaze taking in a multileveled terrace which took advantage of the natural slope of the hill. Another hundred dancers could easily fill this outdoor area, given that they watched their footing, as there were many stairs and changes in elevation. A low wall bordered the outdoor court, beyond which was thick forest on three sides, and cliffs overlooking the loch on the fourth.

Drusilla imagined there must be a wall, beyond the thicket, which swung back around and connected to the keep—which would technically make this a castle—otherwise, this was the perfect backdoor for anyone to enter. She decided to check that out later. Right now, she decided it was more important to examine the cliff side. The only place with no apparent fortifications. That, in itself, was curious enough to warrant investigation.

CHAPTER EIGHT

A FEW STEPS DOWN and Drusilla was standing on the lowermost part of the terrace. A wall, ending in a tower, did indeed come right to the cliff's edge, including within its periphery a portion of the forest beyond the courtyard.

So much for security flaws.

The whole run of wall along the cliffside was waist high, compared to only eight inches or so, bordering the rest of the courtyard. The wind pulled harder here, her dress snapping at her legs, Loch clearly visible below, sweeping out in both directions between cliff and mountains.

In the corner where the low wall met it, there was a door in the keep.

A bit odd, architecturally speaking. But then again, that was the thing about doors, you could put one anywhere you liked.

She examined it and found it to be locked. She had expected nothing less. Her curiosity deepened. Drusilla looked around. She was alone.

She put an ear to the door, listened.

Stillness answered.

She removed picks from her hair, careful not to let them blow away, and went to work on the lock. It was a simple design, as most locks were, and offered no resistance. A few seconds later, she heard that rewarding "snap" and the mechanism yielded to her query. The door opened, not into the keep though, but onto a little square platform of stone open to the cliff's mad descent.

Drusilla checked her resolve, then entered quickly, closing the door behind her, and found relief from the wind. Dry land, she reminded herself, though now loch and sky filled the greater part of her vista.

It's out there. I'm safe back here, she told herself, recoiling into the cool little stone alcove. Just look at your feet.

She noticed the platform was the first landing of a staircase that went down. Below was a wider veranda. She couldn't make out all of it from here, but it was definitely roomier.

Sunlight caught out a dark ripple as it traveled across the loch's bright surface. The effect was to suggest something massive, something serpentine, moving just at the surface. A common effect on large bodies of water. Still, Drusilla's head spun a little, and she suddenly realized the very real danger of tumbling over the edge.

No longer trusting the sureness of her own feet, she pressed herself further into the wall. Feeling foolish. The slight panic such thoughts induced, forcing her to chide herself.

Don't be ridiculous. It's only the wind. Nothing can hurt you here. Stone underfoot. Everything's fine. Breathe.

Drusilla waited for the world to stop moving, then leaned out to reconnoiter her next move.

A dozen or so steps went down to a second landing. This one was larger, and it was occupied. A woman, garbed all in white, stood there, not twenty feet away. Drusilla's heart leapt as she slammed herself back into the alcove, but then it registered.

The woman she had seen standing there on the little veranda, overlooking the loch, was nothing but a statue—wrought in ivory of all things. Being a trader in fine goods, the way the light infused it, she was sure of it at a glance.

Ivory. How curious?

Drusilla poked her head out. Theory confirmed.

She sighed her relief. All right.

She took the first step, descending the side of the cliff. No time for games, she looked only at the stair. One at a time. No big deal.

Reaching the veranda, there was room for about half-a-dozen brave souls here, plus the statue. As it was, it was just herself and the mysterious woman in white.

She certainly was lifelike. A young woman in a toga. Absolutely beautiful. A bit austere. Cold. A wistful hand pointed towards the keep, her expression imploring, a little lost, as though drawing a lifeline from the sanctuary of stone. The other hand pointed towards...

The loch.

Drusilla sat down, another bout of panic-induced vertigo.

She closed her eyes a moment, focusing on the cool stone at her back, and when she felt she could, took in the scene again. It was then that she noticed another staircase descending from this landing. She forced herself to the edge, on hands and knees, and looked over.

Through a series of switchbacks, it went all the way down. Down to a narrow strip of beach walled on three sides by cliff, and bound on the forth by water. Fascinated and fearful, taking comfort in the solid feel of the rock under her hands, Drusilla looked on.

The beach was composed mostly of scattered rocks and dark grey sand, some hundred and eighty feet below. One rock, in particular, though, was striking. It projected high into the air. Drusilla judged it to be more than the width of a man, and twice as high. It looked dark, possibly volcanic.

In an odd way, it seemed to mark something. Like the standing stones at Avebury. Druids had put those there for a purpose. Was this the same sort of thing? Drusilla had to know. She stood up, went to the wall. She wasn't going to learn anything by peering down the staircase in the wrong direction.

All right. She needed a second marker. Think, Dru, think. The statue. Of course, it was pointing. Statue, standing stone, the water...

Follow the line. You're safe. Just think. No room for feeling right now.

Nothing but water, water, follow the line...

The opposite cliff.

Falls.

Across the way, by direct line, were falls plunging off the mountain into the loch. A beautiful, terrible yellow-white ribbon of cascading water.

Chapter Nine

Water is almost always deep beneath a waterfall, and this one plunged directly into the loch. What secrets did it hold, that the ivory hand, permanently frozen in time, pointed to it, and with such a haunted look that it was hard to believe that she was not flesh and blood?

Drusilla took a deep breath. She had stumbled upon yet another mystery. Whether it had anything to do with Camille's disappearance or not, she didn't know.

As she stood there, pondering, she almost forgot her innate horror of the loch. A mystery was beckoning. Across the water, near that far cliff, a black ripple disturbed the surface. Judging by the distance, it had to be large, elephantine large—maybe larger. Then it was gone.

Drusilla's stomach was doing little flips, heart pounding in her throat. The way the water had moved...

Had she seen anything? Water could move in such unusual ways. There were many smaller ripples out there on the loch, accountable to wind or fish. Seals might come inland here from the sea. Perhaps this was a compounded effect, a fluke of wind and water.

Drusilla looked away, back to the statue. Back to her own solid footing, which had begun to sway.

Sometimes she thought she might just as well be crippled. The whole world was made of water. It was everywhere. Of all the things in the world to be afraid of, why water? Why was she so terrified by it?

She wanted to turn away. Instead, she locked both hands on the ledge and let the moment swallow her.

Chapter Ten

T HE CLIFFS WERE DEEPENING to a black silhouette. A glance behind her, eyes straining up till they found the keep's crenelated walls rimmed crimson by the departing Sun, found no solace there. The presence of the water was all pervasive. It need not be seen to be felt. It seeped its way into every last remaining sense.

She looked out again, to the falls, and found only grey against the black mountain, last light playing orange upon the expanse of dark water.

How long had she been out here?

Oh god, thought Drusilla, about to turn, when she saw it again, even closer to the falls now. A ripple in the water's surface. Serpentine—

"How on earth did you get down here?"

Drusilla startled terribly, her hand involuntarily seizing the veranda's wall for safety—head snapping around, facing the owner of the angry voice. It was Bayden, no longer charming, his attitude transformed, become cold and menacing.

Drusilla summoned all her courage, met his eye, and said simply, "The door was unlocked. I wandered off when you began discussing matters of household efficiency with your staff. You'll have to forgive my impatience for such things."

Lies came easily to Drusilla, and this one flowed off her tongue, but Bayden's jaw remained set, his look dangerous. She could tell he was judging her story, unsure of its truth. Good, at least he wasn't sure she was lying. It was time to divert him from any more brooding.

"Who is she?" Drusilla asked, hedging herself away from the edge. The water was so immediate.

Bayden's eyes burned with seeming anger, but his voice was calm, even distant. "Someone I once loved."

Drusilla was of the distinct impression the conversation was over. She moved further from the wall, but Bayden crossed, taking her hand, and pulled her back to the edge. His grip was masterful, demanding. It left little doubt that she was not calling the shots now.

"Isn't it beautiful?" he said, indicating the loch. "Isn't that why you stopped here? At my keep?"

Drusilla's heart raced. Her hand, tiny by comparison, squirmed within his. The dark, undulating waters consumed her vision. She felt dizzy, and fought against the faintness overcoming her. Did he know? Could he sense her fear?

Her knees buckled, vision going starry.

Bayden caught her up in his powerful arms, pulling her to his chest. He was like a rock, an extension of the very stone from which the veranda was formed.

"My Dear," he spoke softly. "You are not yet well. You require rest after such a long journey. I was a fool to think otherwise. Come."

Drusilla was relieved to find he had dropped the subject of her presence on the ledge, and that there would be no more questioning, at least for now. But it was nearly as unnerving to know what a disadvantage he had her at.

For a fleeting instant, she imagined how easily he could toss her out over the wall and be done with her. Instead, he led her inside, calling to a young woman. There were several at hand—all, though not an official uniform, dressed similarly, from pinafore to kerchief—near the servant's quarters engaged in idle chatter whilst busy hands folded sheets. Foxborough Keep did not lack for servants.

"You, Bridgette. Come attend to our Lady Drusilla. She is not well after such a trying journey. Show her every courtesy. Give her our best suite."

Bridgette was young, maybe seventeen, with sandy hair and an open, lightly freckled face framing cerulean eyes. She trembled, dropping the sheet, and bent to retrieve the now rumpled cloth, fingers hammering away like scared rabbits which could not depart her hand, but not for lack of trying.

Drusilla's heart immediately went out to the young maid, so much of her a mirror to her own awkward years.

"But surely, my lord," the young woman spoke nervously, in too much haste, "one of the rooms in the east wing would be better—" She stopped herself, obviously knowing she had spoken out of turn. "Oh, please forgive me," she begged. Then added, still floundering terribly, "It's just, that would be Evelynn's, was Evelynn's..."

The young woman, named Bridgette, looked like she wanted to die right then. Her fear of Bayden, and her current peril, was unmasked and complete.

Bayden was silent a moment. Drusilla sensed hesitation. If he crossed the line of brutality towards this girl, she vowed to intervene by any means necessary. Diplomacy was the preferable route, and probably the only survivable course, but still, she took account of the location of her dagger...

His indecision lasted only a moment, though.

"Do as I say, woman," he said, clearly irritated.

Had he misspoken? Drusilla suspected so, and that now his pride would not allow him to withdraw his words. The lord of Foxborough stood glowering over the onlookers till all eyes fell away. He did not look happy. In those burning blue eyes lay a challenge none would meet.

Another servant, an older woman, took the fallen sheets from Bridgette and picked her up. Bridgette stood there, too shocked to move.

"Go," the older woman said, breaking the spell.

Bridgette scrambled to comply, bidding Drusilla follow her, the poor dear clearly frightened half to death.

Up the staircase they went, past the balcony, and down a hall to a set of double doors framed in a stone arch. The entrance alone spoke of importance. Wealth. This was not a guest's quarters. It was a master suite.

"Here we are," said Bridgette, hesitating, before swinging the doors wide. She had calmed some since leaving the presence of Bayden.

The open doors revealed a scene that instantly chilled Drusilla. This place, this suite, had been lived in, and recently. The faint aura of lavender still clung to the air, probably her perfume or favorite flowers. Bridgette had called her Evelynn. The aroma clung here like a spirit not wont to leave this world.

Drusilla pushed the vague and haunting feeling aside, surveying the room. A large, canopied bed stood against the north wall. A night stand on the far side. Several chairs of fine workmanship placed about. The south wall had an exquisite dressing table, sporting a mirror of quality generally only afforded to kings. There were still bottles and potions of all sorts on the table, neatly arranged just so.

An organized mind.

There was a wardrobe in the southeast corner. Drusilla would open that later, in private. No sense creating rumors. The most startling feature of the room, however, was the wall-to-wall balcony opening onto a view of the loch.

It was twilight out there, the water dark and almost indiscernible. A ghost in the gloaming. The dim outline of mountain against sky evaporated into the haze of a cheery light as Bridgette lit candles about the room.

The balcony had a series of doors which could be closed against the elements. Doors which, like the ones in the ballroom, were made from wrought iron and glass, though these were only of clear glass, and done in a simpler pattern, they would be horribly expensive—or looted. She knew only of the Romans to have such things. In fact, it was her observation that no expense had been spared to make this woman comfortable.

The floor was flagstone, but sported several rugs of oriental design, each large and, well, expensive. And a bearskin rug before a fireplace. Definitely a plush lifestyle.

"Well, if that's all..." said the young woman, looking at the flagstones, knees trembling.

Drusilla turned, wide eyes of the other, so close to tears, meeting her own—seeking permission to flee. She hated to press on, but it was necessary.

"Who was she?"

Bridgette touched a bracelet on her opposite wrist—colored beads entwined in hempen cord. It was a momentary and seemingly unconscious gesture. "I beg your pardon, my lady."

"Evelynn, who was she?"

Hearing the question rephrased seemed to snap Bridgette out of a momentary reverie, but it brought no end to her unease. "We're not allowed," she said pitifully, lower lip joining her knees in a tremble-fest. "Please don't ask me that."

Drusilla crossed the room to the bed, sitting on the edge. Down feathers. Nice.

Bridgette was still in the doorframe, fidgeting terribly now with the hem of her apron. Drusilla patted the bed next to her. The young woman looked at her, scared near witless from the look of her.

"Come here," said Drusilla. "Sit."

Bridgette hesitated, then obeyed.

"Bridgette, I know that you're scared. Believe me, I know a considerable lot about fear. More than my share."

Bridgette met her eyes.

"Oh my god," said Drusilla, seeing the fear ran much deeper than she had at first suspected. "Whatever's wrong, I want you to know you can come to me. I won't tell your secrets."

"Be careful, my lady," said Bridgette. "I don't know what's going on here, but things aren't right." She glanced fearfully to the door. "Please don't get me into trouble. I've got no one."

Drusilla put an arm around the woman, only a handful of years her younger. To her surprise, Bridgette trembled under her touch.

There was something in that reaction...

Drusilla thought about the young woman in her embrace. No different than all the other housemaids here. Similar in age to several others she had seen. Similar in dress. The bracelet meant something to her. An anchor of some sort. As they sat in silence, Drusilla giving what comfort she could, she let her eyes wander idly over the pattern of the beads.

Rose-red, green, purple like the crocus, and violet. Why did that mean something to her? It nagged at her brain—a thing she had heard once... or possibly read.

And why should a simple touch set the young woman to tremble? It troubled her. Was she too accustomed to the back of the hand? Was it simple deprivation?

Drusilla made further study of the beads as Bridgette finally melted into her. Red had grabbed her eye the first time, but it was violet which led the sequence. The first bead after the knot securing it to her wrist: violet, then red, followed by green, then purple. Violets, roses... she could not grasp the meaning behind the shade of green, and crocuses.

The tickle at the edge of her consciousness was now a hum. This had meaning, and she had encountered it before...

Bridgette let out a sigh. Drusilla suspected she was being brave, and that she was holding back so much more.

"It isn't true."

Bridgette looked to Drusilla, a question in her eyes.

"What you said, about having no one," Drusilla went on. "You have me."

DRUSILLA WOKE FROM A long, dreamless sleep. The bed had drawn her deep into its seductive comforts. Stuffed with goose down, heavily quilted from fine white linen, it was a thing of exquisite quality. Four blonde-oak posts, turned and polished to an almost glass finish, held a canopy of gossamer white. She had not drawn the heavy drapes closed, leaving them tied back by their gold cords, preferring the fresh mountain air throughout the night. By the Sun, it was late afternoon.

How long had she slept? Some eighteen hours, she calculated. Nothing she could do about the lost time. Stretching, she took consolation. She did feel rested.

She dressed, then went to the wardrobe. It was, as she suspected, full of clothes—expensive clothes. She wondered what would happen if she put one of the dresses on and wore it in front of the brothers—to provoke a reaction. She wondered, but then decided it was a bad idea.

She dug further into the wardrobe, looking for something personal. In the back corner was a carved wooden box. She withdrew it. It was just the right size for...

Letters.

They were written in French. Interesting. Fortunately for Drusilla, French was one of her acquired languages; being Merovingian, she had grown up speaking Gallo. It was somewhere linguistically between English and French, and had afforded her a head start tackling those two. She settled into a chair in the corner of the room, giving herself a view of the loch. If at all possible, she had to accustom herself to its menacing presence.

Drusilla took the first letter, and glanced at it, skimming it for content, then the next, and so on. Not letters, as she had thought, more of a disjointed diary. As she sat there, reading, a strange and beautiful tale of love unfolded. Evelynn, it seemed, was Bayden's betrothed. He gave her everything money could buy.

From her point of view, he doted on her, and was romantic and sweet. Life was idyllic for her. So what had happened to her?

The last entry talked of a moonlit walk on the beach. Not one they had shared together, but one that was planned. Still in the future. She was looking forward to it with great enthusiasm. It was a secret beach—

Drusilla dropped the page and ran to the balcony. She hesitated several steps from the edge, then fell to her knees, crying. Why couldn't she live a normal life? A life without fear?

Come on, Dru, two more steps. It's important.

She stood, closed her eyes, and let it fill her senses. Waves lapping against slicked rock faces, must and algae carried on a breeze—water, mountain, night. Rising, she took a step forward, laughing near hysteria, then opened her eyes. One more step, come on.

Fear swelled back into her brain, but she took the last step anyway, and looked down, steeling herself against the revulsion she knew would come. There it was. Not the whole beach, just the pinnacle of dark rock, and a hint of an ingress in the cliff face.

Of all the rooms in the keep, Drusilla felt this one had to have as good a view as any. It was doubtful anyone could watch the goings-on on that beach without going to great effort. Why, then, was that letter the last entry in Evelynn's journal? What happened that night? Why had she been memorialized in ivory of all things?

Something about that nagged Drusilla's brain. A particular something just beyond her present ability to recall. The ivory. She had read about it before, somewhere...

She grasped at the memory.

When Drusilla was little, and living in Merovingia, her father had run an import-export business. But his true passion was intellectualism. He often had associates over for dinner with the hopes of a good conversation afterward.

Drusilla would sneak down from her bedroom and listen. Often the conversations were in other languages. They were, after all, in the business of establishing trading triangles for profit. Triangles that spanned half the known world.

When the men would converse, Drusilla would listen. And over time, she learned. And learning, she eventually came to read in those languages. French, Portuguese, English, Latin, German, and...

Greek. Of course—

The Pygmalion.

It was time for Drusilla to pay a visit to the two brothers.

Chapter Eleven

D RUSILLA FOUND THE MacKAY brothers dining in a private hall on the third floor of the keep after some wandering—none of it wasted. She was determined to gain as intimate a knowledge of her surroundings as possible, and with all haste. She could easily have asked any one of the many servants she encountered along the way for the whereabouts of the brothers, however, should things turn badly for her here, it could only serve to know her way around.

She'd found the door ajar, sounds of silver service and crockery, as well as all the lovely scents betraying their location. Stepping into the doorframe, wearing a cloak of shadow, Drusilla took the lay of it.

Narrow arched windows ran nearly floor to ceiling, letting in dusky slivers of the available evening light. And though the room was composed of dark stone and darker wood, she could see the brothers well enough. They piled their plates high, taking of the varied and over plentiful feast before them. An iron candelabra at the table's center put them, and the great splay well within a cheerful pool of light.

Knowing that a direct gaze was the easiest way to draw unwanted attention, Drusilla kept her eyes moving. Deep shadows obscured the edges of the spacious hall, making ascertainment of fine details all but impossible. But it was not details she needed. The larger picture would do.

And whilst her presence remained unknown, it gave her welcome time to reflect on the sight: two men, brothers, big as they were, sitting down to a splay of food that could comfortably feed twenty. She supposed the remnants would be passed amongst the servants later. But in this, there would be no indulging. She knew well that common folk ate simply and with good cheer, participated in physical labor, and over time, had the better health for it.

Drusilla chided herself. Such thoughts were unkind, and worse, unsubstantiated—rushed judgements of men she barely knew. She had known the brothers scant hours, hardly a time frame suitable to form an opinion of any merit.

And it wasn't why she was here. Drusilla had come to learn what news she could of Camille.

Her mind was not operating as dispassionately as she would have liked. It was not like her. Something about this place, this room, in particular, had raised her hackles and put her ill at ease. She tried to see it again with fresh eyes.

From the continued anonymity the doorframe provided, she looked anew. The windows opposite her once again drew her attention. Cool air drafted in, chilling her legs as she stood immobile. She caught scent of the loch as she stood there, could hear it faintly beyond those stone walls. This was the far edge of the keep, the extent of which was bounded by the very presence of that dark, deep body of water. She was ever a prisoner of her dread. Here, it was not so much omnipresent as hinted at, and rather than causing her irrational terror, it merely plagued her serenity.

"Ah, Lady Drusilla, we were hoping you could join us." It was Bayden. Her reverie had gone too long unchecked. She hadn't noticed him look up. "You will join us, won't you?"

His voice pulled her, as if from a fog, into the Sun.

"Are you well?" Again Bayden. How long had she occupied the doorframe, paralyzed to inaction? The subtle power of her dread had worked her into a trance. Her delay could be mistaken in many ways. Trying to reorient herself, she eased her grip from the doorframe, now acutely aware of the spectacle she had raised. Ludo rose from his chair, moving towards her.

She forced a smile. "Yes, well as can be. I am in fact famished and a bit weak for it. It would be my pleasure to join you."

Ludo offered his hand, and she took it, allowing him to guide her to a chair to his right. His eyes looked kind in the moment, that is, until he glanced to his brother who sat to his left. They seemed to darken and take on a wild aspect lacking just moments before.

"I hope I haven't interrupted anything," she said, surveying the food. She was, in truth, quite famished. That much of her excuse had come easily. Already, she was devouring the feast with her eyes.

"Not at all," said Bayden, ignoring the politics of seating. "We were just discussing the invitations. We sent them out weeks ago. Guests should be arriving any time now."

"Invitations?"

"We're hosting a festival," said Ludo.

"And games of sport and courtly fun," added Bayden.

"You might as well join us," said Ludo, "as you are already here."

Drusilla forced yet another smile. It would seem that was to be her permanent condition while ingratiating herself in the role of courtier.

"Already here?" Bayden scowled at his brother. "Heathen." He turned to Drusilla, those brooding blue eyes piercing her most uncomfortably. "Drusilla is a rare and delightful discovery. If she goes home now, I shall simply have to cancel the entire course of events.

"You will stay, won't you, My Dear?"

Something in the way Bayden phrased that question made Drusilla's skin crawl, straining to be free of her skeleton.

"Of course," she gave her best genuflection and smile. "How could I refuse such charming implore?"

"It's settled then," said Bayden. "You shall be our guest of honor."

Drusilla took a sip from a glass of wine Ludo had just filled, so that she would not need to smile again.

The three ate in relative silence at first, but soon as appetites were sated and food became more of an idle diversion and less of a necessity, conversation reinstated itself.

"You must tell us more of your travels." It was Bayden.

"I only recently found my freedom," said Drusilla, reflecting on her life before Britain. "I sailed from Merovingia to Dover, and there to London, I made my way."

"But what lured you from your home? You're obviously a woman of means." It was Ludo. "You must have had all you wanted there." His strange, shifting gaze scrutinized hers. Anything she said now could be dangerous. She felt the weight of his perception as a prisoner feels his jailor.

The truth, in this then, at least.

"I learned to read," she said simply, letting that sink in. Now they were both watching her hawkishly. A baited silence hung amongst the party. She took a bit of sweetmeat upon her fork, inhaled its tender succulence and slowly enjoyed it. They were still waiting when she finished. The pain of it could not be outmaneuvered. A reckoning had to be made, and so she continued.

"Not just my native Gallo and the closely related French, but English too." The truth, but minimized. Contained for damage control. She did not wish to reveal the whole of her hand. They were looking at her with what seemed to be a mixture of fascination and amusement. Merovingian men would not be so amused. She had to smile, this time genuinely, as she continued her tale, changing her age from twelve to fourteen so as to account for less years in this retelling.

"I was fourteen when my mother discovered this. When she realized the extent of the damage, the sheer number of works I had read, she was furious. 'You're ruined,' she said." Drusilla mimicked her mother's voice, plying it with the thick, Gallo accent of her memory. Little stabs of pain shot through her as she recounted the last day she ever spent in her birth home. The last day ever she saw her mother. "'No man will have you now.' Those were her exact words. And off we went to the convent."

"You're trembling." It was Bayden. He rose, taking the goblet of wine from her hand, and set it aside.

Drusilla looked at her hand, willed it to be still. *You're lucky the church will take you,* her mother's voice still rung in her head. An unhappy echo. The last thing she had ever said to her.

Drusilla swallowed. Closed her eyes a moment, calmed herself. "I'm fine," she apologized. "It is not the happiest of memories. Pray, sit, my lord. Do not trouble yourself on my account. There is still much to feast upon, and my tale only gets happier from there."

Bayden took his seat, quirking a smile. Ludo watched her with new fascination. He seemed genuinely amused by something, and she could not quite place it. Still, there was the expectation of more, and it did not suit her to leave things in this emotional state of disquiet. Before she could form the next bit, though, Bayden posed a curious question. Curious, because he seemed conflicted in the very inquiry.

"You are a Christian, then?"

How should she answer that? Religion was always dangerous ground. Arthur had followed Christendom's basic tenets, though there was always the influence of Druidic belief and the wisdom of The Merlin. Drusilla found the convent's version of devotion to be cruel and heavy-handed, yet she believed in God. Perhaps not as they wished, but in her own way. Through Roland, she had learned much from The Merlin. She was as much a Druid as a Christian, she supposed. To her, it didn't matter. God was God, and men had funny ideas about God.

"I am," she said, simply. "Though I have no desire for cloistering. I ran away when it came time for me to make my vows. In truth, I could never have made a very convincing nun. My faith is not absolute." In truth, she had run away, at fourteen, after Carlotta's death. After the terrible things which had made life at the convent unbearable.

Ludo was grinning now. That crooked smile coupled with dark mischief in eyes that yet defied description.

"My brother," said Bayden, "is an unbeliever. I follow Christ, though we are not formal about it here in Foxborough."

He was lying. At least in his conviction. She had seen more than her share of conviction at the convent, and this man did not have it. That Ludo would choose a less structured life, however, was most aptly fitting.

"You learned the reading of three languages without any formal tutoring?" It was Ludo. "How?"

"My father had scrolls, papers, maps. He was a merchant and would acquire them in his travels. Sometimes he brought men home, and I quietly listened to their conversations in foreign tongues. It enchanted me, knowing there were whole other worlds out there to discover.

"But the papers from those foreign lands. And the scrolls. At some point, I just had to know what was in those scrolls."

"You are a delightful creature, Lady Drusilla. No one in this household would begrudge you your self-gained education." There it was again. Bayden could melt her with a word at times, this being one of them. But she reminded herself not to fall prey to his courtly behavior. Too often, she had seen the undercurrent of danger running deep within him.

"How does a runaway come by a small fortune?" asked Ludo, danger coming from him now.

"I ran away from the convent. No work could I find." Here, she mixed truth and invention, needing to provide a suitable cover. "I was starving. I saw the horrors of life on the street, swallowed my pride and went back home, only to find my mother had passed that very week, and I, a small fortune, as you say, inherited, along with land and a title. I was the lady of the house, and free in every way that counted.

"Knowing some English, and wishing for a new start, I liquidated everything, and crossed the Channel. Life has never been better."

"Still, you travel alone, it is unseemly," said Bayden.

"I have my servants," said Drusilla, not liking this new development.

Bayden nodded, savoring a bite of venison. "I only meant that a lady of such high standing shouldn't travel without the aid and comfort of another woman."

Drusilla saw where he was going. She needed an excuse. He was teasing out her social station—checking her story, as it were. She had been unwilling to risk another woman on this mission, and had hoped the people of this remote and rugged country would not question her affairs too closely. She had been wrong.

"My lady-in-waiting of many years," she said, after stalling for time by sipping her wine, "was recently taken ill. She was a great loss to me."

She looked over her fork, idly twisting a piece of venison through the air, trying to appear wistful.

"Irreplaceable," she added with an air of finality.

Bayden looked as though he were gauging her every word. Drusilla looked away, unable to tolerate his unabashed and penetrating stare any longer. Just when she had decided he was an absolute monster, he said something redeeming. She felt guilty for judging him in haste. There was genuine compassion in his voice.

"I'm sorry," he said. "Such things are never easy."

"She was more like a mother to me," added Drusilla, cringing inwardly at her solicitations of pity. Unwarranted at that.

"How much you must have suffered," he rejoined.

At that, Drusilla dared to meet his gaze again. What a strange and complicated man he was.

"Thank you," she muttered, her throat tightening. Drusilla set down the untouched fork, placing her hands in her lap to hide signs of the reaction he elicited within her.

"I only hope Bridgette can be of some small service to you."

"She's been wonderful."

"Good," said Bayden, "then I insist you take her when that sad day of your departure comes."

Drusilla was shocked. "Doesn't she have family?" She knew, already, the answer to that. But she was not wont to supply any hint to him that she had conversed in confidence with the young woman in question.

"Alas, no," he continued. "Only us, and I suspect she much prefers your company."

"But your offer is too generous, my lord," said Drusilla, moved to genuine gratitude by this inscrutable man. She feared him more now than ever before. If he was capable of such subtle shifts in his personality, he might be capable of anything.

"You are capable of providing her upkeep?" asked Bayden.

"Certainly."

"Then the matter is settled. I'll hear no more of it." He wiped the corners of his mouth, and pushed his plate away. "She is yours."

"Thank you, my lord," said Drusilla, inclining her head in a slight bow.

Drusilla vowed to let Bridgette decide her own destiny, but if the young woman wished employment, she would provide it. Something was not right about this household. It was a place of enigma and contradiction. One thing she would not feel bad about, was taking Bridgette away from here.

AFTER DINNER, DRUSILLA WENT down to the servants' quarters to inquire after Linus and Percival, and to find the stables so she could check on the horses and send a pigeon. She didn't have much to report yet, but she didn't want Roland worrying to the point that he raised an army and sent it up here.

Also, she wanted to see if any of the other servants were more willing to talk. She was afraid if she came right out and asked about Camille, she might spoil her chances of getting to the bottom of things.

The first servant Drusilla encountered was a manservant or butler of some sort.

"May I be of some assistance, madam?" he inquired as she approached.

"My Coachman, and the lad, Percival, do you know where they are?"

"They are taking a late supper in the north wing. The kitchen, to be precise."

"And my coach? I have need of my personal effects."

"I can have them sent up to your room. You're in Ev—um, the grand suite. I shall call a porter, or see to it myself personally."

He certainly wasn't the one to talk to. She would try the kitchen. Perhaps Percival or Linus had gathered more than she had. They were both under explicit instructions to ingratiate themselves to the staff, keep their eyes and ears open, and pick up on the local gossip.

Making her way to the north wing, Drusilla found twenty or more servants just getting up from dinner, clearing the plates away, and stacking them for the scullery maid. Drusilla smiled. If ever there was a lonelier position in a castle, it was scullery maid. Perhaps her ear would be hungry for gossip.

"My lady," said Percival, rushing over to her. Linus, spotting her, came too, but at a more dignified pace.

"Percival, Linus, are you two well?"

Other servants were noticing her appearance as well, and seemed to grow uncomfortable.

"Can I get you anything?" the senior servant, a man bent and elderly, asked her.

"I'm fine, please go about your day as though I weren't here."

The man nodded, and bowed deeply, which wasn't much considering his perpetual stoop. "As you wish," he said, and shuffled off.

"Well enough," said Linus, speaking for both of them. "A private word?"

Drusilla retreated to the corner, absently staring out the back window, which overlooked the walled part of the southeast forest.

The three had relative privacy here.

"How are the horses and carriage?"

"They have been stabled," said Percival.

"And the carriage is in the livery," added Linus.

"And the pigeons?"

"The lords of the keep practice falconry. They have been taken to a roosting pen," said Linus. "I saw to it myself. They are quite safe, and the young girl who tends to the birds is as gentle and sweet a soul as you'll ever meet."

"Good. I need to go there. Can you give me directions?"

"I can do better," said Linus. "I'll take you there myself."

"Later, then," said Drusilla. "First, I need to do some dishes."

Both men looked at her, puzzled.

"I must earn my keep," she said with a laugh. It was a ruse. One designed to fool no one. She knew nothing at all was actually required of her but proper behavior. Before either servant could protest, she added, by way of diversion, "Is there anything of merit to report?"

"Nothing yet," said Percival, taking the bait too easily. "It's just that, well, the house seems—nervous about something. Sort of superstitious or tight-lipped, if you will."

Linus nodded, a dubious glance, just to let her know he knew, she was sure, before giving his piece. "They're scared. It's too soon to know why. We're still strangers here."

Drusilla was thoughtful a moment, then spoke. "Go, then, make yourselves available to them. It won't do to stand around with me."

"I'll be near the scullery, in the hall, when you're done with your—dishes," said Linus, almost choking on that last word.

THE SCULLERY WAS ADJOINED to the kitchen, and as Drusilla had suspected, one young girl was in charge of scrubbing the towering stack of plates, the mountain of pans and tankards, the haystack of silver…

Drusilla entered quietly, removing her velvet jacket, revealing well-toned arms, and the white laced, white silk bodice and pinstriped skirt. She searched the shelves and cupboards till she found an apron to protect what she could not set aside, and while she did, the girl, unaware of Drusilla's presence, whistled a happy little tune.

It came as quite a shock to her when Drusilla brought a stack of dishes over and placed them in the soapy water. The tune came to an abrupt end.

"Oh, my lady," the girl exclaimed, falling back and immediately curtsying. She was about fourteen, a fair-skinned redhead with frightened grey eyes.

Drusilla just smiled. "I don't mind doing them all myself, but if you'd care to help…"

The girl stood there in wide-eyed silence a moment, then found her wit. "Of course," she said. "I beg your pardon."

Together they scrubbed in silence for a moment, then the girl spoke again.

"It's really no trouble, no trouble at all. I can finish these myself—"

"I said I don't mind." Drusilla spared a kind look, then continued to scrub. "What was that tune you were singing?"

Flustered, the girl searched her memory. "Bonnie Hill Maid," she said at length.

"Could I hear some more?"

"Um, yes. Of course, my lady."

"If you don't want to…"

"It's all right." The girl smiled, shyly, and began.

In minutes, the two had developed a happy work rapport and had put a sizable dent in the dishes.

The girl finished her tune, and Drusilla volunteered one of her own. Something she had learned crossing the channel with Childebrande.

"Lovely," said the girl, with genuine enthusiasm, when Drusilla finished.

"Why thank you," said Drusilla, in an exaggerated stage voice, giving a little curtsy of her own.

They worked some more, and as they did, Drusilla tried to get the girl talking. They fell into easy conversation, and she eventually turned the talk to her "cousin" Camille.

"Oh, she was lovely," said the girl. "A real nice lady. She didn't stay long, though."

"I had so hoped to run into her," said Drusilla.

"She left near a fortnight ago. She was real upset over the death of that young man, Atreus. That, and the fact all her writing supplies went missing."

Drusilla's heart skipped a beat. Sir Atreus, dead. A deep sorrow filled her.

"Is something wrong, my lady?"

Drusilla composed herself.

"It's always tragic when someone young dies," she said. "Did he suffer?"

"No. At least I don't think so," said the girl. "Fell off the cliff, he did. Lost his footing. It was raining, of course, poor chap. We had a right, nice funeral service for him. Couldn't get to the body. The loch took him. All that heavy armor, it's no wonder."

Drusilla didn't feel well. Atreus had been a friend. Like herself, he had been mentored by Roland, and at times they had shared lessons, training excursions, even sparred together. She felt all the more ill, realizing she would have to break the news to Roland.

"Are you well, my lady?" asked the girl, actually touching Drusilla's arm. "Was he a friend?"

Drusilla brightened her face, lying. "It's a sad tale you tell. I was moved by it, that's all.

"Did anyone see him fall?"

"Only Lord Ludo and a couple of the Elite Guard. Ludo himself reported it to the household, and only a month after Lilly went missing."

"Lilly?"

"One of the village girls, down by the loch. Her father's a fisherman. Won't fish no more. Folks say he may die of a broken heart. She was his pride and joy, and just off to Dál Riata too, to marry."

"That's tragic," said Drusilla, her mind still swirling with thoughts of Atreus, that cliff, Ludo's strange, wild eyes. She still didn't know what color they were. They seemed to change with his moods. What was it Roland had said about that?

Oh, yes. She had heard it from Roland, and Roland from The Merlin. "Eyes that change belong to the personality that is not fixed." That certainly fit. A shudder passed through her body.

"Lilly was very beautiful, you know," the girl continued. "All the missing girls have been beautiful."

"All the missing girls? What other girls?"

The girl looked away and began scrubbing furiously at a frying pan.

"Oh, I've got so much work to do," she said.

Drusilla decided not to push it. Something had the whole household terrified to silence. She doubled her own efforts on the last remaining pots and pans. Better to win friends right now than lose them.

DISHES FINISHED, DRUSILLA BID the young girl goodnight, learning her name was Beth. She then slipped out to the hall, buttoning up her jacket, and located Linus, who was in the crook of a column where it met the stone wall, dozing.

She made a little clicking on the flagstone with her heels until he took notice.

"Oh, um, my lady, forgive me, I was just..."

"Resting your eyes, I know."

"This way, my lady."

Linus led Drusilla out the keep, and into an area open to the sky—livery, exercise yard, and more. First, the courtyard off the ballroom, and now this.

She turned and craned her neck upwards to observe the keep, then ran her eyes along crenelated walls manned with soldiers. She had expected outbuildings, but found towers standing apart from the keep, and a rear gatehouse, equally formidable to the front, all connected by defensible walls.

The keep, that was not a keep, kept growing.

Was this outlying sprawl a centuries-later afterthought? Had the original name been kept for euphony or tradition? Perhaps it was a deliberate downplay to assuage the neighbors any concern that another ambitious king had popped up?

In short order, they were in a loft, in the highest part of the southeast tower, filled with soft hay, cages, and birds. Linus pointed to the one assigned to her pigeons, and she went straight over. The birds lay there, in the bottom of the cage, on their sides.

"Oh god," said Drusilla softly. She lifted one of the sweet creatures from its repose. Its head flopped limply over her finger, glassy eyes staring at nothing.

She tried to think.

Rigor not yet set in... it was recent work—

The horses!

Chapter Twelve

D RUSILLA RACED FROM THE loft, leaving Linus behind and bewildered. She had a good idea where the stables were and how to get to them. She raced along stone corridors, and out into the rear courtyard and exercise yard, heart pounding. Stacks of hay populated one end of the yard, and directly across from the keep door she had exited were a livery and stables constructed to a massive scale. Her eyes scanned rapidly, desperately. Fifty horses or more could be boarded here.

Drusilla was only concerned with eight.

She rushed across the yard, checking one stable, then the next, then the next, fighting the swell of panic that threatened to overwhelm her sensibility. With each stall that she found a horse other than her four, her determination grew, and with it a vow. If anything foul had befallen her horses, there would be an avenging.

A livery man caught her by the arms, stepping in front of her wild flight. Drusilla's eyes snapped to his, savage, impassioned.

"What troubles you?" he asked, holding her in a powerful grip. He was maybe twenty-five, and it was obvious he earned his living by hard labor.

Drusilla thought to strike him down, but calmed herself. She was small by comparison, but she knew speed would compensate. Roland had taught her that. This man was not her enemy, though. She counted the beats of her heart till they yielded to her will. She needed to be rational right now.

"Forgive me, sir," she said, taking a breath. "My horses, are they well?"

"Is that all? You had me frightened half to death, my lady," he said, relaxing, and dropping his arms. "They're right over here."

She was surprised the man had dared to touch her. Another reminder of where she was, and how very carefully she must tread. He led her about twenty stalls down and showed her her horses quietly sleeping. Drusilla closed her eyes. Thank God.

Drusilla reached into her purse and took out a gold solidus, an exorbitant amount of money, and pressed it into his hand.

"My lady," he protested, trying to give it back. It was probably a half year's wages for him.

"See that my horses are kept safe. Be vigilant," she commanded. "You'll get twice that again, when I leave with all eight, well and spirited."

The man bowed deeply. She thought he might be on the verge of weeping.

"I will see it done, my lady."

She patted him on the shoulder. "Thank you."

BRIDGETTE WAS ASLEEP IN the corner chair when Drusilla returned to her rooms. It was nigh to midnight, by her best guess.

Through tears, both heartbreak and anger, she had rehearsed her next move as she had made her way from livery to suite. She had moved in a trance, not remembering exactly how she had arrived at the double doors, deep in her own ruminations.

In one version, she went, herself, to Nairn. In variations, she sent Linus or Percival—to find if any of Sir Atreus' pigeons had been left behind. Surely, he had come to Loch Ness with at least two, but the investigation being so close to his home, perhaps he had not brought all...

It was a stretch.

It would forestall Roland any action undertaken in the absence of communication, though, and that made it worth considering.

Yet this was day eight? Nine? Her mind was a blur.

The trip from London Town itself had been expected to take anywhere from eight to ten days. He would not worry yet. But he would worry soon.

So the plan had merit.

But it also contained an undeniable danger.

Soon, if Drusilla did not stumble upon the information, she would needs provoke it. And once she revealed her connection to Camille, coincidence would be her only shield. If a connection between herself and Atreus was made...

Then she would be revealed, and any hope of her investigation dashed.

Drusilla slipped into the room and barred the doors.

No. She could not go to Nairn. Roland would wait. How long, she wasn't sure. But there would be no more pigeons. The next time she sent word to London Town, it would be delivered by hand.

As the young woman in the chair breathed the soft cadence of sleep, Drusilla let her eyes adjust. Let her emotions cool.

Unexpected shapes slowly emerged in the opposite corner—all her things from the carriage had been placed neatly. Several trunks and a few smaller boxes.

While she had dined, exchanged songs and rumors in the scullery, panicked over horses, and found tragedy in the aviary, other hands had been busy with their work. Seeing to her comfort.

Murdering her birds.

Drusilla took Bridgette's hand, noting again the bracelet, and led her to the down comfort of the bed. The young woman remained more or less asleep throughout—Drusilla laying her down and pulling a blanket over her.

One mystery solved. The Pygmalion. Another remaining. Violets, red roses, something green...

She arranged a pillow under Bridgett's head, and the young woman curled into it, sighing softly. She was obviously none too familiar with ministrations of kindness, but slept on. Drusilla was glad to have at least one of the maidens away from harm. Something was most definitely wrong in Foxborough, and it needed sorting in the most serious of ways. Tonight was not that night, though. She was exhausted. The mystery—all the mysteries—would have to wait.

Undressing herself, she was reminded that the night, like the day just passed, was uncommonly warm, and so again, she cracked one of the balcony doors open a few inches to let in the fresh night breeze. Curling up on the down mattress opposite Bridgette, Drusilla pulled covers over herself, and was soon sleeping.

A LOW, DEEP HORN woke her sometime later. It was still dark, and Drusilla had been sleeping soundly. She sat, trying to guess the time, trying to locate the horn's origin, but there was only silence now. Silence, and then a shrill cry. Drusilla leapt from bed and rushed to the balcony.

Bridgette joined her momentarily, bringing her a dressing gown, and rubbing sleep-filled eyes.

The cry became screams, a woman's voice—a voice of pure, primal terror. Then there was silence again, and a splash. Could it have come from the beach?

"Go to the edge and look," said Drusilla, slipping into the dressing gown. She was a couple paces from the edge herself. "Quickly."

The young woman obeyed.

"There's something large in the loch, my lady. It's gone now."

"What was it?" She forced the words from her mouth, shamed she could do no more.

"I don't know, my lady. It was there. Now it's gone. It was dark. Darker than the water. All I saw was a shape, receding from the water's edge—a kind of hump. I'm sorry, my lady. That's all I saw. Maybe it was an unnaturally large wave."

Drusilla approached the veranda's edge, struggling to break the grip of paralysis upon her, coming within six inches of it, by Bridgette's side. The sky, a mix of silver-tinged clouds and starlight. The water, a dark and rippling nightmare. "Point," she said.

Bridgette's finger extended to that little bit of black rock by the secret beach, and then out towards the falls. Drusilla needed to sit down. Instead, she said, "Fetch my boots, quickly now. And my dagger."

Drusilla went to the dressing table and put her lock picks in her hair. There was just enough moonlight, she didn't bother with candles.

"Your boots, my lady."

Five minutes later, Drusilla was past the lock and on the stairhead. This was no time for a weak heart. Stairs in a meadow, she told herself, and rushed down the first flight. The next bit was more treacherous, the view of the loch dizzying. There was nothing for it though. Down she went, one agonizing step at a time, heart racing, threatening to burst.

The smell of the loch filled her senses. A cool night breeze wafted at her bare legs, fluttering the hem of her dressing gown. Down she went.

Pictures of that serpentine blot of darkness near the falls filled her head. Had Bridgette described the same thing, or was it only waves and darkness tinged with too much fearful fancy?

Drusilla could smell the algae now, the lichens on the rock, the sand. The air was moister here. She was on the final landing, maybe twenty feet above the beach. It ran about thirty-five feet end to end, and was narrow against the cliff, maybe eight or ten feet wide.

The distorted ripple of the full Moon, what was left of it, as it traveled westward and away over the horizon's edge, shone upon the water's inky surface. Tides were such that the black stone stood right at the waterline, waves breaking past it, receding, leaving circular ripples in the sand.

There was something else there in the sand. Drusilla would have guessed it was kelp circling the rock loosely at its base, but this was not the ocean. She didn't think kelp grew here. Reluctantly, she was drawn further down.

Ten steps. Five. She pressed onward, alone in the near darkness. The sound of the waves now her dominant sense. Four steps. Three.

Just do it, she chided herself. The waves were starting to claim the encircling bit, whatever it was. In a moment, it would be too late.

Drawing sharp breath, Drusilla rushed forward, the last steps were carved from the cliff's own stone, and then her booted feet sank deeply into thick, wet sand. She fell to her knees, grasping out with her hand, seizing the bit of...

Rope. Wet, slick rope. It was frayed at the ends, severed unevenly by something razor sharp. She held several broken coils of the stuff. A scrap of something triangular, about ten inches in size, was sliding in the foam at the water's edge. Drusilla dropped the rope and closed her eyes, muttering a silent prayer.

Please, God, no.

She opened her eyes. It was definitely cloth. About a foot out into the water now. It could not be wished away.

Drusilla rushed, stumbling upon her hands and knees, towards the scrap of cloth washing in the surf. It was pulling away, maybe a yard from the shore now.

Drusilla sobbed, crashing into the icy cold loch, water spray filling her senses. She reached out for the scrap of cloth through blind tears. A wave slapped her in the face, choking her, going down her lungs.

God help me, she silently pleaded, opening her eyes, coughing. The water churned all around her now. Her hands and knees sucked into the sand as the next wave receded, pulling her.

Drusilla grunted, a summon of courage, not unlike a battle cry, but quieter, more primal. Her nose and lungs stung from the invasion of water, eyes squinting against the drizzle that ran down her face. Still, she cast her gaze about for the cloth.

A wave knocked her backwards, off her hands and knees, and onto her rump. Water rushed up to her neck. How far out was she? Drusilla's arms flailed as she tried to stand—where was the land!

She wanted to cry out for help. The image of the severed rope circling around that pillar of stone stifled the thought, replacing it with something more terrible than her current predicament—murder.

She had heard cries from the beach, and now she was here, only minutes later, and the maiden who had cried out? Only a bit of rope and scrap of cloth remained.

No. She might be drawing a false conclusion, but the chance she would be calling a killer and not a rescuer seemed very real. She had to get herself off the beach, and fast. There could be no help.

Get your feet.

Another wave knocked her over.

Get to your feet!

Drusilla exploded with everything she had, standing against the battering waves. Turning one way, and then the other, she failed to spot the land. How could she be so far out so quickly?

But then, she realized, however far out she might be, the water was only waist deep.

She felt so foolish. But shame did nothing to erase the panic as another frigid wave crashed about her midsection, taking her breath, and to keep her footing, took her deeper. The loch was claiming her, as it was claiming any evidence of what had transpired here this night.

A singular dread overtook Drusilla. Death was imminent. It was stalking her, hiding all routes of escape. It was playing with her.

Where was the land?

Another wave hit her, the spray, icy fingers blasting her face.

Blinking the water away, arms flailing to keep her balance, she tried to take her bearings. Boots, heavy with water and sand, ground against her skin. Like shackles of lead, they thwarted any effort to turn around, to orient herself to the shore.

Another wave knocked her down as she was twisting, and she went under. Mind absolutely blank with terror, she swallowed loch water, choked it out, and more came in, filling her lungs.

Oh god, she was drowning!

Drusilla's arms flailed madly, with no reason, her boots clawing at the sand for purchase. She had no idea which way was up. The water burned in her lungs, and then her hand grasped something.

The cloth.

Chapter Thirteen

S HE MUST LIVE. THIS was what she was fighting for. All her muscles exploded, pushing against the bottom. The other way must be up. Head and chest exploded above the surface, arms flailing.

She lunged forward, coughing, gasping, loch water spewing from her lungs. She was in shallow water again. About five feet from the shore. How, she couldn't know. She only thanked God and pushed forward, willing herself to the beach. Tossing herself upon the cold, wet, blessed sand.

Pushing herself to hands and knees, the frigid water still lapping at her shins, she coughed and sputtered until there was no more water to give. Still, her lungs burned. Her chest seized, then obeyed, drawing in life.

Something was clutched in her hand.

Drusilla looked down. She still grasped the cloth tightly. It made her laugh. Crawling a little further inland, rolling over, her gaze stole across the loch. It was fairly placid, actually. The waves gently rolled in at her feet.

Lying there, dealing with her fears, thanking God silently for her life, Drusilla saw something dark and serpentine move the water's surface about halfway out, half to three quarters of a mile. She crab-walked away from the horror, eyes locked on the dark shape, unable to scream.

A hump rose from its center, and the whole form submerged, leaving only a disturbance on the surface. Drusilla scrambled to her feet and ran forty stairs or more before calming herself enough to look back.

When she did, it was gone. Whatever had disturbed the deep waters, no sign remained.

Chapter Fourteen

D RUSILLA WAS GLAD TO find the picks still in her hair, her dagger still in her possession, and her mind still in one piece. How easily they could have been lost. How easily her life could have been lost.

She sat at the edge of the high courtyard, upon the low border masonry, emptying water, sand, and pebbles from her boots. She worked vigorously, and it was only that activity which kept her from shivering. Warm as the summer night was, its embrace could not staunch the hemorrhage of heat the cold loch water bled away.

And then an afterimage of things she had just seen surfaced. An incomprehensible nightmare. Drowning. Not knowing up from down, or land from water, confabulating all her fears to something larger than they were...

The dark shape...

Perhaps she had lost part of her mind after all.

She did her best to put it away, put her mind back on the task at hand, wringing her hair out when she heard footsteps in the court. Looking up, she saw Bayden approaching.

She smiled at him.

"There were reports of a disturbance," he said. "The guards are on alert—" He stopped suddenly. "Why, you're soaking wet. Drenched. Whatever happened?"

"The night was most uncommonly warm," she said. "I went for a swim."

"I thought," he began. Hesitated. "It's just you seemed uneasy near the water yesterday. Loch Ness, in particular, is cold and deep, with unpredictable currents."

"It is heights I fear, my lord," Drusilla lied, "not water. I find your loch to be most charming."

Bayden looked astonished.

"I'm afraid it was my cries of delight that alarmed the household. Terribly inconsiderate of me," she continued. "In the future, I shall be more discreet. Please accept my deep felt apology."

She stood up, secreting the scrap of cloth to her dressing gown pocket, and collected her boots. Bayden's boots, she noted, were spotless. Either he'd just dressed to come and investigate the disturbance, or he'd just changed. In either case, he stood before her, unable or unwilling to comment on her apology.

"If that is all, my lord, I am relaxed after such a good swim, and tired to the bone."

He looked to the door. It was closed.

"I found it unlocked, my lord. Much to my delight."

"The waters are dangerous," he said. "You should take more care. In the future, the door will be locked."

"Then could I prevail upon you for a key?" she said, pressing him.

Bayden's eyes were dark and angry in the moonlight. He faced her squarely, standing less than a foot from her. Drusilla's mind flashed to her dagger. She readied herself for anything. Her eyes searched downward, fleetingly, and saw he too was armed. He carried both a sword and a dagger. But more than that, by the way in which he carried himself, she knew he was more than a match for her in single combat.

"If that is your wish," he said, simply. "May I walk you to your quarters?"

"Thank you," she answered. "I'm sure I'll manage."

MORNING LIGHT FOUND ITS way into the room, reflecting off the loch. Drusilla stood on the other side of the glass, watching the brightening day. Even from this side, her sense of unease was heightened.

Bridgette had identified the scrap of cloth as belonging to a village maid named Helen. She was eighteen and lived with her parents. Her father was the local cobbler, and her mother took in washing, sewing, and occasionally told stories to the local youngsters.

Drusilla feared the worst for Helen, and for the rest of the young women of the area. At sunrise, she had risen and dressed in another unique creation, this one, a dress of fine, bright orange linen, trimmed in white embroidery with a white corset pushing her bosoms high, bliaut sleeves, similar, though less ambitious than her yellow and green, falling shy of the knee. Around her neck, she tied a simple orange ribbon.

She wore her hair down today, held back from her face with a simple bronze comb that once belonged to a lady in Rome of Cretian birth. It was the first and only piece of jewelry Drusilla's father had ever given her.

White slippers adorned her feet as she was still drying the insides of her boots by the hearth fire in her room. She didn't want to put them too close to the heat for fear of cracking them. They were, however, treated with mink oil, like all her leather, and should be fine with a little patience.

"Go to town and find out how Helen is," said Drusilla. "Be discreet. Don't raise any suspicions. As an excuse, buy a jug of milk." She pushed a few copper coins into Bridgette's hand. "Buy whatever else you like with the change."

"Thank you, my lady," said Bridgette, curtsying and taking her leave.

Drusilla walked out to the balcony's edge with a deliberation born in the mire of self loathing. The water still made her most uncomfortable, but after last night's episode, she had more courage and a need to face it.

The loch was calm, a gentle breeze blowing, and on the air, the sound of carriages, horses, and many voices. Her curiosity piqued, but she could learn nothing from here. Down the stairs she went, her dagger hanging on a simple, silver chain about her waist, and was greeted, upon reaching the final flight, with a host of new faces.

"Ah yes, your attention, fair guests, one and all," said Bayden in a voice of proclamation that filled the hall. "May I present the Lady Drusilla of Merovingia."

There was applause for her. Drusilla felt suddenly abashed. She could just turn. Retreat back up the stairs. But she must not. She had a part to play, and play it out she would.

She raised a white-gloved hand, giving a courtly wave to the crowd, and descended into their midst.

The house was abustle with activity, servants taking luggage, livery boys tending to horses and coaches, introductions flying faster than the wintering goose. It was a lively and happy occasion.

In the midst of it all, Drusilla became aware of a tugging at her skirts.

She looked down.

A beautiful little girl, maybe seven, was staring up at her with wide brown eyes from under blonde lashes. A cataclysm of red curls crowned her head, cascading halfway down her back. She wore a finely tailored linen dress made more fancy by a beautiful butterfly brooch, done in silver, clasping a woolen cloak about her shoulders. The broach was cut and faceted to give it sparkle and radiance. But it was the girl who sparkled most.

"I saw a kelpie in the loch day afore last," she said in the thick local accent.

Drusilla searched her memory. The reference stirred deep childhood feelings. Her older brother, Bartholomew, had talked of kelpies, amongst other things. He had always been preternaturally obsessed with water and all things aquatic. Kelpies were water horses. How old had she been? Two, maybe three? My god, how could she recall such a thing? And something else, kelpies were supposed to be mythical, weren't they?

"Are you sure?" asked Drusilla, giving the girl her full attention.

"Michael went down to the Moray Firth to fish for Pike," said the girl. "He took me with him 'cause I promised to be quiet, and tie bait for him. I didnae want to, but I wanted to see the ocean.

"When it's clear, you can see Merovingia across the sea. You're from Merovingia, aren't you? Are there really fairies?"

Drusilla was skeptical Merovingia could be sighted from the edge of the North Sea. Further south, it became possible, however. Like all truth, sometimes it wore a cloak of confusion. Perhaps cloaked within the girl's casual reference to the mythic was some seed of reality.

"Tell me about the kelpies."

"Kelpies are supposed to be small, but this one was big. Michael didn't see it, but I did. He says I made it up." The young girl looked up into Drusilla's eyes imploringly. "You believe me, don't you, Lady Drusilla?"

Drusilla smiled, patting the child on the head.

"Of course I do."

Someone else wanted to meet Drusilla. She could sense him hovering at her right, but she would not turn from the girl without a proper conclusion. "Nice to meet you," she said, taking the child's hand.

"Sara MacTavish," said the young girl, giving her best attempt at a curtsy.

Drusilla returned a curtsy, perfected through a lifetime of intrigue. "Enchanted," she said, feeling a genuine warmth for the young girl.

She turned, then, to address the young fop who so ardently wished to make his introduction to her. "I am enchanted," he said, no rush to his words. He spoke well, his Latin accent adding but color. "Raul of Sicily," he continued, finding her eyes. "I wasn't sure the festival would suit me, though I must confess, I suddenly find the prospect most charming."

Abruptly, the relative isolation she had known at Foxborough Keep was at an end. Drusilla was faced with the whole of high society, surrounded by it. The room was awash with high civilization. Courtly affairs were not her repertoire. She would have to tread carefully here, or surely be exposed. She was a runaway thief, daughter of a bankrupt sharecropper, and an overextended merchant who cared more for learning than for keeping sound accounts. An orphan of low birth had no place here, except maybe amongst the serving class, people for whom she had great respect. But she was also a dame of The Order on a mission of profound importance. This, she must never forget.

"Drusilla of Merovingia, though I now call London Town my home." She summoned forth a look of haughty disinterest and tried to appear regal.

"My lady." His bow was deep. Her behavior had not fazed him. He seemed terribly smitten with her despite it, or maybe because of it, and slobbered all over her glove.

Much too ardent for a first kiss. He was, however, not unpleasant to look upon: dark wavy hair, olive complexion, flashing dark eyes narrowed to attentive slits.

"Ladies and lords, all." It was Bayden again. This time he had climbed the stairs to the overlooking balcony, a piece that projected out in a semicircle central to the entire hall.

In all, there were easily a hundred gathered, counting guests and servants. Everyone in their finery, including a few other well-mannered children. The rest, by all appearances, were of the landed and gentry. She was sure mingling and other expectations of social behavior would ensue, but with the appearance of their host, a murmured hush had taken the crowd as all eyes fell to Bayden.

He was dressed much as always, but with an added cloak of red, clasped at one shoulder by a golden broach. It gave him an Imperial look. He paused just long enough to draw a complete silence. "It is with great pleasure," he continued theatrically once that was accomplished, "that I welcome you all here to my home."

There was much applause.

He waited, basking in it, and only as it waned, continued.

"To set things off with a bang, I am happy to announce, after lunching today, we will embark upon a fox hunt."

More murmurs and applause.

"Everyone who wishes to participate is welcome. I have bows and horses aplenty, if you lack. And for you ladies, may I entreat you to the luxury of my home."

More applause.

"There are courtyards, and parlors, and many games and diversions for you here. You may acquaint yourselves one with another, and my capable staff will be happy to give you a full tour."

Great. A tour. Drusilla was so thrilled.

Bayden was joined by Ludo, who leaned over and whispered something in his ear.

"Ladies and lords, dear friends," said Bayden. "May I present my brother, Ludo."

There was great applause now. Ludo wore a mantle of wolf's fur clasped in silver intricately worked in some Celtic fashion. He held up his hands and smiled. Somehow, his grin was always crooked. His eyes seemed to be especially pale today.

"Thank you all for coming," he said. "I look forward to meeting each and every one of you."

This received the greatest round of applause yet.

Was that dark jealousy on Bayden's face?

"Pavilions have been set up on the northeast lawn, and I am told a feast awaits us," added Ludo, drawing an even more uproarious response.

Who knew?

"Let us adjoin then," he finished, and came down the steps, leading the crowd out the front doors of the keep into the Mediterranean courtyard she had first entered upon arriving.

Northeast lawn? Drusilla was unfamiliar with any such place.

Ludo crossed the stone to the keep's wall, and there, in the shade of an olive tree, was an arched door, nearly the color of the wall. It had completely escaped her notice till now.

Chapter Fifteen

Drusilla had long abandoned the idea that her new, temporary residence was a keep. The conclusion had been easily reached the moment she had laid eyes upon the dancer's courtyard. But that, in all her explorations and speculation thus far, she had missed an entire lawn large enough for a hundred guests to luncheon, not to mention the attendant staff required to facilitate such an event, still came as a shock.

And yet, where had she expected a "festival", and "games of courtly fun", to be had?

Or did the door lead outdoors somehow? No. This door was no match for an invasion. This, wherever it led to, remained securely fixed behind castle walls.

Once again, she wondered, why call it a keep?

The brothers MacKay were not advertising to their neighbors their true strength. Did that indicate they were lying low? There was no love for the Empire north of the Hadrian, and yet they were clearly entangled with Rome in more ways than one. It would make sense for them to do so. And though Foxborough had an overplentiful staff, and an adequate guard, it did not house an army or have a monarch.

Keep, though not accurate, was perhaps a more apt summation of the totality of what it was. And in that, she felt she had finally solved another of her pocketful of mysteries.

Still, how much room could lie beyond the little door? Drusilla consigned herself to the notion that she would be pressed into tight mingling today. Such musings did Drusilla no service when, after the modest, arched door was swung wide, and the crowd passed through—till at last she got her own glimpse of what lay beyond—all her preconceptions were smashed.

Acres of gently rolling, manicured lawn spread out before her, bound at the edges by hedge lined walls. Roses, in great variety, grew all along the northwest and northeast boundaries, taking advantage of the southern track of the Sun, and here and there, throughout, could be found fruit trees in full blossom.

She gasped for the expanse of it.

As each guest entered the greensward, they passed first a herald in a bright and festive tunic, trumpet in hand, and were asked to identify themselves. Drusilla was one of the last to pass through, choosing to observe rather than rush ahead. When it came her turn, she was well familiar with the routine and also knew a goodly number of names and titles thereof.

"Your title, madam?"

"Drusilla of Merovingia," she said, staring out at the festivities underway.

The herald smiled at her thoughtfully, then, blowing his trumpet three times instead of the usual one, announced:

"Presenting Lady Drusilla, the Fair."

Drusilla smiled. The Fair. She liked that.

Green lawn, blue skies, puffy white clouds, and not a view of the loch to be had. Drusilla was in Heaven. Above, along the wall, she saw the soldiery and archers standing their duty. Well, almost Heaven.

Brightly colored, striped pavilions were set about, under which were tables laden with food of all variety, from exotic nuts, seeds, and puddings, to roast joint and roasted vegetables, to platters laden high with fruits. Other tables were exclusively for drink, and still others held bunches of grapes of various colors, wedges of cheese, also in great variety, and servants everywhere, ready to pour wine or serve up delicacies.

The servants worked from plain white tents, and several seemed quite pleased to see the appearance of Drusilla. Apparently, she was earning a reputation with them.

Drusilla heaped a plate with food and wandered off under a cherry tree to enjoy it. Nearby, golden gorse grew. Its unique, fragrant yellow flowers smelling sweetly in the high mountain air. She had just sat down when Bayden joined her, carrying a half loaf of bread and some cheese on a silver platter, and a jug of wine with two fluted glasses in his other hand.

"May I join you?" he asked politely.

She patted the ground next to her and smiled invitingly.

He poured two glasses of wine and handed her one. It was something she had brought back from Helven last year and sold in the London market. She suppressed a smile, hiding her satisfaction.

"It's lovely," she said. "A most marvelous way to spend the social season."

"Social season," Bayden laughed. "My, but you do have a way with words. Not something you learned in the convent?"

"Aside from those two years, I have led a privileged existence. London society, in particular, has been very good to me."

"Forgive me, My Dear. I am sometimes rash with my words. I should not assume that you are less than you are. A lady of high refinement."

"Of course, my lord. I have seen both sides of the mirror. Neither is a path insulated from hardship." Drusilla looked away, to the sky above the enclosing wall. Little puffy clouds drifted by in their carefree existence.

"Few of these women, born to their luxury, never spending so much as a day away from it, could speak so true and eloquent as you." He cut away a piece of cheese and a slice of dark bread, offering it to her. He was sitting much too close to her, and he seemed completely unabashed with his gaze.

"I'm afraid my eyes are bigger than my stomach," she demurred. "It'll be all I can do to finish my plate. Horseback riding should never be done on a full stomach."

"Surely you wish to remain behind," said Bayden, challenging her with those infuriating eyes. "With the other wompen."

"I think the activity would do me well," said Drusilla, giving him her most defiant look. "And I'm positive my horse will welcome the excursion."

"As you please, my lady. I have other guests to attend." Bayden rose, turning to leave. "If you're joining us, be ready, in the lower court, about an hour. The hunt waits for no one." As a final warning, he added, "It will be vigorous."

"Perfect," said Drusilla, offering her glass for a refill. She wanted him to know that his words had in no way cowed her.

Chapter Sixteen

D RUSILLA CHANGED INTO HER most practical dress, a full dark-red skirt and bodice, laced in front with gold cord, and a black jacket. She tucked her hair up within a floppy black velvet courtier's hat, securing it with pins.

Her boots were still damp. She gave them a quick rubbing with a cloth and put them on anyway. She was rich. Why didn't she have two pairs of boots? She decided to remedy that in the near future.

Black gloves, dagger on a more secure black leather belt with silver buckle, she was just ready to leave when Bridgette returned, jug of milk in hand and out of breath.

"Do sit down," said Drusilla, "and tell me your news, but quickly." She didn't want to be left behind, and judging by Bayden's reaction to her at lunch, he would take any excuse he could to do just that.

Bridgette set the milk on a low table before following orders and going to the chair.

"Nobody's seen Helen. She's missing. Her parents are heartbroken. Her father came to the keep today, requesting an audience with Lord Bayden, but was turned soundly away. Now he searches with the other townsfolk, while her mother waits at home, hoping she'll return."

Bridgette stopped. She was still a little out of breath. "I'm sorry it's not better news," she said after a pause.

"It was as I feared," said Drusilla. "Thank you, Bridgette. Tell no one of this."

Drusilla unfolded a serviette on the low table where the milk stood. Inside were half the items originally on her plate at the luncheon, untouched. She had smuggled them away for Bridgette.

"Take the milk to the cellar, and keep it cool," said Drusilla. "We'll have it tonight when I return. Then come back here, if you can, and eat something."

Bridgette's eyes scanned the food, and she grinned. "Thank you, my lady!" she said, suddenly no longer wanting for breath. She seized the jug of milk and ran happily from the room.

THE STABLE MASTER INSISTED on helping with the saddle and other preparations, though she was a fully capable horseman and squire. There were social pretenses to keep up, and so she allowed a certain amount of fawning. He showed a deep curiosity in her custom saddle, asking about the gripping horn and the stirrups she had added. She breezed over their importance, implying she was a bit clumsy and they provided welcome aid. Still, he looked at each deviation with great thoughtfulness. Soon enough, though, she and Polaris joined the other would-be fox hunters in the courtyard.

She found she was not the only woman after all.

A spirited looking woman of about twenty sat upon a pure black stallion. Her bright red hair, a wavy mane, and fierce hazel eyes spoke of the independent spirit which still reigned throughout much of this wild land. The rest of the assemblage, about thirty in all, were men, including the MacKay brothers, and her Sicilian suitor.

There were hounds, too. Two breeds. One the locals were calling wolfdogs. Those, Drusilla recognized as wolfhounds. Lank, shaggy grey cousins of the wolf, alert and menacing by any name. The other breed was smaller, a short-hair variety, brown and black in patches, with the nose and ears of a tracking animal.

The rear gate was opened, and the whole procession rode out, abruptly joined by eight others. The bodyguards, each on a dark brown horse with a white star on its forehead. They did not talk or joke like the others. They were, in fact, a quite humorless bunch. In addition to their usual armaments, each carried a bow of yew wood for the occasion.

As they rode southwest into a woodland spotted with meadows and dells, Bayden came alongside Drusilla. He held out a bow. He had two.

"Can you use this?"

"How hard can it be?" she asked, grinning coquettishly.

She took a quiver from him also, then clucked a command to Polaris, and shot ahead, into the forest.

The hounds were baying. They were onto something. Drusilla quickly separated herself from the others. She had no desire to hunt. She was looking for clues, and was determined to survey as much of the surrounding forestland as she could, having now the perfect excuse.

She shouldered the quiver, and hung the bow over her saddle horn, looking about to gain the lay of the land.

In the distance now, one of the dogs yelped. Probably shot by an overzealous, drunken courtier—poor thing. She was glad not to be saddled with that group.

Drusilla rode on, avoiding areas that looked easily accessible, or well traveled. If there were secrets to be found out here, they would be in the hidden places. She headed for a particularly dense part of the forest and soon found herself deep in lush shade.

It was quieter here. Drusilla slowed Polaris to an easy gait. Old oaks and yew grew in abundance, along with dogwood, willows, and pine. There were hickory trees and scrub oak. Occasional patches of sunlight allowed a few wildflowers and grasses to grow, but it was to the deeper, shadier parts that Drusilla headed.

As she traveled quietly, following the deer trails, Drusilla saw several creatures she might have shot: a chestnut-brown grouse too concentrated in its foraging; a small family of deer, who startled and ran only when she was well in range; and a badger.

Drusilla knew better than to shoot a badger, lest she deal it a mortal wound. But she was in no need of food and did not wish to return with better prizes than the men. It was best if they thought her more or less helpless for now.

So it was that Drusilla had to laugh when she saw a fox cross her trail, running scared, probably in the opposite direction in which the other men had gone.

Drusilla continued to explore the deep woods, Polaris choosing his footing carefully, until, after an hour or more, she came upon a curious sight. A small clearing within a ring of trees covered in loam and dead branches. In fact, it was more of a sinkhole. It might be the lair of some burrowing creature, but more likely, someone had hidden something here. The collection of debris did not look random, and there were signs, however subtle, of booted passage.

Drusilla dismounted and bade Polaris stay put. She approached the hole cautiously, clearing away branches, pushing aside the detritus and loam. The smell of smoldered ash reached her nostrils. There had been a fire here.

She cleared away some more and came upon what was burnt. It was not sticks and logs. These were planks of wood, once shaped and painted, and to one piece a metallic ornament, now blackened with soot, was affixed.

An interesting discovery indeed.

She cleared the pit and examined what was left. At first, it was hard to figure out, due to its smashed up, burnt condition, but then she began to see the lines, recognizable shapes. A hinge, a fender.

This had been a carriage.

Drusilla took her handkerchief, and spit upon the ornament, polishing it. Slowly, a brassy undertone began to emerge, and then a shape as ash and charcoal flaked away, and the ruin was restored to some semblance of its former self.

It was a shield with a griffon on a field; three, five-point stars above; a fish below; and the initials L.G. raised in the top corner.

"Lion's Gate," she whispered. Camille's ancestral home. "Oh my god."

Drusilla dug through the wreckage, fervently searching for something more. The wheels were missing, as was about two-thirds of the carriage. Thankfully, there were no bodies, but there were a certain number of personal effects, burnt nearly beyond recognition. A few dresses and blankets, charred and useless; the blackened remnants of a writing quill; and a silver comb, not unlike Drusilla's. She took the comb, wrapped it in a handkerchief, and, hand shaking as the weight of its meaning sunk in, put it in her jacket pocket.

Drusilla fell to her knees and prayed for Camille's soul. Who had done this remained yet veiled. This far from the castle, it could be anyone. What stories would they tell when she began to pry?

She shook with anger, inhaling the ashes of her dear friend's life, and a sob overtook her shoulders. Loam and charcoal crushed through the gaps of her fingers as her fists dug into the blackened earth.

Hope was no longer reasonable. There would be no rescue.

Chapter Seventeen

Drusilla rejoined the others. It was easy to follow their cacophony. Really, all one needed to do was to ride in the opposite direction of all the fleeing woodland animals.

She had splashed her tear-swollen face in a little brook, then found her way to sunlit patches, meandering through thistles, bluebells... heather dipping in the highland breeze. The buzz of bees about their work. The song of birds.

She stayed away until her feelings cooled. And then she found Bayden and Ludo together, and rode alongside them, putting herself in the middle.

"Find your fox yet?" she taunted.

"I'm afraid half the men are tipsy, and the other half don't know a bow from a bough." Bayden chuckled subtly. "But don't despair. I sent one of my huntsmen off to retrieve a stag. There's no reason for us to starve."

Drusilla felt sympathy for his crestfallen attitude. "I drew a similar conclusion myself. It's not a total loss, though. The excursion itself is quite invigorating."

"I'm glad you're enjoying yourself, My Dear."

There was that infuriating familiarity again. All her sympathy was gone. It was time to draw a little blood.

"My cousin must have passed this way recently. She was on her way to London Town. Perhaps you know her? Camille of Lion's Gate."

She watched for the reaction.

Ludo's silence deepened. Bayden got that irritated, dangerous look that was becoming all too familiar. In any case, his mannerisms definitely changed. His resigned, almost bored, attitude had an edge to it now.

"In fact, I'm quite certain she would have come right past your keep. She forwarded me her itinerary," said Drusilla, keenly watching the brothers while hopefully appearing casual, perhaps even a little bored herself.

Bayden's gaze could have melted lead in the moment that followed. Drusilla's mind raced with scenarios should she be required to fight or to flee. She felt her nerves attuning to the conflict, burning and agitated, a surge of possibly needed power trembling beneath the surface.

"Ah, the woman from St. Stephen's upon Moray," said Bayden, suddenly seeming to relax. "She did pass this way... two or three weeks ago. Charming young lady. We attended to her as best we could here in the country. She met with a little—mechanical difficulty. Repairs were made to her carriage, and then we sent her on her way, newly provisioned."

"Well then," said Drusilla guardedly, "I suppose she'll be on ahead of me. Pity. We do get along so splendidly. I had hoped to summer with her."

She shrugged, as though dismissing the whole matter. "I shall just have to winter in London Town and see her then."

Was it a cover story, or from his perspective, the truth? And his need to correct her, or was that just his Christian filter? Her hand was starting to shake with frustration—or maybe it was rage. Rage and the frustration of not knowing where to direct it. To cover it, she gripped the reins tighter and pressed her hand to her steed's warm neck. Buried her gloved hand in his mane of silver gray.

No more could be learned here. She clucked a rapid command to Polaris, pulling at a gallop to mingle with the others, taking great care to watch for stray arrows.

Chapter Eighteen

THE GRAND DINING HALL hosted a table thrice the length of the one she had dined upon only yesterday, and several smaller tables scattered further out to accommodate the hundred or so guests. Servants buzzed about in flurries of activity, ever keeping their places, silently the force which facilitated the event.

A fire, equal to the one in the grand den, blazed merrily, radiating heat outwards into the vast stone hall. Torches burned in their wall sconces, further distributing the light, though shadow persisted everywhere. The smells of torch smoke, and roast meats, and every manner of cooking mingled with alcohol filled her senses even as a babble of happy conversations pervaded.

She was seated left of the brothers, again, next to Ludo at the main table. Seating was not assigned, but for the brothers who held their place of dominance at the center of the great table. Even so, a social stratification of sorts had naturally evolved. That she sat where she did spoke volumes of her success at ingratiating herself here.

Bayden made good on his promise. His huntsman brought a red deer back, and with it, a strange tale. As they all sat around, feasting on fine venison, the few game hens, a partridge brought back from the hunt, and the leftover fruits and sweetmeats from the lunch along with newly conjured stews, soups, and puddings, the huntsman was drawn out to relate his tale. There were murmurs of a strange object he had retrieved during the hunt, and everybody's curiosity was burning.

"I was hunting at the southwest end of the loch, near Smoking Falls, when I came upon a lame doe. She was hopping along on three legs, and this curious white object was sticking out of her hind flank."

He held up the retrieved object. It was twenty-one inches or more, curved and lined along the inside edge with what appeared to be serrations.

"Well, I could hardly leave her suffering there like that, so I crept up on her and laid my glove to the object, yanking it out. That doe, she bolted straight out of sight," he laughed. "Never a thank you, or a never-you-mind to spare."

The guests all laughed at this, but as the object traveled around the table, hand to hand, a hush began to fall.

Drusilla, receiving the object, recognized it at once. Twenty-two inches of gleaming white, the inside curve being narrower, and sporting a vicious row of little barbed hooks. She touched one. It was razor sharp. It was clearly a tooth, and she knew just what kind it was.

"It's eel," she said, passing it along.

"I beg your pardon?" said one of the guests. "It's two feet if it's an inch. Surely you misspoke?"

"My mistake," said Drusilla. "I'm given to a fanciful imagination."

"No harm done," said the guest, but someone else followed his comment immediately with a response to Drusilla's.

"That would make it monstrous," he said. "I mean, look at this thing." He held up the "tooth", giving it a good shake. "It would have to be a hundred feet in length."

"At least forty," said another.

Raul sat across from Drusilla and a few chairs down. He shared a look with her that said he took her observations more seriously than was the general consensus. She found herself glad to have the solidarity and realized she was smiling at him before she checked herself.

The "tooth" continued to circulate, quickly changing the mood of the room. Even the outer tables were catching wind of the conversation, and soon all eyes were upon the head table and the unfolding speculation, a somber air settling over all.

"Do you think we're safe?" asked one of the women, Elaenor of Vascon, averting her dark eyes when Drusilla met them. Vascon was a conquered territory of Merovingia, making Drusilla, by default, her superior. A thing she hoped Elaenor lent no weight to, in this place, far from all their homes.

Another woman, the fierce redhead who had come on the hunt, looked around with mock terror, followed by a wide grin of self-amusement. She giggled coyly.

Contained safe within the ancient masonry, the mighty log sagged a bit more over the iron as the fire consumed it, casting out great showers of spark and ember. With every pop or crack, it slumped a bit more, collapsing slowly to ash. Swirls of smoke and fire raced up the chimney and out of sight, pulled by the cold highland air.

"Don't you worry," said the huntsman. "It's not a tooth. Somebody's obviously having a bit of fun. It's probably carved from a whalebone or walrus tusk. A Pictish dagger, or a spearhead that's come off."

"It looks like a horn," said another man, now holding the tooth.

"Perhaps a unicorn," said Elaenor. Though only a moment ago frightened, she now seemed positively enchanted by the prospects under discussion.

Weren't unicorns supposed to be mythical?

"Let us ask Bayden's opinion," said Drusilla. "It is my suspicion, he knows a thing or two about sculpting in rare materials. Could it be fashioned by the hand of man?"

The tooth was passed to Bayden, and Drusilla pretended to wait with unmotivated interest. She was sure he was hiding a scowl meant for her.

"It's true, I've studied the works of classical sculpture," he said, turning the tooth over thoughtfully. "This appears to be the working of a whalebone, as Master Hunter Connoleigh suggests. Fine craftsmanship indeed, probably the working end of a Celtic or Pictish dagger from antiquity. The handle obviously broke off in the attempt of stabbing the deer, being an antiquity, and already probably fractured from many centuries of use."

Elaenor clapped. "Bravo. Bravo, Lord Bayden," she commended.

Others congratulated him, and he was definitely scowling at Drusilla now when another at the table spoke up.

"There have been sightings and rumors," an elderly gentleman said, clearing his throat and taking a drink from his tankard before continuing on. His was an accent, though refined, bearing definite traces of the local flavor. "It is said that Loch Ness has a sea serpent swimming its deep waters. Sometimes, the creature comes ashore, and takes a sheep, or a deer. It roams the land on flippers—"

"Oh?" said the gentleman, who had proposed the horn theory, interrupting the old man. "You're needlessly frightening the ladies. Flippers, indeed. Preposterous."

Drusilla addressed the old man directly. "Have you ever seen it?"

"Oh, heavens no," said the old man. "There have been stories. The occasional missing sheep. Nothing more. Nothing to trouble your head, dear.

"I apologize, ladies, and it is past my bedtime."

He rose from the table, wiping his mouth, and pushing in his chair. He received several warm goodnights, departing.

Waves of heat poured over Drusilla as the fire continued its ravenous work. She could feel naught but chill, though, as her eyes continued to follow that tooth as it rounded the room, for in truth it could be nothing else.

Taking Bayden's words of assurance to heart, and having been plied this night with every creature comfort and with the added safety of these walls, she suspected most assembled here would return to their bedchambers, and there sleep a contented sleep. She couldn't help but summon up the image of that serpentine form gliding through the dark loch just the night prior. That she should sleep soundly, Drusilla was not so certain.

Chapter Nineteen

T HE NEXT DAY, DRUSILLA was consumed with the idea of exploring the area around the falls. A tooth like the one she'd seen last night could easily belong to a gigantic eel, or something equally monstrous. It's not that she wanted to confront such a creature. And she didn't relish crossing the loch, either. But it would be derelict for her not to. Everything pointed to those falls.

Today was supposed to be a day of games. Merriments. The summer festivities of a bunch of spoiled fops who, wanting for nothing, sought any elaboration, at any expense, to give meaning to lives stripped free of purpose—

She took a breath, closing her eyes a moment, seeking serenity. Far from a fair assessment, it was cruel and mean spirited.

She was getting frustrated by this investigation.

She recanted the thought, silently well-wishing the people she had just met. People, not one of whom, had done her the least harm. No sense indulging in falsely laid blames, or the vanity that she was somehow superior. Such thoughts were of no use and did only damage herself.

But neither could she tarry in the idleness the others would enjoy this day. There were secrets that needed rooting out. Secrets, the playing of games was not going to get her any closer to.

So, she would attend the games, admitting to herself that theirs was the enviable lot, and as soon as possible, slip away and somehow, find passage across the loch.

Drusilla wore her yellow dress with the green sleeves. None of these people had seen it yet. In the whole of her wardrobe, this was her favorite. An absolute stunner.

As she entered the throngs of aristocratic born people, she wondered what would happen if they discovered her low birth. Her past.

It would not go well, surely. She had felt the rope about her neck once before. Sat upon the horse's back, for what she had imagined would be her last time, beneath the hanging tree...

Yet, the people seemed to accept Drusilla of Merovingia with open arms. She was even becoming something of a minor celebrity. These people knew nothing but what she told them.

Yellow and green silk flowed around her in ephemeral flashes of light. Her past could cast no shadow here as long as she wore the dress like it belonged to her.

She stood taller, and moved deeper into the throng.

The games were set to take place in the northeast green, where the welcoming feast had been. Tightly bound stacks of hay with archery targets were assembled at the far end of the yard. Another area had been designated for contests of sword. And though these bouts were conducted with unsharpened contest blades, they could be deadly nonetheless.

For those who didn't wish to entertain such risks, there were diversions aplenty still—for the younger guests, and those more tame. It was towards these that Drusilla wandered.

There were musicians playing lively tunes, jugglers, a maypole with maidens weaving colored ribbons in and out as they danced in the sparkling sunlight. There was a ring toss, lawn darts, and long straight sticks with colorful ribbons tied on the ends. The last had had no associated game, yet the children, in their infinite inventiveness, had conjured more than a dozen variations of play involving the ribboned sticks already.

As Drusilla mingled, artfully dodging her Sicilian suitor, she heard the buzz that there would be a chariot race later that evening. An hour before dusk. Three circuits around the three-quarters of the outside of the keep. Foliage was kept cropped back all the way around the keep for visibility against invasions. It was the perfect racetrack. Turnaround would be made, and poles had been set to mark the points at each end for turning.

The fourth side of the keep, of course, was sheer cliff.

There would be three races, each winner going on to compete in the next.

A chariot race. That was something Drusilla would have to see. She would try to slip away sometime in the early afternoon and be back an hour before dusk at the latest.

"Lady Drusilla," it was her suitor. She sighed, put on her coolest face, then turned.

"Might I say you look particularly lovely today."

"You're too kind."

"Not at all," he said, taking her hand and kissing it. "I think you are easily more beautiful than Helen of Troy."

Drusilla raised an eyebrow. "Did you know Helen of Troy?"

"Well, no," he flustered. "But the stories. Surely your beauty could inspire men to war and to love with even greater ferocity. I know you have that effect on me."

"You are very charming, Raul"

"I speak only from my heart."

"Raul, I wonder if I could trouble you," said Drusilla, dismissing his ardent words with less than an acknowledgment. She wanted only to escape and thus accomplish her task. She needed to dispatch him on some errand. One came to mind. "I'm actually looking for my lady-in-waiting, Bridgette."

"Oh, yes. I know this young woman. I have seen her with you. I will set out to find her for you to prove my devotion."

Drusilla nodded, smiling to forestall her tongue from laughing.

"I would be ever so grateful," she said, trying to hold her composure together. "You can find me at the archery event. I think I'll try my hand."

"I live to serve you, my lady," he said, drinking deeply of her eyes. All of a sudden, she wasn't laughing anymore. He was young, impetuous, too quick to love. But there was no denying, one day soon, he would grow into his charm.

Departing, he threw her a quick wink, and she was surprised at how easily she melted. She smiled weakly, and left quickly. Of all the things she didn't have time for today, romance was right at the top of the list.

The archers were all at twenty paces, taking their turns in fives, shooting at the circular targets. It looked like great sport, but that was not the appeal. Her mind busied, devising a way to use this exhibition to her advantage.

"Care to try your luck, my lady?" the administrator of the event asked her.

"I would."

She took a bow, without any seeming thought, from the rack, and the administrator gave her a quiver.

"Forgive me, my lady, but that bow has a forty-pound draw," he said, masking his nervous demeanor with a downward gaze. "Perhaps this one would be more to your liking. It draws at twenty."

Drusilla nodded stupidly and took the trade. Twenty pounds? Her own bow was sixty, and it had taken her two years to master the strength and grace to use it properly. Being fired by entirely different technique, was the warbow, which she had also learnt. She could handle a hundred-and-ten-pound-draw when wielding the large and peculiar implement belonging to Roland the Just. It was all a matter of recruiting one's whole self to the task. With either the warbow or her preferred longbow, Drusilla was an expert shot, and stronger than she looked. Twenty pounds was insulting.

It comforted her to know her own bow, though hidden, was close at hand, though she dared not expose either her skill, or her possession of such a fine and artfully made weapon. So there it would stay, she affirmed, twisting the twig in her hand to and fro, unless sorely needed.

"Step up to the line," the contest administrator said. She and four other contestants obeyed. "Do you know how to knock your bow?"

"How hard can it be," she said.

"Three shots each," he announced, looking a bit dubious. "Begin."

And they all started to shoot.

Drusilla put her first arrow through a lazy arc, landing it in the lawn five paces in front of her opponent's target.

"Oops," she said.

Her opponents all hit their targets, though there were no bull's-eyes, and no inner circles.

Drusilla put her second shot over the top of her target, ricocheting the arrow tip off the wall. It fell harmlessly to the ground. Her contestants did considerably better.

For her third shot, she fumbled the string, nearly giving herself a welt. It was a close gamble. The arrow landed at her feet. She picked it up, and fired again, hitting her contestant's target, three to the left, so high it barely stuck in the top of the hay.

The contestant on her right had landed all three arrows, one in the second to inner ring. She smiled at him and applauded.

"One contestant moving to the next round," the announcer said.

Drusilla put her face into a pout, then shrugged. Turning, she saw Bayden and Ludo standing there. Double score. She had hoped at least one of them would be witness to her ineptitude.

She handed Bayden the bow.

"It's a little trickier than it looks," she said, a sheepish grin on her face.

Bayden looked at the bow, assessing it. It looked pathetically slim in his hand, then handed it to the event administrator as though passing off a particularly foul piece of refuse.

"I trust you are enjoying yourself?" he said.

"I hope you didn't just see that folly?" she countered.

"Every shot," said Ludo.

"Perhaps I could give you a few pointers?" offered Bayden, looking like he might be undressing her with his eyes.

"Of course," she said, inwardly cringing.

"Lady Drusilla is a woman of many surprises," said Bayden, addressing the administrator. "Let us see how she does with a real bow."

Bayden selected a forty-pound bow of decidedly superior quality to the other one, and handed it to her. He stood behind her, placing the bow in her hands, and showing her how to hold it.

What a lech.

A new set of contestants stepped up, and of course, the returning champ, man on the right.

Drusilla was shown a three finger technique. She desperately wanted to use her two finger draw, and bury an arrow dead center at a hundred paces. She could do it, with ease, from horseback even. But she wouldn't. There was no place for ego here.

A reminder, she realized with some humor, she was in need of.

Bayden sidled in even closer, gently guiding her in, drawing the arrow back to her ear. He smelled good. She hated him.

He stepped back. Good.

"Wait for it," he instructed.

"How will I know," she asked, playing along, allowing her elbow to wobble slightly.

"Wait until your hand's steady, then release."

Brilliant.

What had Roland taught her? "Visualize the end result. See it in your mind's eye as though it's already happened. Then act."

"That sounds so easy," Drusilla had said.

"It is. Trust the simplicity of it. In simplicity, lies the solution to all problems. Only the mind makes things complicated. Think from the heart, Dru. I see greatness in you. Have the faith in yourself, I have in you."

Drusilla let her elbow wobble a little more, seeing in her mind's eye the arrow of the contestant to the right, shattering.

Then she acted, ignoring the fact he had yet to shoot.

Her elbow folded in, and the arrow flew wildly sideways. Just then, the man to the right released his arrow as well, flying straight and true. It was a perfect shot.

Was.

The string slapped Drusilla's forearm brutally, tearing the green sleeve of her beautiful dress. A dress that had cost her an outrageous sum.

She dropped the bow.

The shot was spoiled. His arrow never made it to the target. Well, not all of it. The back half was shattered by Drusilla's arrow, which sailed on to pierce a distant pear tree. Shame about that.

The remaining fragment of the shattered arrow hit the target dead center, but tumbling, and bounced harmlessly to the ground.

Drusilla watched the whole event unfold in slow motion, then time suddenly snapped back, and she seized her arm, welt already forming.

"You're hurt, my lady," said Bayden, rushing all of three feet to her side.

"It would appear so," said Drusilla, looking sadly at her dress. Oriental silk.

"Let me attend to you," he said. "I am responsible. That bow was much too powerful for you."

Drusilla choked back a comment.

"'Tis nothing, my lord. The skin is not even broken."

The man to her right was still staring at the shattered remains of his arrow.

"Here is the man who needs your sympathy," she said, looking to her right. "I beg the favor of the judge. Give this man another shot. I'm afraid I've spoiled his most splendid effort."

The administrator looked to Bayden, who nodded his approval.

"My lady," said Bayden, "you astonish me."

Drusilla slipped away, shortly after the archery incident, finding Linus, and thus sending discreetly for her horse, Orion, asking he be readied with her saddle.

Ten minutes later she was riding down the dusty road, parallel to the cliff, which would take her to the little fishing village which also bore the name Foxborough.

There were about half a dozen boats and a primitive pier system hewn from raw logs, and lacking any finish or panache.

About three dozen houses made up the village, as well as a public house, a small market, and what looked to be an inn. Further down the way were several more scattered cottages.

As Drusilla approached, the people looked rustic and a bit unfriendly. She suspected she'd receive a warmer welcome if she was in rags. And she couldn't blame them. The behavior of the high-born around here wasn't exactly exemplary.

Drusilla rode up to the pier, stopping well on the dry side of the land.

"Stay, Orion," she said, dismounting, and striding up to the first sailor she saw.

"Afternoon," she said, trying to employ as little formality as possible.

The man grumbled something unintelligible and spit on the ground. In Merovingia, he would be beaten to death in the public square for such a display before an aristocrat. Then again, in Merovingia, Drusilla was not who she pretended, and she would be sentenced to die for impersonating a noble.

"You might try a little honey in hot tea," she said.

"Huh?" he grunted.

"It's marvelous. Simply does wonders for the throat. Break that phlegm right up."

"Eh, hehgh, hehh," he coughed. Or was that laughter?

Drusilla smiled.

"What's the matter with your arm?" he asked in a thick brogue, almost as unintelligible as the grunting.

"I'm afraid my sleeve's ruined."

"Nah, it ain't ruined. Nettle'll fix it right up. Does odd jobs, sewing…" he paused as though trying to remember something important. "Oh," he added, looking suddenly crestfallen. "Her daughter, Helen, went and gone missin'. Best if you don't bother her."

Drusilla nodded. "I hear a lot of young women have gone missing lately."

Finally, someone who might open up to her.

"Young girls is always running off. It's their way."

Or not.

"I'm looking for a way across the loch."

"With that horse. Ain't no one's gonna take you."

"Just me. The horse will stay here. He likes it here."

The old sailor laughed again, coughing up more phlegm and spitting. "Honey and tea, you say?"

"Hot," said Drusilla. "Hot as you can stand it. Add ginger or peppermint if you can get it."

He nodded.

"All right. But if you want to go, we'd best leave now. I don't like being out on the loch after dark. You got any luggage?"

"Just me," said Drusilla, warming to the man.

"All right. That one's mine over there," he said, pointing out a small craft that was little more than a rowboat. Correction. Was a rowboat.

Drusilla took a deep breath.

"I'm Shamus," he said.

"Dru," she answered. Formality would only be wasted here.

He smiled, his weathered old face puckering up beneath his whiskers and oilskin hat.

Drusilla approached the boat within two feet of the pier's edge and froze.

"Well, are you gettin' in or ain't ya? The Sun won't wait for an invitation."

Drusilla pictured sitting in the boat. Tried to approach it the way she would do archery. It was no good. She took the last step to the edge, held her breath, and stepped down into the boat, quickly sitting and seizing each side with a hand, clinging to it like a lover.

The boat rocked and swayed. It seemed the whole world would be tumbled upside down.

Shamus snorted and climbed in after her, causing the boat to pitch on yet another axis. He cast off the ropes, and grabbing the oars, pushed off the pier. The little boat glided out into Loch Ness. He slid the oars expertly into the oarlocks and began rowing. Away from the village. Away from land.

"Any particular place you'd like to be put down?"

Drusilla's mind snapped back to attention. "Oh," she said, still trying to orient herself...

So much water. The opposite shore rose and fell, shifting, dipping. Never staying put. Despite that, she found her target.

"Over there." She pointed towards the falls, reluctantly freeing her hand from its deadlock on the boat to do so.

"It's much prettier up that way," said Shamus, "and closer to Inverness, too." He pointed east, up the loch, past Foxborough keep.

Drusilla shook her head.

"I need to go to the falls."

Shamus squirmed in his seat. "How's about we go west a little, throw out the rods, and see if we can't bring in some nice fish for dinner? Good pike this time o' year."

"The falls are right there," said Drusilla, freeing her hand again. Every time she did so, little waves of fright gnawed at her gut.

"Don't normally go over there."

"Make an exception."

"Best if we head back now," he said, clearly making any excuse why he could not go near the falls. He squinted at the sky. "Looks like it may storm."

Puffy white clouds floated across a pristine blue sky.

Drusilla dug into her coin purse. This was obviously a time for universal diplomacy. She fished out a silver coin, trying without logic to plant her feet more firmly to the bottom of the boat. She held the piece of silver out, letting its brilliant luster flash in the sunlight. Raised an imploring eyebrow.

Shamus' old hand reached out, then hesitated.

"Bribery. Shame on you."

She doubled her offer. The land bobbed and weaved at the horizon of her vision. Damn you! Take it!

He grumbled and took the coins. "Only because I like you," he said, shoving the loot away into some deep pocket. "And just for a look," he said, rowing towards the falls now.

"In and out," said Drusilla, inwardly sighing. Inwardly dreading. One more obstacle overcome. But she took no joy in the accomplishment. The worst, she feared, was yet to come, and she had just opened the way.

The falls were beautiful up close. The churning water where they met the loch, terrible. Drusilla tried not to think about it, instead, she focused on her goal. Something terrible was happening to this village, to the people of Foxborough. She suspected there was a human hand in all of it. But there was something more. Maybe it was her imagination, but Drusilla suspected otherwise. The overly large, too dark, ripples in the water. The severed ropes. The superstition about the falls, and the statue's hand pointing that way.

The tooth.

Drusilla shuddered. Everything pointed this way. There was no more time to waste. And what had that horn been—

A great clamor rose in the forest near the falls. A murder of crows erupted into the sky, blackening the Sun, their caws a cacophony of chaos.

"We should turn back." Shamus shouted over the noise, oar clacking against the side of the rowboat. Was he trembling?

The boat bumped into something. Or something bumped the boat. Drusilla gasped, letting out a shrill sound of fright as she clung desperately to the little craft.

"What was that?"

Shamus muttered something, casting his eyes about the loch, pumping the oars, propelling the boat back towards the village.

Drusilla wanted to order him forward, not back, but found, when she tried, that she could not speak. She clung to the wooden seat, searching the now disturbed water as it rose and fell about the little boat.

The falls were getting farther away now. Her mission, along with her resolve—failing by inches, by feet. Soon, her feet would be back on solid ground, but it brought her no comfort. She thought of Roland, and she was ashamed.

Please stop. Go back, part of her mind screamed at Shamus, but she had neither the courage nor strength to speak it.

The boat continued to glide away as fast as Shamus could will it. The falls were an amber-white ribbon of despair, taunting Drusilla, diminishing by degrees, receding to the distance.

Something bumped the boat again, pitching it nearly ninety-degrees sideways. It came suddenly, violently, and Drusilla found herself flailing through the air.

CHAPTER TWENTY

J UST BEFORE HITTING THE water, Drusilla squeezed her eyes shut, and then the cold, wet loch slapped her, enveloped her. She was plunged into its depths.

Her eyes snapped open to dark shades of blue and little crystal bubbles swirling all about. There were shades of green, too, and something mottled, dark brown, almost black, slid by her. It was slick and oily, and had the feel of scales as it rubbed past the raw skin where her sleeve was torn.

Oh god!

Drusilla was still, whether involuntarily or by instinct, she didn't know. Her chest was seized by shock of cold and terror. Holding on to what little breath she had by fortune when she went under, she tried to think.

She wasn't dead, and that alone was something amazing to her. But she didn't know how deep she was in, and panic seized her anew as she realized she didn't know which way was up, or how to get there.

She was going to die.

She thought of Roland and whispered a quick prayer, begging forgiveness as the last of her air escaped involuntarily. Bubbles and dark, shifting shapes filled her vision. Drusilla's lungs ached for air. Air they could not have. She felt like she was sinking. That was when something shifted within her mind. No longer filled with terror and despair, she became angry—kicking, flailing her arms.

Fighting.

She would not betray Roland's sacred trust in her. She would fight with every ounce of her being, and any help God would give her.

As she flailed, feeling the water shift and churn about her, Drusilla's vision dimmed and flickered. There were fewer and fewer bubbles and an ever more encompassing cold, wet darkness. She was bumped again, dragged sideways by the shifting, passing form. Scales raked her, rolled her as they glided by.

Her lungs ached for breath. The world was wet and dark with no up, no down, no proper sense of time. Anger competed with wild panic as she thrashed against the formless enemy that was swallowing her whole.

And then her hand broke the surface. She felt it. It was that all familiar feeling of moving air cooling wet flesh—her wrist. Then her other gloved hand came free, and her face broke into the sunlight, spinning dizzily overhead in an indistinct haze of yellow and cyan.

No crows.

The grey-black blur in her peripheral vision must be the cliffs.

She gasped in air, and nearly blacked out, everything hazing over darkly with dancing red pinpricks scintillating about.

She went under again, swallowed water, freezing and burning her lungs simultaneously, and then she was up again, gasping, coughing, breathing...

Drusilla stole a glance across the loch—water, cliffs, there in her peripheral vision, the falls. Where was Shamus?

She wanted to call out for help, and discovered something odd in her makeup. Pride would not let her. She went under again, a churning vision of blue-greens and bubbles. Up she came and gasped for air.

She forced herself to call out his name calmly. This brought on another fit of sputtering and coughs. She tried to turn, started to sink, and abandoned that thought, reverting to the flailing that was keeping her afloat.

Something grabbed her arm just below the shoulder. Drusilla's head whipped around, prepared to fight for her life.

It was Shamus.

In the boat.

Looking very worried.

He hauled her aboard, and she threw herself to the deck, hugging it.

"I can't swim," Drusilla gasped, coughing up a spray of loch water and spittle. White-knuckled, she pulled herself to the boat plank that served as her seat, trying to reclaim some of her dignity.

"Looks like you were doing just fine, my dear," said Shamus, grinning what looked like both relief and amusement.

Drusilla thought about this, shocked. He was right. She had been swimming.

"This old ship," and he patted the sturdy rowboat with his gnarled hand. "She ain't goin' nowhere. So just you relax, and I'll get you back to dry land in no time."

Drusilla relaxed, sinking into her bench. She was safe. She was going back to land...

"No."

Quietly, she regained a bit of herself with that one simple word.

"But after what we've just been through," Shamus whined.

"No. Take me to the falls. To the land just over there." She pointed out a little grotto where the land made ingress just beyond the falls. Surely they could land there.

She wrung out her hair, rubbed her arms to warm herself. It was an all too familiar ritual.

"Do you have any idea what just happened, dear?" he said.

"I think I do," said Drusilla. "I need to investigate that bit of land. "We'll be back well before dark if we start out now."

Shamus sighed. "You're the boss," he said, looking squarely at her, then down to the growing puddle at the bottom of his boat. She must look something awful. "And a braver lass I've never known," he added.

Drusilla was stunned to silence.

She thought about that as they glided towards the loam-white curtain of water that marked their way, cascading off that black rock. There was definitely a deeply sheltered bit of woods back there, buried under the overhanging cliffs. A secret place. A wild place. Was this where the huntsman found his tooth?

The air smelled good here, like after the rain. Everything was wet and slick. The rocks behind the falls had a polished look to them, glossy, magical.

The Sun, hours past its zenith, cast the trees in long shadows. Drusilla, cold, dripping wet, splashed over the side, pulling the little boat up onto the reedy mud, finding purchase in the roots and stone.

At least she found the exercise invigorating.

"I'll stay right here," said Shamus, looking uncomfortable as a frog in a frying pan. "Don't you be too long."

"Just a few minutes to look around." She smiled at him as added assurance, perhaps as much for herself as for her new friend.

"I've got me this whistle," he said, pulling a carved piece of bone out from his shirt. It hung on a leather cord about his gnarled neck. "If you hear it, you come back quick. You hear?"

Drusilla patted him on the shoulder. "I won't be long."

She turned and went into the thick of trees.

It was hard going. Everything was either slick, mucky, or intertwined here. The trees were tangled and dense, competing for the constant moisture. Roots protruded everywhere, and there was a considerable amount of ground foliage, moss, and ferns.

Drusilla saw signs of a local deer population as she worked her way along towards the falls themselves. There was an earthy smell here, mingling with the water and crisp air. She could see why the hunter liked to come here, but she doubted he had explored all of it. The going was difficult, in places the forest would not yield to passage. She began to doubt she would find anything of use here.

The thing that haunted her, though, was the statue. Bayden's Galatea to Evelynn. Why did she look to the keep for protection while pointing to the falls? There had to be something here.

Drusilla climbed higher, away from the water, looking for a way to get closer to the falls—behind the falls. She was coming up against the same rock face which had prevented her from making direct access when she noticed a deeper shade of black.

Moving towards it, she found that it was a cave entrance, a tunnel of some sort. She wanted to draw her dagger. Who knew what might have made its home in the cave? But it was too slick, and she needed both her hands.

She climbed towards the opening, slipping, and nearly sliding down the slope. Gloved hand clung to a bit of rock, pulling herself back up. She would not be stopped now, least of all, by the land.

Reaching the opening, she peered within, wishing desperately she had a torch. The yawning black mouth did not yield its secrets readily. The opening was only big enough for crawling. There was no sense in ruining her dress any further, It was soaked, torn, and dirty. All those things could be fixed, but crawling through the stone passageway on hand and knee—that would surely put it to ruin.

She shed the dress, folding it and hanging it over a tree limb. Short of an overly ambitious jackdaw or polecat, Drusilla didn't think anything would make off with it.

Buckling her belt required a tighter notch for the lack of her dress, now naked but for her linen underthings, boots, and gloves.

That done, and everything secure, she entered the cave.

It smelled wet, dank. There were echoes of dripping water in here. Light quickly succumbed to darkness, and so Drusilla increasingly relied upon her other senses. Her knees received punishment with each advance. The way was difficult and grew more so with every foot traversed. The rock beneath her hand and knee was increasingly gritty in the depressions and worn smooth at the high points. Taking off her glove, she examined the grit, drawing it between her fingers.

Sand.

A theory came to mind. This was a blowhole for the tide. Drusilla wasn't sure how much the loch rose and receded, but she had heard there were places where a large amount of water could be driven quite high through a small passage of stone. Akin to the difference between how high you could throw a small rock as opposed to a big one.

Did this tunnel connect to the loch?

Drusilla was suddenly seized with a collage of terrors. She had just escaped, by narrowest of margin, the deadly grip of the loch. She wanted desperately to turn back. What if the tunnel suddenly sloped downward, slick and wet, and she was plunged upside down into a dark, deep pool, trapped on all sides by stone? Or what if the tide surged up, and filled the tunnel with water, trapping her...

Stop.

She would not tolerate this thinking. She had a job to do. Her theory was sound and needed investigating. For Camille. For Roland. For her own dignity as a knight of the Round Table, she was honor bound to face her demons, and to prevail.

Saying a silent prayer, she continued.

The tunnel did start to slope down, but it was manageable. Drusilla fought back her fears and continued. Gone was the crisp, evergreen world above, replaced by a deep sense of isolation. Water was more prevalent here. A living thing, issuing from cracks and crevices unseen. Dripping, collecting, running in little rivulets along the downward sloping passage. Every sinew of her wanting to retreat, she pressed on.

The darkness was total now.

Then it sloped some more. Oh god.

Suddenly terrified, she tried to slow her descent, to stop, but it was slick here. So very slick. Rock battered her, savaging elbow and knee. She could find no purchase. Down she went. Her scream echoed through the small tunnel, summoning back the sound of a thousand cawing crows.

Chapter Twenty-One

D RUSILLA PLUNGED OUT OF the tunnel, a disorienting tumble, before crashing into a pool of some sort. Somehow, her legs, not her head, struck the bottom, water spilling over her, taking her under. Hands located the bottom as she flailed wildly, then shot up, legs fighting to be upright, breaking the surface. Gasping air, she looked around, seeing nothing but blackest pitch. She was breast deep in the icy water, her feet upon a bed of shifting sand.

She didn't know where she was.

She had to find the tunnel. Had to get out. Ignoring the various new insults to her body, she turned and turned, looking for something, anything, met only with blackness. Hands found the wall, pawed at it, searching. She must find a way back up. Desperately, she ran the edge and back, seeking any purchase to climb back out. This wasn't like the Sun warmed loch. This was a sinister cold bereft of sunlight. A place forgotten, or perhaps never discovered.

The wall had a slight negative slope. It was slick beyond hope. Impossibly smooth. She was trapped.

Drusilla's chest began to wrack with grief. Silently trembling, she pressed herself against the wall, resisting the impulse to fall to her knees in total submission. To do so would be to lay her head on the block. The axe would soon follow.

She turned to the wall, searching it again. Frantic hands found nothing she had not gleaned upon the first pass, but still she searched with alarming desperation, reaching as high as she could, even leaping to find the slightest handhold from which to pull herself from this nightmare.

The water bobbed and slapped against her as she churned its frigid surface. The chamber echoed back her ragged breath, sounding large and hollow. Searching fingers became claws, digging at the unyielding stone. She thought to bury her dagger in rock, and thus buy a handhold. She knew it would only result in the loss of her blade, however.

She dared not cry aloud, let alone cry for help. She knew all too well what thing might call this home. Still, the emotion that welled up within her demanded release. Pressing her face to the cold stone, body succumbing to the rigor of freezing, she sobbed.

Water continued to lap against her in the darkness, not yet revealing whatever terrible things it concealed. She wanted to claw her way up and out, but it was not a thing she could manifest. She was trapped. There was no way back.

Drusilla's breathing was harsh and ragged; stilted by the cold, it came in short, painful pulls. Arms pressed to the wall, body slumped and forlorn, pressed to the cold stone, her only anchor to the green earth above, she continued to sob. Her heart felt like it was in her throat. She couldn't breathe. There was no going on. She had lost all control.

Stop, she told herself. Think.

But she couldn't. Not over the clamor of her own panic. She must get a hold of herself, before she had any hope of regaining rational hold on the situation.

Follow your breath. That was the advice of The Merlin. She didn't have much else to hold on to in this place. Follow your breath. It meant step outside of yourself and observe. Make no attempt to change what you see. Simply observe.

And so she watched herself breathing at the ragged edge of total panic from a place of detachment. Listened to the pounding of her terrified heart without judgment or any will in the matter. She observed from this place of no mind until the beat of her heart retreated from its high alcove. Till her breaths no longer threatened to black her out.

Good. Far from the serenity she might want, but enough.

She understood, perhaps for the first time, what The Merlin had intended for her in that one simple instruction. Follow your breath. She could think again. The use of her rational mind was returned to her.

With a new sense of calm, Drusilla searched her mind for a plan of action. She found it in the words of her mentor. "When you don't have eyes, listen." Roland had said that to her as knight to squire, one particularly dark night in the forest. His voice came back to her now.

Drusilla was quiet.

There was the dripping. Her own hammering heartbeat—no longer in her throat, but back in her chest where it belonged. The cavern she was in must be big, because the echoes were distant in places. The sound of lapping water began to define the shape of her submerged prison. In her mind's eye, the map of her surroundings took on ghostly form.

Good. Find the near wall and follow it. Drusilla found the wall's edge, moved along it, trailing a gloved hand along its smooth, worn undulating surface. Her fingers ached with the cold. Only numbly did they continue to give her the feedback she needed. Stopping to flex them, putting them to her mouth, she attempted to breathe new life into them.

Time was against her.

Placing hand to wall, she continued her journey. Her legs and stomach, ice, not wanting to obey her simple commands forward. But forward she went anyway. Forward was all she had. Moving this way, Drusilla soon began to see distinct shades of grey amongst the black. Either her eyes were slowly accustoming, or there was light this way. Either case was good.

She took hope from it. Follow your breath.

She moved towards the light, paying attention to every sound, every sensation. Soon, she could hear the white noise of the falls somewhere ahead. Encouraged, she pressed on, shaking her hands out again. Cradling them a moment under her arms as her body shivered, clinging tenaciously to life.

After a moment of respite, Drusilla pressed on, that is, until the water started to deepen. At first, she ignored it, hoping it was a temporary fluctuation. But now, it was nearly up to her neck, gently rising and falling.

It must be connected to the wave motion of the loch somehow, or the rippling caused by the falls. But water could travel through the smallest spaces. What if she couldn't get through? What if it got too deep? And what else was in the water with her?

This was not productive. No one was going to save her in here. No one cared about her fears. She, and she alone, could save herself. Or she could whimper in the darkness till one form of malice or another took her.

The light was her best possibility, she decided. Follow the light. Soon Drusilla was able to see more outlines of rock, shadowed egresses. Slithering forms on the water's surface.

Fish? Eels maybe? Drusilla fought back her urge to scream. The shapes, whatever they were, were relatively small, and they were keeping their distance. That was good, right?

The price Drusilla paid for continuing to follow the unknown source of light was that she was now chin deep and shivering. Her toes were burning. A bad sign. The lapping of the water splashed against her face and made her cough occasionally as it went up her nose or into her mouth.

Her coughs sent echoes through the cavern, and right now, she really didn't want to announce her presence. But as she took another step, the rock dropped away, and only her nose and eyes were above. She could feel her wet hair floating out behind her.

Sputtering, she tried to take that step back, panicked by the thought of being over her head again, this time all alone. Her foot would not find the place, and to her amazement, Drusilla found herself treading water.

What had Shamus said? "You were doing fine."

Actually, she had been floundering quite badly, but she had been swimming.

Swimming. That was a laugh. There was nothing elegant or practiced about what she was doing. But it kept her afloat at great effort. Treading water was hard work, and Drusilla had a decision to make. And though she was loath to do it, she felt panicked to make it right away.

Go back to where she could stand? Let the hours fritter away? Possibly freeze? Embrace her entombment so long as she could stand? Or go forward?

Desperately, Drusilla tried to conceive a better option. There was always another option if one only searched it out in good faith. Except that there wasn't always. As in battle, sometimes there were only bad choices and worse ones. Tarry too long, and the gap closes with brutal swiftness. Indecision is a choice, too, and often carries with it terrible consequence.

In this place, inaction was a death sentence. The choice had narrowed to a razor's edge. For the first time in her twenty-two years, Drusilla chose to swim. Not because she wanted to, but because she must. Her head reeled with fears. Things imagined yet unseen plagued the unsurveilled corners of her mind. In the darkness, all but swallowed whole by the icy, liquid dark, she swam. Her feet were numb and clumsy, arms ached from overwork, but she went forward. Forward towards the light.

The distance was hard to judge, her mind not functioning as clearly as she would like. Any lapse in concentration could be her undoing, and yet her mind continued to wander into less than useful avenues of speculation. To assume she was alone in here was foolhardy. Yet to entertain all the possible ways she could be done in served no purpose. It only divided her efforts, squandering actions, which, at best, were amateur and poorly directed.

Ragged breaths echoed the chamber as Drusilla pressed forward, willing her mind to swim and to do nothing else. Swim. That is all you must do. Nothing else.

She repeated the mantra, and again. Every time her mind would wander, depravedly wondering whether the water itself would win out and take her into its deep and permanent embrace, or whether, instead, some slithering and horrible thing would drag her down to her end.

Swim, she told herself, pushing aside all other thoughts vying for her attention. An attention which must not be divided.

Cold slowly petrified her muscles, causing her to flounder and spend yet more precious effort. What was worse, a new realization crept into her mind, past her mantra acting sentry. All the things she could imagine were not the thing she feared so deeply. The fear, which visited her in the night, evaporating upon waking without leaving its footprint. That was what she feared. The real reason Drusilla had so much utter dread of water was unknown to her.

It was to that thing that her mind obsessed. That destination which had no face, no name or way to place it into any context.

Swim.

It was the only way.

No thoughts. No wasted effort. No space for fear.

Swim.

Through this mantra, this pushing aside of all the panic and wasted effort, Drusilla noticed something which nearly, but for the circumstance, made her happy. At some point in her no-mind mantra, her legs began to help.

It was an astonishing thing.

The task, instead of growing more difficult, became just a little bit easier.

She swam towards the vague source of light. She put arms and legs equally into the task, attempting to keep her body from freezing. But the numbing cold could not be endured forever. That thought penetrated her carefully constructed wall of detachment. This was no mere exercise, given by The Merlin to sharpen her mind. Life itself hung preciously in the balance. New panic blossomed, and she renewed her efforts with a desperation reserved only for times of total need.

Her skin was ice, muscles barely responding to her will. But she would not stop. Would not give in. The sound of the falls was getting louder, and the cavern, though deeply shadowed, began to reveal its secrets. Drusilla suspected she was in the plunge pool behind the falls. Under the mountain. If she was right, then on the other side of that crashing curtain of water was the loch. And several hundred feet up the shore, she prayed, was Shamus.

It wasn't easy for her to imagine him abandoning her. He was a good man, but he seemed particularly superstitious about this part of the loch, and likely, with good reason. She would just have to trust him.

Drusilla ventured a look towards the ceiling. It was lost in blackness, and she got a drip in her eye. Right. Bad idea. Then she noticed a patch of shifting light to her left. It could have been a trick of light and shadow, but it appeared to be a bit of land that sloped gently out of the water.

With renewed hope, she headed towards it, working her arms and legs against the vicious cold of the water. It took more effort than she had imagined. Now that she actually had a visual reference point, she realized just how ineffectual she was in the water.

Just when she was really starting to regret her decision, and wondering whether she would make the "shore" or not, her foot exploded in needles of pain. Sand. She had struck the bottom.

She struggled, flailing harder, and soon had purchase, both feet afire as contact with the sandy bottom lit them up. She didn't care. It was land.

Drusilla waded the rest of the way, feeling great relief as she collapsed upon the sand and pebbles, deep under a canopy of dripping stone and darkness. She lay there in a collapsed heap, shivering. Curled herself into a ball, and rubbed life back into her hands, her thighs. She dared not tarry long.

With a grunt, held in check best she could, for fear of being heard, Drusilla rolled back to her stomach. She was nearly to the patch of light. She reached her hand up to crawl further on land and was met by something hard and unforgiving like a branch, but smoother. Gasping from the effort, Drusilla pulled herself up on hands and knees and crawled into the patch of light. It danced in patterns like water, and she realized it was sky filtering through the falls. Though the Sun must be sinking into the west now, it was still light enough to give her this.

She followed it upwards, back across the pool, maybe a hundred and fifty feet away. An opening in the rock, low and wide, and the rushing white water curtain which led to daylight.

Drusilla's heart leapt. It was distant, and it would be difficult, and right now she ached with cold and exhaustion. But there was hope, if she would only muster all her courage, she could do it.

Drusilla had almost forgotten the cylindrical object in her hand. She pulled on it, and it gave way. She held it up to the light.

It was an arm bone.

Chapter Twenty-Two

D EAR GOD, WHERE WAS she?

In the gloom, Drusilla held the object before her, and there was no denying it—it had belonged to a person... had once, and not so long ago, been a person.

She gasped, dropping it to the sand, and turned around. It took her a moment to adjust her eyes, after staring at the waterfall, but she forced herself to look. Dimly at first, and then, in shocking clarity, a mountain of bones came into view. Partial carcasses littered the area as well—antlers, hides, human skulls...

Drusilla recoiled in horror, tumbling down the sandy slope, gloved hands splashing the pool's edge. She looked back up at the pile. It was monstrous. There must be thousands of bones. Somewhere in that macabre pile, something glinted, then was gone.

Drusilla's heart raced. Eyes?

It shone again, steadily, as she moved her head to a new position. She knew that glint. It was jewelry.

Drusilla had found the missing women.

She thought about the spire of black rock, and the coils of broken rope. Somebody was sacrificing them to this beast. She couldn't be sure about Camille, though. Maybe she had gotten away. It was a slim chance, but she had to allow for it. How could she return to Roland and tell him Camille was probably dead?

Maybe that jewelry could tell her something. Improbable as it seemed, that anything of recognizable worth would have survived, she had to try. Digging through a pile of bones, human remains, was the last thing she wanted to do. This was possibly the answer she had come for, though.

It was necessary.

Drusilla stood, approaching the interlocked white mound. She caught a whiff of moldering deer hide that knocked her back a step.

Returning to the water's edge, this time with purpose, she lifted the hem of her underskirt to get at her shift. With dagger and a few good tears along the bias, she had a makeshift rectangle of linen. Soaking it afresh, rinsing out the dirt and grime, she folded it double and tied the cloth triangle around her mouth and nose.

Satisfied, she returned to the macabre mound and started tossing bones aside, looking for that glint again. Already, she was losing light. She thought of Shamus. Hold on, she silently pleaded. I'm coming.

Tossing a hundred or more bones aside, she found a hand and a ring. She fought back the impulse to retch and pulled the simple piece off the slick white bone and tendon that was once someone's finger. It came off the middle finger of the right hand.

Had it been Evelynn's? She couldn't imagine anything so plain belonging to the woman.

Perhaps Helen's then...

She closed her eyes and steadied her hand before pushing the newfound clue into her purse. It would mean something to one of the mothers. One of the fathers, sisters, uncles, best friends, or brothers. That it would cause them grief was certain. But it might also give them a bookend to close upon their search. To quell the uncertainty, which was a pain unto itself.

Drusilla said a little prayer for the departed and continued.

Another two dozen bones, and the rib cage of a calf, shaggy patches of fur still clinging to it, brought her to an arm, hand still attached. There, around the wrist, tangled with a piece of decaying oarweed, was a bracelet.

"I can't," said Drusilla, falling to her knees and sobbing. But she knew she must. She reached out, almost touching it. Closed her eyes, taking a deep breath. "All right."

She reached to it, disentangling it from the clinging vegetation, working the clasp, releasing it. She prayed she was wrong as she brought it into the fading light.

It was an ancestral piece, a betrothal bracelet long held by Roland's family, passed one generation to the next.

It was Camille's.

Chapter Twenty-Three

D RUSILLA HEARD THE WHISTLE blowing frantically, ceaselessly, after passing through the roaring curtain of water. She called to him once she cleared the sucking force of the waterfall, but the noise of the falls was too great. The rock passage had been less than two feet high, but beneath the water's surface, it was fathomless, easily passable by a large creature.

Drusilla tried not to think about it. The feeling of her feet dangling into nothing was horrifying enough. To paint pictures in her mind of sea serpents gliding by searching, watching from the deep, with a taste for young maidens was too much. She pushed it from her mind lest she come undone.

She treaded hard for the boat. She couldn't see it yet, but she knew where she had left it, just around the bend.

"Here," she called, hearing the whistle again. She had put some distance between herself and the crashing noise of the falls, and could now see the boat, barely, between the rise and fall of the waves.

He had waited for her, but he didn't hear her. His whistle blasted again. She was growing weary, but tread harder against the emptiness below. Sometimes, the easiest thing to hear is your own name. She tried it, calling out as loudly as she could.

"Shamus."

It was getting harder to tread. Please turn around.

The Sun was low. The sky was not yet orange, but she was completely in the shadow of the cliff.

"Shamus."

The boat pushed off from the shore. He had heard her. Her heart quickened. She tried to stay afloat. It was getting so hard. Shamus put the oars to locks and glided out into the loch... away from her.

He would turn around. He was just getting out into the water. But he didn't turn. He was leaving her. The very thought was crushing.

As she struggled, water splashed in her face. She sputtered, fighting to stay afloat. Panic was setting in. The little rowboat was getting farther away.

"Shamus!" she screamed, venting all her rage. All her futility.

He paused, cocked his head, and then the crows took to the sky again, cawing madly. Something had spooked them.

Drusilla flailed at the water, clawing for forward progress, taking more hits of water in the face. Choking back the loch's water, beginning to lose her rational grip on the situation.

The sky was black with crows. Cawing, swirling, they veered off to the east, climbing, moving up over the cliffs and away. Drusilla envied their mobility.

"Shamus!" she screamed again, working her vocal cords raw. There was real terror in her voice now. She didn't like that.

Where was he? Somehow she had gotten turned around. She searched frantically for him, twisting in the cold waters, every muscle aching. On fire.

She heard the whistle again and called back.

"Here."

She twisted some more in the water, then spotted him.

He was coming. God bless him, he was coming.

"We have to go back," she said as Shamus rowed for port.

Shamus mumbled something.

"My dress," she said, rubbing her arms fiercely, shivering and drenched. "I left it across a branch. It won't take twenty minutes."

Shamus looked at the darkening sky, shook his head, and kept rowing.

"Twenty aurei," she said.

"Beg your pardon?"

"Twenty gold coins. That's how much I paid for that dress."

"Well," he mumbled, hiding a smile. "It was a pretty dress."

Drusilla glared at him... and then laughed.

DRUSILLA RODE TO THE keep, shift and petticoats, a filthy disgrace, clinging wetly to her body. The village had been deserted when they had made dock, and Shamus, the only one to see her in her disreputable state thus far. He had taken it all in good humor. She didn't think she'd get as much levity from the noble class into which she was riding.

In fact, she needed little imagination to see the many looks of shock and judgment she would soon incur. And that answered her momentary confusion; they would be at the chariot races. The villagers had been invited, too.

It was a grand occasion.

Nearly every eye would be elsewhere. A few guards and nothing more. That she should return at once to her rooms, scrub herself clean, and dry out by the fire, praying she encountered no one of higher station, was the sensible thing.

Her plan was made.

But visions of what she had just endured continued to surface as she navigated the switchbacks, ever climbing, on the road to the keep. Her friend's bracelet, taken from her friend's skeletal hand—

She suppressed a sob.

And the ring. Another poor soul in her purse.

And she had found these things, not by chance, but because the Galatea in Evelynn's image pointed her the way. The Galatea wrought by Bayden's own hand. Beyond the door to which he held the key.

It was him.

How many sign posts did she need?

Shivering turned to heat as a fire rose up within her. On the forge of anger, her blood did boil. Even her brain transformed, a cauldron of rage.

The sob came.

She rode.

Orion climbed the hill.

It was him.

The first to go missing was Evelynn. His betrothed.

Why did she persist in gathering evidence? Was it all not laid bare at this point? How much more obvious could she demand it be?

Should her next move not be equally obvious? She felt her fists tighten, resolve burning in her belly.

It had to be him. If not both brothers, at least Bayden, then. Were his guards in on it? She doubted it. He was a man like Count Nolan. He kept secrets.

A secret door. A secret beach.

It had to be him.

He had the key.

So what was her plan?

Her blood ran red-hot despite drenched clothes and the chill of the loch still in her bones. This time, she would not need months for the hunt. Bayden was here. Just beyond those walls. Justice was but a single, decisive action away.

She reached into her purse, felt past ring and coin till her fingers found the bracelet. Fond memories of times spent with her companion flitted by like butterflies in shafts of sunlight.

Camille.

Her heart ached.

All that was left of her beloved friend was here in her purse, and buried in the forest, far from the activities of man, to be forgotten. Broken and discarded, the evidence hidden with deliberation. And maybe that had required the help of his guards...

No. Not even that.

One man and a team of horses could accomplish as much.

Drusilla knew it was rash, but could not quell the anger welling up within her. It was a furnace. A cauldron. She should be seeking a fire, but what need she of that? Even her brain felt as though it were cooking, and the colors of the world were leaching away, leaving only red—

What more was there to think about?

It was him!

Beyond Foxborough Keep, somewhere above the cliff face east of the outer walls, Drusilla heard the gathered crowd faintly. She dropped Orion from canter to trot, approaching the portcullis, and then to walking as she was let to pass within.

The feeling might have been spooky had she not known of the race. Only a skeleton crew manned the garrison. But she was not intimidated, and in no mood for entertaining ghosts.

She would find the MacKay brothers and have her vengeance.

"Where are they?" she asked, surprised to find her voice husky and raw. Edged with danger.

Gone was her plan to hide herself away and regroup.

"At the races. Perhaps you'd like to put on a dress first," sneered the captain of the regular guard, and she guessed he thought her one of the villagers.

So this is what it was to be on the other side of things. For her, it had not been forever ago.

"Maybe run a comb through your hair," said one of his subordinates.

"Perhaps you'd like your tongue cut out," countered Drusilla.

"That's Lady Drusilla," whispered a third, though she overheard it.

"As you wish," conceded the captain, the ghost of death visiting his complexion, and he was suddenly contrite. "I'll have your horse stabled."

Drusilla collected herself, despite the boiling pit in her stomach barking for action. She reined in her impulses, if only for the moment. Calm was needed if she was to get to the brothers. She had no advantage but her perceived rank here. She could show no weakness, but rather rely upon their perceived station and duty.

"No," she said.

The soldier reaching for her reins withdrew his hand like he had nearly made the mistake of touching hot iron.

It was a razor's edge she walked. Rein it in!

She forced a placid indifference upon her expression and added,

"Thank you all the same. I'll ride."

She was led through the arched door by the olive tree, both she and Orion ducking low as they passed through. Across the expanse of lawn, the much wider and more heavily fortified door in the northeast tower stood open.

Tawny stone draped her in shadow as she was led in, and it was only the increasing clamor of the crowd beyond the outer portcullis which assured her she wasn't being taken to the dungeons.

Instead of taking a breath in relief, however, she found the muscles of her abdomen tighten. And was reminded, through her wet and plastered, remaining clothes, that and much more was showing.

And then she was on the other side of it, in the shadow of the keep, the whole of Caledonia stretched out before her, cliffside to her left, and the loch, a dizzying plunge below. Both imminently close at hand.

A great crowd, village folk and gentry alike, was gathered in the clearing between the keep's walls and a lush forest beyond. They were not yet organized at the periphery to allow a track for the race to proceed, though the turning pole was erected nearby, and over the heads of those many gathered, two horses, one black, one white, huffing, tossed their heads.

Drusilla's eyes raked the crowd, searching out her prey.

There was an eagerness and buzz as of a great event about to start—the nicker and snort of the two horses who would be competing. The servants she had grown to know so well, attending to this and to that.

Perhaps they would forgive her for what she was about to do.

She watched on, more and more eyes settling upon her, first with concern, then bordering on shock as they pieced together the wrongness of her appearance.

The servants, in particular, seemed afraid, not of, but for her, and she didn't need to wonder why. She had been a champion of their small causes these last few days, and soon, she might very well be removed from their lives. Certainly, any of them would be dragged off for behavior even bordering upon her current display.

And as eyes continued to find her, and with their arrival, the shock and murmur she had only too knowingly expected, rippling through the crowd, Drusilla knew she had pushed the boundaries of social grace too far.

No.

Have sense.

Heart and breath in sync—fast and hard, like a storm of arrows.

She tried to slow it all down, to quell the heat within her.

Only activity, and her raging temper, had kept her chill blood circulating. And now she knew she had acted rashly, and felt the chill wind upon her, and with it, the cooling of her temper.

The colors of the world returned to her. This day was done. Though pressing need within argued for it to be otherwise, it was done. She need withdraw, recuperate, and plan.

The crowd, in the interim of her ruminations, had become more interested in her than that of the impending race. From scandalized whisperings and haughty judgements, to confused speculation and mutterings of concern.

Her escort, a two guard detachment from the gate, had since returned to their post. And Bayden's special guard, though not near her, had her now firmly in their observation, two of them moving, now, her way.

Race forgotten, Drusilla was the attraction.

She must retreat at once, and perhaps, with luck and a cleverly crafted lie, she could blame it on fever.

Highland air, heavier than in the valley, rolled down the mountainside and off the cliff, robbing life from her as it did. She shivered. Orion, in seeming empathy, shook out his muscles, and gave a little snort. She felt his heat and was glad for it.

It was time to retreat.

With luck, and proper measures, chill would not take her to her grave—

And then she saw it.

Turning Orion to leave back the way she had come, she saw them through the pressing crowd—two chariots stood waiting, gleaming white with gold trim in the low sunlight.

Each, a horse tethered and ready, one black, one white. But the wheels had been painted recently, poorly—the thin coat of white, in the late Sun, could not hide the quality work that lay beneath it: robin's egg blue, cream, and silver—and it was that, the ancestral colors of Camille of Lion's Gate, which caught Drusilla's eye.

It was that pattern which gripped her by the throat and barked—action!

Fury roiled back to life like a kettle only momentarily off the flame.

Bayden walked towards one of the chariots now, seemingly content his guards were handling Drusilla. And the big Scotsman, Angus, strode to the other.

Once again, her eyes fell upon that pattern. The bleed-through was only visible in direct, harsh light, but there was no mistaking it. Those wheels, those chariots, had been built from the salvage of Camille's coach.

Drusilla dismounted, and drew her dagger, entering the crowd, who all began to mutter and step aside. The many looks of shock and fear barely registered as anger throbbed behind her eyes.

No matter. In a moment, it would all be over.

A clear path was cut for her.

She moved from shadow to Sun, close to him now. Close enough to pounce on him and strike a deadly blow before anyone could do anything about it. Not even his eight loyal bodyguards, nearby though they were, and beginning to flank her, were close enough to lift a hand against her. She had acted too quickly, and it was now a game of catch-up they could not win.

Chapter Twenty-Four

G UARDS SHOVED THE MILLING crowd aside—path cleared but for a person or two, armored hands unseating swords, all too quickly to elicit any greater response from those gathered to panic. Drusilla would be dead in seconds. Bayden would be mortally wounded before she fell.

Her vision tunneled. There was only herself and Bayden, standing there in a haze of her own red hatred.

Where the guards had to move people, people had moved for Drusilla—and now the path was cleared.

A moment to be upon him, arm coiled like the snake yet to strike, but something stopped her—

Her inner voice of Roland.

She couldn't just murder him without knowing for sure. What if she was wrong?

Might for Right.

"Sometimes that will be a thin line, Dru," he had told her. "There will be times you will be sorely tempted to cross it. Be true to the principle. It will guide you in your darkest hour."

"Drusilla, my dear child..." Bayden turned to her, noticing her approach just as she was sheathing away her dagger. His stare said it all. He was shocked to disbelief, eyes traveling the length of her nakedness.

Half his guard arrived and were summarily waved off by Bayden.

"I just can't get enough of your wonderful loch," said Drusilla, pushing a clump of wet hair out of her eye. In the blindness of rage, she could not have summoned the remark. But even in the ember of its passing, lies came easily to her.

A trumpet sounded, calling the chariots to their mark.

Angus lashed the black horse forward, approaching the line that would be both for start and finish. Wheels turned, hooves pawed the ground, actions that encouraged the crowd to clear the track and reform along the treeline.

"I really must go, Dear," said Bayden, mounting his chariot. "Do stay and watch the race. Yah!" He lashed the white horse to action, moving up to the line as well.

Drusilla's heart pounded in her ears, beating the tempo of war.

"The action's only beginning," she said, words ragged edged. Menacing. Her voice still raw from her desperate cries out in the water, but even more so for the emotion they carried.

Sara sat upon her mother's shoulders, bright-eyed and eager for the race. She spared an enthusiastic wave for Drusilla. Drusilla raised a hand to her and managed a smile that was better than crying.

Liam MacTavish, Sara's father, stepped up to the turning pole just ahead of and between the two charioteers. Persian pipes hung upon his chest by a strap. With a mighty breath, he began to work bag and drones, striking up a solemn tune. As the tempo built, so did the tension in the crowd. The tune came to a crescendo, and then ceased, Liam dropping the pipes to his side.

The chariots leapt into action, thundering down the wide, hardpack road, roaring onlookers on one side, high stone wall on the other. Rounding the back tower, they were gone.

Drusilla scanned the crowd for her lady-in-waiting, each spotting the other about the same time.

"My lady," said Bridgette, falling to a low curtsy. "I do apologize. They've kept all us servants so busy of late. Ordering us here and there—"

"It's all right," said Drusilla.

"Raul said you were in need of me," Bridgette continued, and looked her mistress up and down again.

"Oh, he found you after all," said Drusilla, impressed at his tenacity.

"I did indeed."

Drusilla turned to see her would-be suitor standing there, taking in her bedraggled form. Fine. Maybe now he would lose his obsession with her.

"I find you more beautiful, and may I add," he said, looking her up and down, "more daring each time I see you."

Or not.

"Raul," she said, curtsying best she could in her limp attire.

He took her wet gloved hand and kissed it.

"Have you encountered some kind of trouble?" he inquired. "Perhaps I could be of some small assistance? That I had a cloak, I would offer it."

"Thank you. But I'm quite fine. Bit of a wardrobe malfunction. That's all." She turned to Bridgette, expecting to catch the young woman stealing glances of the handsome newcomer from under those flaxen lashes. She didn't think Bridgette had met Raul yet...

But Bridgette had no eyes for him. Rose-red...

Drusilla shook the thought off like so much rain flung from oilcloth, giving space to remember, on this most crowded day, the reason she had turned to the young woman in the first place.

"Could you go and fetch me a cloak?" she requested. There was no sense spoiling another dress. The loss of her yellow and green treasure hurt too much already.

Bridgette curtsied again, but before she could run off to do as she was bade, a dark thought crossed Drusilla's mind like an inkblot on the Sun.

There remained at the keep, at best, a few soldiers. Maybe a servant or two. What might happen to an unaccompanied young woman?

"Hold," said Drusilla, thoughts unwillingly straying to Carlotta.

A shudder passed through her, this time having nothing to do with the highland wind. Her mind was a chaos of thoughts this day, and adrenaline, though in abeyance, still coursed her veins. She wished she could slink away and reset the pieces—clear the board and start anew on the morrow.

Bridgette awaited new instructions, but it was to Raul, Drusilla made her request. "If I could impose upon you, would you chaperon my lady-in-waiting? I'm sorry to cause you to miss the excitement."

That she should carry out the task herself, she knew, but she could not. The hunt still boiled in her blood, and she would keep an eye on Ludo. And where was Ludo? She thought she saw him in the company of Lady

Elaenor earlier, but now, on reflection, she couldn't be so sure.

She had been half out of her mind earlier...

"It is no trouble. I would be honored."

It was words like that which melted a young woman's heart. But again, Bridgette's reaction, one of gratitude, was directed only at her mistress.

Violets, red roses, something green... and crocuses.

After they departed, Drusilla's mind wandered, trying to fit various pieces into a larger picture that would not emerge. The day had been too long and upsetting already, and it was not yet done.

Visions of that cold, dark place under the mountain came unbidden—the pile of bones. The last, identifiable traces of maidens...

And so it was, she had no idea how much time had passed before the charioteers were back around the wall, kicking up dirt, thudding her way.

Bringing her mind back to the present—the race, it occurred to her—would be much more exciting to watch from the walls, or one of the various towers. Even so, it was thrilling to see all that muscle and machine rumbling along.

Angus was in the lead by two horse-lengths, and made the turn first, his face a grimace under thick red whiskers. Then Bayden made the turn, looking unhappy but not beaten, and they were off again, down the stretch that would take them beyond the sight of the crowd.

Without the chariots to occupy her eyes, Drusilla paused in her broodings to take in the southern crags bathed in the last golden light.

It had been night inside the mountain.

Again, a chill passed through her, and she stamped her feet and rubbed her arms to fend off malady as she awaited the return of the chariots with deep interest.

By the beginning of the third stretch, Angus was ahead by just half-a-horse, and Bridgette had returned with a cloak, Raul staying but a short time before disappearing back into the crowd. Drusilla was glad she hadn't caused him to miss the whole thing. At least he could witness the climax.

But as the riders were turning past the wall, Drusilla could swear she saw Bayden raise his whip to Angus.

She pulled the cloak tighter about herself. Had she imagined it? She looked to Bridgette. The young woman looked worried, but that could be for a host of reasons.

Upon realizing she was being scrutinized, Bridgette offered, "Thank you for providing me with escort. The keep is so empty it felt like a ghost story."

Drusilla touched Bridgette's arm, and smiled for her, and then they both heard the thunder of the returning charioteers and put their attention back on the race.

They watched the two men come in for the final stretch, Bayden in the lead, and Angus wiping blood from his eyes, a horse behind.

Bayden finished the race first, reining his horse in dangerously close to the cliff. It was clear Angus couldn't see. He had crossed the line right behind Bayden, still wiping at his eyes. He had made no attempt to slow or turn.

Drusilla looked to the cliff, then to Angus. It didn't look good. There were mere moments before horse and rider would be plunged to their deaths—

Angus' wife screamed. One of the other ladies in attendance fainted dead away, Sara's mother dropped child from shoulders, sheltering the young one's eyes. Drusilla whistled for Orion, dropping the cloak, and fleeing from the crowd towards the open space in the path of disaster.

Orion galloped up, and she leaped into the stirrup, throwing her other leg over, gripping the saddle horn.

The crowd gasped as the remainder saw what the few had already seen. Angus was riding to his death.

A cluck of her tongue, and the gentle engagement of the reins, and Drusilla was at a full gallop for intercept.

"Move," she cried as a confused onlooker stepped into her path.

She missed him by inches and came alongside the charging horse pulling Angus' chariot. Swinging one leg over her horse's neck, she gripped the saddle horn between her thighs, leaning back and out into empty space. Extending her arms, fingers straining, she grabbed the other horse's reins, pulling hard. The horse nearly stumbled, chariot coming up on one wheel and pitching Angus to the ground.

A cluck of her tongue, and Orion skidded to a halt as she slid back into her saddle, and hopped to the ground. She was mere feet from the cliff's edge.

Angus, still tumbling, rolled to a stop inches away from the plummet.

"Stay," she told Orion, and then, seeing Angus trying to stand, still blinded and teetering, dangerously tempting a fall, she ran to him—

Too late.

He toppled over the edge.

Drusilla grasped at him—her own toes at the brink—grabbed his belt and threw her weight back, despite her effort, certain now they were both going over.

Her toes ground forward, dirt and gravel spilling over the edge, rocking back, digging her heels in. And still she slid towards the edge.

Oh god!

Chapter Twenty-Five

T HE LOCH STRETCHED OUT like two great black wings, waiting to envelop her. Would they be smashed to bits upon the narrow strip of land, or sail clear to be swallowed whole?

Drusilla could let go. She'd be safe...

Except she couldn't.

She cried out, exerting every last fiber of her being, and prayed, toes going over—

And then she managed it, thank God, hauling Angus back, knocking him safely to the ground.

"Cliff," she said, panting, heart pounding in her ears.

He nodded, as if understanding.

"Can you see?"

"Aye, I've just got blood in me eyes. That damned Bayden whipped me." He was cradling his face in his hands. "I expect my forehead's busted wide open."

"Let me see," said Drusilla, the crowd of spectators a closing circle of murmur, animated conversation, and worry.

Angus took his hands away.

Drusilla cringed at what she saw.

"It'll need cleaning," she said, "and a good bandaging. Spider webs if you can get them. They'll bind the wound together."

The gash ran nearly four inches across his brow, slanting down to slice through his eyebrow. A continuing cut was just below his eye, across his cheek. Both were red and swollen, and starting to bruise.

"Aye, you're a wise woman, Drusilla of Merovingia," said Angus. "Was that you who stopped me horse?"

"It was."

"You're a remarkable woman. If there weren't laws agin bigamy, I'd ask you to be my wife."

Drusilla laughed.

"Take care, Angus," she said, giving him an affectionate pat.

"And you," he said. "Don't be taken in by that devil's charm. Lord Bayden is not what he seems."

He had no idea.

"You impugn my honor," said Bayden, making himself known. He was standing with the crowd, observing the interplay, and had probably heard everything. "As lord of this realm, I could have you put to death."

"Then do it," cried Angus, rising to his feet, a menacing bear of a man. More blood pumped from his wound, giving Angus a fierce crimson mask and staining his upper body.

"But you won't," said Drusilla, taking the whip from Bayden's hand and leaving.

Several men were holding Angus back from a charge. He growled at them, shaking them off.

"I think you've overstayed your welcome," Drusilla heard Bayden say as she retreated through the tower and across the greensward.

In response to Drusilla's whistled command, Orion broke into a trot, flanking alongside her.

"I wouldn't stay in your keep another day if the whole valley were under siege," said Angus. She could hear him punctuate the sentence with spit.

Good for him.

BAYDEN'S ANGRY WORDS MAY have been meant for her. With blood in his eyes, Angus may only have assumed otherwise. If so, she was grateful for the deflection. She was by no means done with this business. On the contrary, things were just beginning to heat up, and she needed to be close.

She mulled over the implications as she sat before a fire in Evelynn's room, wrapped in naught but a blanket.

Bridgette busied herself with a scrubbing basin and then draping wet clothes, tending to her gloves and beloved adventure boots, and had even volunteered to sew the removed rectangle of cloth back into the shift once both halves were dry.

Before she had allowed such ministrations, despite her shivering, Drusilla had Bridgette identify the other piece of jewelry recovered from the loch.

The ring was Lilly's, the young woman missing more than a month now.

"Be careful," Drusilla had said. "Nobody must yet know. You would be in terrible danger if word got around you had information about the missing women."

Bridgette left the room, returning ten minutes later with hot soup from the kitchen and a steaming mug of tea infused with local herbs and thick with honey, insisting Drusilla warm herself thoroughly lest she catch her death. The young woman then picked out new clothes, warm, dry night clothes, assisting her in the dressing.

Drusilla pretended aristocracy. Often she had worn it as her mask. Never had she truly experienced it. Not till now. It sat uneasily with her on the one hand, and on the other...

It made her feel so very cared for.

She trembled.

Bridgette took it as a sign she needed more warmth. "Into bed with you now," she ordered, turning down the covers. "I won't have you taking ill."

Drusilla continued to shake, but not from cold. The soup had done its job well enough. The tea had soothed her raw throat, working its own small miracles. She trembled, not from the cold, but from the burden lifted. A lifetime of struggle and hard living melting away as she found herself truly pampered for the first time in her life.

"Thank you," said Drusilla, glancing out the window at the darkness, then to the bed cheerily lit by the fire throwing off its welcome heat.

"To bed," Bridgette repeated. She held out her hand for the finished tea mug, taking it from Drusilla, who climbed within the covers.

The young woman tucked her in to the chin and issued more orders.

"No prowling tonight. You stay right there. Full night's rest. That's what you need."

Drusilla was not about to cease her prowling, but it would do no good to run herself down or get sloppy. She would lay here quietly, taking Bridgette's advice, use the night to recoup. But she would not be idle. Already her mind was plotting her next move.

She suspected Bayden and Ludo of terrible things. Further, she anticipated trouble. Bayden did not strike her the type to let fate decide things. She must be more than vigilant. It was time to cross the Rubicon.

"Bar the doors, then," she told her lady-in-waiting, "and place my dagger upon this table by my side. Then get yourself prepared for bed and take your comfort."

Bridgette eyed the bed, uncertainty in the brief glance, before taking a blanket and setting it in the chair.

"I won't have you sleeping in chairs," said Drusilla.

"I have a cot in the west wing..."

"None of that. Now bar the doors and say no more about it. This bed is more than ample for two."

Bridgette nodded, dropping the heavy bar across the double doors.

Chapter Twenty-Six

"I'M GOING OUT," DRUSILLA announced, walking into the grand den where the two brothers were breaking fast. The heavy maroon drapes were wide, letting in Sun, fresh air, and the omnipresence of the loch.

Roast meats, eggs, rye bread, and barley tea steeped in honey assaulted her senses. The heat of the well contained inferno in the fireplace bathed her in waves of comfort, drawing off the morning chill. Again, she wore her black and red, hair in coils, ringlets descending from the velvet hat. Gloves casually held in one hand.

The brothers were dressed, much as usual, in their open white shirts and form-fitted leather pants, uncommon to this lonely part of the world.

Both looked up, uncommonly interested.

"To hunt," she added, keeping the subject squarely upon the purpose for which she had come. "May I take one of the bows?"

Ludo grinned crookedly. "Do you think it will help?"

"Don't be cruel, brother," said Bayden, then to Drusilla: "Of course you may take a bow. Anything you desire. But do you think it's wise to venture out alone?"

"I didn't leave Merovingia to lead the life of a chaperoned woman," said Drusilla. "Besides, what could happen? I'll have my bow with me. I think I'm starting to get the hang of it."

Ludo nearly choked on his tea.

Bayden's face looked strained. He must be trying to play it straight. "As you wish, My Dear," he said. "Do you have any particular hunting grounds in mind?"

"I thought I might try the woods to the south of here," she said, laying her trap. "Afield of where we hunted for fox."

"An excellent choice," said Bayden. "I look forward to dining upon wild game this evening."

Ludo was gasping now. He set down the tea and mumbled some unintelligible excuse.

"About noon hour, then," said Drusilla, wanting to give them time to conspire.

"I'll send a bow round front to the gate," said Bayden, "with one of the servants, along with a quiver of arrows. Are you sure you won't be joined?"

"Certain," said Drusilla. "The excursion will do me good, I think. Nice to get out alone now and then."

Was that delight on Ludo's face? If so, he concealed it well enough to ensure uncertainty. Bayden's civility was paper-thin. She was sure he was still sore over her exercise of power at the chariot races. She'd undermined him, and more than that, acted in most improper ways.

It occurred to her that only Raul had overlooked her social transgressions, taking even delight at her behavior. And of course, Angus. She turned away from the brothers so neither would see her sudden smile. Angus had actually proposed to her after a fashion. All but. She supposed she had his loyalty. It was too bad he'd also been banned, though she still wondered whether that was meant for her.

Without her intervention, much worse would have come his way. Luck or fate, he'd gotten away with expulsion. No great tragedy. Were it not for her mission, she would have packed up last night as well, and left the jackals to their savagery.

DRUSILLA RODE INTO THE forest, this time taking the Major. There was the stable master and his exercise yard, but most of her horses hadn't had a chance to really stretch their legs since arriving at the keep. At the least, each of her Coursers would get their turn if she could manage it.

She thought about the Hobbys, but, much as she would like to give them equal time, they were not battle tested like the dappled greys.

Drusilla trotted along the better used forest paths, making herself easily accessible to anyone watching. She wasn't disappointed. Once well out of earshot of the keep, she became keenly aware she was being followed by multiple horsemen.

She picked up the trot a bit, just to be sure. There was no mistaking it. She dismounted, and sent Ursa Major off a few yards out of the way to graze, taking up her bow and shouldering her quiver.

"Here foxy, foxy, foxy," she said, holding the bow badly, and playing her part.

Shortly, eight men rode up. They wore traditional Roman armor with the accouterments of round shields, Roman short swords, the ever formidable gladius, and helmets with nose pieces concealing their identities. One look at their horses, though, brown with distinctive white-starred foreheads, and Drusilla knew they were Bayden's personal bodyguards.

The Picts had refused Roman rule not once, but three times, spilling much blood and turning Caesar's forces back. Was the Celtic armor they normally wore, the disguise—the only thing that would be accepted in this rugged outland—and this, the Roman kit, the true face?

Here, before her, stood the best of the best. And they had left Bayden's side to come after her. Most telling. She pretended not to notice them at first, then turned.

"Oh, hello," she said. "Don't mind me, I'm just scaring up a little game."

One of the men dismounted, coming forward and drawing his sword rapidly to strike her.

Drusilla had no chance against these eight men. No chance except her bow, a weapon in which she was exceptionally talented. She stepped back, knocking her arrow, drawing—

The string snapped!

Chapter Twenty-Seven

THE ONLY CHANCE SHE had. Her bow. And who had handed that to her? A soldier. One of Bayden's men. And who had given it him? Not even a conclusive chapter to end her story.

Drusilla ducked the sword blow, stumbling backwards.

The string had snapped at the bottom of the bow—sabotage in the knotwork.

She felt foolish.

And she knew she was going to die.

Roland had taught her better. It was upsetting. She'd undergone a full apprenticeship, serving as his squire five years.

"Never take an untested weapon into battle." He had drilled the concept into her head. And she had left her life to chance.

The soldier swung again, a downward stroke to finish things quickly.

She ducked under the blow, drawing her dagger in the same swift motion, and sunk it up under his breastplate, pushing it in deeply. He fell back, dropping the sword over her head, into the forest dirt. As he fell away, she twisted the knife brutally. Blood gushed out over her hand and blade, littering the road in crimson.

He stumbled to his knees.

The other seven dismounted, slapping their horses away.

The wounded man reached his hand out, grasping the air in front of him, then fell dead.

The seven men moved into a semicircle, each with shield and sword, closing on her. The odds were laughable. Still, Drusilla would give them nothing.

Running would be prudent—except each saddle was equipped with a recurve short bow and quiver of arrows. She would never make it.

She stepped back, finding the fallen gladius. Trading the dagger to her left hand, she slid her toe under the balance point of the sword, near the hilt, flipping it to her dominant hand. She gave it a twirl to assess it. Heavy, but well-balanced. It looked sharp.

Another untested weapon.

It would have to do.

"Afraid to fight me one at a time?" she asked, hoping...

One of the men stepped forward. Good. Ego was a beautiful thing.

He came in with a thrust. She parried. He countered with a shield bash, sending her stumbling backwards. She slashed her dagger through the air, fanning blood in a carefully aimed arc. It peeled from her blade and spattered his eyes. His reaction was almost undetectable, but in that moment, she drove her sword through his neck, and stepped back.

He flailed out wildly with his own weapon. Had she been there, she would have been struck. Would have been killed. She had expected the reaction and was not there. Knowing how an opponent might react was half of battle.

Insight, not chance.

There was no place for luck in battle. To beat these men—what had the scullery maid, Beth, called them? The Elite Guard—she would need to be better than them. Her training had been very demanding. Exceedingly thorough.

Was it enough?

Even if it were so, she was desperately outnumbered. Six men faced her now. She was down one weapon, her recently acquired sword having wandered off with its new owner, fallen in nearby forest.

Which man was leader? If she could break their morale... Anything to improve the odds by even one more man.

All six steadily closed on her. There would be no more chivalry—

She was rushed.

She picked the man who came at her with the most confidence, reached to her belt, and tossed her velvet pouch of glass in his face. Scintillating shards exploded, stunning him.

She dropped the cord, and tossed her dagger to her right hand, leaning away from the sword stroke of another oncomer.

With the snick of her wrist, steel cut tendons as the gladius passed her waist, missing by an inch.

The man's hand went limp, sword flying away.

That was two swords in the forest.

He tried to bash her with his shield, but she ducked under the arm belonging to his now useless hand, and slashed the back of his knee as she passed close enough to smell his leather.

She didn't wait to see him fall, but immediately attacked the man behind him. He didn't see her emerge from behind his companion until it was too late, so she merely stabbed him in the jugular, and continued on her way.

It was never good to be anywhere near a dying man. That's when they were always the most dangerous.

Behind them all, she spun, and seeing four of them on their feet, still trying to orient themselves, she darted to their mounts.

Despite the horses making no move to shy her, she knew better than to mount an untested horse, and these men almost certainly knew this particular forest better than she. As much as she wanted to flee, it was a fool's errand. But a bow—

Drusilla unhooked a short bow and grabbed a handful of arrows, turning back to the fray.

One man on his knees, back to her, fountain of blood escaping through clutching fingers at his neck. Another twisted on the ground, having crawled a ways, grasping at a sword with a hand that would not close. Not one of the remaining four assisted their fallen comrades, despite having the numbers.

Instead, they charged.

Drusilla knocked an arrow and let it fly at the closest man, piercing him through his open mouth. He fell face-first into the dirt, driving the arrow the rest of the way through the back of his skull, knocking off his helmet.

Time was not on her side, options narrowing to a razor's edge.

Tilting the bow sideways, she knocked three arrows, an advanced scattershot technique, letting them loose. Three hits on two men, one fatal, hitting his windpipe. The other man was hit right shoulder, left biceps. Force divided, no one arrow hit with full impact, but at close range, great force had not been necessary. The soldier held onto his sword despite the shoulder wound. Angry. Never breaking his pace.

She readied another arrow, the other man only a few paces behind him. She knew better than to rely on penetration where armor was concerned, especially with a bow that drew this easily. It was maybe forty-five pounds. Helmet lowered defensively, he presented mostly armor.

As he neared melee range, Drusilla found her opening as his banded skirt moved, putting the arrow through his groin artery. His forward momentum snapped the arrow imbedded in his leg, and he stumbled, crashing to the ground inches from her feet.

She stepped through his flailed arm and stomped down on the back of his neck, hearing a satisfying crunch.

The last man skidded to a halt a dozen feet from her position and turned to run.

"Stop," she said calmly.

The man hesitated, then spun, hucking his sword at her like a hatchet. It came with speed and perfect aim. Drusilla blocked instinctively with the bow, sword nicking past her without drawing blood.

But as satisfied as she was with her fast thinking and faster reflexes, an instant later, she heard the terrible twang as the second bowstring snapped!

Now she knew what had been nicked as the sword passed by.

She let the bow drop, picking up the sword. Harder was to push regret aside, but even more necessary. A battle is no time for emotions, Roland had told her.

Immediately, she chucked the sword back at the man, thinking it poetic.

He caught it. Actually caught it. And charged her.

He was good. Better than her, no question.

Drusilla ran.

Deeper into the woods, she led him, letting the soldier chase her. She would use the terrain against him. He was more heavily encumbered, and would tire, or make mistakes.

Except that he didn't.

He kept coming, at times getting dangerously close. She leapt over a fallen tree, ducked under a low branch, then crashed through some thicket, but he kept coming.

Drusilla chose increasingly difficult terrain, hoping to wear him down, but he was undeterred. Finally, panting, she realized she was the one getting tired. He had fought one person. Her. She had just finished off seven, more by luck than she cared to admit, and he was obviously in excellent condition.

That she had survived at all was testament to her calmness and quick decision. She owed that and more to her extensive training. But every moment this continued stretched the odds towards a breaking point. Drusilla didn't like the unpredictable in battle. She must finish this, and quickly. She looked for opportunity. Something she could use.

Up ahead was a dead tree with some low branches. It should be fairly brittle. That would be perfect.

She ran around it, dropping her dagger, snapping off a branch as she went, and as she rounded the backside, grabbed a handful of dirt. Her branch was nearly seven foot long. She was ready.

Popping back around the other side of the tree, she saw her pursuer almost upon her. She tossed the dirt in his eyes, and he stumbled. She gave him something to land on.

The branch pierced his abdomen, just below his breastplate, and actually suspended him a moment before sliding through. She doubled back, grabbing up her piece of steel. She checked the impaled man, to be sure, and found him dead.

Quickly, she searched him, finding only coin, which she took. Satisfied, she immediately headed back up the makeshift path towards the road. The man whose wrist and knee she'd slashed would still be alive and possibly cause for concern. She didn't think any of the others could have survived, but you never knew.

And they could have friends.

Something drew her eyes as she strategized. At first, she thought it was blood spatter, but it was something much better. A gift from nature. "Oh," she said, delighting at the sight of succulent little spheres, glistening red and mock-delicious, amongst a thorn bush, not five feet from where she'd impaled the soldier. "Poison berries."

She grabbed a handful, pocketing them for later.

Drusilla arrived back at the road, slightly winded, finding the remaining man propped against a tree for support, all his weight on one leg. His shield discarded, he held a sword in his off-hand.

Unless he was ambidextrous.

Drusilla would take no chances.

"Who sent you?"

He was silent.

"Whose idea was this?"

More silence.

"Then you can die in silence." She approached him slowly, picking up a fallen sword as she went.

He put the blade through a flourish of moves that proved he was still most capable of dealing death.

It's fine.

Drusilla forced herself to relax the grip on her own sword. Watched the movement of the blade, flashing gold, in the afternoon Sun. Timed it, picked her moment...

Entering with her own blade, she sped its course around the pattern, working with, rather than against the motion, forcing the speed, ramping it up. The man lost his grip on the blade, and she stabbed him through the eye.

He reached out to strangle her, groaning in pain, sword still projecting from his head, but she was already four paces away.

Scanning her surroundings, Drusilla listened, intent to discover the telltale signs of further ambush. Far off, a crow cawed, probably communicating the find of new carrion to its companions. The last man thudded to the ground, driving the sword through the back of his helmet.

These men would soon be picked clean, but first honors were hers.

Drusilla searched each man, looking for written orders or any other clues to the attack. There were none. More coin, some dice, a few personal charms. She took the coin, leaving anything personal or identifiable behind.

Next, she collected the bow the brothers had lent her, and the arrow she had tried to fire before discovering the sabotage, placing it back in her quiver. Both could easily implicate her in the events here. Much better to keep her adversary guessing.

Had she left anything else of hers? She reviewed the battle, step by step mentally... The glass pack.

She located it.

She could have finished the last man with a bow. Each horse had one. Fool.

One more chance she had taken, she hadn't needed to. Battle was fast, and she had come out of it alive. No more recriminations were needed.

Now what could she use?

A round shield? A gladius? She didn't know if she would need them, but it couldn't hurt to be prepared, so she took the best one of each, and a scabbard too, and hid them in the woods in a place she could remember. Then she unsaddled and unfettered all the horses, and gave them slaps, sending them off towards Dál Riata.

Her work was done here. Except for a few scratches from the tree branch, and a bit of blood, she was none the worse for wear.

She called to her horse, suddenly glad these men had been in a foreign land too long, and unable to openly practice the art of war as they had been taught. They carried no spears, chose close quarters over archery thinking she would be easy quarry, and rather than come at her at once, they had given her not one, but two opportunities at single combat.

Maybe it was she who had overestimated them. They hadn't even attempted proper flanking, despite having the numbers. Perhaps they were from Rome. Maybe the gear was passed down, and they had only heard the stories.

Maybe, and she made herself laugh, they were the rejects of Rome.

And what were the MacKays, then? Their connection to Rome was strong, but was it blood? The Roman general in the portrait in the grand den seemed to argue so. Had both brothers sent these men to kill her, or only one of them?

She had laid the trap, but many hands, and perhaps even a greater number of ears, would have been privy to her plans. Neither MacKay had put that bow in her hand. A soldier had. A guard.

It was only yesterday she had threatened to have a guard's tongue cut out. When anger had run riot over rationality. When she had come seconds from murdering the lord of their castle. The controller of their purse.

What lengths might they go to to see that she never bring threat upon their house again?

Drusilla sighed. She had hoped her plan would prove the brothers guilty, or innocent, once and for all. Instead, she had proven what a mess of things she had made in Caledonia.

Still, someone had taken the bait.

She brought Ursa Major to a halt by a clear brook on the way back. And as he drank his fill and plucked about for wild carrots and tender grass, she washed away the blood.

Funny, the brook held no menace for her. Sunlight danced off the water's ever-changing surface, gliding over well-worn stones colorful with moss. Even as blood colored the water, staining it a temporary red, she found it relaxing, serene even.

Only deep water troubled her. Perhaps it had always been that way. Maybe there was never to be an explanation. It was simply her cross to bear.

She was coming back empty-handed, as befit her cover. She was terribly inept with a bow. Instead, a new plan began to formulate in her head. One which required flowers...

Chapter Twenty-Eight

A scratching sound woke Drusilla sometime in the dark hours. At first, she thought it a tree branch upon the window, but then Bridgette's soft breathing brought her back to full awareness.

No trees.

She was in Evelynn's old room, perched high above Loch Ness. She was instantly alert to the possibilities of danger.

Footsteps padded away from her door.

Drusilla was up, seizing her dagger, clad only in her nightdress. Bridgette slept on. A dim light, stars reflecting on loch, gave the room subtle illumination. It was enough. She stealthed past the comforting rugs, and across the cold flagstone, laying fingers upon the crossbar, securing the door.

It was then that she noticed the rectangle of paper upon the floor. The scratching sound...

She snatched it up. An envelope. Within, a weighty card of some sort.

Letter and dagger in one hand, she threw open the door. Behind her, she heard Bridgette moan softly, rolling over in the luxurious bed.

A small pool of radiance floated down the hall outside. A single candle. Drusilla, stepping into the hall, prepared for confrontation, dagger back in her right hand and ready.

A serving girl, one whose name she didn't yet know, set the candleholder down at the next door down the hall, and from her pinafore, produced another of the envelopes. She slid it under the door, producing the telltale scratching, and, not noticing Drusilla's silent vigil, retrieved her candle.

Down the hall, the ephemeral pool of light floated. To the next door, and another envelope, all seemingly without distinction.

Drusilla withdrew to her assigned chambers, barring once again the door. There, in the near dark, Bridgette was sitting, legs still beneath covers, rubbing at sleep eyes.

"I'm sorry I disturbed you," said Drusilla, moving to the bedside.

"My lady," Bridgette moved to get up.

"Stay," said Drusilla, placing an assuring arm upon the young woman's. "There's no need."

"What is it?" the wide-eyed Celt asked, staring at the envelope Drusilla still held, unexamined.

"Light a candle," said Drusilla. "It appears we have mail."

Chapter Twenty-Nine

A T THE GAMES LATER that day, Drusilla slipped in as unobtrusively as she could manage, finding a quiet spot to ruminate. Plucking a green apple from a nearby tree, and standing in its shade, she made her observations. The emphasis today seemed to be on contests of sword, both on foot, and mounted. It was to be chariot racing again in the late afternoon; the second round. Instead, and without any offered explanation, rounds two, three, and the finals, meant to each take place a day apart, had all been canceled.

Drusilla put together what she observed with the rumors already learnt within the keep's walls. The stray couple passed her. Conversations were overheard. A picture emerged. Later that week, there would be jousting and a baking contest. But the buzz and murmur about the grounds was all about the late-night visit each had been paid, and the invitation found slipped under the door. The entirety of festivities was slated to conclude with a grand ball on Midsummer's Eve, which the letter stated was in twenty-six days.

The trouble was, Midsummer's Eve was little more than a fortnight away. She did the calculation in her head again. Nineteen days, to be exact.

Bayden was a meticulous and calculating man. Drusilla did not think it mere oversight. Nor did she think he merely wished to extend the length of festivities an extra week. Something else was cooking in his brain. But what? What was so special about the twenty-sixth day from now that trumped accuracy and the holding of events on the longest day of the year?

Drusilla strolled the manicured green, far from the crowd, mulling the problem over once more. Absently, she bit into the apple in her hand. It was sour, and she wished she had a pinch of salt for it, the way she and her father used to eat them—

The Moon!

Two days ago and a night, Drusilla had been on a beach, hands and knees sucking in the soft, wet sand, staring up at the full Moon. Poor Helen had been sacrificed that night. And in twenty-six days, somebody else would be next.

The ball was not taking place on Midsummer's Eve, but on the night of the next full Moon, though the brothers were calling it just that: A Midsummer Night's Ball. It was to begin as the Sun touched the horizon; Roman dress was required. Drusilla found it more than a little worrisome that the MacKays exerted so much influence over the local population that they could openly embrace their love of Rome when Rome was so very hated north of the Hadrian wall.

The household staff had been made available to anyone not already possessed of attire appropriate to the evening. Tailors and seamstresses already bustled about, taking measure and filling orders for togas and sandals. In their desire to please their hosts, or perhaps simply of a herd mind, not one of them made protest, but indeed, seemed to embrace the idea with great enthusiasm.

Drusilla, however, had her own ideas about procuring proper dress. A plan she would implement later this day or upon the morrow. For now, she needed to play her part in a carefully woven plan, and for that, she needed to mingle.

It was another day of pleasant weather, she noted, finally returning from her far off mental machinations, looking out rather than in. The northeast lawn was spectacular in the sunshine. Morning fog had burned off. Occasional moody clouds wended by, but winds were minimal. It didn't look like to storm. Drusilla wondered what kind of reception she would get, taking another bite from her apple. After last night's fiasco, she didn't expect much from the well-bred.

As she walked, she found her mind straying to her Sicilian suitor. She spotted him and felt a little rush pass through her. Not the sort of distraction she needed. Before he could spot her, she cleverly maneuvered the grounds, even while feeling the strange longing of wishing he would find her. For what she had in mind today, his appearance would only hinder. She needed, instead, to find the brothers.

A hooded crow strutted along, head darting into the neatly scythed grass, foraging. She gave him the core of her apple, which he snatched up greedily and flew off.

Fife and lute wafted across the grounds, growing louder as she approached the main area of congregation. Several of the gentry, those who had scoffed her at the chariot races, seemed to regard her with forgiveness or even deference as she passed them. Not what she had expected. Perhaps a night of reflection had given them perspective.

No.

It was she who had underestimated them, too quick to judge, and on more than one occasion. And after last night, that she could walk amongst them, receiving, as she was, nods of acknowledgement and kind smiles...

Drusilla dabbed at her eyes with a handkerchief and tried to put her mind back on today's plan. Roland would be expecting a pigeon today, if not tomorrow. How long would he wait, when one didn't come, before enacting drastic measures?

There would be nothing concrete for him to base a decision upon. Pigeons could be intercepted in the wild. A small margin for such occurrences had to be allowed for. Would he give her a week? Two?

If Roland came, he would not come alone. That Drusilla could resolve matters before it came to war was the best-case scenario.

To do just that, and speed things along, she had selected to look particularly devastating for the occasion—a dangerous and calculated risk. She felt that mind games were in play, not wanting either brother to think he was wearing her down. And if it came down to one or the other, it was Bayden who was her target.

He had carved the Galatea-Evelynn. He possessed the key to the secret beach. It wasn't much to go on. But it was enough, she believed, to warrant her actions.

She wanted him off balance.

Keeping with that, she had put on Evelynn's prettiest dress. It was white linen, embroidered with little lavender flowers trimming the sleeves, hem, and neckline. Drusilla remembered the room had smelled of lavenders also, and so, searching the dressing table, found lavender water, bathed herself in it, and with Bridgette's help, put to use the lavender flowers she had gathered the night before in the forest. Together they weaved a wreath of them and made her a May crown. She wore her hair down, in long curls that nearly reached her waist, with a few strands pulled teasingly across the sides of her face.

"You'll drive him mad," Bridgette had said in the way of a warning.

"You said things were not right here in Foxborough," she answered, donning a pair of Evelynn's white slippers, finding them to be close enough to her size to be comfortable.

Bridgette's eyes filled with fear.

"'Through every generation of the human race there has been a constant war,'" Drusilla said, the words of Alexander the Great rising to meet her need this day. "'A war with fear. Those who have the courage to conquer it are made free and those who are conquered by it are made to suffer until they have the courage to defeat it, or death takes them.'"

She found a ring in Evelynn's jewelry box on the dressing table, with an amethyst of approximately lavender color. She put it on her left pinky, and looked to her lady-in-waiting—the fearful young woman who would divert her eyes, bend a knee, and suffer.

"I would, this day, take courage, in the prayer that fear be vanquished from this land."

Through stoic tears, Bridgette met her face and nodded.

Drusilla handed her a handkerchief, then looked upon her own visage in the gold-backed mirror—a piece that could have belonged to Alexander.

For a fleeting moment, she thought it was the ghost of Evelynn looking back. She hoped it was. Emperor. Ghost. Her lady-in-waiting... she welcomed whatever help she could get this day.

The eight-guard cadre was conspicuously missing. But other eyes followed her across the lawn as she began to mingle amongst the crowd. Sword fights stopped, archers put down their bows.

Was it her, or did they recognize whose clothes she wore? She preferred to think the former, but the latter was a strong contender for the truth.

She looked at the tally board for swordplay. Bayden was leader amongst them all, possessing an unbroken record. Ludo was in the top three. Her suitor, Raul's name, was missing—possibly the only man not playing at these games. She wondered at that.

Bayden spotted her. He was taking a break from swordplay, and when he noticed her apparel, he looked absolutely furious. He stalked across the lawn, joined by Ludo halfway, who looked quietly amused.

Drusilla waved, deciding to head them off in a particularly charming fashion. Play to the opposite of their expectations.

Bayden was literally seething when he reached her. She couldn't imagine what was going on behind those volcanic blue eyes, but it was murderous. He was burning holes in her when his gaze traveled to her wounds.

"Your hands," he said.

So focused upon her new ensemble, she had forgotten her scratched hands. The remaining telltale of her recent encounter.

"I ran into a little scrape in the woods yesterday," she said. "Nothing I couldn't handle."

"How was your hunt?" asked Ludo, eyes a wild blue, or was that green?

"My bow string snapped," she said. "It was quite a disappointment. I don't know a thing about bow repair. I collected flowers instead." She rolled both eyes straight up, indicating the crown.

"Flowers," said Bayden. He seemed to be reaching the end of his patience for her.

Good. Let him play his hand. In fact, time to twist the knife.

"Where are those special soldiers of yours? The ones that follow you everywhere. I haven't seen them all day."

Both his hands curled into fists, and it looked as though he might burst a vein at the side of his temple. A ripple traveled across his close-shaved jaw, eyes narrowing to murderous slits. Ludo looked a little more crazy than usual, too. She really had struck a nerve.

"They were killed," said Ludo, stepping in for his brother. It seemed Bayden was too angry to speak at all.

"Oh my god," said Drusilla, imitating concern. "How absolutely dreadful. How did it happen?"

Would they lie now? Make something up? She wondered just how they would handle this. It would tell a lot.

"We don't know," said Bayden, his voice edged with venom. "It would have taken a small army. They were well armed. Well trained. Some of the best men I've ever occasioned to know."

"I'm truly sorry, Lord Bayden." Drusilla held her hand out towards him in sympathy.

He pulled away, looking sullen, troubled.

"They were killed with their own weapons," added Ludo, a nervous smile twisting his lips. It was impossible to say what he was feeling.

"Perhaps we should cancel the festivities," said Drusilla. "This should be a time of mourning."

"They were soldiers," said Bayden, anger flashing back into his eyes, rippling throughout his voice. "Please, enjoy yourself. I shouldn't have burdened you."

Bayden looked at her dress again, Evelynn's dress, and there was hate in his eyes. He turned and left. If he was innocent, she had tortured him mercilessly. Unforgivably. Somewhere, deep down, she believed otherwise, though.

Ludo looked at Drusilla.

"She was about the same size as you, you know," he said, his eye twitching, crinkling into an almost-wink. He smiled his crooked smile and left her there to ponder the enigma that was the MacKay brothers.

Drusilla had no more interest in the games. She had done her damage. It was time to snoop.

Now if she could just escape the event without bumping into her—

Sicilian suitor.

"Hello," she said, extending her hand for the inevitable kiss...

IT HAD TAKEN A clever bit of maneuvering to escape the games and all their attendant social intrigues. Even so, a half-hour later, Drusilla found her opportunity and slipped away. Wandering the keep, she artfully avoided all possible contact, even to the point of hiding in doorframes, or behind pillars and furniture as people passed by. She had no more time for social niceties. She was on a hard fact-finding mission.

Encountering Bridgette, she pulled her aside.

"Where do the lords sleep? Bayden, Ludo?"

After collecting the information she needed, she made her way to Bayden's room in the high northeast tower. He had the whole floor. The door was locked. That didn't stop Drusilla.

Inside, it was like an armory. Weapons of every type littered the walls. There was every kind of armor and shield—a golden breastplate that would befit even an emperor...

More loot from Rome? A family heirloom? She recalled the portrait of the Roman general in the grand den.

She traced a finger along golden contours, Evelynn's lavender jewel, and the golden light playing off each other, and she felt as though a ghostly hand moved with hers.

Drusilla looked around, but she was alone.

She looked next at the weapons, spooked, and needing to keep the search moving. It would not do to tarry here.

Next to an array of spears, a Roman pilum caught her eye, and she was glad she had not faced one of those in the forest. It went far to strengthen her conviction. The men she had faced in the forest were pretenders. Skilled warriors, but far from a contubernium—the term came from some old text she had read, and it jogged her.

She should have pieced it together sooner. Ten legionnaires, eight of combat, and two of support. Ten contubernia made for a centuria. Ten tens. One hundred legionnaires.

Centurions.

These men traveled as eight. They were not what she had thought. They might imitate Rome here, but they were not Rome's doorstep.

And that they had tried to execute her for an idle threat was losing favor as a theory of choice. Someone had sent them. They were the messengers.

So who had sent the message...

Drusilla's eyes fell upon the bed. It, too, was fit for an emperor. Huge and stately, done in dark, masculine colors with a heavy top quilt and canopy. An abundance of pillows. She searched the mattress, searched trunks in the room, and the desk. He was well supplied for writing letters, a signet and sealing wax for making pacts and treaties. There were clothes and a washbasin, a small polished bronze mirror, razor strap and straight razor.

Nothing out of the ordinary, though, other than an obsessive interest in ordinance and armor. Most conspicuously, there were no tools for sculpting. Not sketches, nor clay, nor stone.

Maybe he wasn't the author of that incredible homage to Evelynn in ivory.

He did have a three hundred and sixty degree view of the keep, though. This was the roost of the entire structure. And from the west windows, small arched cutouts in the stone just wide enough...

She had to know.

But to know, she would have to lean out.

Chapter Thirty

There was nothing particularly daunting about heights, given that you didn't act foolishly or take undue chances. But the window did not overlook just the cliff. Directly below was the loch.

Drusilla wedged herself into the casement, and saw that it was wide enough for a man, even Bayden, to do the same. Unlike Bayden, however, it was wide enough for Drusilla to fall out of, should she lean too far.

She hooked fingertips on the wall and extended her arm until she could get her head past the thick stone blocks. The view was dizzying, but still, she need lean further if she were to look straight down.

And it was at the end of her arm's reach, heart pounding at the possibility that her fingers might falter, that she got her view, and her reward. If he were curious—and being wider of chest than she, having no fear of falling out—Bayden had a perfect view, straight down, to the hidden beach.

The night of the screams—she had to wonder why he hadn't just looked out the window, maybe he had—he had certainly known just where to find her. She felt the press of time. To be caught here was unthinkable. She would think more about the events of that night later.

Drusilla made a quick search for false panels, loose stones, hidden doors. There was nothing. Time to see how Ludo lived.

She found his quarters one floor down, as Bridgette had described. She had passed it on the way up, wanting to see Bayden's place first. In case it was the only one she got to, she felt it was the more important.

Ludo's room had two locks on the door. She had never seen that before. It cried paranoia. She would have to be on her guard. With a mentality like that, traps and snares were not out of the question.

Quietly, she passed into the room, and was immediately disappointed. The room was quite spartan, smaller than Bayden's in every dimension. From the looks of it, he was sleeping on a cot. A few blankets were at one end, neatly folded. He also had appointments for shaving, and washing up. In one corner, a small wardrobe with a limited selection of clothes.

Ludo was a boring man. She would never have guessed it.

She checked his view, the window casements almost identical in construction, but differing in orientation; his view of the secret beach was partially obscured—the pillar of black, occluded.

It only became visible by leaning almost half her body weight through the narrow opening and into empty space. That made it questionable whether Ludo had ever seen the stone from his window at all. It was possible, but had he, like her, risked the fatal plummet to see that little bit he might not know to even look for?

Drusilla pulled her head in, and put hands to knees, letting her head stop swimming, letting visions of the loch below fade from her mind, before moving on. She'd seen what she had come to see, and especially for Ludo's quarters, she'd collected more maybes and nothing concrete.

At this point, she had a whole basket of maybes. It almost didn't seem worth it, and she thought of retreat—before the inevitability of getting caught closed in around her—but decided it was her unease of the loch nudging her to leave when she had yet to be as thorough as she had been with Bayden's quarters

Dismissing her urge to be done, she checked for secret doors, loose stones, the usual—you just never knew—and was wildly rewarded.

At the back of the wardrobe was a sliding panel. It was locked, the mechanism behind a sliding dovetail. It led to a small hall. She had to push aside some of the clothes to let more light in, revealing the passage to only be four feet. It ended at an iron door that looked very substantial, but picked easily enough.

Beyond the door it was, of course, quite dark. Drusilla went and got a torch from the wall of Ludo's outer room, and already knowing where he kept his flint and striker, lit it. Careful not to burn the clothes, she returned to examine the room.

Oh, Ludo's a sick boy, she thought, unable to fully control her revulsion. There were chains bolted to the walls, manacles and shackles attached. Leather restraints. A locking iron mask, and, dear god, an iron casket lined with spikes. Every manner of hook, knife, scalpel, whip, chain, needle, and implement of torture was here.

There were a few slits for air, high, where wall met ceiling, nearly parchment thin. She doubted much sound would escape them.

Was this just a fantasy for him, or had it been recently used? Did he even know about it? It hadn't been exactly easy to find, and they were not the original owners of Foxborough Keep. She checked for signs that would answer her questions.

Everything was well oiled. It could have been here weeks, or centuries. Like his room, it was all neatly kept, though much more cluttered in here. She had to conclude that it remained an unknown.

Drusilla shuddered. The place was giving her the creeps. It certainly wouldn't do to get caught in here. Suddenly, she needed to get out.

She closed everything, aware of her own heart pounding in her throat. She drew slow, deliberate breaths, gathering her wits, thinking out her retreat. Unfortunately, she had no way of returning the locks to their secure position. That would have to be a puzzle for the brothers to work out. If they were like the majority of people, they would just use their key, assuming it was still locked, and never notice the difference.

Coming down the stairs, Drusilla encountered Ludo.

"I was just looking for you," he said.

Her mind flashed back to the torture chamber. Slow breaths.

"Me?"

"I was told you wandered off from the festivities. I admit they're a bit dull."

"After Bayden's news concerning the guards, I just wasn't in the mood," she said, a forced calm defining her voice.

"What brought you to the tower?" he asked.

She had hoped he wouldn't.

Drusilla smiled to buy time. A woman could always buy time with a smile. Smile slow, think fast.

"I wanted to see the loch from the highest point possible," she said, deciding on a plausible story. "Unfortunately, all the doors were locked."

"Were they? Let's go check."

CHAPTER THIRTY-ONE

T HERE WAS NO UNDOING this. Ludo would test the doors and know she had lied.

Drusilla's heart skipped a beat. She bit her tongue. Anything she said now could bury her. Or land her in irons behind muffled stone walls. The torture implements she had just viewed—the needles—transposed themselves, unbidden, upon her vision. And those tiny ventilation slits in the near dark...

She felt ill.

Ludo took her hand and led her back up, turning the knob to his room. The door swung in.

Drusilla decided then and there, if he tried to force her in, she would kill him on the spot.

"Interesting," he said, dragging her up to the next floor. "This would be the highest point in the keep. Let's just see."

"Open. What a surprise." He pushed her into Bayden's room, following after her. "You wanted to see the view. Here it is."

Drusilla hesitated, staying away from the windows, and a good distance from Ludo—her dagger ever foremost in her thoughts—but still, she tried to buy time, to search out the more subtle solution. The outcome of any battle was never certain.

"Oh, that's right. You're afraid of heights. You see, my brother tells me everything."

Her eyes darted involuntarily to the window overlooking the secret beach. A window she had already tested for fit, and knew she could be passed through it.

Was her case hopeless? Drusilla's mind raced, knowing there was a plausible explanation for nearly any situation. One just had to be clever. Living under lock and key in a convent for years had taught her that.

"Please," she said, stalling for time. "Don't tell Bayden about this."

"Hmmm," he said, that crooked smile forming over his face. She had still to know if he was an idiot or a genius. She suspected a little of both. "All right. You tell me your secret. You tell me how you go anywhere you want to around here. You tell me why you're really up here, and I'll keep your secret."

Oh, thank god. Drusilla hoped she didn't look too relieved. He really didn't know. It was possible he didn't know about the torture chamber either. It was possible he was just, well, a bit off.

Drusilla had a card to play. It was a serious trade-off, but she thought it would work. Besides, she had no time to come up with anything better.

"I'm a thief," she said.

Ludo's crooked grin cracked wide. A look of open amusement.

"I'm not really an aristocrat. I'm the daughter of Frankish peasants."

"Drusilla the Frank. Not quite so charming, is it?"

She wasn't sure if she had him yet. Not quite sure if he believed her. She had to crank it up a notch, use his ego—the Achilles tendon of all men, if employed with proper finesse.

"I came here to steal from you, but then I fell in love with you. Please don't tell your brother. He frightens me so."

He seemed pleased with this, but pushed her further.

"Then why come up here? I mean, if you've had a change of heart?" His words were logical, thought out, but he was already looking at her in a different way. Behind those crazy eyes, a new passion was smoldering, ready to ignite.

What had she gotten herself into?

Even now, though, she felt better about the situation than before. And she still hadn't thought of any better excuse she could have made. Always stick as close to the truth as possible when lying. Wasn't that the adage? Love was a stretch, but was it really that much different than fear and loathing?

Had she dodged the hunter's arrow only to put her foot in the snare?

"I was snooping," she said. "Old habits are hard to break. I had to know how you felt about me. I didn't know which room was yours, so I searched them both."

"I like your room better."

"I had no idea..." said Ludo.

This was working out better than expected.

"... you were so devious."

Or not.

"Why did you dress like Evelynn?"

She remembered that first meeting with the MacKays, they each kissing a different hand. She was playing with fire, she knew, but it was all or nothing at this point. A complete gamble, based on what little she thought she knew of Ludo's mind.

"To alienate your brother," she said. "He has too much affection for me. I wanted to hurt him."

Ludo chuckled.

"You really are too much."

Was that good or bad? He seemed amused. Ludo could be so inscrutable.

"Can you really pick locks, or did you steal a key? We've both been wondering."

"Must I reveal all my secrets to you, dear Ludo? A woman should have some mystery."

He paused, thinking. The silence was excruciating.

"You're right," he said at last.

Another silent sigh for Drusilla.

She felt like a Catholic school girl again, lying to the Mother Superior. She had never imagined that aspect of her education would constitute such a boon to her particular tradecraft.

"And the swimming?"

"Oh, I just love to swim," she said. Of all the lies, this was the most outrageous, and seemingly, the most easily accepted by him.

"Come," he said, taking her hand, gently this time.

Ludo led Drusilla downstairs to the grand den.

Glass eyes followed her, firelight dancing in their glazed, dead stares. Ludo crossed to a decanter of cut glass and poured amber liquid into two matching goblets. More of her glass. Now she thought of it, the hauntingly real, convex eyes of these hunting trophies were likely glass from Helven as well. She had supplied the market with bags of them. And as the glass trade went, she was its only supplier, as far as she knew, here in Britain.

That they had made it as far as Caledonia filled her with a sense of pride.

"A toast," he said, handing her a goblet and bringing her attention back to the snare. "To new-found love."

She took a sip, staring into his eyes. Honey mead, and of a fine quality. She moved to a small table between two chairs, setting her drink down. Desperately, she scanned the room, hoping for anything to slow the ardent behavior of Ludo, if only by degrees.

There, above the mantel, was the enigmatic hunting horn. She quickly moved her eyes on from there. That was another mystery she did not want him to know she'd taken an interest in.

Then there were the scrolls. Such a wonderful assortment of scrolls. She doubted much refuge could be found in the written word this afternoon, however. This game between them had surpassed the intellectual stage. She needed something more visceral. They were alone without much chance of interruption, and she, having already falsely declared her love, stood upon dangerously shifting sands.

But there was a familiar sight, she thought, as her search continued.

"Is that chess?"

He set his drink down near hers, eying her crookedly.

"You're not saying you actually know how to play?"

"Badly, but yes. Would you mind, terribly?"

Ludo brought the board and pieces over. "You actually know how to play?" he asked again. "This is a rare delight."

She hadn't needed to let him win at chess. He was remarkably good. A nice challenge. In fact, of five games, she had only won one, and that by a castling maneuver which achieved a revealed checkmate. He had shown admiration for her move, and then soundly beat her two more times before they both moved on to backgammon.

She passed several hours with him, playing various games and acting the part of a coy lover. It was time to move things along, however. Her stalling tactics would become transparent sooner than later, and were he to, at any point, doubt her sincerity, she would be plunged into extreme danger.

"Dear Ludo," said Drusilla, sipping at the same drink she'd managed to nurse along.

"Yes, my love," he said, taking her free hand in his. Looking at her with those crazy, green? eyes, and taking another draw of his own third drink.

"I think we should play our love coolly until the ball, and then, if you are still amenable, announce it to the world."

She gauged his reaction carefully, hiding her interest behind another sip. Was that elation she saw?

"Why not announce it now?" he asked, drawing her a little closer. "The way I feel for you is not going to change in a span of weeks."

"I am still worried about your brother. Let me create a greater distance with him. It would not do to alienate and anger a future in-law."

With that, Ludo coughed up a bit of his drink, turning his head slightly, and wiping his mouth with the back of his hand. When he turned back to her, he was transformed.

"This is most good news," he said.

She realized she'd said the magic words.

"I thought, in your wisdom, you would see it that way," she said. Then added, squeezing his hand a little, "Let us enjoy our courtship, and not rush things. We'll not get a chance to relive these three weeks."

Ludo drew her to his chest and kissed her slowly upon the mouth.

The kiss was tender, slowly moving to the passionate. Drusilla was caught up in the moment, enjoying it, when that torture chamber flashed back in her mind. She shuddered involuntarily, hoping, after the fact, he would think it purely the effect of his passion on her.

She smiled at him, leaving her unfinished drink upon the table, leaving the room. Reaching the door, she looked back at him. He was still watching her.

"Sleep well," she said. "I shall look forward, most enthusiastically, to our next encounter."

Ludo's grin distorted half his face. "Your kiss leaves me speechless…" and he did struggle to find the words. But when he did, they were astounding. "I am consumed by your beauty, and your mind, more so than any woman I have ever known."

Drusilla felt a bit faint. She would have to watch herself with this man. He was dangerously charming in his offhand way. And if he was innocent of all her suspicions…

She gave him her best curtsy and ran away.

DRUSILLA RETURNED TO HER—to Evelynn's room. She was becoming entirely too comfortable here. The late afternoon Sun poured through the wall of glass doors. It was time to strategize. She threw herself upon the sun-warmed bed, propping herself on pillows to think.

Neither brother was clearly guilty, though both were prime suspects. Several local women, all maidens, and Camille, whose misfortune it was to experience mechanical troubles—

Camille, not yet married…

Drusilla took a moment. It was too hard. And what of Camille's coachman, for surely she had one. And poor Atreus. Had he been murdered, too?

The witnesses, for knowing too much. And Atreus for digging into the truth. Young maids, for that is what they all were, not girls, nor matrons, but those in the flower of their youth, deliberately sacrificed to—she forced herself to think it—a creature in the loch.

The sensation of its oily scales sliding along her bare skin came back to her. She pulled the pillows a little tighter to her body, wiping the back of her mouth with her hand in disgust.

Then there was the horn she'd heard so clearly that night. Was it the same one from the mantelpiece, the "wyvern" horn? And weren't wyverns supposed to be mythical? Its sound was unique. Had it been used to summon the creature, or to summon the guards to alert?

And then there was the secret beach. No one but the huntsman seemed to dare venture near the falls opposite it. So there were few to look across the way and spot activity upon it. It was cut off from any casual stroll along the shore. Maybe from a boat, but if Shamus was anyone to judge by, none were out on those waters after dark.

Bayden had a key to the secret beach. Did the guards, or her fiancé? Oh, what trouble she'd caused herself...

Might she be overlooking a suspect as yet unnamed so?

She knew there was a killer, at least one, who had access to the beach, by land or by sea, she couldn't be sure. And she knew the creature, possibly by no fault of its own, now had a taste for human flesh, and must be destroyed. Every moment, another young woman could be in danger, but Drusilla could not act indiscriminately. When she meted out justice—and she would—it must be to the correct party. All her intrigues and searching so far had led to no clear perpetrator. But there was a way to find out...

Drusilla napped until dusk. She would need all her strength come nightfall.

Chapter Thirty-Two

D RUSILLA WOKE TO BRIDGETTE trying to cover her with a blanket. It was nearly dark.

"Evening," said Drusilla.

"Good evening, my lady. Can I be getting you ready for bed?"

"No, dear friend. I'm going out."

Bridgette's eyes went wide. "At this hour?"

"Fetch my cloak, and my red and black dress." This night would be rugged, and she wished for pants. But, as befit her cover, she had brought none.

"Of course, my lady."

Drusilla liked having Bridgette around. Perhaps Bayden had been correct about needing another woman's company. She relaxed into her role, and began mulling over the case as the young woman ran a brush through Drusilla's hair, and then something occurred to her.

"How old was Evelynn?"

Bridgette ceased braiding—frozen in place. Even now, and even between them, the subject remained taboo.

"It's important."

Bridgette resumed the work, making Drusilla's hair into a high crown of night. Finally, she drew a breath of courage, and told what she knew. "About your age, I would guess. Five or six years my senior. A stunning woman. If not high-born, she carried herself so."

Helen was eighteen, but still lived alone.

Lilly, eighteen, still a maid, but off to marry soon.

Maidens.

And how old are you? she wanted to ask Bridgette.

She left the words unvoiced. By her guess, Bridgette would be the youngest of the bunch. But she didn't think that mattered. Whoever was doing this was picking maidens. And Bridgette was old enough for that.

But what of the first?

"And Evelynn? Was she a widow? If she was my age…" Drusilla was well aware of just how near the end of marriageable age she was. Old maid, and other, more cruel terms came to mind. "The others, they weren't…?"

"I think I know what you mean," said Bridgette. "No. She had never been married. And the others, though they may have had sweethearts from afar, were not wild."

Bridgette resumed her activity, getting Drusilla ready for the night's "prowling" as she was wont to phrase it.

Dressed, hair braided and coiled close to her skull, dagger hanging from its sturdy leather belt, Drusilla was ready. It was time to make things happen. She turned to Bridgette, who handed her the dark riding cloak.

"I want you to stay here. Bar the doors. Young women have been going missing. I intend to find out why."

"But the danger, surely—" said Bridgette.

"I am the one who is dangerous," said Drusilla, donning the cloak, and placing two firm hands upon Bridgette's shoulders.

"Do you know your Arthurian History?"

"Yes, my lady."

"Then you know what was most important to Arthur? More than anything."

"The sword, Excalibur," said Bridgette.

"No."

"The lady, Gwenevere. Surely, she was most important," said Bridgette, romance sparkling in her eyes.

Again, Drusilla shook her head, and said no.

"His knights?" said Bridgette, losing confidence quickly.

"An idea," said Drusilla. "An ideal."

Bridgette looked deeply into Drusilla's face with those pretty blue eyes, imploring for more.

"Might for right," said Drusilla.

Bridgette looked awed, nodding her head slowly.

"I am here to make things right. Bar the door. Stay inside till I return. Is it true you have no family here, no lover?"

Drusilla looked at Bridgette's bracelet, causing the young woman to look at it too. There was a melancholy in her eyes, but she answered steadfastly, "It's true, my lady. I only have you."

"Then if I'm not back by sunrise, go to my servants, Percival, and Linus. Give them this message. The three of you are to flee this place, back to The House of Roland in London Town, never to return. Do you understand?"

"Yes, my lady. But surely, you will return." Bridgette sounded more than a bit scared now.

"In all likelihood, yes," she smiled. "But do as I say. Lord Bayden has released you from his service into mine. I have it on his own word."

Bridgette's eyes went wide, her jaw gaping. She looked pleased with the news to the point of shock, then suddenly threw her arms about Drusilla, embracing her. Drusilla could feel the young woman sobbing lightly upon her shoulder.

"Please don't go tonight," Bridgette said at last, pressing ever closer, seeking comfort. "Let's just all leave. Right now. I'll pack everything. You won't have to do a thing but come along—"

"There are things I must do," said Drusilla, gently putting Bridgette at arm's length. "Now bar the door behind me. Don't let anyone in. I'll knock twice quick, once at a pause, and twice quick again seeking entrance. If anyone else tries enter, you hide in the wardrobe. And come morning, if I'm not here, if you can't find Percival and Linus, you leave anyway."

"Yes, my lady."

"How many knocks?"

"Two quick, one surrounded by pause, two quick."

"Good."

Drusilla patted the young woman on the shoulder and left.

DRUSILLA WENT TO THE grand den next, "borrowing" the wyvern horn from the wall. It was lighter than it looked, and very solid. Seeing it up close, she was certain it was both natural, and belonging to no beast she had ever seen or heard described. Another mystery for another time. She put the cord around her neck, and concealed the rest of it, the best she could, beneath her cloak.

Next, she went to the stable yard. A young boy on watch woke the stable master. He seemed to be taking security much more seriously since her previous night visit. Good.

"May I help you, my lady?" said the stable master.

"I'm sorry to have woken you," she said. "Can you have my horse, Perseus, he's the one on the end," she pointed, "saddled and ready right away? I need to visit my carriage and will be back momentarily."

"Of course, my lady, right away."

"I trust your utmost discretion?"

"Of course, my lady. I'll see to it the boy knows as well."

"Give him this for his silence," she said, flipping him a denarius. "And see that I pass the rear gate on your authority, unidentified."

His jaw tightened, eyes darting to the guard tower which dominated the northwest sky. Despite any trepidation he might be feeling, he gave a solemn nod, hand closing over the silver coin. "Yes, my lady, it shall all be done according to your will."

DRUSILLA FOUND HER CARRIAGE in seemingly good order, but when she lifted the floor panel to retrieve her sixty-pound bow, and good hunting arrows, she found only an empty space. Anger shot through her stomach, forming a knot where only determination had been before.

Somebody had been over this carriage with a fine-tooth comb. Somebody paranoid, threatened enough by her presence to take such precautions. And, whoever it was, must now suspect she could well use a bow.

She sat on the running board of the carriage with a sigh. Anger would not restore her bow to her. It was gone. She closed her eyes a moment, letting quiet flood back into her center.

The night air was cool. Drusilla pulled her cloak tighter about her. She did not relish her task this night without her good bow. Considered abandoning her idea and returning to the warmth and comfort of her chambers for some extra rest and a rework of strategy. She couldn't do that, though. The idea was sound. She had the sword and shield in the forest. It was a start, but not enough. They would serve as a defensive backup. What she really needed, though, was heavy artillery.

The garrison at Foxborough Keep was too well guarded. She had already cased it in her tour, and multiple subsequent skulkings, about the grounds. She contemplated the risk of creeping past Ludo's door, picking Bayden's lock in the hope he slept, and stealing in to pluck a bow. It seemed much too risky. Just thinking about it raised dozens of unpleasant possibilities.

She looked around the yard, sealing her carriage up, and returning to the horses. There were pitchforks... too unwieldy. Hay hooks? Much too close quartered for what she had in mind. Or there was...

Shamus. He was a paranoid chap. Surely he kept something...

"It's me, Dru, open up."

Drusilla banged on the door again.

"G'away," he grumbled from the other side. "It's dark."

"It's quite urgent I see you—now!"

There was an aggravating pause, then the scraping of a bar being lifted from the door.

"I hate having friends," Shamus said, stepping to one side.

Drusilla entered, looked around the little one-room cottage letting her eyes adjust, then spotted it.

"That," she pointed.

"What, my salmon gaff?" She was surprised the word was the same in Gallo and English.

Drusilla nodded, paused. "Do you have a bow, or a spear?"

"Got no use for such things. I think maybe that dip in the drink did you more harm than good. Must still have loch water in your brain."

"Shamus," Dru said, "I don't have time for pleasantries. Can I borrow your—gaff?"

"Whada'ya need it for?"

"Hunting. Give it here. I'll bring it back in one piece or pay you double its worth."

That got his attention.

"Well, go on then, take it," he said, handing the eight-foot, wickedly barbed pole over. The brass tip shone in the faint starlight. It looked to have a razor's edge.

"Thank you, Shamus. Go back to bed. Tell no one of my visit."

"Who would I tell?" he grumbled. "Crazy woman."

Chapter Thirty-Three

D RUSILLA RODE AT A gallop, once she was clear of the keep walls, and into the forest, to the place where she had hidden the sword and shield. Once again, she was become night, her eyes adjusting to the din of starlight. There, in the shadows and brush, the sword and shield were still there.

Good.

She retrieved them, securing each in turn to the saddle, and rode further down the way until she found a clear bit of meadowland. The slope to the loch was gentler here, and there was no obstruction of trees. Though should she need its cover, the forest was near enough at hand.

Gone was Foxborough. Neither village nor keep would accost her actions here. She was on her own.

Drusilla dismounted, leaving Perseus a good hundred and fifty feet to the land side. She walked to the water's edge. That familiar, old feeling of dread returning to her in spades as she approached the water. She pushed it away. She was done with fears. She had a job to do.

The ground was soft here. A patchy rain had laced the night in dampness and drizzle, cold highland air, invigorating, carrying scents of evergreen and the freshly turned loam. Drusilla lifted the hunting horn to her lips and blasted out a call. It was the same low, mournful tone as the other night when Helen had been sacrificed. For she was sure now that's what had been done.

She waited a moment, watching, paying particular attention to the falls. The call echoed back from the far cliff. The placid water carried the sound well. Drusilla lifted the horn again, then noticed something dark and sinuous winding through the water, from the falls, creating little

S-shaped disturbances in the surface.

Her heart began to race.

She looked back to Perseus, his silhouette on the hill top distorted by the salmon gaff projecting upwards from the sheath normally used for lances. Another untested weapon. Roland had never told her how many times sound rules of combat would have to be bent or broken for lack of time.

Looking back to the loch, she could no longer see the serpentine disturbances. Halfway out, there were large ripples where the creature must have submerged. She raised the horn to her lips, then hesitated. Had it turned back? Or had it gone under to make for ambush?

The rain was coming harder now, making itself known upon the surface of the loch. Obscuring the evidence of the creature's passage. The air took on a chill aspect.

She had waited too long.

Drusilla spun back towards Perseus, running for all she was worth. As she mounted the hill, she heard a great splash at the water's edge. Panic told her to look back, but instead, she whistled for Perseus.

The horse started, looking spooked. There was a moment of uncustomary hesitation in his gait, so contrary to his training.

Behind her, Drusilla could hear the flat slapping of something large upon the land, and the hissing exhale of breath. She ran as hard as she could, mud sucking at her boot heels, pulling on reserves she didn't know she had.

The slapping turned to low, rapid thundering. The creature was charging. She could feel its hot, rank breath on her neck and scalp. She drew her dagger, ready to turn.

The twenty-two-inch tooth flashed back to her memory. The dagger in her hand was ten inches. She felt helpless, alone—foolish, knowing she called her own executioner...

And she was going to die.

Chapter Thirty-Four

Drusilla pressed through the mud, slogging upwards, fighting for higher ground. Ground that was buckling under her feet to the pounding onslaught of the creature at her heels.

Again, foul heat drilled down on her neck, the rattle of exhalation testament to something monstrous in scale. Again, she fought the urge to look upon it, knowing any delay would be her last—

And then Perseus leapt forward, whinnying as he galloped down the hill towards her.

Oh, thank God!

He snorted as he turned, reaching her, almost...

Drusilla leapt forward, grabbing the saddle. Hot breath roasted her back as she seized the saddle horn, and planted a boot in one stirrup, hanging on for dear life.

Perseus didn't need to be told what to do, already bolting away at an angle, Drusilla felt the creature's jaws snap shut, inches from her. Swinging into the saddle backwards, she slammed the dagger back to its sheath, drawing the sword.

Looking up, she was confronted with a terror that burned permanent holes through her psyche.

A sinuous, slick neck, thick as a hundred-year maple, rose, narrowing only slightly, past flapping gills to connect with a dark, horse-like head monstrous in proportion. Twenty-six inch teeth lined its perpetually gaping maw, and its huge, oval eyes stared at her with malice and clear, deep intelligence.

The beast was looking her right in the eye.

Drusilla clucked to Perseus to keep going. Pulling the shield onto her arm.

The creature lowered its head as it flapped along the meadow with both serpentine undulations, and four mighty, diamond-shaped flippers. The head shot forward on its supple neck, jaw snapping. Drusilla ducked back, shielding herself as she was bathed in more rank, hot breath, and struck out with the sword as the creature came to the end of its reach, barely thumping her shield.

The sword bounced off its tough hide, maybe shaving away a few surface scales.

Maybe.

She doubted the creature took much notice of her effort at all. She wondered if her arrows would have fared any better. When the creature blinked, she noticed it had two sets of eyelids. She'd heard of that in crocodiles before. The second membrane, a clear tissue, thicker than her sideways hand, plus the even thicker outer lid, dark and bumped with pebble-like calluses, might even protect it from a direct strike.

The shield bore the brunt of the assault, minor as it was compared to what this beast must be capable of. Even so, it displayed a nice dent. Her arm ached dully, pulsing beneath sleeve and shield. It, too, would bear the mark of punishment.

The creature immediately went in for another lunge, Perseus pulling ahead just enough to clear the attack. Drusilla could feel the terror rippling through her stallion's body.

She had to gain an advantage, and quick. Maybe if she could put some trees in the way, equip her gaff?

She clucked, and Perseus pulled to the left, uphill. She figured that was her immediate advantage. A beast that size couldn't climb hills as fast as a lightly encumbered horse. As they turned away from it, she noticed the full scope of the creature, being slightly sideways to her now. It was maybe sixty feet nose to tail, a queer hybrid of a thing. The tail, in particular, had the same type of membranous, undulating fin she had seen in the eels at Elvers Pool, and of course, with its mighty flippers and dark, mottled coloration, it was reminiscent of a seal or sea cow. But the face, long, narrow, predatorial, with rows of razor sharp fangs each the length of a short sword...

Drusilla flipped around in the saddle, sitting frontwards now. Quietly, she clucked out commands to Perseus, who still trembled with fright.

"I'm here, boy," she whispered in his ear, calming him.

They galloped across the road, her stallion kicking up clumps of rain wet sod and hard packed mud, and down into the lightly forested area on the other side. Into the trees, careful to choose her passage so that the creature could follow, but with more difficulty.

Spotting an ancient oak tree standing by itself, Drusilla reined Perseus around, standing just behind and to the side of the tree. It was eight or more feet across the base, and near a hundred feet tall.

Drusilla saw the creature bounding—slithering across the meadow.

Weren't dragons supposed to be mythical?

It was circumventing the larger trees she had put in its path, crashing through the branches to the side, and smashing right over the smaller saplings. Drusilla didn't even want to contemplate how many tons it weighed.

She tossed her sword and shield aside. They were useless, and readied the salmon gaff.

The creature was coming down the slope now, less than a hundred feet away.

"Steady," she whispered to Perseus, who was trembling but standing firm.

The creature bellowed, something between a lion's roar and a hiss, lunging its head forward.

Drusilla clucked, and Perseus side stepped, strafing right behind the oak. The creature compensated, last minute, following them, and ducked to avoid smashing out its mouthful of glistening white sabers. The forehead of the monster smashed into the mighty oak tree, shuddering the very ground, and nearly throwing Drusilla from her horse.

The tree cracked.

Oh my god, thought Drusilla, looking at the seam rip wide down the center of the massive tree. Earth beneath rider and mount surged upward, staggering the two as ancient roots lost their foothold.

The sound was terrible.

Perseus whinnied, struggling to keep his feet. The creature spun its weight, shaking its head. It acted a little stunned. It certainly wasn't hurt badly.

Trusting her mount, Drusilla watched, hoping in that fraction of time she had bought, to learn something, anything she might exploit to her advantage. It was then that she thought she spotted a large pulsing vein in its neck, maybe the width of her thigh.

No time for deliberation. She rode out, clucking a command to her stalwart stallion, hurling the gaff through the air.

It stuck, sinking into the brown-black, glistening flesh. She clucked Perseus back a few steps and circled, riding clear.

The beast hissed, smashing the lower branches of the tree as it spun first on her, then seeing her retreat, upon its own wound. Displaying incredible flexibility, the beast snatched the gaff in its teeth, yanking it out and tossing it aside.

A drizzle of blood oozed from the wound, pulsing to its heartbeat in little spurts.

Drusilla wanted to retrieve the gaff, but it lay tossed on the other side of the beast. Instead, she retrieved her sword and shield while the creature licked its wound with an enormous purple tongue.

Drusilla assessed her options. She had irritated the creature, maybe even shown it that people could fight back. If she had her bow, and an unlimited number of arrows, time, luck, and the creature didn't retreat, maybe...

Drusilla was no coward, but the beast had just cracked a hundred-foot oak tree in half, partially uprooting it. And now it was looking at her again, angrily, its wound salved.

It was time to go.

She rode back around in a circle, the creature lunging towards her position just as she abandoned it, came around the other side of the tree, and straight towards the gaff. The beast was intelligent. It would remember the gaff.

She tossed sword and shield again, they were dead weight, and picked up speed. Lifting her knee up and over the saddle horn, hanging on by nothing but that and her other stirruped foot. The saddle horn was wet and slick. A skirt was not the proper dress for this sort of stunt. Leaning out and down, straining to keep her grip, Drusilla snatched the gaff up as ground rushed by.

Her leg slipped more. She fought against the forces which threatened to spill all but her entangled foot to the ground. Whatever else happened today, she didn't care to be dragged by a frightened horse. With monumental effort, she slid back into her saddle, pulling her body upright, fingers clutched tightly about the gaff.

This would have been easier with pants.

Behind her, the very earth quaked and thundered. Tree branches and underbrush snapped, giving way to the beast.

Glancing back, Drusilla saw the creature, close at hand now, having turned itself around in discovery of her ruse.

"You want some of this!" she cried out, spinning around in her saddle to face backwards again as Perseus headed northwest towards the road in the direction of the keep. Drusilla shook the salmon gaff at the oversized eel, taunting the beast.

"C'mon!" she cried, looking it in the eye. Fifty feet separated her and the rain-slick beast. Water drizzled into her own eyes, weighted her hair and cloak. She shook it away. They were on the road again, the creature in full pursuit. It seemed to be tiring slightly. Perhaps it wasn't happy to be so far inland.

If she could just get it to chase her to the walls, perhaps the archers would perforate it before it could knock them down?

But the creature slowed again, bellowing, and then stopped.

Drusilla spun in the saddle. Ahead, the keep stood, flames atop the high towers, torchlight pouring from several of the windows. Something was astir.

Behind her, she heard a terrible crash.

She turned to see the creature smashing through a stand of saplings and undergrowth, back towards the loch. She thought of chasing it. If she could just get a lucky shot in. Or a good thousand—

Who was she kidding?

She slowed Perseus to a gait.

"We won, boy," she whispered in his ear, giving him a good pat on the neck.

She thought a little more about the battle. The creature had slowed just about the time the keep had come into view. Maybe that's what had changed its temperament.

"Don't like people?" she mused. "Or… maybe you don't like fire."

The rain pelted down steadily now, chilling the air further. She pulled her cloak about her. She still had to return the gaff before returning to the keep. It was just as well. She needed the time to recover her wits. What she had just seen stretched belief.

And at the same time was wholly undeniable.

SHAMUS SEEMED RELIEVED TO have his prized hook back. He didn't even ask her what she'd done with it, or if she'd been successful. He wiped it clean with a cloth, not even questioning the blood or tongue-slime. Though mostly washed clean by rain, there was still the odd bit.

Rain pelted the outside of his small cabin. Drusilla's mind was still on a bender, trying to absorb what she'd seen.

Dragons were real. At least great worms were. The shock of it was immense, but there was no more time for processing it. She felt the urgency of knowing what had woken the keep return in full.

"Thank you, Shamus," she said, rising from the small stool where she'd taken a moment's rest.

He grumbled something unintelligible.

She thought, just maybe, he was beginning to enjoy having a friend. "Good night."

"Night," he muttered as she showed herself out.

She approached Perseus, standing loyally in the cold night rain. "C'mon, let's go see what the disturbance is."

Chapter Thirty-Five

D RUSILLA ENTERED BY THE back gate, directly into the livery again. The stable master had waited up, and the guards were conspicuously missing. He had done his job, probably at great peril.

"You two look well exercised," he said.

"A little night air is always invigorating."

The stable master squinted skyward into the rain, blinking against the downpour. "You'd best go straight to the house. I'll tend to your horse." He took Perseus' reins as Drusilla dismounted. "There's been a disturbance. Your room was broken into."

Bridgette!

Drusilla didn't wait for an explanation. She broke into a dead run, boots kicking up splashes of water collected in the uneven hard pack, heading for the house. The hunting horn made its presence known, thumping at her side as she went. She couldn't be seen with it.

Finding the first servant she saw upon entering the house, she paused, pulling it off her neck and handing it to him.

"This goes above the mantel. Do you know the place?"

The servant nodded.

She slipped him a silver coin. He looked at her quizzically.

"For your silence," she said.

He nodded vigorously and took off at a sprint down the hall.

Drusilla ran to her room, finding a guard posted there, along with a maid who was straightening up. The brothers were there too, surveying the damage from the shattered doorframe. The double doors of the entrance were splintered in, and the place had been turned over. Someone had been looking for something.

Torches were burning in their wall sconces, and half the candles had been lit as well. The maid looked too frightened to do anything but straighten. She was furious inefficiency.

Drusilla ran to the wardrobe, which was smashed in, and tossed aside the clothes that weren't already scattered.

"Lose something, My Dear?" asked Bayden. There was cruelty, and something else in his voice. Accusation.

Drusilla looked up, her eyes pure venom. She stilled her hand from going to her dagger.

"Show some respect, brother," said Ludo. "She's a lady. Please address her as such."

Oh, yeah. Drusilla had forgotten Ludo was her new fake boyfriend.

She smiled at him, straightening to her full height, and realized she was leaving puddles wherever she stood. "Thank you, my lord," she said, curtsying low to him.

"What's this?" asked Bayden, a dangerous tone in his voice. "A bit of chivalry?"

"Where's Bridgette?" Drusilla asked, allowing for no nonsense in her voice.

"Oh, her," said Bayden. "She's missing. Run off, probably." He was watching her, like a cat watches a mouse after pinning its tail.

"Missing?" said Drusilla, voice rising. She turned in a small circle, indicating all the damage. Splinters of the door were everywhere. "I suppose a girl, not yet a woman, did all this as a lark before running off?"

"Be calm," said Bayden. "I have the whole house up. We're doing everything we can."

Drusilla wanted to spit more venom at him. In truth, she wanted to beat the truth out of him. Instead, she apologized.

"Thank you. May I make an announcement to the staff?"

"Certainly," said Bayden, looking like he'd rather not agree.

There was mischief in Ludo's brown? eyes. The more badly she behaved, the more amused he seemed to become.

"If you wouldn't mind assembling just a few of them," she said, "Say, half a dozen or ten. What I have to say will be brief, and I'm sure word will quickly spread to all ears."

"As you wish, my... lady," he said, turning to leave.

Ludo crossed the room, taking her hand sweetly. "It will be all right," he said. "You should change into something dry."

She nodded, putting her hand over his momentarily, before pulling away, going to the balcony. The glass doors were all shut. Drusilla opened one and went outside, looking towards the loch. The rain had abated. Placid waters shimmered in the crescent moonlight.

Bayden returned with six servants. With the guard and maid already present, that made eight plus the brothers.

She came back into the room. Drusilla decided to make this very simple.

"Twenty gold aurei to anyone who finds Bridgette alive. Five for any information that helps me, or anyone else, find her," she didn't want to say it, but she had to, "... otherwise deposed.

"Bring your information directly to me. No one else."

Bayden looked angry, but he was silent. Ludo was slightly amused. With her, or with his brother's foul mood, she couldn't say.

"Now go," she said. "Spread the word. And, thank you."

DRUSILLA WENT QUICKLY FROM the room, running the instant she was clear of the shattered doorframe. Running before she could be questioned, or stopped.

She went straight to the courtyard. A fire was burning in a brazier, one of the flames she had seen from the road, and there were guards here. She didn't care. But if she could do this without them, it would be better.

"Have you searched the forest?" she asked urgently. They both shook their heads no. "Go," she commanded, hoping her pretended station held sway.

Both men lit torches and stepped into the little, walled-in woods.

Quickly, Drusilla pulled her picks from her hair, and opened the door. She noticed the lock had been changed. Bayden must have initiated that based on the theory she carried a key. Or perhaps he hoped this lock would prove more a test of her skill. No matter, the new lock gave way as easily as the old.

Passing through, she pulled it shut, and flew down the stairs with no concern to her own safety.

The beach was deserted, but there were footsteps in the sand. Most were washed away, but a few remained, and they led to... another passage in the stone of the cliff.

Why hadn't she noticed it before? Because she had been busy dealing with her fears.

Before exploring the passage, which was more of a natural crack in the stone that entered into the cliff at about a thirty-degree angle off parallel, she fell to her knees and examined the footsteps. Two men wearing boots, and a woman, or young man, in flat shoes—flat shoes like the ones that Bridgette wore...

The smaller person appeared to have put up a struggle, at times being dragged by the men, at other times, walking on their own.

Into that crack in the earth, someone had been dragged.

Once more, and again without fire, into the mountain, she would follow.

Chapter Thirty-Six

W HY MUST THE IMPORTANT things—the truly pivotal moments of life—be undertaken under pressure of time? The sand that measures life is always scarcest when it is most needed.

Roland had warned her of such things. And so the deep sigh she let pass her lips now was not one of exasperation, but of consignment. No amount of wailing against the Fates would reorder the events of the night.

Behind her, the cold tide rolled up, not quite reaching the place where Drusilla stood. The stairs to her right, carved out of the cliff itself, led back to relative safety, the promise of comforts. And even the option to flee back home.

To London...

Away from this madness.

Only a measure of minutes previous, so small they counted for nothing, she had done battle with a creature such as only exists in legends. It could not be far. The water, almost at her heels, was its perfect camouflage.

And now, with her back turned to those waters, she measured each print in the wet sand for width and length, against points on her own hand, wrist, and arm, memorizing the three dimensions, and also, committing to memory their basic shape. Because she would not turn back.

She would not retreat to London Town.

She would not flee.

The dimensions of these boot imprints would be important—a theory already formed in her head. She pushed it aside. This was no time for theorizing. The wrong theory would only cloud her judgment and possibly throw her off track.

Enough of that.

Time to explore that crack. It would be black as pitch in there. She regretted, for the second time in as many days, that she had not thought to bring a torch. There was no remedy for that now, though, so on she pushed, taking the plunge into darkness.

The opening was well enough camouflaged. Just a natural fissure in the rock. Drusilla flashed back to the boneyard. She chided herself and continued forward. The walls were about three foot wide, and soon she found her feet leaving the sand. Within, as she had expected, she encountered total darkness, instead, feeling her way along, trying to concentrate on negotiating the rising stone. It was slick going at first.

The evidence of the tide, of recent encroachment of loch water within, assaulted her senses, accompanied by returned visions of watery entombment. She ignored them, consciously slowing her breathing. About thirty feet in, the rise was no longer natural, but seemed to be hewn into stairs. As she climbed in the darkness, Drusilla realized she had definitely discovered another of the keep's secrets.

She had probably climbed a hundred feet or more, and must be mere stories below the keep, somewhere deeper inside the mountain than she had started, when she came to a dead end.

Having no visual cues to go by, she removed a glove and felt the blockage. An iron reinforced door. Locked. No. Double locked. The same type of paranoia that had found its way into the design work of the castle.

Picking a lock in the darkness is just as easy as in the light. Picking two locks adds no difficulty. It merely takes twice as long. Drusilla was soon through and to the other side.

There was light here, faintly burning, not the smell of candles, but of a small wood fire. There must be ventilation to the outdoors, or the whole place would be choked in smoke.

Drusilla worked her way down a rectangular hewn hallway, coming after forty feet or so, to a tee. This hallway was wider, about five foot. One way, cold and silent, the other, the direction of the fire.

Following the light, Drusilla began to pass several other reinforced doors with iron bars for windows. This was a dungeon.

"Bridgette," she whispered into one, then the next, going down the hallway. Every cell echoed back hollowly.

The rough-hewn stone, smoothed in places from centuries of use, began to reveal their finer features. Every step brought more light.

Drusilla stopped, listening, hoping to avoid an ambush or other unpleasant encounter. In the half-dark, ahead towards the light, she could hear quiet whimpering.

Drusilla's heart leapt with the joy of hope. She drew her dagger, and rushed silently forward, keeping herself at top alert.

She emerged into a room that was roughly circular, about twenty-five feet in diameter with higher ceilings, about eleven foot up. There was a dais in the center, complete with chains and manacles. Torches lit a menagerie of torture implements and weapons lining the walls, with three other hallways leading off, like the one she had entered from. There were a few wooden chairs—for torture spectators, she supposed—and a rack for stretching people.

Wonderful.

That's it. Everybody down here, not in chains, has to die.

She scanned the wall, looking for a weapon she liked, when someone entered from another hallway. He looked like your typical executioner: a hulking build, wearing all leather with thick, high boots, bare, muscled arms, and a mask.

Drusilla hated masks. Not all masks, but masks that made people look inhuman. Masks designed to inspire terror like this one. It was black leather with eyeholes, and covered only half the face. It had brass eyebrows, arched and sinister, and two brass devil horns, little prongs set atop the skull.

"Can Bridgette come out and play?" she asked.

The man spun, momentarily startled, then grabbed the largest handy weapon from the wall, a halberd, and charged.

Drusilla decided she could do this with her dagger. She leapt to the center of the room. In two easy strides and a leap, she was atop the dais.

Mask-Man tried to chop out her legs, giving his best lumberjack swing. She jumped over the passing blade, lancing him through the eye with a lightning quick jab. She jumped back and dropped off the far side of the dais, keeping her blade.

The man howled in pain, and somewhere down the corridor, to the right of the one she'd entered, a young woman screamed.

Bridgette?

The cry echoed throughout the caverns. She listened. There were no other responses—just the grunting misery of Mask-Man.

She wanted to rush to Bridgette's side, to offer her comfort, but she still had work here. Any distraction would likely be her death. Bringing her mind back to focus, Drusilla circled as the man straightened himself. She had to admire his pain threshold.

"There's blood on your mask," she said, dodging him as he charged, enraged.

Good. Put him off balance.

She moved to his blind side, careful not to step where he had passed. No sense slipping in blood. It never helped things.

Mask-Man tossed the halberd edge on, so that it was the axe blade which came hurtling at her. Drusilla pressed herself to the wall to avoid being cleaved in two, blade passing so close to her face she could smell the oiled metal as it sliced the air before crashing into the wall just beyond her.

And though she had been missed, it felt as though someone had dealt her a violent blow from behind!

Confused, she came away from the wall and knew—as metal slid free of her back, requiring some force to dislodge it, and the rattle of a chain—she had been stabbed. Something amongst the wall's clutter had impaled her.

Mask-Man grabbed a great sword from amongst the plethora of choices for his next assault. From clumsy to ridiculous. Somebody should have taught this wallflower how to fight. She was glad no one ever had.

She stepped away from the wall to see she'd been huddling with a flail. It had an old look to it, an air of disuse. Beautiful. She felt a little drizzle at her side as echoes of the pain continued to throb and spike, vying for her attention.

It would not do to be distracted. She would tend to it later.

The man rushed her, holding the great sword straight out, intending to lance her, it seemed. She hopped up onto the dais again, somersaulting over to the other side of the room. By the time the man stopped his charge, looking for her, she was plunging her dagger into his kidney from behind, over and over.

The second he tensed to react, she left it buried in his side, jumping back, grabbing a weapon at random from the wall.

Rather than swing on her, he crashed his back into the wall, trying to crush her with his own weight, which was considerable. Drusilla, however, was no longer there.

He came away from the wall with a double-headed flail and a mace stuck in his back. He did not look happy. The whole mask, one-eye thing, was working for him, though.

Drusilla looked at her new weapon. A fire poker.

Great.

The man charged her again, still in command of his great sword. The kidney stabs should have left him stunned, gasping for breath, dying. Yet still, he came at her. She ran around the dais, evading him. Blood was gushing from his kidney now, and he crashed into the wall again, taking a deep cut to cheek and mask from a meat cleaver. But still he rose.

Drusilla raised an eyebrow.

She was just thinking what to do next, when she spotted throwing knives on the wall. She tossed the poker and grabbed a brace of knives, throwing.

At first, her aim was deplorable. She hit a leg, then a foot. He definitely didn't like that one. He howled, an enraged, dangerous beast filling the halls with more terrible sounds.

Another scream echoed back and kept coming this time.

"You're upsetting the prisoner," said Drusilla, tossing her third knife. Each throw was an exercise in discipline, the wound under her shoulder blade flaring with new heat as though something sharp remained behind. The knife sliced across Mask-Man's lips, then bounced off the wall. A fourth throw hit him in the stomach. He fell back against the wall again.

She tossed the last two simultaneously, hitting him in the neck and chest.

Mask-Man was coughing up blood, twitching slightly. He was no longer howling. In fact, he was being quite good.

She walked over, twisting her dagger as she ripped it out of his side, knocking his head against the stone wall with her other hand.

He sat there limply, still half-gripping the great sword, as his last life's blood spilled out. Drusilla quickly measured his foot. Much too big. He was not one of the men from the beach.

Ignoring her own pain, Drusilla raced along the corridor from whence the screams were coming, finding herself in a well lit room, and the source of the woodsmoke.

It was a cluttered workshop—the missing sculptor's studio. The ceilings were vaulted here, being twenty-feet or more high at their apex. The room was forty feet or so on a side. An odd shaped room, given to no easy description, and being possessed, like the upper courtyard, of many terraced levels.

Blocking direct access to the highest terrace was a larger-than-life glass mural of Aphrodite. Behind the colored glass was the wood fire she had smelled, burning in an open hearth, giving the art-in-glass life and color. A hole in the ceiling vented smoke off to somewhere else, pulling it with a considerable draft. An altar, laden with flowers, sat at the foot of the mural.

Drusilla thought back to the Pygmalion story.

Several ruined attempts of statues littered the area, all given to an identical theme. There, on an easel, was a portrait of Evelynn in rich, lifelike detail. A masterwork in egg tempera.

She knew because the woman in the painting wore the white dress with the little lavender flowers. A chill passed over her, the scent of lavender finding her senses, and she took a moment as time hung suspended, to look for the ghost she could not see.

And then time resumed, or so her mind told her, and she saw that she was standing upon a lunar calendar, done in tile, ornamenting the floor. It was a living work, the next full Moon having Bridgette's name already laid, but incomplete.

Her blood began to heat. Consciously, she relaxed white-knuckle fists. Had each previous full Moon had one of the missing women's names? There were discarded tiles near the new work, as though one name had been pulled up to make way for the next—for Bridgette's...

A pattern of ritual sacrifice was suggested. She wanted to be sick, but instead cast her eyes about, ever vigilant.

"Drusilla!" Bridgette cried out.

Drusilla's head snapped to a corner, where her lady-in-waiting was chained to a wall, former dress reduced to tatters, body bruised but whole. She took a quick step towards her, but Bridgette cried out again—

"Behind you!"

Chapter Thirty-Seven

S EEING BRIDGETTE IN CHAINS, in that terrible place under the mountain—a place where screams meant nothing, and no one in the sunlit world above could hear—was horrendous. And though Drusilla had expected half as much, no sane mind from the world above could be prepared for it.

An instantaneous revulsion overpowered her, and with it, a simultaneous need for vengeance. But there was time for neither as Bridgette, wide-eyed with terror, cried out her warning—

Drusilla spun, dagger unsheathing in a flurry. A man, resembling the first in the broad strokes, only smaller, slighter, and definitely more stealthy, had crept to within mere feet of her position. He held two daggers, blades backwards along the forearms, and was crouching—milliseconds from a pounce!

He didn't have milliseconds.

Drusilla's dagger continued its arc, shearing Horned-Boy's aorta and part of his trachea. He raised his hands with lightning speed, daggers flying towards Drusilla, then gurgled, blood fountaining from his mouth, a crimson foam, and fell back, crashing to the floor.

Daggers scattered from his hands.

Bridgette whimpered.

Drusilla watched a moment more to make sure he was dead, scanned the room and hall for any more unwanted company, then turned to Bridgette.

"I don't know where the key is," said Bridgette. "I think Lord Bayden has it."

Drusilla's jaw tightened. She was impressed with the young woman, still thinking clearly after all she'd been through.

"Don't call him lord ever again," said Drusilla.

"Yes, my lady."

"Two men brought you here," said Drusilla, half hoping she was wrong about her would-be boyfriend Ludo.

"Yes," said Bridgette. "He had the help of his brother."

Drusilla felt sick anew. She wiped the back of her mouth again with the back of her hand, and spit on the floor.

"I'm sorry, my lady," said Bridgette as Drusilla removed the picks from her hair.

"Why is that, dear friend?"

"I was supposed to spy on you. Lor—just Bayden was so furious when I continued to report only things of no consequence to him. He accused me of protecting you."

"And?"

"It's true. I didn't want to hurt you. I even made up things, like how you were enjoying the games just to have something to say to them."

Drusilla smiled, tears welling in her eyes as she bent to the manacle at Bridgette's hand.

"But the key," protested Bridgette.

"Keys are for the unimaginative," said Drusilla, freeing the lock, revealing the hempen bracelet with its color beads now scratched and bearing the signs of abuse the iron had wrought.

It made her furious.

Slowly, she lowered the arm, seeing that it pained Bridgette to do so any faster. Tender flesh made red. Tender colors cracked and broken…

Violets, red roses…

"How long have you been here?"

"Only hours, I think," said Bridgette. "I did as you said. They ordered me to open the door, though I can't imagine they knew for sure I was within. I hid in the wardrobe, just like you said, but they found me after breaking down the door."

Another manacle gave way. Time to work on the shackles. Bridgette resumed her account while rubbing at her wrists—inspecting her damaged keepsake. "They gagged me, but I think Ludo wanted me to see. L—Bayden tried to blindfold me as well, but Ludo stopped him.

"They must have ordered all the servants out of the east wing. We didn't encounter a soul."

One of the shackles was free now. The swollen ankle of the young woman trembled involuntarily in Drusilla's hand, her body a patchwork of bruises and cruel marks. Nothing that wouldn't heal, given time and proper ministrations. Nonetheless, the sight of it stung her eyes to the verge of more tears.

Drusilla checked her emotions. She didn't yet feel they were safe. Far from it.

"They beat me and tried to frighten me into telling them where you were. Somebody saw you leaving tonight. I don't know who. They said they have eyes everywhere."

That little piece of information concerned Drusilla. She thought of the stable master and of her horses. Of her pigeons. Those dear pigeons. Her allies, at best here, were few. And danger everywhere.

Each pin fell into place with less than conscious effort as she mulled over her situation. It painted an increasingly grim picture. Then, with a soft, oiled click, she released the last shackle.

"And?" she asked, putting the picks back in her hair.

Bridgette rubbed at her ankle. "And Ludo kept on and on about his missing wyvern horn, and they said they'd be back later to torture me into telling what I knew. They showed me needles and all sorts of wicked instruments."

Drusilla measured the boots of the man lying next to her. Too small. She didn't mistrust a single word Bridgette had spoken. On the contrary. Bridgette had displayed uncommon loyalty and high character.

She had also concealed from Drusilla her secret reports to Bayden. Or to Ludo? She may yet be under some coercement. Could they yet hold leverage against her? Or worse, Drusilla didn't wish to think it, but could she yet be a willing conspirator? Was it two brothers, who seemingly were at odds, working together? Or was one playing the other, using Bridgette as an accomplice?

That would leave an as yet unidentified man at large. How complex the web of deceit before her, she couldn't know with certainty. Before condemning two men to die, she wanted to be thoroughly certain.

Her mind spun with the possibilities. For one, and most pressing, Bayden knew Drusilla could pass locked doors with impunity, and further, that she had trod upon the very beach lying just outside this secret place. Was her presence here now part of his orchestration? Or Ludo's? Or the third man, if there was one? Escape was paramount. The other considerations, and there were many, by necessity, must wait.

Bridgette's eyes were wide, and she, too, looked on the verge of crying. Drusilla took her into her arms and comforted her. The young woman sobbed silently, but only for the briefest moment. Pulling away, she found her feet with Drusilla's help. The puncture wound in her own back flared with the effort, reminding Drusilla full well it would need tending, and soon. An injury like that could easily inflame and turn lethal.

She took a last look at the Aphrodite mural, memorizing the outfit. The Roman dress ball was in twenty-two days. Maybe she could use it.

"We must leave here quickly," said Drusilla, leading Bridgette away from the macabre scenery.

Reaching the hall marking the first stage of the way out, Drusilla said, "We may get out of here cleanly. If not, stand well clear of any battles. Try not to be made hostage, and if, only if, I can no longer defend you—do not let them take you alive."

Bridgette looked very solemn. "All right," she said simply.

"If you can use a weapon, take one now," said Drusilla, pointing to the wall of chains, blades, bludgeons, and other implements of death. Drusilla didn't think Bridgette would take her up on the offer, but the young woman surprised her, striding over and plucking a light mace from the wall.

Good woman, she thought. Times would be less dark with more people of her spirit.

Four passageways. Drusilla knew the way to the beach. Bayden also knew that she knew.

"C'mon," she said suddenly, leading Bridgette down the way Mask-Man had come, snatching a torch off the wall. Maybe she could outfox the brothers and avoid a direct confrontation while Bridgette was with her.

The passageway went straight for a while, then descended, curving east. It branched out several times, looking like it had once been a mine. In places, there were shafts running straight down, or straight up, but no crossbeams or pulleys. If it had been a mine, it had been in disrepair for centuries.

Drusilla was questioning how far they would have to travel, and whether she had made a good decision, when they came to a pullied freight elevator. The find was in good repair. The brass was oiled, and the wood painted a bright orange.

"Up or down?" she said aloud to herself.

"Down," said Bridgette. "Maybe it goes to the village or another beach. Up would go to the keep."

Drusilla could understand her not wanting to go back there.

"Good," she said, not entirely sure she liked the decision, but liking the idea of indecision even less.

Echoes of rage came wafting down the shaft as they descended, pulling rope through block and tackle. Bridgette pressed her body closer to Drusilla's, pulling faster at the rope.

Drusilla couldn't be sure, but she imagined the two brothers finding their jailors butchered and their prisoner escaped. It couldn't be a happy moment for them.

They reached the bottom of the shaft, opening a most curious scissor-gate. She'd never seen such a thing, but supposed it served to keep the unwary from stepping under the elevator as it came down, and stepped into a small cubical of a room with two shafts running off. The torches were pulling towards one, so they went that way.

"I can smell the loch," said Bridgette, excitement in her voice.

Drusilla had noticed the fresh, humid air, too. She had never thought she would be happy to see Loch Ness. But right now, if they came out anywhere on the land side, however skimpy, she would be glad.

Her wound throbbed, occasional stabs of pain vying for the attention it could not yet have. She should have stepped out instead of in. Flattening herself against a wall of weaponry had been a poor choice, but she couldn't berate herself for what was done. The arrow of time flew in but one direction. Drusilla refocused her thoughts, scouting the way ahead, as the evidence of the nearing loch assaulted her senses.

Bridgette followed close behind, never lagging or displaying the slightest waver in her resolve, and did so nearly as quietly as herself. Again, she was impressed by the talents and courage of the young woman.

Crocuses...

Was her mind still working on that puzzle? And why would it not come?

The air grew more damp, and the torch pulled its way ahead, burning brighter. Fire picked out gathered condensation along the ceiling, its drips glazing the walls and feeding the uneven places of the floor in shallow puddles. They pressed on, choosing each footfall carefully. Wherever this was leading, Drusilla had no desire to announce her coming. And Bridgette, ever close behind, seemed of the same mind.

At length, they came to a solid door with just enough draft to let the air whistle through. The top and sides were shored up with substantial jams. Iron reinforcements pervaded. It was, as expected, also locked.

Drusilla passed the torch to Bridgette, putting an ear to the door. Stilled her breath. Silence greeted silence. She hadn't thought to take any keys off Mask-Man or Horned-Boy. She had yet to encounter the situation of needing one.

Seconds later, she was through to the other side, Bridgette silently tagging at her heels. She felt a bit of pride in that. She imagined she'd brought Roland a measure of the same.

The door reminded her of Ludo's secret torture chamber. On the other side was a short shaft of stone, and then a panel of wood. Were they on the other side of a trick wardrobe?

Bridgette looked nervous, quietly watching her work.

"Don't worry, we're almost out of here," she assured the young woman, a quiet whisper in her ear. Testing around, she found the release, and swung the...

Fruit shelf open. They were in a cellar stocked with food and old cast off pieces of furniture and fishing gear. It was a damp and musty place. Cool air, not unlike the tunnels they had just emerged from, but heavier. Humid.

She could feel the weight of a storm, and the presence of the loch.

Creeping to the stairs, Drusilla listened again, letting Bridgette hang back with the torch. Someone was sleeping up there, the muffled patter of rain nearly masking it. She made a "shush" motion to Bridgette with her forefinger and lips. Reached back and took the torch from her young companion's hand. Rolling it, with a sizzle and waft of smoke, in the water besotted earth floor, she plunged the room into darkness.

Slowly, eyes adjusted to the gloom. The crack which was the world above slowly revealed itself. It was less than starlight on a moonless night, but it was enough. Carefully, she lifted the hatch.

The scent of the loch was strong here. The lapping of its shore, muffled by the wattle-and-stone walls. Small, wood-shuttered, paneless windows blotted out the cloud-choked sky. This must be one of the cottages in the village.

It was a small room with a hearth, a couple of trunks, and two cots for sleeping. Only one of them was occupied. He was a large man, covered by a nightshirt and ragged blanket. On a stool by his bed was a brass-horned leather mask, and a ring of keys. Hanging over the wall, a cat of nine-tails and a meat cleaver.

Second shift. Resting up before a nice day in the dungeon.

Drusilla crept out of the hole, lowering the hatch, and went to his bedside. He grunted, muttering something in his sleep, and wiping his nose with the back of his meaty hand.

With excruciating care for silence, she unsheathed her dagger. Exquisitely sharp metal sliding through leather to freedom. She knew it made less sound than her own breathing, which she artfully matched to the sleeping man's cadence.

Rain pelted the roof. Her legs were taut with the effort of her disciplined crouch. Years of horseback riding had given her a ready strength and uncommon constitution.

She plunged her steel through his aorta, laying glove to his mouth.

Twisted the blade. Blood let flow freely, escaping along with his life. The man thrashed about for a moment like a fish hauled suddenly out of the sea, then went limp.

She exhaled.

It was done.

Wearing red and black and already being wet, the blood shouldn't betray her deed this night. Drusilla cleaned her knife on the man's nightshirt. Her clothes, she would launder and darn at her earliest opportunity. Their colors, the rain, and the welcome cloak of night would be her allies tonight.

Drusilla checked the front window. It was shuttered, but she was still able to peer through age-cracked splits in the wood. They weren't in the village, but only a thin strip of land separated them from the loch. They must be somewhere downshore. The rain smelled good after being underground, surrounded by all the ugliness men could invent. She cracked the door open and saw that the village was just a few hundred feet east up the pebbled beach.

Fetching Bridgette, they made their way by stealth and patience all the way to the forest behind the livery entrance to the keep. Bridgette didn't once question Drusilla's lead. Not a word did she mutter as she emerged from the hole in the ground to freedom, her first sight, the man slain upon his bed.

Watching her close, in case she need contain her companion's reaction, Drusilla saw the young woman's eyes drawn to the mask. A subtle terror washed her expression. Her grip tightened on the mace. She looked to Drusilla, and terror gave way to gratitude.

DRUSILLA FOUND A GOOD hiding spot for the young woman amidst the firs, and told her to keep quiet and to wait. Rain sheeted off the overhead branches as the two women huddled within.

Her mind moved, swaying back and forth between the recent past and the present, putting together the meaning behind Bridgette's love-token.

It had come to her during their skulk along the shore of Loch Ness in a flash of realization even as the valley had bleached to white, and the rumble of thunder had driven them along.

And now, finally understanding just how isolated this poor young thing must have been, not just of recent, but for a truly long time, she was leaving her alone and shivering under a wayward pine.

"I'll send food and my man, Linus. You'll accompany him to London Town, and I'll join you in a few weeks, after the ball."

Bridgette nodded, and they embraced.

Having emerged from the torturer's cottage, they had, together, stolen along the cliff's edge. Rain battered them. The sky electrified moments of their passage, and they would freeze, hoping not to be seen as the night became as day.

Beginning again after one such moment, Drusilla's hand fell amongst feathery stalks growing to her waist. Pungent scents of anise and lemon filled her lungs.

It was then that she knew. It was then that her heart broke for Bridgette.

"Take my cloak," she said, shaking it out at the edge of the pine's sheltering embrace, and wrapping the young woman in it. Bridgette tried to refuse, but Drusilla was firm in her insistence.

She left her friend, approaching the keep.

The green of dill...

Passed through the rear gate and into the livery, ushered in by her ally there.

Let Bayden's spies watch her return. Though she now knew this method of coming and going was compromised, there was little she could do about it.

Her mind returned to her final conversation with Bridgette.

"I am taking you away from Foxborough, but I must do so with a clear conscience."

"What troubles you?" asked the young woman shivering in her cloak.

"That I would be taking you from the arms of a lover. One, perhaps, you could not speak of..."

"I spoke true. I have no one."

Drusilla lifted Bridgette's wrist, the one bearing the now damaged bracelet. "Who gave you this?"

"She is gone, my lady."

And even though tears are often lost in the rain, Drusilla was witness to those which did now fall from those beautiful cerulean eyes.

The innocence of violets. The romance of red roses. Dill, an aphrodisiac... words floated back, stolen from her father's library: "Sweet mother, I cannot weave—slender Aphrodite has overcome me with longing for a girl." And lastly, crowning it all, the pride of purple crocuses—fidelity, joy, and love.

The passage returned to her:

"all the violet tiaras,

braided rosebuds, dill and

crocus twined around your young neck"

The author—Sappho.

She had read it in the Greek, and at too young an age for it to contain the fullness of meaning it now did.

"Any sign of her?" asked Drusilla, passing Bayden on her way back to her room, letting tears of her own fall unacknowledged down the rain-soaked disguise of her face.

Bayden glared at her, in a particularly foul mood.

"Nothing yet, my lady. Although I'm sure your coin is working wonders for the search."

Drusilla left him, not even bothering to explain where she had been. The whole household was up, looking for Bridgette, except of course Bayden, who was pretending to look, and Ludo, who would be looking for his precious wyvern horn everywhere but where it was—back on its hooks above the mantelpiece.

That was, unless things were more complex than she supposed...

CHAPTER THIRTY-EIGHT

DRUSILLA RETURNED TO HER chambers. A guard still stood watch over her room. A maid nearby, prim and erect of posture, hands joined behind her back, waited also—a young woman of about sixteen Drusilla had seen about, but didn't yet know the name of. The young woman kept her eyes averted, but watchful, to receive commands.

"I must undress for bed." Drusilla looked at the guard in a way she hoped made him uncomfortable. "Pray take your station further down the hall."

"Yes, my lady." His cheeks colored. With a deep bow and hurried step, he was gone.

The maid looked ready to follow her in. Another agent to report on her? Almost certainly. A potential next victim, now that Bridgette was missing from the dungeon? Probably nothing so obvious. Somebody else, another poor maiden, less connected to the first—less connected to Drusilla—would be picked.

But to be near her, when Drusilla, herself, was increasingly a target, would endanger the young woman, spy or not.

"Thank you for attending me, but I have no need for a lady-in-waiting."

The young woman looked immediately distressed, but stood her ground.

"I assume you were assigned to me," said Drusilla.

"I was, my lady."

"What is your name?"

"Maisie, my lady. Short for Margaret, if you prefer. I'm to assist you until Bridgette is found."

"Return to your former duties, Maisie. And live a long life. This is no place for you."

Drusilla looked to the broken doorframe, and then the smashed-in wardrobe.

Something changed in Maisie's eyes. A pallor of fear blanched her skin. "But my orders—" Maisie silenced herself, eyes still fast upon the splintered wardrobe, before they found their way back to her slippers.

"I have countermanded your orders, and if anyone should question that, they may redress me personally."

"If you would prefer someone else?"

"Search for Bridgette if you wish to be of assistance, but send no one else. They will all be turned away."

"Yes, my lady," said Maisie with a deep curtsy, and then in a slip of the tongue, betrayed her true feelings. It came out as scant more than a whisper. "Thank you, my lady."

There could be no mistaking it, the girls of Foxborough were terrified.

As Maisie departed briskly, relieved, the burden of spending a night in that smashed up room lifted, the room where Bridgette had gone missing—and the servants must have their suspicions about that—Drusilla toweled herself dry enough for her next task, so as not to ruin her supplies, then went to her chests and withdrew ink, quill, and paper.

The room was already outfitted for writing, so she would use Evelynn's blotting powder, wax, and for her seal, she always used her own Order of Arthur ring. Its edge on one side was crenulated in a very specific way that Roland would know. The other side in a different fashion.

To use one signified a message worthy at its face value. To use the other side, meant that the message was written in distress and to disregard its contents. Instead, the recipient should look for hints and clues possibly disguised in the text and elsewhere. To send a letter using neither, meant anything goes, and could not be trusted, although it may contain merit. One's judgment would be taxed most heavily under such a circumstance.

The chair's back aggravated her injury, so she sat leaning forward slightly as she worked. Drusilla composed one message plainly, actually, more of a diagram for a mask, measurements, and other specifics using Evelynn's seal. And wrote the other in a secret code, using Druidic runes and a pre-memorized cipher known to all who pledged their loyalty to The Order of Arthur.

The first letter was for her footman, Percival, to take to Lion's Gate, where she knew there were craftsmen who could fashion extraordinary things.

Thinking long upon the second letter and her required strategy before plying ink to paper, Drusilla considered the great loyalty, even love, the brothers commanded amongst the community as a whole. Ludo, especially. To kill them publicly would go very badly for her.

Drusilla took up quill and pen, and scrawled out this message in the predesigned code:

My dear friend, Roland,

It pains me to pen this communiqué. I would carry the news myself, but for that I cannot be certain I will survive to do so. A dangerous game is afoot here at the loch. The pigeons were killed my first day here. I pray you have not already moved to action.

How do I begin to express my condolences for what I must now inform you? Your dear, sweet Camille has fallen to the treachery and madness of men. I suspect with good reason the guilty parties to be none other than the brothers, Bayden and Ludo MacKay. But though my case grows ever more strong, there are yet elements of uncertainty. I hesitate to convict without the definitive proof which would lend such act the necessary, righteous authority. For this reason alone, I wait, remaining ever watchful, seeking that final piece of evidence that will release my hand.

Please accept my friendship at this time, and my most heartfelt sympathy.

I suspect dear Atreus was murdered as well. In any case, he is dead, and beyond our help now. I am sure he sits well in the kingdom of God, as does our friend Camille.

If guilty, my path ahead is clear. I must kill the MacKay brothers in baffling fashion, in plain sight, and not be caught, nor suspected, for such is the love of the community for them... **even the ignition of war is not beyond imagination.**

Do not do anything drastic. There is no need for your action. By the time the Moon waxes full, you can be assured that they have been dispatched to the well deserved Hell of their own making. I will personally see to it on my dying honor!

I hate to impose at all upon you in this most difficult of times, but I may need your help. It is most certain that the loch is host to some manner of sea serpent. I have seen it up close, and there is no case for denial.

More horrifying, there is indication that it has acquired a taste for human flesh!

I may be required to destroy it. I can handle the two brothers—such is my specialty. But the lake monster, which measures sixty feet or more, and has no aversion to human encounter, is entirely another matter.

Please advise. You have always been wiser in such matters than I. Time grows short.

D.

Finishing, Drusilla stripped out of her blood soaked clothes. Both her own, and the men she had done battle with. The heavy cloth peeled away ingraciously, painfully where flesh, blood, and cloth had had time to dry and cake together. What was left behind should have been an even canvas of fair skin, not the mottled crimson and dark brown she found, or the ruinous patchwork of discoloration adorning her shield arm.

She chose to ignore the latter for now. Bruises, such as they were, would resolve of their own accord, and therefore, were not her primary concern. Using mirror and washbasin, she inspected the damage, revealed in the gold-backed glass. A small puncture greeted her sight, ringed in angry red.

Her mind flashed back to the moment of impact—back to the dungeon...

She shook it off, and returned to her work.

Reaching the wound was no easy task. It was just behind and below her right shoulder blade, and felt larger than it looked. Taking a deep breath, she prodded it. It was tender to the touch. She pressed harder.

Pain flared.

Something sharp, as she had suspected, remained within. A sliver of metal was not out of the question. The flail, like many of the weapons in that pit of Hell, was roughly hewn and carelessly tended to. The possibility that something worse remained behind must also be acknowledged.

Drusilla slumped into the chair, drawing several sharp breaths, thinking. Recalling all she had been taught by the Druid healers.

Taking a clean cloth, she soaked it in the washbasin and cleaned the wound as best she could. Pressing the sides of the puncture, she bled it. And though it already ran red, as was her training, alcohol would be required to ensure against fever and infection.

Using a second cloth, she bathed away the rest of the blood, most of which was not hers, staining her washbasin as red as the dress she had just peeled away.

She dumped the water out over the edge of the keep, naked, transfixed by the dark waters below. She let the rain wash her clean, too terrified to be much bothered by the heat robbing storm. Inhaling deep, she tried to slow the world down. For a moment, she escaped it all.

Too soon, however, Drusilla was overpowered by the omnipresence of the loch. A sense of urgency overcame her. An urgency to distance herself from her mere proximity to it. Bridgette still waited, out there in the miserable damp, in the wet earth and forest litter beneath a mighty fir.

She left the washbasin to continue its collection of new water, closing glass doors to the rain, putting herself on the dry side of them.

Her wound would need dressing. A clean handkerchief from amongst Evelynn's things would temporarily suffice. She dried herself, shivering, though a fire burned beneath its mantle. Keeping the pristine cloth between her wound and shift, Drusilla pulled the laces of her underbodice tight, then donned fresh clothes pulled from one of her several traveling trunks.

She had deliberately not unpacked the better part of her things as a reminder to never get too comfortable in these surroundings.

The dress she selected was tawny, made from a heavy muslin and stitched in heavy black thread, with black laces crisscrossing the front. Her only other wrap was more cape than cloak, though it was possessed of a hood of light material, dyed most auspiciously a deep purple.

She could borrow Evelynn's heavy cloak. It was even lined in a beautiful silver fox fur, but tonight was not the time for poking the bear. Her own things would have to do. Draping the cape over her shoulders, she concluded, the night was cold, and anything was better than going without.

Hiding the newly minted letters in her bodice, she left the room again. Passing through the splintered ruins of the double-doored archway served as a visceral reminder that she was but scant more safe here within the keep than under it, in its woefully active dungeons.

Again, she thought of Bridgette, out there in the woods, hiding, cold, in the rain. Her step quickened. At least the oilcloth cloak would give her a chance of coming through it.

The guard eyed her suspiciously as she came down the hall.

"I cannot sleep. My dear Bridgette is out there somewhere."

"The whole of the keep does all they can to find her, my lady."

"Agreed. Everyone but me."

She walked past him, and down the staircase, making the turn to the servants' quarters.

A few discreet inquiries later, and she located Linus, then Percival, giving them, each, their instructions. She sent Percival to Lion's Gate, to acquire all that would be needed to affect the Aphrodite costume—including a gold coin to be beaten thin, and overlaid upon a mask covering her upper features, and another to be leafed thin upon parchment and made into radiant squares of confetti.

That left her with not enough coin to pay out the promised reward should someone locate Bridgette. It was a calculated gamble, but one she need take to put the rest of her machinations in place.

She spoke first to Percival. "Ride swiftly and avoid any encounters. Go to a goldsmith first, and lacking to a silversmith, or a smithy of any kind. Then to a seamstress, and then to anyone else you deem useful in this task.

"Here is some coin. Pay extra if it will speed things along, but use discretion. Do not throw your money away, and let no one know how much you carry.

"Take one of the horses, take the Major and go, now."

"Yes, my lady."

The lad had a solemn look about him. She was asking him to embark on a midnight quest in this wild land so unfamiliar to him. If he was afraid, he hid it well.

She was proud of the man she saw emerging from the boy, knowing she had had a hand, however small the influence, in shaping him.

The other letter she gave to Linus, and some coin as well. "Take the carriage, and two teams of four horses. Leave Perseus. He needs a rest. Buy two more horses from the livery man, and go with immediate haste to London Town. Give this letter to no one but Roland the Just."

"Yes, my lady."

"And, Linus."

"Yes?"

"You will have company. When all is readied, I will take you to her, and see you off."

Drusilla had a small window of time before Linus and the carriage would be readied. She thought about what Bridgette had said. That she had been charged to spy on her and report her activities to the brothers. If that was true, she could scarce trust any of the household staff. But she needed to tend her wound, and for that, she skulked about until she had gathered both clean linens and a bottle of strong spirits.

The work could be done herself, but not as easily nor as well. Any wound could be life-threatening if it became inflamed. The Druidic wisdom was to clean wounds with alcohol, and to keep them clean. She didn't know why. The Merlin taught many things which, though mysterious, bore good fruit.

She needed help.

Bridgette was her first thought, but quickly dismissed. Once out on the road, any dallying would be unwise. All of Foxborough was on high alert, its masters in a paranoid and dangerous mood.

Drusilla found herself down the hall, near the quarters of other guests, contemplating her dilemma. Over the past days, she had learned much of the layout of the keep and its inhabitants, temporary or otherwise. She stood outside Raul's room. Soft candlelight radiated and pulsed, seeping beneath the door's sill.

Her breathing was quickened, feet frozen to inaction. She needed help, she reminded herself. Taking note of the position of her dagger, she knocked upon the door. Sudden panic seized her by the throat as she realized she didn't know what to say...

The door opened.

Raul stood there, naked to the waist, rock-hard muscles glinting in the pulsing candlelight. Over a fustanella, the Roman equivalent of the locally popular kilt, he wore a leather-banded pteruges.

Armor.

What came as more of a shock, his legs were not the spindles she had expected, but were well-defined and hard with muscle. Feet bare, he was solidly planted. In his hand, a gladius. He held it at his side almost casually, yet everything of his bearing told her he was well versed with it.

She tried to speak.

Nothing happened.

"Forgive me, my lady," Raul said, quickly laying the sword aside, to rest against the doorframe's inner lip. His eyes darted to the bottle of alcohol in her hand, slowly traced their way up and back to her eyes, perhaps lingering a little too long upon her lips as they made the journey.

Something in that stirred Drusilla to shake her mind loose. She summoned up false superiority, drawing upon the practiced part with which she was becoming all too familiar.

"The hour is late, I know..."

Raul interrupted her. "I have only just returned to my room. I thought to take an hour's rest before continuing my search. It was a weakness. I beg your forgiveness. I felt fresh eyes might..."

Drusilla reached out, took his hand, staying his words. He had been searching for Bridgette, she believed in earnest. Here was her ally. How could he be anything else?

"Be not troubled."

"But surely—"

She put a gloved finger to his lips, stepping forward and pushing the door closed behind her.

"On this, you must trust me. Be not troubled. Make pretense to search. Nothing more." She was close to him. Close enough to feel the heat pouring off his half-clothed body. She knew the impropriety of the situation was alarming, and that should she have read this man wrong, she was in grave danger.

Drusilla could not bring herself to believe it so. Within these stone halls reigned madness and corruption most foul. She had to believe it was not all-pervasive.

She stepped away from Raul, over to the small window at the back of his room, past the bed, which overlooked the rear courtyard and livery. Linus would be down there right now, hitching up newly acquired steeds. The keep militia would be crawling about, making it their business to know all that transpired.

A draft brought with it the smell of damp moss, stone, and rain-soaked mud. The window was a narrow arch of stone, slick with pelting rain. No pane adorned its interior. Quickly, she drew the shutters closed, all the while listening for footfall or the scrape of a gladius upon stone as it was retrieved by its owner. She wanted to trust him... A part of her still kept vigil.

She turned.

Raul was watching her with curiosity.

Between them, the bed was still made. His stripped away shirt was folded neatly over the back of a chair by the bedside. Sandals placed neatly beneath. The whole of the room was but a fraction that of Evelynn's suite. The ceiling lower. The comforts more sparse and basic in design.

Who was this man? Why was he here? What relation to the MacKays? If their father was the man in the portrait, a general serving Emperor Heraclius, in Constantinople, or one of the far-flung territories... Perhaps that was the connection?

The sandals registered in her brain. They were centurion, part and parcel of a Roman soldier's kit. Yet he did not participate in the games of martial sport. He had always worn clothes which hid his well-honed muscles. She had assumed wrongly he was a soft man given only to the leisurely side of life.

She had been wrong about many things. Had she been wrong to come here?

Time was short. Linus would soon be ready for her. Bridgette waited freezing in the forest. Trust or don't trust. Time ever marched ahead, indifferent.

Raul had made no move to approach her. He stood, watching. Waiting. But then he spoke, as if composing himself after a long contemplation.

"I would not dishonor you."

Simple words.

Five simple words. Her heart leapt. Here was a man who lived by an ideal worthy of Camelot itself. Here was a man for whom chivalry came before the baser lusts.

Drusilla's cheeks went hot. Her breath came, but raggedly. She looked away, to the windowsill, the bed... her eyes lit upon the chair. She crossed the room, not meeting Raul's gaze as she set her things down upon the simple wooden construct.

"I have little time," she said, organizing the small bundle upon the chair.

Other than a table smaller than the washbasin, which sat upon it, and a tiny nightstand where the candle burned, there was no other furniture in the small quarters.

"It would not be wise for us to drink alone," Raul said, unable to gain her gaze, though she was painfully aware he sought it.

"I would not think so, either."

There was no more time to waste. She turned, faced him, met his gaze. There, in his eyes, was want and discipline in equal measure, though she was sure it was a raging battle whose tide could turn at any moment. She knew this, at least, to be true of her own frail resolve.

"I have need of your help, and of your discretion. I would not act improperly. Can I count upon you?"

"My lady, you have but to ask."

"In the absence of Bridgette, I come to you. It is a small matter, but one I must have help with." She was stalling, and she knew it. This was no easy thing.

"Put a name to it," said Raul. "I am your servant."

She smiled. She couldn't help it.

"It is the practice of my people to clean and dress wounds, beginning with alcohol."

"You are wounded? I could call for a surgeon…"

"No. I have asked for your discretion."

"You have it."

"It is a delicate spot."

"My eyes shall not stray from the work at hand."

Drusilla nodded her consent, and turned her back to Raul. Laying cloak and belt across the edge of the bed, she began to unlace her dress. Laying it, too, aside, there remained only her underclothes. At the races, he had seen as much, but they too must come away. She forced her hands to do the work, though they trembled unbidden.

The puncture was in more intimate a spot than she would have liked. As the bodice loosened, her breath quickened, so too, her heart. Her eyes stole down to the dagger at her belt. No longer on her hip, but still within reach. She took a small measure of courage from it. But her back was turned. Raul was the stronger, a soldier. He had the advantage. Her next action was not a demonstration of trust, but rather a willful act of faith.

Moving her small bundle to the edge of the bed, she straddled the chair backwards, and set the bodice aside. Drusilla slid her shift down about her waist, feeling her breasts escape their confinement into the cold and drafty freedom of the room. Closed her eyes against the predicament of her near complete vulnerability. Swallowed at the lump in her throat, realizing it, too, was bare.

She was as naked as Raul, and all too aware of his proximity.

Heat poured from his chest to warm her back. Gently, he peeled away the handkerchief, which had served as her battle dressing, and laid it aside. His hand hovered over the dark bruising on her arm, stopping, momentarily touching, expressing a tenderness, then moving on.

The simple heat from his hands was healing. She stroked the fabric of his shirt draped before her, out of his sight line, glad he did not probe her for answers she was not wont to give.

"It is deep," he said, his mouth less than a foot from her ear.

Drusilla held perfectly still, unable to force her eyes open.

"It looks to have been done cleanly," he added.

"I fear a shard of iron remains within," she countered, knowing the worst was yet to come. "You must search it out before we are done."

"Would you rather lie?"

Drusilla steadied the tremble of her lip. "No." She gripped the rungs of the chair's back tightly. "Please proceed."

His hands felt cool against the heat of the wound. His prodding, though gentle, caused her to wince, a thing she hid, as he worked the tender flesh, lighting up raw nerves, searching out the culprit she now knew was there. And, in that, it was a waiting game—a cruel anticipation until the thing was found.

She didn't have to wait long. The razor within her made itself known, and she began to tremble. Again, she felt the drizzle of hot blood running free, the stab of the foreign metal, within her, doing new damage.

She wanted to keep her eyes closed, but instead, watched the undulating shadows flicker and crawl across the wall and floor. She needed to keep watch. She was exposed and deeply vulnerable.

Terrible thoughts crossed her mind as she speculated upon the evidence at hand, ever sublimating the pain to which she was subjected.

Raul was not rich like the others in attendance here. She had assumed him to be of nobility, of the landed gentry at the least. His presence here was an enigma. He had a connection to Rome hitherto unsuspected. Bayden and Ludo had grown up in the chaos of fallen Rome.

Raul's hands moved away, and she felt their absence as a flower feels the setting Sun. And then she heard him draw a knife from its sheath.

Involuntarily, she tensed.

Raul had no business at a gathering of the social elite. She moved her hand to her own dagger of steel. Gripped its wire-braided hilt.

Listened.

"I must probe the wound," he said. There was something reassuring in his voice. Something deeply caring and protective.

"Use mine," she said, setting her own blade free.

A final leap of faith. She was terrified.

She turned to meet his eyes, found them, anchored to them, a small ship adrift in a storm seeking harbor. "It is sharper."

Raul set down his knife, a Roman-made piece, a soldier's knife, and took hers.

"Steel?" he asked, marveling at the blade. Turning it over to test out its balance.

"It cuts easily," said Drusilla, feeling more naked now than if all her clothes were on the floor.

"I shall take great care," he said.

His hands were steady and gentle, the alcohol soaked rag cold as he went to work, the wound more painful since the last time she had tended it. She was enduring it well, the occasional spike of pain causing her to want to wince, and as quickly, she suppressing it, hiding her discomfort, keeping her silence as his hands passed over the small, exposed area of her body needing attention.

As one hand worked, the other rested, hot upon her side, below her shoulder blade, upon her ribs or back variously. Where it needed to be, she fully understood, but much too close to her breast for her to ignore.

He was on a knee for the support, she imagined, he needed to accomplish the delicate work.

She narrowed her eyes to a slit, letting the warmth of candlelight bathe her. Focused on that to aid her mind in enduring the task at hand.

Ever, her mind came back to the heat of Raul's hands, and the inferno they stirred within her. Though she fought for inner tranquility, Drusilla's rapid pulse and ragged breathing argued otherwise.

At least, she thought, he might mistake her kindling passions for suffering. Mistake her own heat for pain. She did not wish him to know the effect his simple touch had upon her.

Suddenly, red-hot pain, flaring her vision white, made her forget her lover's quandary. Wincing, she squeezed tight her eyes, sparkles and blackness, as once more her own knife sliced into her back. Her grip on the chair rungs was iron.

"You endure pain like few I have ever known." The knife withdrew, giving her some relief.

He would not pay such a compliment if he knew how close she had come to screaming.

Controlling her breath, not wanting him to ever know, and certainly not trusting the normally steady quality of her voice, she remained silent.

"There's the devil," he said after a moment.

Composing herself, Drusilla turned, looking at the blood-slicked steel tip of her knife in the dancing candlelight. There, cloaked in crimson, was a tiny splinter of darker metal. The culprit dislodged.

Drusilla nodded.

"Well done," she said, voice betraying her, despite her best attempt to mask the effects of the ordeal she'd just suffered, then added, "Is there more?"

The question was loaded with dread, but it needed asking.

"I do not believe so."

She felt tension fall away, and in that moment realized her nakedness, turning back to the wall before her.

"Pray, apply more alcohol."

Raul wetted a new cloth, then came that familiar sting as alcohol met wound. The pressure now carried with it no sharp insult. It needed only time and care in keeping it clean now to heal. Such was the Druidic wisdom.

Drusilla reached around, pressing cloth to injury, fingers momentarily brushing Raul's, cheeks hot with fire.

"I can manage from here," she said.

His hand withdrew.

"My lady."

She slid one arm, then the other, back into her shift, always a hand securing the cloth beneath, then wriggled into her under bodice and began at the laces, cinching the affair tight.

Raul crossed to the shuttered window after cleaning and oiling her knife, laying it next to the remainder of her dress and improvised medical kit upon the bed. As she worked the rest of her outfit, he spoke in a cautious, measured tone.

"Are you in some trouble? I would help."

She glanced up. His eyes were averted in chivalrous fashion.

"I am honored." She finished with the dress, sheathed her knife, and retrieved her cloak, donning it. "I rely upon your discretion. Trust that I have matters in hand."

He looked to her, locked her gaze with those piercing dark eyes that had been stranger to her a mere handful of days prior.

Her resolve was all but gone. She wondered, fleetingly, if she had found more than an ally in Raul. Heat raged through her body. Her thighs burned. Her chest was fire. Discretion was quickly fading in the blinding candlelight.

Raul nodded.

Seizing the barring mechanism, Drusilla quickly, and without ceremony, fled the room.

Chapter Thirty-Nine

T HE NEXT MORNING, DRUSILLA awoke, alone. She cast her glance about for Bridgette...

Recognized she was disoriented, memory of the previous night flooding back. She had tilted with a dragon, butchered evil men, and sent away her one comfort in this place. She had also bared herself to the waist in Raul's chamber. The memory of his hands upon her still caused her to tremble upon recall. A glance to the shattered doorframe broke that spell, reminding her that a guard would be posted nearby, just beyond sight.

She laughed.

It was all too much. And now, she must rise and go about her day as though the world sailed still on even kilter. She opened the glass doors, letting in the rain fresh air. It looked as though more was imminent.

The loch itself was dark and placid under a grey sky, touched here and there at the edges by sunlit brilliance and patches of bright blue. The deep, heavy valley soaked with rain was crisp and vibrant green. Far away, a crow cawed, echoing sinister.

She collected her rain-filled basin, washed up, cleaning again her wound and giving it a new dressing. Accomplishing that, she selected a spring-green linen dress, bordered and embroidered with little white flowers. The bodice laced up the front across a white center panel with white satin laces.

Drusilla employed her silver chain to suspend her dagger, and slipped on delicate white gloves. She couldn't see ruining another thing—the loss of her green-sleeved dress still stung—and so wore her boots, which she had dried and oiled the night before, rather than risk muddying Evelynn's white slippers, which would have looked better in completing the outfit.

Satisfied, Drusilla paid visit to the tailor next. Parting with a few coins, she commissioned a new oil-skin cloak. After being measured, she made her way down to the kitchen, volunteering herself for several small tasks. Knowing permission would likely be denied, she didn't ask. Donning an apron and plucking up a large chef's knife, she simply went to work. There were onions to be peeled, carrots to be sliced and chopped round. She diced several beets, readying them for the boil, washing and saving their tender green leaves for a separate dish.

It was hot and damp near the boiling pots. Drafty elsewhere. Outside, the weather was moody, alternating between noncommittal rain, and reluctant sunshine.

Having not yet been accosted by any of the staff, who watched her warily from as far away as they could comfortably still conduct their own business, Drusilla started on her next task—making a broth from the collected drippings of last night's roast. Mincing a combination of herbs and a bit of salt to season it, she thickened it with flour as she hummed absently. Gradually she became aware of many eyes upon her. With an implacable look upon her broad face, the head cook, Agatha, stepped forward and took the stir spoon from her hand. Tasting.

The rest of the kitchen staff waited, watching in baited silence. They seemed to fear displeasing Agatha almost as much as they feared the lords of the keep.

Agatha looked thoughtful as she rolled the flavors around in her mouth. "Is that beet juice?"

Drusilla nodded. "Just a hint."

"And basil?"

"It is," Drusilla confessed, starting to feel the same tension exhibited by the staff, all packed into a tight semicircle around their immediate boss.

"I wouldn't have thought of that." Her expression was a perfect dead pan.

Drusilla worried she might have offended the older woman. It would not do to lose the support of the serving class here at Foxborough. She had precious few allies as it was.

"It's better than mine."

Stares turned to wide mouth gapes. The staff crowded in further, trying to see exactly what had been done. Glances bounced from Agatha to Drusilla and back again, seeking more.

"Everyone step up and have a sip. And take note. This is your lesson for the day." She turned her eyes upon Drusilla. "And as for you, young lady. Sit down and have your breakfast. You might as well eat with us. You cook like us."

"Yes, ma'am." Drusilla curtsied, finding, at last, the mirth in Agatha's eyes.

Having breakfasted, she walked out to the greensward to see what the general mood of her hosts was.

There were more games and merriment. Rain was an occasional companion, never showing itself in full force, always loitering nearby until its next appearance. When not sheltering under the pavilions indulging in the endless parade of food, there were contests to be had and sporting events to spectate.

Drusilla was sipping on some hot tea, just brought up from the kitchen, when she spotted little Sara MacTavish. The girl's eyes lit up, and she ran to Drusilla, colored-ribbon stick trailing out behind her.

"Lady Drusilla," the child breathed, coming to a stop out of breath. She bounced on her toes, beaming as a stray patch of sunlight erupted onto the greensward.

"Can I tell you a secret, Sara?"

The little girl nodded enthusiastically, eyes wide.

"Promise?" said Drusilla, stooping a bit and extending a pinky.

The child put her pinky forth, interlocking hers with Drusilla's, and they sealed their pact with a shake. Sara waited, eyes greedy.

"I saw a kelpie last night."

The little girl was astonished. Delighted.

"Was it the same one?"

"I don't know. It was very big, and not too friendly. Stay away from the loch. I think I left it in a grumpy mood."

Sara MacTavish nodded her consent.

"You don't mean the flippered thing, do you?"

Startled, Drusilla spun around, rising to face Raul. Her heart quickened.

Raul bowed deeply. "My apology, dear lady. It was not my intent to startle you." He reached for her hand—which she offered, secretly anticipating what she well knew came next.

He kissed her white-gloved hand, never breaking eye contact. His other hand, never straying from its hidden place behind his back.

"We were speaking of kelpies," said Drusilla, watching his reaction closely. "Privately."

"Forgive me."

"Have you ever seen one?"

"I'd never heard of one before coming here. But the world is too wide for me to pass judgment." He pulled flowers out from behind his back. A colorful assortment. He separated out three, from the two dozen or so, and gave them to Sara.

"My lord," she said, taking them with a smile. Her curtsy was improving.

He presented the remainder to Drusilla. He behaved much as though nothing so much as a "hello" had transpired between them the night before. True to his word, he displayed utmost discretion.

"My lord." She curtsied in perfect form, providing, by example, an education for the young girl at her side. "They are beautiful."

"They pale next to you." Her knees went a little weak.

"Your words are most appreciated." Drusilla looked to a far off cherry tree, feeling the heat of his ardor upon her. "Pray, excuse me. I am late for an engagement."

And once again, Drusilla made haste away from her Sicilian suitor.

She had successfully avoided Bayden this morning. It was now approaching noon, and she felt she must test the waters. Making her way through the various merriments, she found the brothers sitting top center in the bleachers, constructed the night previous, for spectating the jousting tournament, which began today and ran all week.

She climbed the white wooden stairs before either saw her, and sat herself next to Ludo under the yellow and white striped canopy. He looked up, smiling as she took her seat. "I had feared you'd run off in the night. Your carriage is gone."

He looked very vulnerable in that moment.

Bayden looked over at her now as well, said nothing, but gave her a nod of acknowledgment. She returned it with a half smile and dip of her head.

Surely, neither one would think her absent. They had only to check the shattered remains of her room to know that.

"You can't think I'd abandon you and your lovely festival," she countered, making sure her gaze took in both of them. She spoke loudly over the crash and thunder of horse and metal upon the field. "And the ball on Midsummer Night's Eve is an evening I wouldn't dream to miss." She brushed Ludo's hand, almost accidentally. She withdrew her own hand only after knowing it could not be perceived as anything but coyly deliberate.

Bayden promptly rose and left the games.

She looked slyly to Ludo, and they both giggled over it. He seemed genuinely pleased. There was no way he knew she was pretending with her affections. And the added display of cruelty only fueled his ardor.

After the jousting, he led her to a semi-secluded spot, eyes a wild grey-green? His look devoured her. It seemed he could wait no longer to take their relationship further. He leaned in to kiss her. She demurred.

"I shall give you such a kiss on Midsummer Night's Eve, that you shall never forget it, my love."

Ludo smiled to his eyes, looking at her fondly. He seemed to be making mental calculations. "The night of the ball?"

She nodded.

"It shall be our engagement kiss, then," he said, taking her hand, and undressing it, slowly, with tenderness, a finger at a time. He then adorned her naked finger with an elegant band of gold, a Roman engagement token.

By custom, in conclusion of taking their vows, an iron band would follow—to be worn when performing household duties that might mar the gold—and she would belong to him. Like the slave collar from which it had evolved, it symbolized ownership. Unlike the slave collar, she had, at this point in the negotiation, right of refusal. Things were more subtle nowadays between men and women. Though, underneath it all, the result was much the same.

Not wishing to look morose, Drusilla held the ring up to the light. It shone like a rivulet of liquid sunshine come to light upon her finger.

"I had it made for you. They have an excellent smith at Inverness. I hope I have correctly estimated the size."

"It's perfect. Such attention to detail. You take my breath away." She added, trying to focus her revulsion into a convincing soliloquy of lovemaking. "I shall be counting every hour."

She put a white-gloved hand on his cheek, and pulling him nearer, kissed the other, being careful none watched them.

After he left, she secreted the ring to a pocket and put her glove back on. It would not do to play their hand too soon. What if he was innocent? The chance was minuscule, yet she plotted against them both as though it were a certainty.

Ludo was too cruel a man for her to love in earnest, should he prove to be innocent. Bayden, too possessed of a cold streak which manifested itself when least called for. And thinking of suitors and their suitability, her Sicilian came to mind and with it a rise of temperature. It was a thought she promptly pushed away. She did not have time for these foolish courtships. She had shoes to measure.

Drusilla's early departures of each night's festivities were bordering on the commonplace. No one accosted her when she left, returning to the keep proper. Inside, she made her way towards the tower where the brothers slept. She must be careful. She had no good excuse for being in this area, and though the eight bodyguards were dead, new men had been promoted to the rank. And then there was the regular soldiery. There were plenty of hazards to avoid.

Shadow to shadow, she moved down halls and up stairs, till at last she came to Bayden's room. She was about to pick the lock when she realized the folly of the action. Any door they found unlocked, now, would point directly to her. She had to find another way.

She retreated, pondering the problem, and in her wanderings, came to the grand den. She sat herself at one of the small tables near the fire, enjoying the heat.

Shadows danced and leapt across the walls, glinting off glass eyes in the dark and rustic study. Dark curtains flapped soddenly as wind and rain, carrying with them scents unique to the loch, made their ingress. Images of the other night haunted her. The encounter with the beast had been indelible.

Unlike... footprints, which would be in grand supply today as the rain sodden earth was trod upon.

It was time to return to the greensward.

BAYDEN WAS LEADER AGAIN in swordplay, Drusilla noted, checking the tally boards. No entry from Raul. A thing she was glad of. After last night, she knew better than to think he was hapless with a sword, though she wouldn't care to see that skill matched against either MacKay. It sickened her to think of someone like Bayden marring Raul's finer features in some barbaric display.

The deep gash across Angus' face came unbidden to her memory.

Ludo had dropped from second to third in the rankings. A local man named Collin had surpassed him. She had seen him fight. He was very good. Better, even, than the men she'd fought in the forest. But unlike Ludo or Collin or any of the other men, several she considered her betters in combat from what little of the events she had watched, Bayden was undefeated. If she ever came to blows with him, she was done.

Drusilla wandered the grounds, absorbing the festive spirit, sampling the baked goods, sharing a smile here and there with the other participants. It was a thing sorely needed, especially after the dark witnessing she had done in the underground only last night.

Rain started up again, driving the crowds back under pavilions or into the main building. But still a festive atmosphere reigned. Even the haunting melody of panpipes seemed in no way to dampen moods. Perhaps it was the free flowing alcohol. Perhaps they were simply having a good time, not burdened by the cares which weighted her down.

She looked about, finally spotting what she sought. Under the pavilion nearest the pear tree with an arrow imbedded in its bole, Sara MacTavish and several other children took their refuge. Sara was eating a pear, probably procured from the nearby insulted tree when Drusilla walked up.

"Lady Drusilla," she exclaimed, and forgetting her courtly manners, ran up and gave her a big hug.

Drusilla returned the affection, hitching up her skirts to kneel before the girl. The wet grass felt good on her knees, a reminder of simpler times.

"I have a task for you," she said, "if you'd like to accept the challenge."

Sara's eyes went wide. She nodded, eager to please Drusilla.

"All right, but you must tell no one of it. If you do a good job, there will be a prize. Do you accept?"

"Yes, Lady Drusilla. I'll do my very best, and tell no one. What is the prize?"

"My best blue ribbon, which would look lovely in those gorgeous red curls of yours, and a coin from my hometown. It has a picture of a mermaid on it." She'd picked it up when tracking Count Nolan, her starting point being Ys, six, almost seven months ago now.

"A mermaid, really?"

"Yes. Ys has a legend about a mermaid, and so they put one on their coin. I think you'll like it."

"Oh yes! What do I have to do?"

Drusilla leaned over and whispered in the little girl's ear, then gave her a fifteen-inch stick and a piece of charcoal.

Sara nodded, having received her instructions in secret.

"Remember," Drusilla cautioned. "If anyone asks, it's a game. Nothing more. Then drop the stick and run off."

"All right, Lady Drusilla. I won't fail you." She looked very solemn.

Drusilla smiled, rising to her full height. "Go on then. I'll see you at the maypole when you're done."

"What was that all about?" asked Edmund, another of the children.

"Just a game. Do you know how to pitch pennies?" She pulled out a handful of bronze coins, giving each of the children three, and facing the wall, gave them their first lesson in gambling.

"This is hardly proper behavior," said a familiar voice behind her.

Drusilla thought she might be in trouble for corrupting the children, but on turning, was met with a radiant smile and a wink. Raul fished into his own purse and pulled out more coin, stepping up to take his turn.

"It was nice of you to let the children win," said Drusilla, walking with Raul during a reprieve in the downpour. The earth smelled fresh and clean. Birds were singing merry tunes and trolling the lawn for worms.

Drusilla stopped short as they reached the maypole.

"Are you saying that I threw the competition?" he voiced with mock injury. He even made the face to go with it, or rather a poor attempt of it.

"You were bested by a six-year-old," she said, realizing he was the perfect height for her, having an advantage of maybe two inches. Her smile was a combination of things, and for the moment, she let it pass without analysis.

"Well, he was very good," said Raul, trying to maintain his serious demeanor, but breaking into a smile of his own instead.

Suddenly, she realized what she was doing? She could not be seen flirting shamelessly by the maypole with Raul, or anyone else for that matter. It would dash all her hard won intrigues to bits. The very real danger Ludo presented would return in full force.

Her arrest, her murder...

"I should very much want some tea," she said, feeling quite abusive, and knowing it was a thing he could not obtain readily.

"Yes, of course, my lady," he said. He seemed quite disappointed by the sudden reversal, but masked it well. "It would be my pleasure."

He left her standing there alone amongst the young lovers, all paired off but her, at the maypole. The Sun still shone, though bordered closely by a patchwork of heavy grey clouds. And though she stood in the brightest part of the day, surrounded by vibrant green lawn, she felt as though her Sun had gone away.

"Lady Drusilla," it was Sara tugging at her skirts. How long she had stood there, she didn't know. The shade of clouds had overtaken her spot. Rain had come, she vaguely realized that now, and tapered off to a drizzle of no conviction, which any moment would be gone again. It had been that way all day long.

More to the point, Raul hadn't returned yet. It couldn't have been more than twenty minutes. How long remained before his return was the question. A pressing one. She needed to leave.

Scanning the field, Drusilla saw Ludo, in the distance, walking purposefully her way. Turning her attention to the little girl, she smiled.

"Were you daydreaming?" asked Sara. "I had a frightful time getting your notice."

Drusilla nodded.

"I have your stick. All marked, X's and O's, just like you said."

"Good girl," said Drusilla, patting her on the head and taking the stick. She broke it in two, putting it in her purse, trading it out for the promised ribbon and coin."

"A real mermaid," said Sara reverently, looking at the coin. Drusilla pressed three more into her hand, Roman as coins made of bronze. "What are these for?"

"Your friends will have a new game to show you. They're like game pieces. You'll need them. Don't mix them up with your mermaid coin."

"I won't, Lady Drusilla," said Sara solemnly.

Ludo arrived.

Drusilla made her curtsy, Sara mimicked best she could, understanding she was dismissed.

"Thank you, Lady Drusilla," she called back, running off to find the other children.

"You certainly have a way with children," said Ludo.

Drusilla acknowledged him with a warm smile. "She's an exceptional little girl. Quite lovely."

"What was that stick she gave you?" He inched up a little closer, scrutinizing her or maybe just wanting to be close.

"The scales of justice."

He regarded her quizzically.

Raul was across the greensward, headed back towards her, tea cup in tow. It was time to go.

"You know children. So given to whimsy." She left him pondering that, and pretending she hadn't seen Raul, strode quickly at an angle away from him, burying herself in the social throng. She wished the clouds would burst. Anything to cover her escape. Anything to avoid what she must now do to Raul.

As it was, she could neither get to the exit gracefully, nor avoid her Sicilian suitor. The trouble was Ludo. Anything that happened now, he would be witness to. That she had left him without a word of goodbye was marginal enough behavior. This could sink her. Her life may very well depend on making the proper show of hand.

She couldn't think.

He was coming. She was out of options.

"My lady," he said, extending the cup.

"My lord," she said, nodding in passing with ever so slight a genuflection, not for a second acknowledging the tea or his intention to engage her.

He stood there stunned.

She felt terrible.

On she walked.

Within the keep, she pressed her back to a cool stone wall, breathing deeply. She had narrowly escaped disaster, and was more wound up for it than she would have been had it come to an exchange of iron and steel. Her heart hammered in her chest. She peeled away a glove, felt her neck. It was flushed, burning hot. She pushed damp hair away from her face and slumped, taking slow, deep breaths.

The look on Raul's face as she snubbed him invaded her serenity. He had been crestfallen. She opened her eyes, unable to stand the image.

Pulling herself upright, she scanned the hall both ways, and headed for Evelynn's room. Carpenters were at work repairing the doors when she arrived. She doubled back and headed for the veranda. She considered how vulnerable she was right now, without Linus, Percival, or Bridgette. No pigeons. No lifeline. She and she alone could make this mission a success, or end up like Sir Atreus at the bottom of a cliff.

Drusilla stared out over the loch to the mountain on the other side as she sat upon one of the terraced steps of the veranda by herself. The storm-burdened sky broiled and churned, casting shifting dark shadows upon the land. She took stock of her assets. There was Shamus, and her horse Perseus. She'd made an ally of the little girl, Sara MacTavish, but that had gone as far as it could. Putting her to use once was completely excusable as a "game". Were she to repeat such an action, notice might be taken. She could not endanger her.

Her thoughts went to Bridgette. She had put her in danger, and nearly lost her. As it was, the young woman's life would never be the same. No. Drusilla was on her own. The last help she would receive, that is, until Percival returned from Lion's Gate, and Linus brought back word from Roland, was in her purse.

The mountain looked lonely, the sky ready to burst. Soon all the guests would be within, and the world would be left to itself. She took the stick from her purse, fingers bypassing the band of gold, her engagement ring within.

The two halves of the stick still clung to unity by a strand of bark. She reconstructed it, fitting the two halves together, and examined the markings. Smudged and sooty, but still legible, these X's and O's would decide the fate of two men.

No match would be conclusive. It was the work of a child, after all. A match, however, could only happen by direct correlation. The odds of a random match just didn't seem at all likely.

Drusilla used points on her hands and compared them to first the X's, then the O's. Bayden's footprints, the X's, were a perfect match, confirming Bridgette's story. She didn't want to believe Ludo a part of it. Some small hope had held out against his involvement in the affair, despite the sheer weight of evidence to the contrary. The O's, however, were conclusive.

The scale tipped to guilt.

There was relief in knowing. She could now completely trust Bridgette. Her final instructions to Linus had been to treat her kindly but with due suspicion. "Be well on your ware," she had told him. "A small chance exists that she is yet a double agent serving our enemy."

She was glad that was not true.

Now, there was only the game. How to stay alive and in good graces with the brothers till the Midsummer Night's Ball? As a contingency, she had already made plans for their dispatching. Plans that now held no moral reservation.

Then why did she not feel the conviction of her reason? Some measure of uncertainty still divided her resolve. Drusilla struggled to pinpoint it. Her mind was still a muddle over recent affairs with Raul. Additionally, the storm was making her shield arm ache. The bruise must be bone deep. In the heat of battle, she had sublimated its true measure.

Pain mingled with her emotional turmoil, making rational thought an uphill effort. It would be folly to reason this any further right now. That much she knew.

Dark rain clouds pressed heavy on the land. It was uncommonly cold for a summer day, reminding her she was no longer in the blessed south of this isle. Drusilla wrapped arms around knees, feeling the chill making further ingress into her bones.

She had three weeks. Three weeks. More than anything, it was now a waiting game. Lightning cracked and thunder rolled somewhere north and over the mountain. She couldn't yet act. She wasn't ready. She would watch the brothers. See what more she could learn. Perhaps there were yet other confederates. Other pieces to this puzzle, undiscovered. No action need yet be taken.

Rain broke free from the sky, pelting down across the loch and the high courtyard where she sat now shivering, cocooned in deliberate inaction.

As the rain began to soak her, spotting the tawny flagstones, she recalled the night before, standing naked on her balcony, letting the heavens wash away all the blood. She had come here to learn the truth. She knew the truth. Additional intelligence would only confirm that.

Returning to Evelynn's room, Drusilla found the doors complete, the workmen gone, and a single servant, a young woman she knew worked in the kitchens, loitering just outside the door with a cup of tea. Pangs of guilt returned in force.

"Lady Drusilla," the young woman said, curtsying low.

"Malory, isn't it? Pray, what can I do for you?" Drusilla regarded the young woman thoughtfully. Were it not for circumstances of a near random nature, this woman of sixteen might well have been as close to her as Bridgette had become. And Bridgette? She shuddered to think that Bridgette would have been little more than an anonymous housemaid, still living under the weighty menace that plagued the local area.

The young woman handed her the tea. "Compliments of Raul of Sicily."

"Thank you," said Drusilla, accepting the steaming cup, silently vowing to protect this young woman as well. There wasn't a maid for miles safe from this new threat. The MacKays were not safe either. She would see to that.

CHAPTER FORTY

D RUSILLA DIDN'T EAT WITH the others that night. She went down to the kitchen after drying herself and taking her warmth a good while before the hearth in Evelynn's chambers, collected a hot bowl of broth, a kettle of tea, and retreated again to her quarters. Ludo sent a servant to inquire after her needs. She sent the young woman away with a thank you, and spent the evening alone, staring at her fire.

She had no memory of falling asleep, but woke in a fitful state sometime after dark, still clothed, upon the bearskin before a now dwindled flame dancing ethereal over a bed of blackened cinder.

Vague dreams had haunted her sleeping hours. They evaporated like the morning mist when she tried to recall them, leaving behind naught but a growing malaise.

The following night was much the same, excepting that, having no wish to alarm Ludo, she made a return to society, dining with the others when the day was done.

Her bruise was fading, purple giving way to yellow, though the bone still ached when the weather turned inclement, which was often. And though her bruise gave ground to good health's return, her heart did not mend so quickly. Every time she encountered Raul, she was either in Ludo's company, and could not pay him the consideration he deserved, or she was alone, and still feeling the wrong she'd done him, would make quick her escape.

The days till the ball were lessening, even as her resolve grew with each encounter. With each new day, she saw nothing to contradict her earlier theories concerning the brothers. Soon, Drusilla would put right to all that was wrong in Foxborough.

Days passed. The storm weather abated. Drusilla took the opportunity to go riding. She and Perseus spent hours in the sunshine, down in the lowlands amongst grazing sheep, and the hardworking peasantry of the land working the fields and tending their various beasts. She hadn't been sleeping well. Perhaps the excursion would clear her mind and wear her out, giving way to a deeper rest.

She gave Ludo just enough of her affections each day to forestall a reversal of his. Raul, she gave nothing but the trailing edge of her cloak, ever retreating at first sight of him.

Each night, Ludo had sent a housemaid around to inquire after her and see to her needs. Last night's visit had also come with a letter. Breaking the wax seal revealed a diagram done in shorthand. An opening move and his initials. Underneath, a blank page.

So they would play chess by correspondence. It was just as well. Anything to keep this intrigue going until the night of the ball. She had the serving girl wait but two minutes while she composed a reply. Her move expressed in the same shorthand and her own initial.

Drusilla and Perseus moved along a weathered ridge, below which, somewhere in the unseen distance, cattle lowed. Stands of trees stood in small clusters separated by large swaths of meadowland, peppered with the occasional bog and hidden patchworks of marshland. Together, they picked their path carefully, staying primarily to the high ground. This was treacherous territory for the four footed.

The world here was quiet. Inviting. The exercise a pleasant escape for an overburdened mind. Drusilla knew how to tend the beasts of the field, how to work the soil to bring forth its bounty. She could ride off into one of the nearby villages, make herself useful, and...

Her mind was drifting. A moment of escape. Nothing more. She had no desire to abandon her quest. To leave the young women of Foxborough to the jackals, which preyed upon them, all the while hiding in their midst.

A meadow pipit hopped along, near a dandelion in bloom. With a hop, its brown and white head darted down into the thick marsh grass, emerging with a prize. A small winged insect in its beak. Other pipits chirped and called back and forth to one another. Drusilla rode on.

The afternoon continued to lull away her cares till Drusilla was in a state of no mind. Perseus continued to pick his way along, keeping close to the ridgeline, which slowly gave way to gentler hills. Where a succulent bit of greenery would present itself, he would pause to nibble before moving on. There was no pressing business to be had this day.

Drusilla closed her eyes, enjoying the song of a distant mountain lark. A cool breeze wafted gently down from the nearby mountain, pulling at her hems, fluttering the rim of her hat. It felt good in contrast to the sunlight, which danced over closed lids, warming her face.

Her breathing slowed—

Drusilla's arm flailed out, grasping for any purchase. Desperate fingers found saddle horn, gripping tight. Her right foot was twisted in the stirrup, her left leg, skyward bent, and almost out of the saddle completely. With concentrated effort, she pulled herself back upright, shaking off the uninvited fog of sleep.

Careless.

She was alone, save for Perseus. In the countryside. Somewhere. She had been so careless.

She rolled her ankle over a few times, then put it back in the stirrup. It would be sore tonight. A small penance if it reminded her of her duty here.

Drusilla scanned the horizon, pulling tight, once more, the reins of her mind. The afternoon Sun was still high above the western horizon. Her nap must have been but momentary.

More assuring, there was no sign of anyone watching. No sign she had been followed.

She adjusted her hat, and clucked a quiet command, turning Perseus about. Her excursion was over.

Late in the afternoon, weary and well exercised, Drusilla planned to retire to bed early. She laid her newly made cloak over the chair where Bridgette used to doze. Her mind had numbed to the whole situation. She wanted to let it all slip away. Such thinking was a trap. She brought her mind back to sharp focus. She was in the lair of the enemy.

Pay attention.

Subtle incongruities nagged at her. She scanned her surroundings, looking for it. The room was not right. It was a maid's duty, at Foxborough Keep, to replenish water. Replace towels with fresh new ones. To tidy up in general. She had grown accustomed, though not entirely comfortable with, the many indulgences of gentried life. This was something more.

Drusilla wanted to strip off her boots, cast aside her clothes, and crawl within the comforting embrace of down and soft linen. She could hardly do so while hairs on the back of her neck stood on end. What was it?

Doors of glass were as she left them. Her boxes and trunks neatly ordered and in their proper spots. Had she become paranoid? Nothing stood out as particularly wrong. She had let down her guard today. That alone could account for her feelings of unease.

It didn't matter. She looked on. Something was assaulting her finer senses. She would continue her search till she rooted the culprit out.

Fresh firewood had been delivered. It stood neatly stacked in one corner. She continued to search the room with her eyes, tired though they were, disturbing nothing. Desk. Washstand. Pillows... and there it was. The edge of the bed, where the heavy down quilt draped gracefully over the edge, bore a most singular indentation to the fabric. A perfectly angular indent of particular height.

To test the theory, Drusilla pulled the cover off her nearest box, a small wooden crate of ornate design. She thought what a careful person might do, if striving hard to leave no trace of passage, whilst turning her room for clues or incrimination. If one was kneeling before the box, and having removed its lid, it would need to be set aside to free both hands for further search: set either upon the floor, atop the bed, or leaned against it. She tried the latter. The indentation of the fabric fit perfectly with the height and angle of the lid.

She had found the source of the mark, and looking within the box, noted that while the snoop had been careful, their attention to finer details was wanting. Every item had been examined and put back. Every item was subtly shifted or folded in a way betraying the spy's hand.

Someone had been through all her things. Turned her entire room with great care to cover their actions.

While she had carelessly passed the days, waiting for her moment to strike, her adversary had been active. Her guard let down, they had made inroads on the battlefield which must come. She was weary, and in need of sleep, but first, she did as they had. Turning everything she owned, everything in this room, to verify they had done the same.

Drusilla secured the room, and placed her dagger beneath her pillow before undressing further. She had not slept well in days. She needed to think things through more thoroughly. Her clarity of purpose felt somehow muddled. She lay upon the down, pulling covers over to warm her cold flesh. There were things that yet needed reasoning out. Things she should make certain of. She tried to order those thoughts. Somewhere, in the muddle of her own mind, a darkness seldom enjoyed in life took her.

THE ROOM WAS DARK. Quiet. Drusilla's mind was not.

As full wakefulness came back to her, a realization, until now nagging only at the periphery of her mind, asserted itself. Twisting her insides. Boot size was not enough.

Too many people shared those characteristics alike. She had been ready to convict on that merit alone. That and the word of Bridgette, compelling though it was. She was taking the word of a seventeen-year-old, self-confessed of being their confederate, unwilling albeit, in the matter of men's lives. She had to have more.

Her sense of conviction shattered, she sat up in the large and lonely room, staring into the deep shadows of the night.

The air was cool. Her head and neck fevered. It was enough. But it could not be. Not might exercised out of suspicion. Not right by suspicion and circumstance. Not right because of an accuser who may well be far from guiltless and without lacking motive.

No.

Might for right.

Might must only be exercised as the strong hand of justice. She must know. In no equivocal terms, she must know. Nothing short of that was right. Nothing short of knowledge was worthy of the label justice. Of the principle of right.

Drusilla rose, and standing against the chill of the room, which felt cool and good upon her brow, moved to her water basin, washing away the night terrors. Splashing cold goodness upon her face, letting it wash away the base impulse that was driving her to rashness. The bracing air served a harsh reminder of the hour. Ignoring her discomfort, she threw on her dressing gown, and not so much as a bother with slippers, slid out into the hall, which was darker still.

Moments later, she found herself standing once again in front of Raul's door. Immediately, she regretted her lack of footwear, but the dressing gown was modesty enough for now.

She rapped at his door, and again, when she did not get an immediate response. She heard him wake with a start, his bare feet dropping to the floor. An instant later, she heard the gladius lifted gingerly from a spot near the door.

The latch slid open, and Raul, clothed again only to the waist, pulled open the door. Despite the sleep still lingering in his eyes, he seemed genuinely pleased, as always, to see her. He nodded, laying gladius aside.

"My lady. How may I serve you?"

Drusilla cast a furtive glance down the hall in both directions, and seeing no one, slipped quickly inside, pushing shut the door.

Only the faint light of stars penetrated the gloom. But it was peaceful here, too. Isolated. Not like her room, which stood ever naked to the elements and the deep mountain loch.

"I beg your indulgence. I know the hour is late, and my behavior most questionable. And regretfully, I cannot explain myself at present, but—"

Raul took her hands in his, stilling her eruption of babbling.

"You have but to name it."

There it was again. That quiet strength he'd hidden so well when first she'd met him. His patience, though she'd roused him from his sleep and none too gently. And chivalry. Of all his qualities, it was that she admired most in Raul.

"Light your candle, then. I would measure your shoes."

Chapter Forty-One

D RUSILLA SLUNK BACK INTO her own chambers. Barred the door. Draping her dressing gown over the chair, she crawled back under the down quilt and huddled against the cold.

Raul's feet were of identical measure to Ludo's.

Her theory had been a lot of stuff and nonsense. Certainly not enough measure to convict two men to death.

CHAPTER FORTY-TWO

T HE HOVEL, FOR IT could not be called much more than that, was
nevertheless neatly kept. A functional home with herbs growing
near the windows, chickens pecking about a fenced yard, vegetables and
fruits growing on the side sheltered from the loch and around back. Still,
there were signs of neglect. Recent signs that only one who'd also worked
the land would see.

These signs did not escape Drusilla as she stood before the small cob
house, its thatched roof still wet with the morning rain which had only
just subsided. She set the basket of things, needing both mending and a
good scrub, down on the single slate slab which passed rather charmingly
for a porch. Most notably amongst her clothes was her red and black
dress. She had spared her own washbasin. Too many questions might
have been raised her fifth or sixth trip down the stairs for fresh water.

The rust red chickens reminded her of home, in Ys, growing up. There
were also black chickens, and one that was almost golden in the right
light. She swung the stick and twine gate open, securing it behind her,
feet sinking deep into the wet shore grass, stirring up a small cloud
of recently-busy grasshoppers who now fled to the relative safety of
five-feet away, disappearing once again into the thick greenery.

A few of the chickens bawked and looked to her hands, watching her.
They hadn't been fed in a while, though with all the insect life about, they
were hardly starving.

"Sorry," she apologized. "I haven't got any seed for you."

The chickens lost interest in her quickly, continuing their late morning
forage. Drusilla crossed the barren patches, where the chickens had
scratched away a living, and stooped to poke her head within their coop.

She hitched up her dress, the tan-and-black one, and made her way inside, head kept low for fear of striking it on the rafters of the low roof. Two days worth of laying in each of the nests. That concerned her. The more eggs per nest, the greater the chance of one becoming broken. And once a chicken acquired a taste for eggs, there could be no undoing it.

She lifted the first of the eggs.

Cracks in the roof work allowed Sun to stray in in slanted beams. She held the specimen up, and each egg thereafter, letting the light of day shine through. A dark circle with a clear center within would herald new life. Any fracture could spell trouble for the behavior of the chicken, and their future usefulness as egg producers.

Her inspection proved nothing irreparable had occurred in their caretaker's absence. Satisfied, she added each egg to her gathered skirts until she had them all collected: about a dozen-and-a-half. Drusilla guessed this had been Helen's job, before she had gone missing. Now, a grieving mother did the work, and, at least on this occasion, had not found the energy nor will to carry out such a simple yet important task.

All the nests accounted for and tended, it was time to make her presence known.

The woman who answered the front door was of a matronly shape, but that she had recently lost weight showed in her sagging features. Seeing Drusilla, she quickly put on a half-convincing cheer, dusting off her pinafore with two age-gnarled hands.

"My lady," she spoke in a revered hush tinged with fear, curtsying low.

"Madame," said Drusilla, glancing down at the eggs. "Would you?"

"Oh, yes, yes," said the woman, rushing all of ten feet to the tiny kitchen, all part of the single one-room structure. The small family-made home. She took down a hanging wicker basket, scurrying back to Drusilla's side, where together, they made the transfer of speckled eggs.

As the woman hung the basket, now abulge with its new claimed bounty, Drusilla collected her laundry basket and brought it in.

"Forgive me the intrusion. I'm Drusilla."

"M'lady." Another curtsy

"You must be Nettle?"

"I've been called worse." The woman smiled at her own joke, but there was no mirth in her eyes.

Drusilla had no wish to open the recent wound this lady was so obviously still suffering. Her eyes cast about the small hovel, buying seconds as the silence between them widened.

The tiny house was smaller than the suite Evelynn had once called home, and more recently which Drusilla enjoyed, yet this was a house shared by three. Until recently...

Sun streamed in one of what passed for windows in this miniature abode. The shutters were open to the morning breeze, an omnipresent view of the loch dominated. Normally that would have been enough to jar her back to the present. But what arrested Drusilla's attention was three little rag dolls lined up along a sill made of split pine, and worn smooth not by craft but by decades of utility.

Each doll was hand sewn, lovingly crafted. She could see it in each of their dear little faces. A redhead, a brunette, and a strawberry blonde. Each with her own painstakingly crafted dress, stockings, shoes with tiny buckles, and pinafores of white linen.

The needlework was exquisite. The little faces bright and happy. Who could take the life of someone who only added light to the world?

Drusilla closed her eyes a moment, letting the crisp highland air calm her spirit.

"She makes them from rags." It was Nettle. Her voice came in trembling waves through the sun-spotted darkness of Drusilla's closed lids. "I take in laundry. I did. I haven't since..."

This would not be easy. Could not be. A mother had lost her daughter, and in the turmoil, the support of her husband as well.

"Every Foxborough girl has one. And even one or two as far as Inverness. She takes rags. Nothing more than an old cast off or two, and from them..."

Nettle broke off, too distraught for speech.

Drusilla looked to her, standing there, hands working themselves into a fit, waiting quietly now as she knew she would.

"I'm so very sorry," said Drusilla, knowing even before she uttered it just how truly inadequate those words were.

Nettle teared up nonetheless.

FOXBOROUGH KEEP LOOMED LIKE a dark predator over the small fishing village as she made her way up the path and back into the monstrous lie that was her current lot in life. But as she climbed up through the field grass and wildflowers, she saw that its dark stain did not blot all. There was an extent to their reach, a limit to their abuse of power.

Nettle had many stories of the loch serpent. As she washed and mended the things Drusilla had brought her, she related a few of her choicest ones at Drusilla's encouragement.

The stories were similar to her own first encounters. Imagined shapes in the shifting dark water. Hinted at purpose. She told of a young man who watched from behind a towering fir as the beast took one sheep from amongst his small flock. But there was nothing of real substance to anchor on. Drusilla's own experience, one she kept entirely quiet about, encompassed far more than all the stories and legends combined that Nettle could recount or spin. In particular, she suspected the last of the stories was richly embellished.

"It spoke as plainly as you or I, telling the young man upon the road he could keep his life, but only if he brought the beast three fell dear, and a maiden with long golden hair before the next full Moon."

Nettle's eyes widened as she seemed to recall the fanciful tale. "Oh, but that clever Jack, he never for a moment intended to give up his lady love. Each fawn he brought the beast on consecutive nights was tainted with a slow-acting sleep potion. The first disguised with cloves and honey, with which he had prepared the succulent feast. The second with..."

Drusilla had heard similar tales. Usually, the subject was a child-snatching ogre, a bridge-guarding troll, or village-terrorizing giant. In each case though, the clever hero outwitted the greedy beast, and in the end, vanquished it to a well deserved fate, or in this case, lengthy slumber.

She doubted there was any veracity to the tale at all. But irregardless, the beast was awake now. And she didn't think it had the mind or language skills for parlay.

Sounds of the festival now competed with songbird and rustle of wind as she drew nigh of the keep's high walls. Their tawny stone looked almost white as she passed from the shadow of a great maple tree into the full light of day. Extending beyond the walls of Foxborough, mighty firs stood sentinel, like Titans of old. Her daydream dispelled, she steeled her mind against the task of the coming days.

It was time to turn the spigot.

The brothers had secrets they guarded more closely than their own life's blood. Passive observation had no more to give. An active campaign of spying and sabotage was in order. She would orchestrate events such that they felt the pressure of her presence. No more could they wander off without feeling her eyes upon them. Their private lives would begin to evaporate at the edges, and as they did, the brothers themselves would become more paranoid and subversive. Such was human nature.

People, she had learned from the careful art of observation, were, at their core, truthful creatures. All deception exacted a cost. Deception was a constant labor. Turn up the pressure, and there will be cracks. And what issues forth from the fissures will be truth. For that is what is at the heart of all mortal men.

It was time to bleed some truth.

Chapter Forty-Three

Drusilla's campaign against the brothers had done nothing to place her in the good grace of Bayden. Each time she allowed herself to be spotted by him, his glare seemed to deepen, and the gulf between them grew ever wider. Ludo took amusement from the whole affair. She often winked at him, or gave him other indication to believe he was the sole object of her stalking.

His crooked grin was generally a mixture of his fondness for her and his delight at her subtle cruelties towards Bayden. Yet all she really wanted was the truth and to be done with it all.

The sky had been moody all day. The threat of storm intermingled with violent outbursts, which lit the highland landscape, and plunged it into a twisted series of mad caricatures. Sudden shadows. Ghastly fades to white. Driving rain followed by drizzle.

Most of the festivities had been relocated to the great hall with smaller groups splintering off, occupying the sewing room, one of several parlors, and during times of respite, a few brave souls out in the courtyard sipping variously, hot broth or spiced ciders whilst wrapped tight in their heavy cloaks, relating old war stories one to the other.

Drusilla mingled a while, refraining from adding tales of her own deeds to the mix. In time, the sky darkened again, and a bitter wind drove in from the northwest. The surface of the loch picked up once again, transforming from rain speckled calm to a heavy chop. The assault came like an endless army sweeping down from the north. Ceaseless sheets of rain battered the keep. Rank after rank, white-crested waves, breaking against rock and village below.

A flash emanated somewhere in the next valley, casting the ridgeline in sharp contrast. The rumble that followed, though still far off, was felt in the very flagstone upon which Drusilla and the other guests stood. It occurred to her that this settlement, remotely tucked into the north country, would not stand the test of time. Rome had fallen to the barbarian hordes, yet the city itself still stood. It would always stand. The alternative was difficult to imagine. Foxborough, however, was built on a cliff edge, the village below upon a fragile strip of stone and sand barely above the water level. At the moment, in fact, it was a shallow flood plain.

The hill would not stand forever.

A good portion of her own fair seaport, Ys, had already been claimed by the sea. Only for its sprawl, had portions of it survived the rogue wave which had visited them a generation earlier. Built on sound foundations upon the higher ground, much of the town remained to tarry on.

Foxborough keep, in particular, was a worrisome thing. Sitting right at the edge of the cliff was bad enough. But now, having experienced first hand, how hollowed out it was below—the network of caverns and man-made dungeons, only a fraction of which she had explored—gave Drusilla every reason to believe, in the long span of history, the loch would claim it too.

She pulled her new cloak tighter about her standing in sheeting puddles and runoff, the collected water finding its way back to the loch, and the sea beyond. All the other guests had already retreated to the interior of the keep, congregating wherever there was a hearth and free flowing drink.

It was cold, a rare moment of solitude. Constant vigil had taken its toll. Slipping into the heavy shadow of the rain slick ballroom, Drusilla took a last look at the dark sky and decided to return to her chambers for an afternoon recharge. She would resume her skulking after a nap.

A QUIET RAPPING AT her door woke Drusilla.

Outside, the storm continued to rumble, shaking the very stone of the keep. The sky was dark, though the Sun still stalked the heavens.

Quietly, she seized her dagger of steel, padding silent across the floor, and released the crossbar. It sounded like Percival from the knock, but care had to be taken nonetheless.

The lad was drenched. At his shoulder was an oversize satchel bag just visible beneath his oilskin cloak, looking much drier than he.

Drusilla motioned Percival in, shutting the door behind him and taking his cloak, then urged him in whispered tones to sit before the fire, now burnt down to embers but still giving off good warmth.

Without a word, she stole into the hall, closing the door behind her. A quick wander round the corner found one of the servants. It was Elsie. Maybe a year or two older than Bridgette. Touching her shoulder, the young woman started. Drusilla had become so accustomed to skulking. Her every move flowed from silence.

"Forgive me," she apologized.

"M'lady?" Elsie curtsied low, holding the corners of her pinafore. "I was lost in my own thoughts. 'Tis I who beg your apology."

"None is required. To be lost in thought is one of life's finer pleasures."

The young woman smiled at that, quickly averting her eyes once again. "How may I serve you?"

"I'm cold to the bone, and a bit famished." Drusilla thought wistfully of Bridgette, hoped she was adjusting to London Town. Wondered if she might even be finding the gentler temperament of its people to her liking...

If all was well, they had arrived days ago, Roland had a response for her, and Linus, hopefully with a second driver, and a fresh team of horses, would already be on his way back to her—

"... hot supper."

Drusilla realized the maid had said something to her that ended in the only two words she had registered.

"I apologize," she said.

"Oh, but for nothing, m'lady."

"And tea. I could very much use a cup of tea."

"Of course, m'lady. Right away."

DRUSILLA TURNED THE BLADE over in her hand again, drawing her thumb crosswise over the serrated edge. It tested true. The quality of work was exquisite. Her Aphrodite costume, a thing of rare beauty. She and Percival sat upon the bearskin before the fire, he, supping upon the last of his soup, Drusilla inhaling the steam coming off her mug.

"Be careful of the crown," he said. "To match your drawing, the artisan had to grind the shells to the new shape, and said the upper edges are fragile."

Nature's fury rattled the windowed wall, followed by yet more lightning and another round of thunder. There was no sign yet it would let up as day slowly crept towards night.

Drusilla examined the seashell-themed tiara, shells ascending in scalloped waves to a central point as regal as any monarch's crown. It was a thing of beauty, and now she knew why it had come in a special made, velvet-lined box.

The kit, especially for the box and sword, was not small. She would need a place to hide her new acquisition till the day of the ball, which was still half a week off. Were it discovered, given what she had seen in the dungeons below, her life expectancy would quickly be reduced to zero.

She cast her mind about... thinking of an appropriate hiding spot. Her room certainly wouldn't do. Recent events had proven that. Her bow had been stolen from its secret compartment. Equally disturbing, her room had been turned inch by meticulous inch. Her hiding spot would have to be brilliant—

Percival broke her silent contemplation.

He looked past glass doors sheeted with rain. "It's like camping," and he patted the rug, glanced to the fire. "Only better."

The young lad stood, stretching his long legs.

"Leave the bowl," she said. "I'll check that the way is clear."

"And my job now?"

"Same as before. And keep a vigil out for the return of Linus. He is still away to London Town. I need to know the very moment of his return."

"I will see it done."

She looked the lad up and down with a sense of pride for the hand she'd taken in mentoring him through his burgeoning adulthood. "Did you grow another inch?"

"There is a good cook at Lion's Gate." He grinned.

Seeing Percival off and seeing to it no one else did, Drusilla barred the door once again and went back to her ruminations. Where to hide her new kit?

In the house of her enemy, she must secrete it away. Discovery, while in her possession, was death.

Chapter Forty-Four

D RUSILLA DARED NOT SLEEP that night for fear she would fall into a slumber which would carry her through till morning. Her work must be done tonight—accomplished by stealth. A quiet household would be best.

Light instantly displaced shadow, playing across the loch, viewed from the rain-bleared glass panes of Camille's room. The Sun had long since set. Darkness reigned under cloud-sodden skies in the absence of lightning. Thunder shook the castle as storm and bluster rattled the fragile panes and continued to menace the very ironwork which housed them.

During lulls in the natural display, Drusilla listened for evidence the house was settling down for the night. Someone or another, mainly the servants, were up at any given hour. That much could not be avoided. To be seen, or worse, questioned whilst transporting her new kit, could not happen.

Hearing no activity, Drusilla stole into the hallway on a mission of initial reconnaissance. A man and a woman, courtiers she had seen flirting upon the greensward on multiple occasions, were leaned, one upon the other at the end of the hall, giggling quietly.

Drusilla retreated.

And waited.

Nearly an hour and several fact-finding forays later, the hall was clear. The house silent save for the persistent rumble of the heavens.

Drusilla had already procured a large sewing needle from the quilting room, and a skein of thread. She collected the satchel containing her Aphrodite costume and her newly forged sword with its fascinating scaled edge. All things in tow, hidden best she could beneath her cloak, she ventured out and into the belly of the keep.

Skulking along the corridors and down the servants' staircase, she went, hiding in doorframes or behind columns of cold stone at the passage of the occasional guard or servant. The latest guard had stopped to adjust his costume, pulling at a leather strap at his side, then began fidgeting with his sword belt.

Drusilla waited patiently, modulating her own breath to his. Using his presence as camouflage for her own. She was trapped in a corner. Should he come this way, there was no retreat. But he had no reason to come this way. No reason to turn.

But he did.

His eyes swept over the spot she hid.

Drusilla remained motionless, no longer breathing, eyes squinted to slits to mask their reflectiveness. He stared a moment into the spot she occupied, wrapped in her dark, earth-toned cloak. It was a deeper brown than the surrounding stone, but it just might do in the poor light of the keep's interior. She kept her gaze lower than his. Unmoving, without challenge. It was enough to watch his feet. They would betray any move he made. Only vaguely, at the periphery of her vision, could she see the rest of his body.

And then his posture changed. Relaxed. He turned away from her and moved on.

Drusilla breathed.

The guard had been the final obstacle. Drusilla found herself alone before the great door leading to the den. The beasts carved into the dark oak looked sinister in the shifting, low light. No sound but the storm beyond, no light but that which nature painted the night, she pushed through and into the room. It smelled of leather, and rain, and parchment. Embers glowed in the great hearth. A new stack of logs waited to the side of the mighty fireplace, next to big iron hooks for hauling them into the flame.

Lightning flashed, illuminating several dozen glass eyes. An afterimage persisted, fang and claw and fur, as thunder peeled and rattled through the room, subtly disturbing all its contents.

Drusilla was attempting to adjust her eyes to the gloom when another bolt lit the den—the brown bear, massive forepaws in the air, mouth gaping, flashed into existence and was as quickly gone.

Drusilla moved to the corner where it stood, mounted upon a slab of stone, anchored by thick iron rods which disappeared into its legs at mid-calf. She picked a spot and knelt before the poor stuffed creature, removing a glove. Delicately, she drew her hand across the fur. Searching. Searching.

Till she found the seam.

She drew her dagger, spared the bear a moment of her sympathy, then sliced in and upwards, splitting the stitches as she went. A few moments later, she was surrounded in mounds of sheep's wool as the bear shed its winter weight.

The spot she knelt upon was drafty. The den was on the same side of the keep as her assigned quarters. But unlike her posh arrangement, no glass lined these long, narrow windows. Only the heavy maroon drapes stood against the elements. Effective to a degree.

Drusilla shoved her new, sheathed sword up and deep into the bear's chest, below the rib cage. The scent of the storm mingled strongly with that of the loch here. Being on the ground floor, only the height of the cliff and those curtains separated her from the loch. The first day she'd arrived at the keep, she hadn't taken any special notice of the curtains. The raging bonfire, and the close proximity of the two MacKay brothers, had occupied the center of her attention. It had been a sunny day, calm and unobtrusive. Now, with wind whipping up the rain-soaked edges, they seemed like living things.

An extension of the deep waters just beyond.

More stuffing littered the space between Drusilla's knees as she tried to keep it from scattering in the cold draft. She plucked an errant piece skittering across the floor and pressed it back into the fold. There would be too much, she realized. As tightly packed as it had been, it couldn't all go back in. She thought to burn the excess in the fireplace. Burnt wool would not make for a pleasant smoke. And though the flue was drafting well, it would still taint the local surroundings.

She decided it was too much a risk. She would pack it out and dispose of it some other way.

In she shoved the rest of her kit, the Aphrodite costume occupying the spot where the bear's stomach had once been. The room lit, faded back to darkness. A thunderous boom followed shortly after. Time for needle and thread. She put her glove back on.

As Drusilla worked the needle in and out of the tough hide, it reminded her of simpler times. The storms in Ys came right off the sea. Mending was a common task when ocean waters rose and skies blackened. She had filled many hours pulling thread as nature put on its fitful displays.

Only a handful of inches to go. The hide was tough. The work slow-going. Still, another fifteen minutes—

Footsteps.

Two men.

Drusilla put a tack stitch in halfway up the open slit, then pushed the needle into one of the two remaining holes, hiding it and the excess thread away. Ruffing the fur to disguise the flaw, her eyes darted about the room, footsteps drawing near.

The two men slowed as they approached the door to the den. Stopped outside.

They were coming in.

There were many hiding places in the room. None of them good. Not if they lit candles or stoked the fire. Not if they had come here for some specific object. Who knew what corner of the room might gain their attention.

Too late for the door. A hand was already upon it.

She closed her eyes a moment, exhaling a quiet breath that was almost a sob. The best choice was the one she could not make. Yet she must, and quickly.

Gathering up the wool in her skirts, into the windowsill she went, pushing past the heavy damp cloth with one hand. Eyes straining not to see what was everywhere. Storm-filled skies and a horrifying plunge to the angry waters below.

Chapter Forty-Five

T HE STONE WAS RAIN-SLICK and mossy. Drusilla slid out and nearly over the edge the second she stepped upon it. Her skirts unfurled and whipped about her legs as both hands shot to either side of the window.

Bits of wool were instantly swept up and away, gone in a blink. The maroon curtain, which may as well have been black from this side, slapped closed behind her, leaving her white-knuckled and panicked, clawing gloved fingers into any crevasse of stone that would stay her ejection.

Wind sucked and pushed the curtain. She pressed herself low and to one side of the window, which was just wider than her shoulders and nearly twice her height. Every time the heavy cloth slapped Drusilla, she feared her position would be revealed.

Somewhere, in the forest on the far side of the loch, lightning struck. Thunder boomed across the water, reverberating through her chest. But it was the flash which alarmed her.

With every stroke of lightning, Drusilla's silhouette would be imprinted upon the inner chamber of the den. With the storm all about her, the only hope was to keep as low and still as possible, relying upon the menagerie of objects within to mask her presence.

The old stone was less than perfect. Drusilla found ingresses amongst the stonework, anchoring her fingers, pressing shoulders and feet into opposite edges to the point they were soon going numb.

Rain drove against her. The heavy wet curtain continued to batter and push at her. Nothing more could be done.

Being situated the best she could, Drusilla strained to pay attention to what transpired on the other side of the curtain. Drinks were poured.

Chairs were shifted, then ignored. The two men paced back and forth. Two lions. It was the brothers.

Ludo chucked a log absently onto the fire. Funny how she could now tell their two gaits apart. Men she'd only known weeks. He picked up a piece of iron, presumably the poker, and prodded new flames to life.

"It's late, Brother." It was Ludo. He sounded irritated.

Another log, this one bigger, was hoisted onto the fire with the iron hooks. It was Bayden. The log was enormous, easily outweighing her by half again. He did it easily.

He picked up his drink again. Said something that was lost in a great peal of thunder.

Drusilla pressed herself further into shadow. Could she seep into the very walls right now, she would. The threat of discovery was omnipresent. The musty weight of the deep mahogany curtains pressed against her, lit by a further off flash. Another succession of lightning cast the whole of the valley in white-hot light, reminding her of the razor-thin edge she walked between life and a disastrous end.

Thunder echoed between the mountains and rolled over the loch picking up an eerie timbre before rattling the stonework to which she clung. Flames burst to life as one of the brothers doused them in alcohol, emptying his glass upon it. Fire roared, then crackled, as the normal state of combustion resumed, albeit at a much more active pace.

Rain continued to drive against the curtain and the window's new occupant. Drusilla would be soaked to the bone before this affair was over. That is, if she wasn't hauled into the den. A possibility she didn't care to entertain. Or worse...

She looked to the waters below, starkly white under the electric sky, and immediately regretted it. The knot in her stomach tightened. She closed her eyes, preferring instead to devote all her attention to listening.

Over the crackle of a great log being consumed most actively by flame, she listened to the exchange between Ludo and Bayden and tried to shut everything else about her predicament from mind.

"She watches us like a hawk. I tell you, Brother, she knows. She is responsible for everything."

Their voices were both muffled by cloth, and storm, purposely cloaked in whisper. But that the speaker was Bayden was still unmistakable.

"I suppose you still fancy she killed eight armed men—veteran troops, I might add, of the first order—single-handedly." It was Ludo championing her, even as Bayden launched another accusation.

"As I have said before, dear Brother," that little bit must have been through gritted teeth, the words grated so, "she may have one confederate, or many. That is why we cannot simply dispatch her."

"Or is it because you fear her?" said Ludo, clearly taunting. "After all, any woman capable of killing even two of your best soldiers in one engagement could certainly put an end to you."

"You know I'm better than any ten men," said Bayden. The thought of it was sobering, for she knew he was not boasting. He paced closer to where she hid.

Just hang on.

Drusilla pressed further into the stone until she knew it would leave bruises. Her fingers ached with the effort she exerted upon them.

Hang on.

She felt her lower lip trembling, the sob which wished to escape driven back to boil in her stomach. Air, charged and fresh, carried the scent of the loch. Her grip tightened until the very bones and sinew of her hand threatened to snap.

A few inches of rain-slicked stone stood between her and the unimaginable. Squeezing her eyes shut, for she could take it no longer, she held on.

When Bayden spoke again, it startled her. He was just on the other side of the curtain. "I'm sick of it, Ludo. Her days are numbered on one hand. After the ball, I'm going to give that wench, Drusilla, to the beast. No finer offering could be made. Surely Aphrodite will hear my prayers then."

With Bridgette gone, Drusilla was the next target. A chill more frigid than any the storm could summon, passed through her.

"Find somebody else, Brother. Drusilla's to be my bride."

"You always were a little touched in the head. I'll do as I please. Find somebody else to love you. She only plays with you."

"Lies," said Ludo, raising his voice. His glass smashed into the fireplace. Flames exploded, sending a blast of heat even the curtain could not mask.

"Not so loud, Brother."

"There's no one around." Ludo lowered his tone nonetheless. Even so, there was increased menace behind it. "If you hurt Drusilla, chasing your demented theory about her, I will kill you, Brother." He spat the last word like it was a bitter poison too long in his mouth.

He was loyal. Devoted. Admirable qualities if she didn't know what a monster he was.

"I seem to remember, you were all for sending the Elite Guard out after your dear Drusilla," said Bayden, pouring himself more of the combustible liquid. More lightning erupted in a chain reaction traveling from one end of the valley to the other.

As the thunder quieted, she heard Ludo speaking softly, his voice raw with emotion, edged with regret and new-found conviction. "That was before she loved me, or at least, before I knew. She's not the saboteur you're looking for."

Drusilla was satisfied, beyond any question now, that they were guilty of all she had suspected and more. It was no longer just Bridgette's word, nor the measurement of their shoes. The way was now clear for her final tasks here. She might kill them sooner, but Linus was not yet returned, and the village might not be too friendly to her after witnessing the demise of their beloved lords.

Chapter Forty-Six

D RUSILLA MASSAGED THE BACK of one hand with the thumb of her other. Both ached from last night's exercise in survival, and she had added new bruises to her back and rump to boot, so vigorously had she pressed herself into the window frame. It had taken her hours to get properly warm. And though sleep, when it had finally come, delivered her a much needed, deep and dreamless escape, it was not enough, and ended too soon.

The rooster's crow had wrested her from sorely needed recuperation, and a restless mind had kept her from seeking new repose. So, joining the others much earlier than was her custom, Drusilla had watched events upon the greensward all morning and into the early afternoon. She needed to make certain plausible gaps in the social interplay existed into which to weave her own fiction.

The field of grass was particularly vibrant, the sky all but devoid of cloud. It brought her no joy. Of all the beauty of the day, she could stand least to look upon the flowers. Every color in nature had chosen to bloom anew after the storm. Come alive with the very vibrancy of life itself.

She had not seen Raul today. Drusilla could not blame him. Not after last night. Not after her late night visit to his room, after the brothers left, and she was able to pry her fingers from the window masonry and skulk back into the interior of the keep after processing some of what she had overheard in the whispered conversation that night...

Her heart ached.

Sara MacTavish's bright young face appeared at her side along with a tug at her skirts. What was she even wearing? Drusilla had dressed, more or less, in a fog. The white dress with the green embroidered flowers. Her hair pulled back with a simple ribbon. What color she didn't know.

Sara was in all white. Expensive white, but simple. Around her neck was the blue ribbon Drusilla had given her.

"Why are you sad, Lady Drusilla?"

A pang of grief shot through Drusilla.

"I read a very sad poem last night," she lied. "Have you heard of Tristan and Yseult?"

Sara shook her head no.

"Do they die?"

"A bit morbid for a day like this," said Drusilla, looking skyward.

Sara's eyes followed hers upwards, and together they watched a lazy cloud slowly morph from one imagined thing to another. She hoped the little girl was seeing things which brought her happiness. Drusilla sucked in the start of a sob before it could escape her lips. She saw nothing in the clouds. Her mind was numb with despair.

Timelessly, the sky changed. Even the subtle angle of the light and shade of blue transformed. New clouds formed out of nothing, while others paled, and faded back into the blue. Sara was first to break the shared silence.

"Can you really read?" Her voice was tinged with awe.

"I really can," said Drusilla, looking kindly upon the girl. "Can you keep it a secret?"

She nodded.

"There are some brilliant flowers over by the cherry tree. Would you care to undertake an heroic quest?"

"Yes, Lady Drusilla." The girl's eyes sparkled with the hope of adventures and glory. She felt empty. Feelings that rose to the level of hope were far removed from her current fugue state.

"Do you know what golden gorse is?"

Sara shook her head no.

"Whin?"

Again, no.

"Snapdragons?"

"Oh, yes. They're lovely."

"These are a bit like the snapdragon, but they grow on a savage bush full with spikes. You must be very careful when you pick them not to prick yourself, nor to bruise the petals. They are delicate."

"I will be careful."

"Good. The flowers, themselves, are yellow. I need a dozen or so. It is late in the year. They will not be in bloom much longer. Can you do it?"

The little girl had a new look of importance. She straightened to her full height, which wasn't much, and answered solemnly. "I can."

"When you have the petals, take them to the kitchen and have them made into a tea. Leave the tea with instructions that it be brought to my room at nightfall.

"Are you enjoying the game I taught your friends?"

"The one with coins?"

"The one with coins." Drusilla smiled.

"I am. Very much so. Thank you, Lady Drusilla." Sara gave her best curtsy.

Drusilla removed six bronze pieces from her purse, handing one to the little girl. "For the services of the one who makes the tea."

Sara nodded.

Drusilla gave her another. "For the servant who delivers the tea."

"Yes, my lady"

And then she handed over the other four.

"And what of these?" asked Sara.

"One each for you and your friends."

"Oh, thank you, Lady Drusilla." Another curtsy.

"You are most welcome. Now go. Fulfill your quest. And mind the spikes"

"I will." Sara ran off towards the northeast run of wall, which would, if memory served, contain the golden gorse bush.

She watched until the girl was little more than a puff of white and riot of golden-red amongst the variegated and shifting gentry.

Without Sara to distract her, and Ludo not yet separated from the crowd, Drusilla's thoughts returned to last night, and her despair deepened. She felt hot tears welling below the surface, and turned away from the throng, fighting to keep them at bay.

Having stolen her way back to the relative safety of the keep, bone-chilled and drenched through, she had skulked under cloak of darkness, leaving only wet footprints, not to her own chambers, but instead to Raul's door.

She could hear his quiet breaths, her wet ear pressed to the oak. Sleeping. She wanted so badly to leave it. So badly to just slip away and ignore the problem. The hall remained deserted as she wrestled with the logic of the situation.

Bayden, and Ludo too, until recently, suspected Drusilla to have at least one co-conspirator in some dark campaign leveled against them. They didn't believe she was here for the lake views, or for the festivities. Ludo believed her to be a thief, and a cruel and devious woman now under the spell of his love. Bayden believed much worse of her. The night's overheard conversation had taught her much. The most valuable lesson being the hardest to reconcile.

Those closest to her, were, by association, in the greatest danger.

Whom might they suspect. Certainly Raul. If she were an outside observer looking in, Drusilla herself could believe no less than that he worked with her. The harmless flirtations she had allowed were not so harmless.

To protect Raul, and to keep Bayden guessing rather than acting, Drusilla needed to put an end to her young suitor's hope. And she needed to solidify her position with Ludo. Enough conflict and doubt already existed in his mind, plying his will to her purpose would require but a nudge. A most artfully played nudge.

But that night, as she sheltered near Raul's door, a puddle of rainwater collecting around her, Drusilla had no thoughts of how she would nudge Ludo. Last night had been about Raul. Putting proper distance between herself and her Sicilian.

Keeping him safe.

She sat in the grass, picking a dandelion, twirling it absently in her fingers. Tiny insects, denizens of the lawn, moved about as oblivious to her idle movements as she was to the events of the day. Last night still haunted Drusilla. Last night recurred in her memory over and over. A bitter charade.

Somehow, in that night born of urgency, Drusilla had found her courage. Leather on oak, she gave the door a light rap, ever fearful of discovery.

Like the soldier she suspected he was, Raul was quick to rise. Quicker still with his gladius as he plied the door open a couple of cautious inches.

Seeing it was her, Raul laid the sword aside. Placed it to its familiar notch beside the door, and took her wet-gloved hand, kissing it slowly, making all the more difficult what she must do next. Making her breath come short, and her chest burn. Dark eyes stared into hers. She wanted nothing more, at that moment, then to escape into that darkness and be done forever with this ludicrous skullduggery.

"My lady."

Drusilla could not find her voice. He was bare to the waist, as each time before, wearing only his Roman kilt. Her hand trembled in his. She was so cold except for his touch. Except for the fire he lit so readily, so deep within her, wherever his touch fell.

"You're soaked to the bone." He took her other hand in his as well.

Her knees melted.

Raul exchanged both her hands to one of his. His gentle strength cradled her, kept her weakened legs from buckling. With palm and fingers of his other hand, he took her temperature. His touch was hot upon her brow, and only served as bellows, fanning the heat within her. The look of concern in his eyes was unrivaled in the whole of her experience.

An unknown passage of time elapsed as her will grew ever weakened. It must only have been seconds, but it felt like hours. A noise down the hall brought her back, and with her return, panic. This was exactly the sort of nonsense which would get one or both of them killed.

Drusilla's eyes darted down one end of the corridor then the other. There was no one. The sound had echoed from somewhere slightly further afield. Still, there was no time to waste. She broke free of Raul's hypnotic touch and skirted around him, pushing the door to his chamber wide. Without word, she beckoned him follow with haste, then shut and barred the door once they were both securely within.

Drusilla crossed the room, shuttering the window. Shuttering the outside world.

He lit a candle as she shut out the last of the light. Stared at her and the water she had tracked across his small room. Drusilla remembered the next moment with regret.

"I felt the need for a little air. I took a walk." As lies went, it was subtle. But lying to Raul was different than the many similar lies she had told Ludo. The score of lies she had heaped upon Bayden.

Lying to Raul hurt her heart.

"You'll catch your death." He unraveled the small roll which served as his pillow. A blanket emerged. Putting it around her shoulders, he dabbed at her hair and neck. With great care, Raul gathered up a section of her hair, wrapping it in the blanket become towel. He took up a new section of each and repeated the process. The gentleness with which he attended to her was intoxicating.

She held back a moan.

Whether he believed her lie or not, she couldn't tell, but as he set aside the now thoroughly wet blanket, exchanging it for the heavier one upon the bed, she felt doubly the sting of deceiving him. Yet deception was her primary defense, a habit long ingrained.

It was the only tool she had in her arsenal which could protect him.

"We should get you downstairs, to a fire—"

"I cannot be seen with you."

She blurted it out, and immediately wished she could take it back. The words wounded him more than he could hide. Raul stiffened a bit. She wanted to apologize, to soften her words with assurances. To tell him it was all but a charade. She dared not.

She wanted to tell him everything.

Duty prevented it.

"Undress," he said.

A bolt of fear shot through her. Fear and desire. The first fading away like the afterimage of a lightning strike. The latter rising in a swell that coursed upwards through her body. She looked at him. Into his eyes. He was all seriousness now. Like her, duty masked his true emotions. Before her stood the soldier.

"Extra clothes are in a ruck sack under the bed."

He lay the spent towel aside, plucking up his shirt, opened the door after listening for movement without, and was gone.

Quickly, Drusilla moved to obey his command. She let her wet clothes fall to the floor, and with them, shed most of the water weight she was carrying. Where Raul had gone, she could only speculate. The door stood closed but unbarred. It didn't feel right to lock him out of his own room. Nothing felt right anymore.

She finished drying herself with the heavy blanket, a thing which would also do should someone enter. Anyone but Raul, and the rumor which would follow, would be the death of them both, however. Finding her prudence to overrule her courtesy, she barred the door, and set aside the wet blanket. She would listen for Raul's return.

If he returned. That brought on an additional pang of guilt. Had she driven him away? Would he return this night, or wander off in his wounded state, seeking some other refuge? Had he simply surrendered the room, his room, to her?

She couldn't know.

Damp ringlets of hair clung to her neck, shoulders and back, and also her bare breasts, rewetting already chill flesh. She needed clothing, or fire. Something more than the cold stone under her feet and embrace of highland air could provide.

Naked, she peered under the bed, seeing the ruck sack pushed to the far center, against the wall under the headboard. She grasped the heavy sail cloth of which it was made, wincing as her arm reminded her it was still bruised deep beneath the surface, and pulled it to her.

Undoing the knot, a shepherd's knot, she dug in, searching for a suitable outfit. She found a simple tunic which would do. A sash. An oversized pair of woolen socks. Boots. A pair made of sheepskin with leather ties. More than she could have hoped for.

The boots were woefully too big, but it didn't matter. They were warmth.

Her own boots, still on the chair, were situated so they would drip-dry in the most effective manner. Cross-legged, Drusilla sat on the bed in Raul's clothing. A bed which was little more than tightly strung rope and a woolen base cloth. The rest, he had already stripped away for her benefit.

She had come straight to him.

She chided herself as she sat waiting in the near dark. A single candle flame bounced and fluttered in the draft between closed door and closed shutter. She should have gone to her room first, dried herself, and only then come here. If he didn't return, she would have to leave soon. Drusilla had more she wanted to say to him. Raul deserved more than she had given.

Too obsessed with her own thoughts, Drusilla didn't notice the approaching footsteps which must have preceded the knock. She stiffened. Rose from the bed. Firelight danced outside the door, stealing beyond cracks of imperfection.

If it was anyone but Raul...

She picked up the gladius, plucking it gingerly from its corner, and lifted the bar. Standing in her oversized boots, bare armed and exposed mid-shin to mid-thigh, she peered out into the hall.

It was Raul. Thank God, it was Raul, and he had brought fire.

She ushered him quickly within, barred the door behind him as he set the brazier upon the stool. He poured the oil, then lit it with the torch he carried.

Flames leapt into existence.

"You make better use of my clothing than ever I could," he said.

She laughed quietly. A laugh which was cut short as she remembered the remainder of her task here.

"Something bothers you," Raul said as the two of them arranged her things about the fire. "You behave as a woman in a very hard place. There is nothing you could ask of me which I would refuse."

"How did you come to Loch Ness?"

Raul looked up. His face looked pained... momentarily. He hid whatever troubled him about her question behind a smile.

"You were a soldier," she ventured. Everything was arranged and drying. The flames felt good. She was desperately cold. She wanted to be in his arms. The impropriety of the thoughts she was having shocked her. But they did not feel wrong, and that shocked her, too.

The Sun warmed her shoulders, children laughed nearby, but thinking back to that night, new chills passed through her very bones. The guilt that twisted and writhed at her core had only deepened since last night, working its bitter poison into her blood.

"Wait. Take your warmth." Raul stood, and again left the room. Again she barred the door, not against him, but against all others till he should return.

She returned to the fire. She had pushed him too far. Whatever his past experiences, he clearly did not wish to relive them. Still, he did not belong here. He was not like the others in this high-born crowd. She was not like the others, but pretended to be so.

Why did he?

Drusilla moved the stool carefully and with it, the flame. She flipped each piece of clothing, laying them upon new spots upon the floor or across the chair, leaving wet little puddles where they had been. She hadn't dared wring them out, for fear she'd be spotted at the window.

Slowly, the fire did its work. Warming her. Drying her clothes. Drusilla stayed busy with the blankets. Being wool, and thick to boot, they would not be dry anytime soon. With the added damp and chill of the storm, it was unlikely they would be dry this night. Still, she tried.

Drusilla thought back to that night, arms wrapped about her legs, surrounded by the field of vibrant grass and sunshine. Feeling the day's warmth on her skin. Could she have done anything differently? It was not a useful line of inquiry. She had done what she had felt she must.

And now the world, vibrant after days of rain, looked uninspiring and dull.

Raul had returned with cups of hot broth. The two of them shared the meal in a silence that felt like the weight of a thousand wool blankets pressing down on her heart. Smothering the life out of her.

Raul was the first to set down his cup.

"I was conscripted," he said. "Taken at fourteen from my family and farm."

That was why his soldier's rucksack was secured with a farmer's loop. Why had she not seen it earlier? All the evidence had been before her eyes.

He pushed the empty cup further away from him, tried to smile. It collapsed into an attempt to hold the pain at bay.

Drusilla wanted to reach out, to comfort him. The duplicity of her situation prevented her. She was here to foster separation, not closeness.

"I'd been with the army four years. It was late summer. We crossed the Ural, making about twenty miles a day. Our expedition took us up and into the Caspiane, near the Göktürk border. There was rumor of an eastern invasion. I suspect our mission was to suss out the strength of that rumor.

"We pitched camp just before losing the light. No bonfire. We had most of a hundred men, and a general traveling incognito amongst our ranks—and I don't think any of us, aside from our centurion, were supposed to know even that much.

"There'd been a few minor skirmishes, with a couple men injured in one engagement. Nothing serious. We were deep in foreign territory. We had the strength of numbers, good equipment, and superior tactics.

"No one thought we were in any real danger.

"Still, four men were left on watch, plus two to keep the horses and mules still and comforted. We were being careful. We were being quiet. I guess that's what had me spooked."

Drusilla looked into Raul's eyes, but he kept his gaze on some spot far away. He looked like another man. A younger man who was reliving a nightmare at her request. She felt ill about it, wanting to make him stop. Surely this went beyond the purpose for which she had come.

"It's all right," she said. "I'm sorry I asked. You don't need—"

"The sentries were dead before any of us knew a thing was wrong," Raul continued, hardening the line of his jaw. "The stable lads, too. And God knows how many others. When I woke, it was already a bloodbath. I managed to find my weapon before the Hun cutthroats found me. There were only eight or ten of them left. They had attacked our camp with less than a score of men. With their curved blades and arrows, and their soft boots, they had taken us.

"I never liked being a soldier. It's not the life I would have chosen. I liked less the idea of being a slave. To run probably meant an arrow in the back. Surrender never occurred to me. I doubt very much it was an option. My only thought was these men would not decide my fate. And so I picked up my sword, and I fought.

"Through some sense of duty, I protected our general, though he could fight as well as any man. Together, we killed off the last of our attackers.

"His name was Kay.

"He said he owed me his life. I only did what any man would have done. Nothing more. But he wished to repay me. With as many of the horses as did not run off, we broke camp and returned to Constantinople, taking turns at watch. Surviving other attacks and trials along the way.

"The general asked me what he could do to repay me for his life. 'Anything in my power to grant,' he said."

A long silence stretched out in the cold little room. Raul seemed still so far away. Lost in a fugue of his own troubled past. She had done this to him. She needed to bring him back.

"What did you say?"

"I would lead a quiet life."

He could have asked for gold, or for rank. A general of Heraclius could surely provide either of those. Or women. Land...

And yet, Raul had asked only for a quiet life.

Raul rolled his empty cup upon its base idly, then plucked it up, standing abruptly.

"The local word for 'son of' is Mac." Leaning, he took Drusilla's empty cup from her as well.

MacKay.

"Why can you not be seen with me?" Raul could no longer mask his pain. He wore it openly, every inch of him declaring it.

"Because I am betrothed," she answered. "To Ludo, son of Kay."

Chapter Forty-Seven

B AYDEN WAS ON THE move. It was time to go. Drusilla dropped the dandelion with a last wistful glance, rising to her feet by the strength of her legs alone.

The contest of blades was done, the winner announced. The day belonged to Bayden. Drusilla had enjoyed almost complete solitude as everyone else, who could, had attended the games. Ludo had returned to the main house. Bayden, ribbon in hand, a colorful token given him by Lady Elaenor, had headed to the pavilion serving as a staging ground for contestants and their squires.

Drusilla stole across the greensward, careful not to solicit the attention of the other guests, to the pavilion. There were guards present, preventing her from more than a peek within.

She caught Bayden's eye.

Bayden nodded to the guard, and she was allowed to pass within.

The floor of the pavilion had not gotten proper sunshine for weeks. The grass was wilted and yellow and had been mostly covered over with sweet smelling hay. Benches and makeshift tables for the benefit of the squires were set about under the canvas shade.

Bayden stood at one of these, sword already laid aside, stripping off his armor. He worked without a squire, the guards keeping a respectful distance at the edge of the structure. Drusilla, however, stole further in.

"I've been absent from much of the games of late. I wanted to apologize." Drusilla ignored what she really knew about the man, and pretended only that he had been a gracious host, and she, an ingrate.

"There's no need." He undid the last of the straps holding his boiled leather chest plate secure.

"But I feel there is." She stepped closer. Close enough now, that she could reach out and touch him if she desired. "You've done exceptionally well, and I have witnessed but a small portion of your victories."

"I seem to remember your displeasure at the chariot contest in particular."

There was that. It was an effective parry, but she would not be deflected from her target. Time to twist the spigot.

"I'm sure your brother must have confided in you our good news."

Bayden's face was implacable. His grip on his chest plate, however, was focused rage. There could be no mistaking it. Peeling it away from his well exercised body, he set it down a bit too roughly.

She knew he knew. How would he play it?

Drusilla ran a finger along the discarded breastplate, stopping where her finger dipped into the cleft in the chest. She took another step forward, placing her uncomfortably close to the man who planned to murder her. Uncomfortably close to the coiled muscle and daunting form of her enemy. Heat poured off his body.

It felt visceral. The waves of heat were the physical manifestation of the menace he held in check. For now.

The voice within her screamed, stop. Her gut told her to retreat. Drusilla twisted more. Stepping so close she could see the waver of his blue eyes, the hatred in his tightly contracted pupils, she forced herself to meet it.

If he wanted to kiss her right now, if he wanted to kill her, there was absolutely nothing she could do to stop him.

"I am not blind."

She turned her face coyly away from his. "I don't want there to be a rift between us." She looked down his body, following the center line of his chest to his abdomen, to the heavy buckle of his sword belt. "I understand how hard it is for you to share in your brother's joy when you still grieve for Evelynn."

She spoke softly enough that the soldiers standing guard outside the pavilion could report that words were exchanged, but not what it was that was spoken. As for Bayden's perception of what she was doing, the hush in her tone could easily be explained away by the delicacy of the subject under discussion. Bayden's outburst, however, was just the sort of thing she had hoped for. The sort of thing she could use.

"Evelynn—" It was a barely repressed shout. Bayden looked confused for a moment, or maybe it was merely discretion kicking in. In either case, he lowered his voice, and only then did his private guard relax. Drusilla heard swords reseating within their sheaths.

"Evelynn," he said more softly, "is not your concern." Pain tinged his voice. He pushed past Drusilla.

Whatever Drusilla told Ludo would have to mesh with what any witness now saw. She let herself stumble. Fell into Bayden's massive arms as he caught her. His grip was iron. She brought her cheek next to his, whispered in his ear. "I'm sorry."

His grip relaxed. She didn't wait to see if that was a temporary thing. Drusilla had no desire to see what he might do next. She pulled herself upright, gently pushing away, without meeting Bayden's eyes a second time, and rushed out.

She stared up at the sunlit sky, but all she could feel was the crushing walls surrounding her.

Chapter Forty-Eight

D RUSILLA FOUND LUDO SHORTLY after the incident. She needed to be the first to reach his ear. Before Bayden had the opportunity to fill his brother's head with a version of the truth different than that which she was here to provide. Ludo was on the veranda, overlooking the loch, standing apart from a few others also enjoying the view.

She caught his eye, not saying a word. She stood behind one of the columns on the dance floor, making certain none of the others spotted her. That she was still trembling from her encounter with Bayden should play nicely to her favor.

Ludo set down his drink, a look of deep concern on his face, and came to her. She led him off, and down the hall to a quiet corner where they were unlikely to be accosted.

She sunk into the shadow of stone, cooling her back, pressing her hands against the wall to steady them. Ludo looked at her curiously. "What has happened, my dear Drusilla?" He took one of her hands in his and cradled it.

She sighed, indicating with reluctance her willingness to speak. "Your brother will never let us have peace. Not a moment of it." She closed her eyes and waited for him to prompt her continue.

He stepped closer to her, sheltering her with his own body. He lifted her hand and kissed it. "My brother will come around. He only needs a little time. He would not abandon me. Not once he sees our union is inevitable."

"I wish I could believe that. I'd very much like to think we could all be one happy family."

"Why do you doubt it?"

"Just today," she said, pausing as though the telling was difficult. She looked up into his hazel? eyes. For a moment, she found the intimate feelings she could genuinely have for him were he not also the enemy. It was easier with Ludo. She hoped he could see her affection for him in her demeanor. "I went to the pavilion, to congratulate him, after his victory at sword. I wanted only to make amends for my many long absences from the games. Instead of making things better, he told me he sees how we look at each other, and that he would not stand for it. Then he said, if I was going to love anyone, it should be him. But it scared me most, when he called me Evelynn and forced a kiss upon me."

"He kissed you?" Ludo was livid with rage. "I'll kill him with my bare hands."

"No, please," said Drusilla, gripping his powerful forearm with both her hands. "I could not stand it if you were hurt. Please, there must be some other way."

"There's not."

"Stay your hand, please, I beg you," she cried, laying on the drama with the craft of many years' perfection.

"What would you have me do?" he said, wringing his hands through his hair. Breaking her grip upon him.

"If you are certain there is no other way... no reconciliation—"

"I can see none. He will harry us to our graves if we let him," said Ludo. "It's so typical of him."

This was the transformation she had desired. Now, and only now, that he was thoroughly baited, and the idea had come from him first, did she volunteer the idea.

"Then let me do it."

He looked at her, shocked at first, unreadable. His strange grey? eyes scanning her expression. Drusilla feared she had read the situation wrong. Hoped this would not get ugly. Out of control.

"But how?" was all he said.

Oh, thank God. He was actually smiling.

"I will do it most artfully, my lord," she had noticed in the past, he always liked it when she called him lord. "And no one will know it was my hand.

No one, not even Bayden."

"I'd like to see the look in his eyes," said Ludo. For him to know it was me."

"I know a poison," she said. "I'll whisper it in his ear as he's dying, after it's too late."

She thought Ludo was going to cry. He looked so twisted, and mad, and happy in that moment. He nodded joyfully, seizing her with both hands, and gave her a quick kiss.

Chapter Forty-Nine

RETURNING TO HER ROOM, Drusilla found a cup of tea waiting. The golden gorse. Sara had completed her quest. She placed the saucer aside, releasing steam from the golden liquid. Inhaled its fragrance before taking a sip.

She had not seen Raul today. Not so much as a glance...

She took another sip, feeling hollowed out and alone. Drusilla hoped the legend of the golden gorse was not exaggerated. She took another sip, staring out over the late afternoon waters of the loch.

Not a drop would she waste.

Chapter Fifty

T HE MIDSUMMER NIGHT'S BALL was scant hours away. She prayed Linus returned by then, but whatever may come, tonight was the full Moon, and if her calculations and understanding of Bayden's twisted Aphrodite worship was correct, he would do everything in his power to make a sacrifice tonight.

To sacrifice her tonight.

Without Linus, and the special help or advice he would bring from Roland, she was at a loss as to how to handle Bayden and the loch serpent. Whether or not he arrived in time, she must be ready. Drusilla had run a hundred scenarios in her head. None of them gave her more than a long shot at walking away.

If she had no other choice, she would do it anyway. Bayden would not live to see the morning Sun. Nor Ludo.

She stared out across the loch, and the Sun reflecting warmly off it. She was low, by the shore, a large stone, her chair. This would be her last day, as well, without Linus. Without the added help she needed to take on such a powerful foe and not draw the attention of the Elite Guard. It was the cost of war. These men had committed crimes. Were bent on a path of crime. It was her duty to end it.

Drusilla thought of Raul, and her heart ached a little more than the moment before. She had crushed him in her campaign of secrecy and lies. Crushed him and left him wounded in her wake. If she did not live throughout the night, she wanted him, above all others, to know what it had all been for. To know that she had never loved Ludo. To know that she was not a murderer, nor a fickle woman.

It was important to her.

It could not be.

Secrets were her tradecraft.

Drusilla picked up her skirts, brushing them off as she straightened. She looked beyond the waters to the greenwood, but turned instead to the keep upon the hill. The house, and below it its catacombs, which housed madness.

Drusilla gathered flowers as she climbed. A vast assortment of wildflowers in every color, before reaching the weather-beaten tawny walls of Foxborough Keep. Within, there was an energy to the place. Servants rushing about completing tasks, making ready for the grand ball tonight. Into the servants quarters she went, wearing her tan and black, the simplest and most plain of her outfits. She did not wish there to be a great line dividing her from those she esteemed most highly, here at the edge of the Pictish wilds.

Drusilla set the servants' table with the bouquet of wildflowers, filling a small pot with water and making new cuts in their stems to keep them fresh longer. As she did this, and several other small chores, she talked amongst the staff—specifically, certain of the young women she had gotten close to, having made herself useful over the last several weeks, helping with one task or another. To these few, she watched for opportunities to have conversations of a more private nature. Remembering how Bridgette had been used as an instrument to spy upon her, she was very selective about what she asked for, and in whom she confided.

Later that afternoon, having done all she could to advance her chances, odds she still felt were woefully low, she made her way out onto the greensward. The final day of festivities, and she had already missed half of it.

She found Ludo easily enough. Walked with him. Showed him the affection of an eager lover still hiding her true intentions from the world. Subtly, they exchanged flirtations, occasionally brushing fingers one with the other. Laughing a little too loud at each other's witticisms.

The day meandered on, and she and Ludo parted ways, promising to meet at the ball.

"Tonight, we begin our new lives together," she told him, watching the fire it lit in his eyes.

Drusilla wandered the field, too often catching herself scanning the faces for a certain Sicilian who was conspicuously absent. She stopped at a little pavilion giving away sweetmeats and roast hazelnuts. Not quite in the mood, she smiled and moved on, finding, instead, a small patch of rhubarb growing along the western wall.

She bent, and cut a stalk, casting aside the poisonous leaves. Peeling away the tough outer skin, she bit into the exotic treat. It was crisp and succulent, and made her mouth water, so tart it was. She should like to salt it. She cut a second stalk, planning to take it back to the house, when a little voice interrupted her.

"Agatha told me that golden gorse is for heartbreak. Lady Drusilla, is your heart broken?" It was Sara. Drusilla stood to greet her. The girl reached out her tiny hand, touching Drusilla's. Her eyes were wide, sympathetic.

Drusilla tried to smile for her and couldn't. "The tea helped," she lied.

"I'll gather more petals. Agatha says she doesn't mind, and will do it for no money. As many cups as necessary."

Drusilla knelt and hugged the young child. "You've been a very good friend." Using the back of her gloves, Drusilla dried her eyes so that Sara wouldn't know she was crying. "But I think this is something I need to feel if I am to truly heal. No more golden gorse."

CHAPTER FIFTY-ONE

"THE LADY, DRUSILLA THE Fair."

Drusilla scanned the room, filled now with people, echoing with laughter, drunkenness, and music. She tilted her head to the herald who had just called out her name, and who had given her the flattering title, "Fair" only a month prior.

She felt naked, and not just for the lack of her steel.

Looking out through the gathering, taking bearing of all in attendance. The white togas, while shockingly immodest, looked positively celestial amongst the ten thousand candles or more that lit the hall. It struck her, that should the very stars fall from the heavens, they would be no more splendid.

Sweeping the crowd, her eyes found Sara's parents, Liam and Mary, near the drinks table. Mary had her hair up in twists, a blue ribbon interwoven throughout. Drusilla recognized the shade, and knew that Sara had lent it to her. Both smiled warmly at her, and raised a cup to her. Lady Elaenor stood near Bayden, flirting with him. While most of the men wore togas, too, Bayden was dressed like a Roman emperor, right down to the crimson cape and gold-inlaid armor.

No ego there.

The Elite Guard were close at hand, shadowing his every move. The servants all wore their usual outfits to distinguish them from the guests. The guards wore their Celtic kit. There was no mistaking who was amongst the elite here, and who was here to serve.

Drusilla, too, wore white. The simple toga Nettle had made for her, and sandals crafted by her husband, the cobbler, who had returned to duties long neglected after the disappearance of their daughter, Helen. She had chosen to give them her coin rather than employing one of the tailors made available to her here within these walls.

It was a small gesture. They had suffered a loss beyond the power of recompense. But it was a thing within her means to do. And so she had done it.

Her thoughts returned to the ballroom, and to the deeds required of her this night. That she was dressed so simply, would make slipping away at the appropriate moment all the more tenable. In that critical moment, she needed to be invisible. She needed a great deal to go right tonight if she was to avoid the fate Bayden planned for her.

She had piled her hair high, like the pictures she had seen of Greek women, a simple white ribbon wound throughout, having learned, from young ladies amongst the staff, that it would be the most popular style tonight. And so, to further blend with the masses, she had opted for the same.

Dark ringlets touched her bare shoulders. A few loose strands brushed her collar bone. A simple cord around her waist, and knotted at one side, held a small coin purse, near invisible, made by Nettle of the same cloth as her toga. It held her costume together, having no stitching up the sides.

Drusilla did her best to ignore the fact her arms and all but a scant few inches of her legs were completely bare, glad the puncture wound in her back was nothing but an angry pink scar now. It might easily be sighted. So much of her flesh was on display this night.

It was the least modest thing she had ever paraded before the public view. But nothing made her feel more naked than leaving her dagger behind. She was "aristocracy". She could get away with wearing her dagger if she but chose to—but to do so subtly sold the wrong message. Tonight, she must radiate submission. Nothing must whisper in Ludo's ear, "Be on guard."

Beyond the dance floor were the columns separating the indoors from the moonlit night. There, standing near one of the columns by himself, was Raul. Drusilla's heart leapt involuntarily. Words caught in her throat she had not intended to say. Words which she had yet to admit were within her.

He was dressed as simply as was she, except the sandals were a thing long in his possession. A remnant of his centurion days. No longer did Raul hide his lean yet powerful physique from the others. His secret was laid bare. This was a man of capability. A soldier who had withheld himself from the various combats, not for lack of skill, but by deliberate choice.

Here was a man who had no ego for proving himself.

Their eyes met momentarily. Hers was a look which she hoped did not betray her conflicted emotions. She strove to keep her nod his way, well seated in the territory of cordiality. Nothing more. Any abuses she had put him to could not be mended this night. She suspected, by the look he returned her way, they could never be made whole again. His smile did nothing to mask the wound, inflicted by her, which he carried.

The redheaded woman from the hunt walked up and engaged him. Drusilla tried not to be obvious as she watched their exchange. The woman said something to Raul, stealing a hopeful glance back at the room's center, where dozens of couples dipped and swirled about the checkered, grey and gold floor.

He was polite, though she could not tell the exact words exchanged. Then he walked away, alone, leaving the beautiful redhead standing there, rejected.

Drusilla wanted to run to him.

Instead, she forced herself to continue her sweep of the room until she found Ludo. It appeared he had been making his way skillfully towards her while attempting not to appear over eager. True to their pact, he was playing his part coolly. Till tonight. Till he announced their betrothal, and she murdered his brother in plain sight, and they ruled Foxborough together as its undisputed masters.

Drusilla had other plans.

"You make a masterful gladiator," said Drusilla, hands joined high as they circled in dance. It was their third of the night. "I am indeed the luckiest woman here."

The leather he wore smelled nice. More than once, innocent thoughts of all the little things he had done for her crept into her consciousness, and helped with her ability to project adoration his way.

His amber? eyes locked with hers as they switched hands and circled the other way, moving in and amongst the other guests.

Though she wore a toga as simple, or in many cases, more so than the other women of this party, some of whom had adorned their outfits with lavish broaches or jewelry, Ludo still paid her the highest deference. "You look divine," he said. "You are royalty amongst commoners."

The comment upset her. She was a pretender, and there was nothing common about these other people, least of all, the ones he labeled servants. But she had a role to play.

"Soon there will be no more hiding," she whispered in his ear, and went to get two goblets of wine.

Wine was perfect. It was opaque, strong flavored, and already of a bitter nature. Earlier in the evening, she had prepared the berries from the forest, crushing them, seed and all, to a pulp with her mortar and pestle. When she poured the juice of the crushed berries into the wine, there was scarcely a change of color, let alone clarity, and she suspected the flavor would be masked to all but the most discerning of pallets.

Regardless, she would not let Ludo's mind focus on such subtle and mundane things. She planned to keep his attention squarely on more intriguing matters.

She put on the bracelet, Camille's bracelet, making her actions appear perfunctory such that no one noted her slightly deviant behavior. Reaching into the pouch at her side, she pulled out the gold engagement ring he had given her, slipping it on the appropriate finger of her other hand.

Two rings: one steel, one gold.

One moral. One deceit.

The musicians began another piece, a lively tune with a heavy reliance on the pan pipes, fife, and drum. It had a wild feel to it, unrefined. Forcefully alive, like the people of this land. She returned across the floor, smiling at the redheaded woman who had found another conquest to pursue, then, more radiantly so, to Ludo, handing him his drink.

"What's this?"

She wasn't sure what he meant by it, but it was time for a little misdirection. She flashed him the ring. "It's time for our toast. Share a private drink with me before you make the announcement. I need take courage from our pact. And you know I have much work to conclude tonight."

He lifted his glass to her. "To courage."

She entwined her arm with his, wrapping her drink around his arm and back again. A most intimate gesture, bringing them face to face.

Inches apart.

"To our future," she smiled, drinking of her own glass.

He quirked that crooked smile, hesitated. Did he know? Her heart pounded fiercely in her chest. So much so she feared he would hear it. So closely they embraced, she feared he would feel it.

And if he didn't drink?

If he knew...

Chapter Fifty-Two

H AD SHE DONE ENOUGH to encourage Ludo? It was to their betrothment they drank. Why then did he hesitate, unless she had given him some subtle cue to beware? Why did she hesitate to give him that last little push, Drusilla wondered?

Had their pretended love clouded her judgment?

Instinctively, her mind went to her dagger, noting regretfully, its absence—and then, how impossibly far and well guarded the location of each point of egress.

There was no way she was getting out of this alive if she had miscalculated.

"To our love," he said, and drank.

As they both lowered their goblets, arms still entwined, he looked at her with blue-grey eyes, the color of the stormy sea. She could see it. He genuinely loved her.

Her breathing was ragged, eyes surely broadcasting her treachery. Panic welled up from within her. It could not be taken back.

Her mind was a ruin of confusion.

"What troubles you?" he asked.

"I am so happy," she lied, feeling an onslaught of guilt, an ugly ribbon of regret twisting her insides. "To our love."

She tilted her goblet back a second time, drinking deeper, greedily, encouraging him by subtle cues to do the same. He followed.

His footing shifted, buckled slightly inward. He looked up at her, those same, now constant, blue-grey eyes. His lower lip quivered as he tried to make words. Panic flashed across his face before the paralysis began to take its ugly hold.

He gasped twice, then managed a single, ragged word.

"Why?"

She glanced to her wrist, still entwined with his, now holding some of his weight. His eyes flicked down, saw the bracelet. She stepped closer, holding more of his weight. His second leg buckled just a little. He could neither stand, nor choose to fall. He was in the grip of it. When this stage passed, he would collapse.

But first the rigor.

"You recognize it, I see," she said. "Camille was most dear to my closest friend, and you took that from him."

His knees buckled. She eased him to the floor, calling out. "The drink has gone to his head, I'm afraid." She fanned Ludo as he lay there in a catatonic trance. "Please, somebody, fetch him to bed."

In those blue-grey eyes was terror imprisoned within a disobedient shell.

She leaned close to him, whispering in his ear. "I know about all the girls you took."

Chapter Fifty-Three

Drusilla feigned taking Ludo's temperature, sweeping her hand down over his eyes, closing them for the last time. She fawned over him till servants and concerned onlookers alike swept in to fill the gap.

She relinquished her position at his side to a well-muscled lad of eighteen who earned his physique through hard labor serving the household. A young man who generally went unseen. However, as he hefted his master up and onto his feet with the help of another, he became the visual draw of the occasion. And in that moment of diverted attention, Drusilla was not.

She slipped out in the immediate chaos that followed Ludo's collapse, and made for the kitchen. Beth slipped Drusilla into the pantry. Beth slipped in too, and together, they quickly took down her hair, stripped off her toga and sandals, and put her into the drab garb of a servant. With the kerchief and pinafore, head held low, eyes directed downward, there would be very little to recognize her by.

Drusilla slipped off the golden engagement ring. The ring she had been meant to wear to the end of her days. Guilt stabbed at her again. She pushed it aside, even as she pushed the ring deep into her pouch. A thing to be forgotten.

Such thoughts would not plague her long. She'd never get close enough to Bayden for poison, even if she had any more left. He was coming for her. His distrust of her gave him a vigilance which could not be circumvented by conventional means. That she should survive this night was doubtful. Still, she had to try. It was with a heavy heart, that she consigned herself to such fate. She would have liked, very much, a second chance to make things right with Raul.

Another of the serving women, Elsie, poked her head into the pantry. She was out of breath, a look of great excitement on her young face. She spoke too quickly, but the message was unmistakable. The long hoped for news. "Forgive me, m'lady, it's your coach man. He's returned!"

There was hope.

She explained that it was Percival who had sent her with the message, and that he could not come himself because he was being watched too closely. Elsie seemed very pleased at her own usefulness, and also a little starry eyed at the mention of Percey, as she informally referred to him.

Drusilla easily slipped past the guard now. Being a servant meant being practically invisible. She raced out to the hall to meet Linus.

"Just got back," he panted, holding out a leather satchel until now tucked under his arm. "Trouble on the road." She saw by the look in his eyes, he meant an assault, not a thrown shoe, or broken axle. Thank God he'd come through it. She was glad, too, he hadn't seen her in her toga as he looked her up and down with a smile. "I see you've been demoted in rank."

She patted him on the arm. He'd always been such a good man. She was glad to see the extra activity hadn't spoiled his sense of humor.

"Bridgette loves London Town," he continued, "but all she talks about is 'When Drusilla gets here.'"

Drusilla acknowledged with a smile. Her heart leapt at the prospect she would survive this night, see Bridgette again, make it back home. But much had yet to be decided this night. "This needs my immediate attention," she apologized. "Thank you, Linus. You've done splendidly."

He bowed to her, handing over the weighty satchel. "Handle this with great care," he cautioned. "It's fragile and dangerous."

Oh goody, a dangerous present from Roland—her favorite kind!

"Be on your guard, Linus," she said in parting. "Everybody's in a dangerous mood right now."

She fled to the only spot she felt might be truly safe right now, to look at the letter. She headed for the scullery.

Bayden passed her in the hall, looking livid to the bone. He was in a rage, his private guard trailing close behind. She put on her most demure look, curtsying him as he passed. He didn't even see her.

Servant equals invisibility, she thought. It was true. She had cast a spell and turned herself invisible. The Merlin himself would be proud of her. She found the scullery to be empty, save Beth, who had gone on ahead of her, and who would now act as her lookout.

"I'll just be under here," said Drusilla, indicating a gap in the supply crates.

She sat, carefully unpacking her new acquisition, and laying its contents out before her on the cold flagstone floor. Within the satchel was a heavy, rectangular object wrapped in a thick wool square of cloth. The object inside, a small, locked chest with no key. The chest was made of steel, with a superior lock. There had been no note about that.

A most clever and secure way to send her "gifts". If the contents really were fragile, and she had no cause to doubt but that they were, then any rough handling or forced entry was liable to destroy them. And depending on just how volatile they were...

Well, it could be most unpleasant for the curious party should they choose to smash it wide with a hammer.

Roland was well aware of her particular skill with locks. So this was merely an added precaution. Drusilla worked the lock, then reverently, opened the chest. Within was a letter sealed in wax, and beneath it, fitted tightly with sawdust to the confines of the steel, a wooden box.

Whatever was in that box could wait. She knew the importance of gathering intelligence before acting. Often it was paramount to success.

Gently, box before her, she set the cloth and satchel aside. Above her, chaos echoed and reigned within the keep's stone walls. She ignored the bustle and activity, instead turning her full attention to the letter. A careful inspection revealed that the letter was Roland's, and that it indicated a communication to be taken at its word. Only then did Drusilla break the wax seal to learn what wisdom might be contained within.

She scanned it quickly as she could, interpreting the runes, and working the cipher in her head as she went. It was something she was already practiced at, so it gave her little trouble.

It went as such:

Dear Dru,

My heart is broken at your news, but a man's grief must always be measured by his ability to carry on. For your sake, and for the ideals of Camelot, I will save my broodings and misery for the private hours. Thank you for your condolences. You, indeed, exemplify all that is good and noble in ways both womanly and knightly. I am proud to be your sponsor.
As you may know, such beasts have been dealt with before. Lancelot did combat with a mighty worm, and was most grievously wounded, nearly unto death. God rest him. All the old knights are gone now. But not all the collective wisdom.
The Merlin himself shared a secret recipe with my sponsor, and now I will share it with you. He learnt it from the chemists of Alexandria and has entrusted it under strict provisions to our cause.
I have sent, with this letter, all the accouterments you may require to constitute this most deadly concoction. The Merlin called it 'Dragon's Breath'. The alchemists of Alexandria called it 'Liquid Fire'. Once constituted, it will burn on exposure with air, and so great care must be taken in its preparation and handling.
Dragon's Breath cannot be extinguished by water. It sticks like honey, and burns hot as coals, and most vigorously, too. I would send a prepared batch, but it is too fragile for safe transport over such a distance. Instead, you must mix it from what I send you.
I have taken extra care with the final, volatile ingredient.
Since the final ingredient activates the concoction, and you would be instantly consumed in its deadly flame—that ingredient, I send to you, encased in beeswax. Be sure to check that it is perfectly sealed before dropping it in, and that the container overfloweth at that point, containing not a single

bubble of air. Then seal the glass ampule in which you will mix the other ingredients to specification. The beeswax will soften and give way. A gentle shaking, taking great care, can accelerate the process. Once integrated, you will have created a deadly, fragile projectile of death—Dragon's Breath, to battle a sea dragon. It is fitting.

Follow the instructions perfectly, included in this small chest of ingredients and equipment, and then destroy them, and this letter. It is best that such a secret never become known to civilization at large. They have not earned such power. It would only be abused to the horror of many, and the gain of few. Such is not our way, nor our wont.

God speed you safely back home to us here in London Town,

Yours most affectionately,

R.

Postscript, If I do not hear from you in a month, I am coming to kill Bayden and Ludo myself, even if it means war.

Laying, now, the letter aside, she turned her attention, at last, to the remaining contents within the box of steel. A glass ampule, wrapped in green silk, no larger than a drinking mug, and about as wide, narrowing to two thumbs width at its mouth. A pretty little piece of lightly tinted glass. Drusilla remembered buying it in Helven. In the candlelight, it glinted faintly purple and gold.

It now contained a highly viscous, honey-like liquid. Next to it was a carved wooden box about the size of her dagger's pommel. She laid the top aside, and found within, the wax sealed capsule. Within its translucent surface, fine white granules, and some, too, of blood-red, were encased. She ran fingers gingerly over the wax surface, inspecting it for the slightest flaw. It proved whole.

With great delicacy, Drusilla laid out vessel, each ingredient, and the various small instruments required. She read over the included set of instructions, then began.

The work was painfully slow, littered with exacting procedures and adamant warnings. She knew them important, lest Roland would not have included them.

Vapors similar to soap, sulfur, and lamp oil... or maybe pitch, assaulted her senses, though none she could definitively peg as such.

The house was in an uproar, she knew, yet this could not be rushed. But the time she spent here would be well rewarded. Of that, she had faith.

When she was done, she would have her Dragon's Breath.

"So this is going to slay a dragon," said Drusilla, staring through the glass at the flame behind it.

Repacking everything but the instruction sheet, letter, and the now deadly vial, Drusilla shouldered the satchel, speaking quietly to herself. "I was never here," she said, rising and walking to the flame which burned darkly beneath a massive iron cauldron filled with scalding hot water meant for washing up. Putting the sheets of parchment to flame, she watched patiently as they were consumed to ash.

She found Beth, fished out a coin, pressing it into the young woman's hand. "Take the box, and return it to my coachman, Linus."

There was something else in her pocket, next to the golden ring.

When Beth was gone, she pulled it out, knowing what she would find. Her final letter to Ludo. A chess move which secured her victory in their penned exchanges. And other sentimentalities. This too, she touched to flame, watching in a melancholy as it burned away.

Chapter Fifty-Four

O NE MORE CHANGE OF clothes, one more big task, she thought. Drusilla headed for the grand den, gently agitating the glass vial of death as she went. Standing tippy-toe upon the hearth stone, she plucked the wyvern horn from its hook.

She stuffed it gently into the satchel next to the now volatile Dragon's Breath. She was placing a lot of faith in that little vial, but this was one time she wasn't worried about taking an untested weapon into battle. She trusted Roland with more than her life.

She was willing to die for him.

Drusilla stepped behind the stuffed bear, hiding herself from the room, and slashed open the recent stitching. She pulled out the wrapped cloth package within, and unfolded it, laying out its contents.

Her Aphrodite costume.

She stripped down once again—it occurred to her that her entire plan consisted of costume changes—she put on the toga. She felt almost revered, donning the clothes of none less than the Goddess of Love.

The wig was real human hair, a light, strawberry blonde, even longer than her real hair, which was considerable. She had to flatten her own hair, and pin it back in a low bun at her neckline to hide it. Some maid had sold her locks for a few gold coins at best, and Drusilla had paid more than twice that, but as she watched her transformation in the reflection on a shield, she was stunned.

Even without the gold-leafed mask, and its golden ribbon tie. Even without the golden sandals, jeweled belt with pink clamshell buckle, and dangling locket charms—even without the golden arm bracers, the effect was transforming, charming, and splendid.

The toga was the finest white silk with embroidered flourishes and borders done with gold thread. She liked it almost half as much as her lost green and yellow dress. She applied the finishing touches. The golden boots, the seashell belt. It was something quite special.

Magical.

The picture hadn't shown Aphrodite carrying any weapons. It also hadn't featured a view of her back. So, it was an open question. Most of the gods carried weapons, so why not Aphrodite? Drusilla, therefore, sported a back slung sword, gold pommeled with mother-of-pearl inlays, its serrated, bronze blade, silver plated and polished to a sheen. She retrieved the sword from the bear, giving it a solid tug. Out it came through the slash in his belly.

She would have preferred an ex-caliber blade, or even a steel one like her dagger, but it was impractical under the time constraints, and against the rules. She understood why.

So, instead, she had had the armorer put a serrated edge on it. Something she had only seen in certain teeth of predators. The sea dragon came to mind. She had already tested it, the night Percival brought it to her. It had been a good gamble, proving wicked sharp.

Not wanting to go completely steel-less, she had had a new leather sheath made for her dagger, which held it in place quite tightly upside down. The sheath, itself, had straps that fixed to her thigh, and hid the dagger under the toga on the side where it dipped asymmetrically as in the glass picture.

Having her steel close at hand, she felt a little less naked.

Picks in hair, fake hair, that was; mask of gold—not a terrible, dehumanizing mask such as she detested, but one of exquisite beauty; the regal tiara... Drusilla hated to admit it, but the squandering of her life's fortune on a single outfit had been worth every denarius.

It would not have done to cut a single corner. This was a game of all or nothing, and second prize was death.

She had set aside two gold coins for the stable master, and a few more for emergency occurrences, but she would have to travel to Helven when this was all over. Take them some British goods, and make another glass trip. It would set her mind at ease to replenish her purse, its customary coin.

And then she thought of Raul. If she were to survive this night...

She pushed the thought and its attendant emotions aside. Best to keep her mind on the mission.

If successful, in the aftermath of her actions tonight, the keep would be without a master. But that would be an internal matter for the people to decide. Perhaps a better man, like Angus, would rise to the occasion. Enough thinking. Drusilla had a plan. It was time to execute it.

She hid the ampule containing dragon's fire in a pouch at the back of her belt. Who was to say Aphrodite didn't have need for storage pouches? The wyvern horn, she slung over her back, hiding the now superfluous satchel, along with her maid's outfit, within the bear. Her newly acquired, strawberry-blonde locks did much to camouflage the wyvern horn. She hoped the toga, what little of it there was, would work to her advantage. With so much flesh on display, she hoped no eyes would examine too closely the thing she concealed.

She was ready.

Chapter Fifty-Five

P ASSING THROUGH THE BALLROOM again, the announcer asked Drusilla for her name and title, not recognizing her. He had always shown her deference, but so complete was her transformation, even he, at close proximity, was fooled.

"Aphrodite, Goddess of Love," she said, disguising her voice, giving it a softer, more melodic quality.

He blew the trumpet in a spectacular flourish, one normally reserved for emperors and high kings!

"Her most Supreme Divineness," he belted out. "Aphrodite, Goddess of Love!"

All eyes fell to her.

Silence washed through the crowd as time itself seemed to contract. Bayden was there at the far end, his private guard of eight near at hand. He saw her, and she knew for certain, from his reaction, that a little piece of his sanity was lost right then.

She unfurled her love pouch. It was the same design as her glass pack, but on a larger scale, and was filled with tiny squares of gold, tens of thousands of them. The room exploded with them. The pink velvet with its white cord fluttered down from the ceiling where her toss had taken it.

The crowd was awed, and began to amble about as though in a dream. Eyes shifted from ceiling, raining gold, and back to her. Murmurs erupted as they looked to one another for confirmation of the reality of the event, then back to the dazzle of gold, and the woman who pretended to walk amongst them, a goddess.

Drusilla winked at the announcer, as Bayden started towards her, then headed to the courtyard, a rain of resplendent gold showering the room in her exit. The night was cool and pleasant. Stars and full moonlight glittered and danced upon the loch. Even with bare arms and legs, she was hot under the wig. She ran fingers through her hair, removing the picks.

Raul approached her.

How did he always recognize her? He fell to his knees before her, dressed in his simple toga and centurion sandals. But to her, he was no soldier. He was a prince.

She held the picks behind her, working the lock, her back to the door. This was the challenge she had often hoped for. The timing of its arrival, less than fortuitous.

"I must say," said her prince, "I prefer your natural splendor, but nobody else could have arrived as the Goddess of Love herself and not been untrue to that precept."

Drusilla's heart fluttered. The lock had yet to yield. She was sure her cheeks were flushing with color, and Bayden had to be halfway across that dance floor. And with Bayden, his eight loyal men were never far behind.

"Arise," she commanded, working the lock. She found the added distraction of Raul's presence made the required concentration a struggle.

He stood, but made no move to take her hand and deliver a kiss upon it. Instead, demonstrating an unfamiliar restraint, he bowed to her. She had informed him of her betrothal, and he had shown the proper deference. She had presented herself as a goddess, and he had stooped before her.

Six simple words, "You have but to name it," returned to her mind in force.

It was all her own fault. She had driven him away by cold calculation. Still, she secretly longed to undo all the hurt. Longed for the touch of his lips. That he should kiss her upon greeting, had become more than customary. It had become a thing most fondly anticipated.

He glanced askew, before privately offering his condolences. "I am so sorry that your fiancé has fallen ill." He could have said, *fallen prey to the drink*. He could have made any number of cruel remarks. Instead, as always, he was perfectly chivalrous.

Drusilla craned her neck forward, finding his mouth with hers. It was not thought out. It could hardly be proper. She suddenly found that it was something she needed, had needed, for a good while now. And she no longer wished to fight against the will of her own heart.

His arms wrapped about her waist and pulled her in. Their bodies melted into one. She felt the pins of the lock fall back into place as her hands went limp. Barely, she had the presence of mind to keep hold and prevent the picks from clattering to the stone.

"I love you." Drusilla said it softly. An intimate exchange for their ears only. A burden lifted she hadn't known she'd been carrying. She felt immediately lighter. More alive.

"I have loved you, Dear Drusilla, since the moment I first laid eyes upon you. And I have only grown to love you more with every day."

More alive than she had ever felt in her twenty-two years of living. That he could love her still after all her bad behavior. She wanted nothing more than to linger in this moment.

And then she remembered Bayden, and her dark purpose this night. Fingers deftly reacquired picks. Once again, she worked the lock.

She had been right from the start. She had no time for romance. Time was scarce. She had much work yet to do. Sorrow returned for what she had already done. For killing Ludo, who lived yet, but only just. She took comfort in the knowledge her actions had been an instrument of right.

Raul would act without a thought for his own safety if he became entangled in tonight's affair. She must send him off without arousing his slightest suspicion. She had always acted in a capricious manner in her past dealings with him. No better plan could she think of now.

She looked up at the full Moon. The sky had scarce a cloud to block it, or the million stars upon the black canvas of night. "Will you fetch me a pomegranate from the entry court? Such a tree grows there. I haven't dared take one myself. They take such care with the gardening."

That should keep him out of harm's way long enough for her to take care of Bayden. She couldn't bear to think of him coming to harm trying to champion her in the coming conflict. His presence would only complicate her job.

"You shall have it," he said, rising to his full height, taking her a final time in passionate embrace. She gasped as their lips parted, and the lock behind her yielded. Her arms too weak to raise to him.

"Go, My Prince." Her voice but a whisper. She was breathless.

He bowed to her and departed straight away.

Out of the corner of her eye, she caught Bayden crossing the courtyard. Suddenly, she found her strength.

She slipped through the door once she was certain Bayden had seen her, and dashed down the first flight of stairs, replacing the picks as she went.

Looking back, she saw Bayden rushing down the first flight, past the Galatea-Evelynn, then down the second flight, and the third, always checking to see that he was following her.

Music floating on the night, murmurs of delight, cries of wonder, all receded until they were but ghostly echoes, as new sounds came into focus. Footfall on stone, giving chase. The surf sloshing ashore, crashing upon the rocks below.

"Wait," he cried out. "Evelynn's back this way."

He continued to chase her.

She continued to run.

"I've done everything you've asked." A sad desperation began to corrupt his normally commanding tone.

Asked? This man, this madman, was much more unbalanced than she had dreamed. She almost felt pity for him, but then she remembered Camille and she had no sympathy.

She raced to the bottom of the steps, and out across the beach. Enigmatic smile, hinting at withheld secrets, even as her eyes invited him to follow. Strode out into the low surf, freezing water rushing over her sandaled feet. Sliding back into the deep...

Drusilla knew the legend of Aphrodite, her birth from the waves, from the deep. Going deeper in, she let the frigid water wash over her legs. Watched as Bayden approached now, looking a little confused, a little scared.

"I have given you everything," he said, falling to his knees on the sand. "I'm begging you."

She looked at him, burning him with her gaze. Took another step backwards, into the water. She'd been here before. She knew exactly how deep it was. The depth of a lake didn't shift as its waters, did it?

She fought back the rise of panic, the urge to rush back to shore, Moon sliding weirdly over the water's surface...

Bayden stumbled to his feet again, holding his arms out as he took another step. "What can I give you? Name it, it's yours."

"You can give me back Camille," she said, swinging the horn around, and raising it to her lips.

The low bellow produced by the horn echoed across the loch, resounded upon the slick black rock of the cliff face before her. It was a unique and undeniable sound. The sound she had heard the tragic night Helen had been taken.

The whispering sounds of the band ceased. Voices above went still, casting the night into eerie silence.

And then murmurs of curiosity arose from far above.

"What are you doing?" Bayden cried, taking another step towards her. His eyes shifted nervously to the waters.

Drusilla was scared too—scared to the very threshold of what her sanity could bear, but she hid it. She buried it so deep within her, in a place of strength—given her by right of her training in the forests of Tintagel near Camelot.

Murmur became alarm. The people above were spooked.

But the game was only started.

Drusilla played her role, the bemused and cruel Greek god. She didn't know if the creature would come, with all the people, all the activity here. All the candles...

On the walls above, ten thousand little fires burned. But hunger was a powerful motivator, and the beast had been conditioned.

It wasn't its fault, really. Its nature had been corrupted.

"It was terrible," he cried. His eyes shifted. Mania eclipsed by a scarred and haunted look. "The walk along the beach that night, moonlight on the water. Evelynn, enthralled by the sheer beauty of it...

"When your Kraken took her, I knew it was the gods. Exacting retribution. We had both just become Christians. All that I've done since has only been to make it right."

Drusilla was getting worried now—worry on top of suppressed dread. The loch was deep, but it wasn't very wide. The creature, the Kraken as Bayden referred to it, could be very close by now, even if it had started out in its lair. She had to speed this up. She had learned everything she needed to know.

The first death, Evelynn's death, was an accident. It was that event that had driven him over the edge. He saw his conversion to Christ as a betrayal to the ancient gods—the Greek gods, turning a British miracle of nature into a Greek monster to be feared and worshiped. In short, he was a killer. He was crazy, there were good reasons, but now it was time to end it.

"Human sacrifice?" she asked. "An effigy in cold stone. Did you really think that would work?"

"Yes," he sobbed. "It still can. You, you could make it work. You did it for Pygmalion."

Drusilla laughed at him. It was so ridiculous, so tragically stupid. It was time to get out of the water. Being eaten would also be stupid.

She gave the horn one more blast—all or nothing.

"You have been judged," she said, tossing the wyvern horn in the air—drawing her sword.

Bayden looked struck down by her words.

She cleaved the horn in two on its way down. The sword was no longer untested. In fact, she was quite pleased with the results.

Something tendril-like wrapped around her ankle. Drusilla suppressed her revulsion—fought back the rising panic. She had since learned, by first-hand experience, that bladderwrack and oarweed did indeed grow in freshwater. This was no time to collapse in fear. The moment had come to put her enemy completely off balance for their final showdown.

"I killed your brother."

"No," said Bayden, looking up with half-glazed eyes from the spot where loch had just swallowed the broken halves of the horn to the shimmering goddess before him. "He sleeps upstairs in yonder tower."

"A sleep of death," said Drusilla, stepping towards the shore. She resisted the fantastic urge to look behind her, to check the creature's location—to flee headlong from the cold and dreadful waters. This was in God's hands now. As far as she was concerned, she was a mere instrument.

"No, he sleeps," cried Bayden, trying to reason out the meaning of his tormentor.

"Like Helen sleeps? Like Lilly?"

He looked at her, realization dawning.

"Drusilla?"

Chapter Fifty-Six

H ER ADVANTAGE GONE, DRUSILLA pointed the blade at Bayden's chest. He drew his, and they circled off.

"I told him, I told him it was you," said Bayden, coming in on her right. They exchanged a lick of blades.

"Well, how does being right feel?" she asked him, pressing her attack.

He executed a perfect reversal, and drove her footing back several paces.

"When I've given you to the goddess, she will be most pleased. Who better than a pretender to Aphrodite's true form to satiate her vengeance!" With that, Bayden began to deal heavy blows that were cruelly fatiguing.

"I will have my Evelynn back. Your coming here proves it. Nothing could be more perfect."

"You're mad," she said, sensing she was coming dangerously to the end of the sand.

"No," he thrust his sword, "I'm about to be vindicated. All my labors shall be rewarded tonight." And again, he drove his blade forward with more skill and more power than Drusilla could deflect.

She went for a risky coup de grâce, realizing she had next to nothing going for her at this point, and failed. He easily swept her sword aside, her beautiful new sword, plunging it into the deep. She saw it arc away, into the sky, over what just might have been a sinewy form snaking through the waters.

There was no way to be sure.

It was far off, and she was paying more attention to his blade. Still, her skin crawled just the same. A twinge of raw dread swept through her.

Something deep within her psyche broke.

Sucking back her fears, she ducked and rolled under the next blow, drawing her familiar steel dagger. Poised herself for his next attack.

He paused and laughed, actually laughed at her.

"Your technique is bad, you unschooled little tramp!"

He fetched her blade with his, twisting and manipulating it just so, that first her wrist was forced to follow sunwise, then widdershins; the blade then separated from her grip, flung into the air under his deft guidance.

He seized it and tossed it flagrantly behind him. Drusilla took the opportunity to grab a fistful of sand. He slapped it away with the back of his sword. The blow stung her bare flesh. So savage was the pain, which shot through the bones of her hand, her eyes teared up.

She tried to lunge at him. A final, desperate move. Bayden dropped his own blade, manhandled her to the ground, brutalizing her with slaps until she was dazed.

She was losing everything in this moment. Even consciousness was a tenuous thing, slipping disastrously from her grip. Drusilla fought for purchase in the world, struggled to exert her will in the matter...

But it was no good.

Her face stung, vision a series of dark blurs and red pinpoints. Her body went limp under the assault, and she felt herself being dragged as the last shreds of light and awareness gave way to dark.

Chapter Fifty-Seven

Drusilla's vision opened like a tunnel.

Immediate awareness of a large and powerful man hulking over her, his iron grip pressing her against the unyielding surface of cruel, wet rock at her back. His brutality, unconcerned by the many bruises she already had.

She fought against him, awareness of her peril seeping back to her consciousness, as wave upon crashing wave, broke over her legs. Receded across the narrow strip of wet sand.

How she had gotten here was unclear.

And then memory slammed back into her like an unexpected bolt of thunder, and she knew she had lost. The fight. Bayden overpowering her. And now he was lashing her to the slick, black standing stone by the same heavy rope she had found bits of on the beach a month before.

Her arms were pinned, trapped low at her sides. The hemp bit meanly at her skin. She had a sickening view of the loch. The creature was definitely coming.

Distantly, she heard voices upon the veranda above. Muttering. Gasps. She and Bayden could not be seen upon the private little beach, but the creature, it would be visible to the gathering above. It appeared there would be an audience for this little spectacle after all. Bayden must have noticed her eyes straining upwards.

"I locked it on my way down." He held out a key hanging on a leather cord about his neck.

"You never did get me my own key," she said, having partially recovered her senses. Her sword hand throbbed painfully, swelling by the moment.

She suspected bones may be broken.

"I give you talent," he said. "But that's one secret you're going to have to take to your grave. No one's going to save you now. Ludo and I are the only ones with keys. And I assure you, by whatever talent you pass locked doors, no one up there shares it with you.

"Even if they chose to break it down, they would be ten minutes or more doing it. You saw how solid the door was."

He was right.

The simple truth of that stung. She was alone with this monster, who had an escape through the caves should he choose. That left the creature. Moonlight and stars illuminated the dark waters. The cord bit cruelly into her flesh as she struggled to find some means of wriggling free. Too much depended upon her to allow failure. Not just her own life. Beth might be next, or Malory. Yet need alone did not provide a way.

Think, Dru, think, she begged of herself.

Out, across the loch, a dark and oily shape moved the water in strange ways. It was coming. She had seen the intelligence in its eyes in her previous encounter with the beast. It would remember her. Remember that she had taunted it, injured it even. But it would not need any incentive to kill her. This was its nature.

Bayden turned to look at the oncoming sea serpent—his Kraken, and while his back was turned, Drusilla worked with all her might to free a hand. Just one hand.

"Why did you come here, My Dear?" he asked, still gazing at the oncoming monstrosity.

My Dear?

Drusilla's anger, and with it, her resolve, doubled. In her passion, she yanked her off-hand free, feeling her flesh bruise as it slid free the harsh rope and wave polished rock. She reached back to her pouch, and grabbed the Dragon's Breath. Liquid fire.

The creature was here.

Bayden stepped back and to the side, shielding himself behind an outcrop of stone.

The smooth glass felt cool under her fingertips.

Drusilla had a decision to make. Her other hand, still pinned, had gone numb. It hung uselessly at her side, lashed without mercy to the black stone. There could be no escape. One hand was all she had. Her only card to play.

On the one hand, she could destroy the creature, but there were probably more. The huntsman's tooth was twenty-two inches. What she had faced on the glen bore teeth considerably larger. Or she could kill a monster—Bayden.

She only had one shot.

Somehow, she just couldn't go to her reward knowing that she had left Bayden alive to hurt more young women. He would, and she knew it. If dispatching that monster to Hell meant she would be eaten alive by a lake creature, so be it.

"You hurt a man more dear to me than life when you killed Camille," she said to him, hiding her hand as though it were still bound.

The creature slid out of the water, its neck emerging, rapidly towering to a great height as it flapped up the beach towards her. She felt faint.

Distorted shouts and cries could be heard from the courtyard above.

Bayden stood back, just far enough that he was in no danger, giving her and the whole proceeding, his full attention.

The creature bellowed, raising its head to strike. "You're a monster. Burn in Hell!" said Drusilla, tossing the little purplish vial at Bayden.

He ducked!

Oh my god, he ducked!

CHAPTER FIFTY-EIGHT

THE CREATURE'S HEAD SHOT down.

Drusilla steeled herself against the end, feeling worse for her failure than for her own lost life and horrific end.

The vial shattered on the rock behind Bayden, hot flames erupting. Gouts of red-orange destruction, pulsing violet-white at its center, splashed out with explosive force, covering his entire back with hot sticky death.

He screamed, every nerve in his body sizzling away, as he stumbled forward.

The creature, mere inches from Drusilla, snapped its head back, alarmed as the whole beach was bathed in an eerie, bright flame.

Bayden stumbled about, trying to get to the water, screaming unintelligible madness!

The creature retreated from him, terrified.

"So there is something that scares you, big guy," said Drusilla.

One shot.

She shook her head. Maybe there was a place for luck in battle.

Bayden plunged into the icy water, but the flames sizzled and steamed and kept burning. "Liquid fire, it will burn even in water," Roland had said. The Merlin and his alchemy. The secrets that she and The Order kept.

Pulsing, writhing light shone beneath the waves as the fire burned on, illuminating the night in eerie fashion. It was a horrible sight. Ghastly. She could understand now why the world was not ready for this terrible—wonderful secret.

Bayden's agonized form went still, continuing to burn, even as the surf carried him out into the loch. The sinuous creature submerged, snaking away. Possibly never to trouble the people here again. Who knew? It had been given powerful conditioning not to.

Like Drusilla's four fine steeds, she knew the nature of the animal mind well enough to know that might be enough. Let it stick to hunting pike and sturgeon, and the occasional sheep or deer.

Her legs were bare and cold, her free hand savagely raw. Above her, Drusilla heard the door shatter. That was good if all parties concerned understood what just went on here.

The chances of that were slim.

She reached up, removing the seashell-themed tiara from her head, and with regret for what she must do, smashed it upon the rock. Shells broke easily, leaving sharp, irregular edges. With them, she sawed away at her bondage. By the time the first of them, Raul, had reached the beach, desperately crying out her name, she had left only footprints.

Chapter Fifty-Nine

D RUSILLA FOUND A STONE upon the cliff near where Atreus had fallen. It was a sturdy rock, about the size of a cow, lying on its side in the summer heat. It overlooked the loch from considerable height. Bandaged hands took up the sculpting tools, hesitating.

She could chisel a warning to future generations, warning of the creature population swimming Loch Ness, and roaming its nearby countryside. Assuming her warning was heeded, and not taken for someone's lunatic fancy, it might do some good.

More than likely, however, it would be taken as a pointer, by some future madman, a signpost:

> **Monsters here, get your monsters.**
> **Nothing terrorizes the local village**
> **like a good, house-trained monster.**

She decided against it. There was more potential harm than good that could come from such a warning. Like the ex-caliber, and the liquid fire, the world was simply not ready yet for truly dangerous bits of information. Weapons, fire, the taming of horses, and the wheel—writing and navigation—these things were already out of the box. Pandora's curiosity had created a brave new world.

But that didn't mean Drusilla had to add to it. Hardly. She would acquiesce to Roland's general wisdom, and guard the secret for the foreseeable future. The world would learn soon enough on their own, the secret's of Loch Ness, and she guessed, the other things as well.

Instead, she carved simply this, putting to use the same tools which had carved the Evelynn-Galatea, but for a much finer purpose. She took all afternoon to work the stone with thought, reflection, and care:

> **Camille of Lion's Gate—full of life and**
> **friendship—beloved of Roland,**
> **Evelynn, who adored lavenders and**
> **believed in the promises of romance,**
> **Atreus, heroic Knight of the Round Table**
> **who did give his life for right,**
> **Helen, who made sweet dolls for every**
> **Maid, her inner light a joy to All,**
> **and Lilly of Foxborough, another flower**
> **tragically claimed just at her full bloom.**
> **To these five, claimed by the Loch, and**
> **those whose names we did fail uncover,**
> **we remember, and wish speed into God's**
> **hands...**
> **You will be missed. You are loved,**
> **always.**

Drusilla set down the chisel and hammer, laying them before the stone, and looked out upon the loch, remembering, as the Sun slowly sank into the western horizon bathing land and water in the orange of Heaven.

DRUSILLA HAD THE DREAM again. A meadow gently sloping down to a lake. She was there with her brother, Bartholemew. He was playing with her, tending her while her mother worked the fields on a sharecropping tenantship sunup to sundown.

Bartholemew was probably nine or ten. Ten, she remembered. How old had she been? Little Dru was only three.

"Watch me," Bartholemew cried with delight. Splashing into the lake, his shoes back at the picnic blanket with Dru, his pant legs rolled up.

Little Dru clapped merrily, watching her brother play in the water. He had always been fascinated by water, drawn to it. He knew of every tale, every creature, mythical or otherwise, associated with the water. He was to apprentice with his father when Dru reached five and could follow her mother in the fields. He was to be a merchant mariner, working his free trade on the oceans, lakes, and rivers he loved.

"I'm going to learn to swim today," he said to little Dru, wading further out into the lake. "Father says it's easy. He's just never had the time to show me."

He was beaming with joy, watching Dru from the water.

She plucked a grape off its stem, and ate it, eyes glued to her hero—Bartholemew.

"Bartholemew," Drusilla moaned, tossing and fretting in her sleep as the carriage rolled along through the deep wood.

"You just watch. When father returns, I'll show him I've already learned to swim, all on my own."

Dru waved her hands happily in the air.

"Swim," she cried. "Me too, me too."

But Bartholemew ignored her simple request. He was too busy learning how to do it himself to stop and involve her. He never took his eyes off her. He had been taught great attentiveness. Instead, he faced her as he backed slowly into the lake, growing more and more distant as he slowly submerged. To his thighs, to his waist, gradually going deeper...

And then he simply plunged out of sight, the water swallowing him whole.

Little Dru began to cry, watching the water churn and boil. A few times, she saw a hand break free, and then, after a while, there was stillness except for her crying.

She called out his name, but there was no answer. She wanted to go to him, to rescue him, but she was sorely afraid. Father had talked to her before about being brave. So she knew, right now, that this was the opposite. This was what it felt like to be a coward.

She didn't like how it felt. She knew that Bartholomew needed her, yet she did not respond.

Dru sat there for hours, the light in the surrounding woods growing dim, casting eerie shadows forth. She sat there afraid, not eating, not moving from the blanket where Bartholomew had put her.

She wanted her brother back. But as the light grew dim, and night was falling, he did not come to her. He stayed in the water. Maybe he had found a magical kingdom with kelpies and mermaids?

Maybe he was dead? Dru knew that would mean he wasn't coming back—ever.

She cried again, feeling more alone than she had ever felt in her life. She began to sob, even after her mother lifted her from the blanket in the darkness, looking all about and calling Bartholomew's name, urgently at first, and then with panic—crying out her brother's name in terror, holding the screaming Dru to her side absently as she searched in vain for the other...

DRUSILLA WAS SOBBING.

"Bartholomew..." she whispered in goodbye, waking to the lull of the carriage passing along the forest-lined road back to London Town.

In the shaded dark of the carriage, patches of sunlight glinting by through cracks in the curtains, strong arms drew her up and pulled her close.

Her mind was still fogged from the dream. She didn't know who held her, nor did she care. She felt comforted, and holding to that alone, let herself drift back into a darker sleep now. A dreamless, restful sleep, where she only knew contentment in the moment.

When she next woke, the strong, cradling arms still holding her in unwavering devotion, she remembered her prince. She placed a loving hand over his.

"Who's Bartholomew?" Raul asked her gently, after a moment of silence.

"My brother."

"Do you fear for him?"

"No longer," she said. "He's with God now."

Her prince held her closer.

"You are such a strange and beautiful woman," he said. "To know you is my deepest honor."

She twisted so that she might gaze upon him, and smile. "Have you slept?"

"You were troubled, so I kept watch."

"It is my honor to know you," said Drusilla, touching his face with her hand. Feeling his warmth. Making sure he was real.

"Sleep," she said. "It is many days yet to London Town. Make comfortable, for this sleep has been owed me decades coming now, and I would share this deep bliss with you."

Chapter Sixty

D RUSILLA PRESSED BRACELET AND comb, now polished and shining, into Roland's hand. They embraced, holding each other tightly, Roland's shoulders wracking with silent grief. She would not begrudge him that. He was her oldest surviving friend, and dear to her beyond measure. And though he knew already the worst of the news, the magnitude could not be easily borne. That she must add, now, to his incomplete knowledge of events was a task unavoidable. It would surely wound him further. But only in this way, like the removal of a splinter, could his healing truly begin. And she would be here for him as long as it took. The least she could do for Roland was to make sure he did not bear this grief alone.

"Do you know...?" His words caught in his throat and he began again. "Do you know what befell my sweet Camille?" He was turned, his back to her now, a few feet away, staring out a window over the River Thames. His voice was steady, she knew, only by great effort, his body held a little too rigid. Attempts to hide his grief.

"Sit down, old friend," she commanded, "and I will tell you the tale. But take this comfort to heart now, before we begin. Those who did this already reside in Hell."

Chapter Sixty-One

Late afternoon sun glinted through the dappled greenery of the forest known as Sciryuda—the woodland belonging to the shire. Drusilla laid her trusted boots by the side of an old elm, and dropping her dress and bodice neatly by the way, strode naked to the water's edge.

She dipped her toe in. The water was cold, stimulating. The cool air felt divine upon her skin. A part of her wanted to run. Drusilla pushed the feeling aside, dismissing it soundly. That was in the past now.

Sun bathed her fair complexion, warming her even as cool mud seeped between her toes. Drusilla looked out across the small lake, its gently rippled surface beckoning—friendly. She smiled, took a step. Water rushed around her ankle, embracing her.

Golden light played merrily with the water's surface, obscuring all that lay beneath. Drusilla was unafraid. She thought about the happy moments of her life, wading in another step. The water caressed her exposed flesh.

In that golden, shimmering moment of time, Drusilla went swimming.

About Nora Dempsey

I have always been deeply fascinated by the obscure edges of reality. Inspired by those who lived before us—whether they drew actual breath ... once upon a time, or were given it by those who preserved civilization with their retellings of those who did act with courage, and a sense of right, in the face of overwhelming odds.

And not just those who came before, but those brave souls living now, and those yet to come. I write fantasy, science fiction, thrillers, mystery, fairy tales, and more. Short stories, chapter books, games, screenplays, and novels—the medium is not as important as the subject. The subject is always the same. The reason we read, the reason I write, is to give space for heroes.

I hope my stories inspire you. Help you to be the best you you can be. I hope you never stop reading. I don't ever plan to stop writing.

I have several, award-winning screenplays out there, by the way—if you're a producer reading this—under the name I reserve for such contests: Halle McGowan. Check out my work at Coverfly.

Now, back to you, dear reader. It means the world to me that you've picked up this book. I hope you've thoroughly enjoyed it, or are about to ...

With deepest gratitude—Nora Dempsey

Reach me at NoraDempseyWrites@gmail.com